DIPLOMATIC IMMUNITY

LOIS McMASTER BUJOLD

DIPLOMATIC IMMUNITY

A Baen Books Original

Baen Publishing Enterprises
P.O. Box 1403
Riverdale, NY 10471
www.baen.com

ISBN: 0-7434-3612-1
ISBN 13: 978-0-7434-3612-0

Cover art by Stephen Hickman

First paperback printing, June 2003
Fourth paperback printing, August 2010

Library of Congress Catalog Number 98-14345

Distributed by Simon & Schuster
1230 Avenue of the Americas
New York, NY 10020

Production by Windhaven® Press, Auburn, NH
Printed in the United States of America.

A WEAPON OF MILES DESTRUCTION

"Did—did my ice-water bath treatment help, then?"

"Yes, absolutely. The drop in core temperature stopped the cascade in its tracks, temporarily. The parasites had almost reached critical concentration."

Miles's eyes squeezed shut in brief gratitude. And opened again. "Temporarily?"

"I still haven't figured out how to get rid of the damned things. We're trying to modify a surgical shunt into a blood filter to both mechanically remove the parasites from the patient's bloodstream, and chill the blood to a controlled degree before returning it to the body."

"Won't that do it, then?"

Clogston shook his head. "it doesn't get the parasites lodged in other tissues, reservoirs of reinfection. It's not a cure, but it might buy time. I think the cure must somehow kill every last one of the parasites in the body, or the process will just start up again." His lips twisted. "Injecting something to kill already-engorged parasites within the tissues will just release their chemical loads. A very little of the micro-insult will play hell with circulation, overload repair processes, cause intense pain—it's . . . it's tricky."

"Destroy brain tissue?" Miles asked, feeling sick.

"Eventually. They don't seem to cross the blood-brain barrier very readily. I believe the victim would be conscious to a, um, very late phase of the dissolution.

"Oh." Miles tried to decide whether that would be good, or bad. His train of thought derailed itself as he imagined little gengineered parasites multiplying frenetically through his blood stream, *blip-blip-blip*.

He thought, *Am I going to live long enough to say good-bye to Ekaterin?*

DIPLOMATIC IMMUNITY

CHAPTER ONE

In the image above the vid plate, the sperm writhed in elegant, sinuous curves. Its wriggling grew more energetic as the invisible grip of the medical microtractor grasped it and guided it to its target, the pearl-like egg: round, lustrous, rich with promise.

"Once more, dear boy, into the breach—for England, Harry, and Saint George!" Miles murmured encouragingly. "Or at least, for Barrayar, me, and maybe Grandfather Piotr. Ha!" With a last twitch, the sperm vanished within its destined paradise.

"Miles, are you looking at those baby pictures *again*?" came Ekaterin's voice, amused, as she emerged from their cabin's sybaritic bathroom. She finished winding up her dark hair on the back of her head, secured it, and leaned over his shoulder as he sat in the station chair. "Is that Aral Alexander, or Helen Natalia?"

"Well, Aral Alexander in the making."

"Ah, admiring your sperm again. I see."

"*And* your excellent egg, my lady." He glanced up at his wife, glorious in a heavy red silk tunic that he'd bought her on Earth, and grinned. The warm clean scent of her skin tickled his nostrils, and he inhaled happily. "Were they not a handsome set of gametes? While they lasted, anyway."

"Yes, and they made beautiful blastocysts. You know, it's a good thing we took this trip. I swear you'd be in there trying to lift the replicator lids to peek, or shaking the poor little things up like Winterfair presents to see how they rattled."

"Well, it's all new to *me*."

"Your mother told me last Winterfair that as soon as the embryos were safely implanted you'd be acting like you'd invented reproduction. And to think I imagined she was exaggerating!"

He captured her hand and breathed a kiss into its palm. "This, from the lady who sat in the nursery next to the replicator rack all spring to study? Whose assignments all suddenly seemed to take twice as long to complete?"

"Which, of course, had nothing to do with her lord popping in twice an hour to ask how she was going on?" The hand, released, traced his chin in a very flattering fashion. Miles considered proposing that they forgo the rather dull luncheon company in the ship's passenger lounge, order in room service, get undressed again, and go back to bed for the rest of the watch. Ekaterin didn't seem to regard anything about their journey as boring, though.

This galactic honeymoon was belated, but perhaps better so, Miles thought. Their marriage had had an awkward enough commencement; it was as well that their settling-in had included a quiet period of domestic routine. But in retrospect, the first anniversary of that memorable, difficult, mid-winter wedding had seemed to arrive in about fifteen subjective minutes.

They had long agreed they would celebrate the date by starting the children in their uterine replicators. The debate had never been about *when*, just *how many*. He still thought his suggestion of doing them all at once had an admirable efficiency. He'd never been serious about twelve; he'd just figured to start with that proposition, and fall back to six. His mother, his aunt, and what seemed every other female of his acquaintance had all mobilized to explain to him that he was insane, but Ekaterin had merely smiled. They'd settled on two, to begin with, Aral Alexander and Helen Natalia. A double portion of wonder, terror, and delight.

At the edge of the vid recording, Baby's First Cell Division was interrupted by a red blinking message light. Miles frowned faintly. They were three jumps out from Solar space, in the deep interstellar on a sub-light-speed run between wormholes expected to take four full days. En route to Tau Ceti, where they would make orbital transfer to a ship bound for Escobar, and there to yet another that would thread the jump route past Sergyar and Komarr to home. He wasn't exactly expecting any vid calls here. "Receive," he intoned.

Aral Alexander *in potentia* vanished, to be replaced by the head and shoulders of the Tau Cetan passenger liner's captain. Miles and Ekaterin had dined at his table some two or three times on this leg of their tour. The man favored Miles with a tense smile and nod. "Lord Vorkosigan."

"Yes, Captain? What can I do for you?"

"A ship identifying itself as a Barrayaran Imperial courier has hailed us and is requesting permission to match velocities and lock on. Apparently, they have an urgent message for you."

Miles's brows rose, and his stomach sank. This was

not, in his experience, the way the Imperium delivered *good* news. On his shoulder, Ekaterin's hand tightened. "Certainly, Captain. Put them through."

The captain's dark Tau Cetan features vanished, to be replaced after a moment by a man in Barrayaran Imperial undress greens with lieutenant's tabs and Sector IV pins on his collar. Visions surged through Miles's mind of the Emperor assassinated, Vorkosigan House burned to the ground with the replicators inside, or, even more hideously likely, his father suffering a fatal stroke—he dreaded the day some stiff-faced messenger would begin by addressing him, *Count Vorkosigan, sir?*

The lieutenant saluted him. "Lord Auditor Vorkosigan? I'm Lieutenant Smolyani of the courier ship *Kestrel*. I have a message to hand-deliver to you, recorded under the Emperor's personal seal, after which I am ordered to take you aboard."

"We're not at war, are we? Nobody's died?"

Lieutenant Smolyani ducked his head. "Not so far as I've heard, sir." Miles's heart rate eased; behind him, Ekaterin let out her breath. The lieutenant went on, "But, apparently, a Komarran trade fleet has been impounded at some place called Graf Station, Union of Free Habitats. It's listed as an independent system, out near the edge of Sector V. My clear-code flight orders are to take you there with all safe speed, and to wait on your convenience thereafter." He smiled a bit grimly. "I hope it's not a war, sir, because they only seem to be sending us."

"Impounded? Not quarantined?"

"I gather it's some sort of legal entanglement, sir."

I smell diplomacy. Miles grimaced. "Well, no doubt the sealed message will make it more plain. Bring it to me, and I'll take a look while we get packed up."

"Yes, sir. The *Kestrel* will be locking on in just a few minutes."

"Very good, Lieutenant." Miles cut the com.

"We?" said Ekaterin in a quiet tone.

Miles hesitated. Not a quarantine, the lieutenant had said. Not, apparently, a shooting war either. *Or not yet, anyway.* On the other hand, he couldn't imagine Emperor Gregor interrupting his long-delayed honeymoon for something trivial. "I'd better see what Gregor has to say, first."

She dropped a kiss on the top of his head, and said simply, "Right."

Miles raised his personal wrist com to his lips and murmured, "Armsman Roic—on duty, to my cabin, now."

The data disk with the Imperial Seal upon it that the lieutenant handed to Miles a short time later was marked *Personal*, not *Secret*. Miles sent Roic, his bodyguard-cum-batman, and Smolyani off to sort and stow luggage, but motioned Ekaterin to stay. He slipped the disk into the secured player that the lieutenant had also brought, set it on the cabin's bedside table, and keyed it to life. He sat back on the edge of the bed beside her, conscious of the warmth and solidity of her body. For the sake of her worried eyes, he took her hand in a reassuring grip.

Emperor Gregor Vorbarra's familiar features appeared, lean, dark, reserved. Miles read profound irritation in the subtle tightening of his lips.

"I'm sorry to interrupt your honeymoon, Miles," Gregor began. "But if this has caught up with you, you haven't changed your itinerary. So you're on your way home now in any case."

Not *too* sorry, then.

"It's my good luck and your bad that you happen

to be the man physically closest to this mess. Briefly, one of our Komarr-based trade fleets put in at a deep-space facility out near Sector V, for resupply and cargo transfer. One—or more, the reports are unclear—of the officers from its Barrayaran military escort either deserted, or was kidnapped. Or was murdered—the reports are unclear about *that*, too. The patrol the fleet commander sent to retrieve him ran into trouble with the locals. Shots—I phrase this advisedly—shots were fired, equipment and structures were damaged, people on both sides were apparently seriously injured. No other deaths reported yet, but that may have changed by the time you get this, God help us.

"The problem—or one of them, anyway—is that we're getting a significantly different version of the chain of events from the local ImpSec observer on the Graf Station side of the conflict than we're getting from our fleet commander. Yet more Barrayaran personnel are now reported either held hostage, or arrested, depending on which version one is to believe. Charges filed, fines and expenses mounting, and the local response has been to lock down all ships currently in dock until the muddle is resolved to their satisfaction. The Komarran cargomasters are now screaming back to us over the heads of their Barrayaran escort, with yet a third spin on events. For your, ah, delectation, all the original reports we've received so far from all the viewpoints are appended to this message. Enjoy." Gregor grimaced in a way that made Miles twitch.

"Just to add to the delicacy of the problem, the fleet in question is about fifty percent Toscane-owned." Gregor's new wife, Empress Laisa, was a Toscane heiress and a Komarran by birth, a political marriage of enormous importance to the peace of the fragile union of planets that was the Imperium. "The problem of how to satisfy my in-laws while simultaneously presenting the appearance of Imperial evenhandedness to all their Komarran commercial rivals—I leave to your ingenuity." Gregor's thin smile said it all.

"You know the drill. I request and require you, as my Voice, to get yourself to Graf Station with all safe speed and sort out the situation before it deteriorates further. Pry all my subjects out of the hands of the locals and get the fleet back on its way. Without starting a war, if you please, or breaking my Imperial budget.

"And, critically, find out who's lying. If it's the ImpSec observer, that's a problem to bounce to their chain of command. If it's the fleet commander—who is Admiral Eugin Vorpatril, by the way—it becomes . . . very much my problem."

Or rather, very much the problem of Gregor's proxy, his Emperor's Voice, his Imperial Auditor. Namely Miles. Miles considered the interesting pitfalls inherent in attempting, without backup, far from home, to arrest the ranking military officer out of the middle of his long-standing and possibly personally loyal command. A Vorpatril, too, scion of a Barrayaran aristocratic clan of far-flung and important political connections within the Council of Counts. Miles's own aunt and cousin were Vorpatrils. *Oh, thank you, Gregor.*

The Emperor continued, "In matters rather closer to Barrayar, something has stirred up the Cetagandans around Rho Ceta. No need to go into the peculiar details here, but I would appreciate it if you would settle this impoundment crisis as swiftly and efficiently as you can. If the Rho Cetan business becomes any more peculiar, I'll want you safely home. The communications lag between Barrayar and Sector V is going to be too long to for me to breathe over your shoulder, but some occasional status or progress reports from you would be a nice touch, if you don't mind." Gregor's voice did not change to convey irony. It didn't need to. Miles snorted. "Good luck," Gregor concluded. The image on the viewer returned to a mute display of the Imperial Seal. Miles reached forward and keyed it off. The detailed reports, he could study once he was en route.

He? Or *we*?

He glanced up at Ekaterin's pale profile; she turned her serious blue eyes toward him. He asked, "Do you want to go with me, or continue on home?"

"*Can* I go with you?" she asked doubtfully.

"Of course you can! The only question is, would you like to?"

Her dark brows rose. "Not the only question, surely. Do you think I'd be of any use, or would I just be a distraction from your work?"

"There's official use, and there's unofficial use. Don't bet that the first is more important than the second. You know the way people talk to you to try to get oblique messages to me?"

"Oh, yes." Her lips twisted in distaste.

"Well, yes, I realize it's tedious, but you're very good at sorting them out, you know. Not to mention the information to be obtained just from studying the kinds of lies people tell. And, ah—not-lies. There may well be people who will talk to you who won't talk to me, for one reason or another."

She conceded the truth of this with a little wave of her free hand.

"And . . . it would be a real relief for me to have someone along I can talk to freely."

Her smile tilted a little at this. "Talk, or vent?"

"I—hem!—suspect this one is going to entail quite a lot of venting, yes. D'you think you can stand it? It could get pretty thick. Not to mention boring."

"You know, you keep claiming your job is boring, Miles, but your eyes have gone all bright."

He cleared his throat and shrugged unrepentantly.

Her amusement faded, and her brows drew down. "How long do you think this sorting out will take?"

He considered the calculation she had doubtless just made. It would be six more weeks, give or take a few days, to the scheduled births. Their original travel plan would have put them back at Vorkosigan House a comfortable month early. Sector V was in the opposite direction from their present location to Barrayar, insofar as the network of jump points people navigated to get from *here* to *there* could be said to have a direction. Several days to get from here to Graf Station, plus an extra two weeks of travel at least to get home from there, even in the fastest of fast couriers. "If I can settle things in less than two weeks, we can both get home on time."

She breathed a short laugh. "For all that I try to be all modern and galactic, that feels so strange. All sorts of men don't make it home for the births of their children. But *My mother was out of town on the day I was born, so she missed it*, just seems . . . seems like a more profound complaint, somehow."

"If it runs over, I suppose I could send you home on your own, with a suitable escort. But I want to be there, too." He hesitated. *It's my first time, dammit, of course it's making me crazy*, was a statement of the obvious that he managed to stop on his lips. Her first marriage had left her riddled with sensitive scars, none of them physical, and this topic trod near several of them. *Rephrase, O Diplomat*. "Does it . . . make it any easier, that it's the second time, for you?"

Her expression grew introspective. "Nikki was a body birth; of course everything was harder. The replicators take away so many risks—our children could get all their genetic mistakes corrected, they won't be subject to damage from a bad birth—I know replicator gestation is better, more responsible, in every way. It's not as though they are being *shortchanged*. And yet . . ."

He raised her hand and touched her knuckles to his lips. "You're not shortchanging *me*, I promise you."

Miles's own mother was adamantly in favor of the use of replicators, with cause. He was reconciled now, at age thirty-odd, with the physical damage he had taken in her womb from the soltoxin attack. Only his emergency transfer to a replicator had saved his life. The teratogenic military poison had left him stunted and brittle-boned, but a childhood's agony of medical treatments had brought him to nearly full function, if not, alas, full height. Most of his bones had been replaced piecemeal with synthetics thereafter, emphasis on the *pieces*. The rest of the damage, he conceded, was all his own doing. That he was still alive seemed less a miracle than that he had won Ekaterin's heart. *Their* children would not suffer such traumas.

He added, "And if you think you're having it too luxuriously easy now to feel properly virtuous, why, just wait till they get *out* of those replicators."

She laughed. "Very good point!"

"Well." He sighed. "I'd intended this trip to show you the glories of the galaxy, in the most elegant and refined society. It appears I'm heading instead to what I suspect is the armpit of Sector V, and the company of a bunch of squabbling, frantic merchants, irate bureaucrats, and paranoid militarists. Life is full of surprises. Come with me, my love? For my sanity's sake?"

Her eyes narrowed in amusement. "How can I resist such an invitation? Of course I will." She sobered. "Would it violate security for me to send a message to Nikki telling him we'll be late?"

"Not at all. Send it from the *Kestrel*, though. It'll get through faster."

She nodded. "I've never been away from him so long before. I wonder if he's been lonely?"

Nikki had been left, on Ekaterin's side of the family, with four uncles and a great-uncle plus matching aunts, a herd of cousins, a small army of friends, and his Grandmother Vorsoisson. On Miles's side were Vorkosigan House's extensive staff and their extensive families, with Uncle Ivan and Uncle Mark and the whole Koudelka clan for backup. Impending were his doting Vorkosigan step-grandparents, who had planned to arrive after Miles and Ekaterin for the birthday bash, but who now might beat them home. Ekaterin might have to travel *ahead* to Barrayar, if he couldn't cut through this mess in a timely fashion, but by no rational definition of the word, *alone*.

"I don't see how," said Miles honestly. "I expect you miss him more than he misses us. Or he'd have managed more than that one monosyllabic note that didn't catch up with us till Earth. Eleven-year-old boys can be pretty self-centered. I'm sure *I* was."

Her brows rose. "Oh? And how many notes have you sent to *your* mother in the past two months?"

"It's a *honeymoon* trip. Nobody expects you to . . . Anyway, she's always gotten to see the reports from my security."

The brows stayed up. He added prudently, "I'll drop her a message from the *Kestrel* too."

He was rewarded with a League of Mothers smile. Come to think of it, perhaps he would include his father in the address as well, not that his parents didn't share his missives. And complain coequally about their rarity.

An hour of mild chaos completed their transfer to the Barrayaran Imperial courier ship. Fast couriers gained most of their speed by trading off carrying capacity. Miles was forced to divest all but their most essential luggage. The considerable remainder, along with a startling volume of souvenirs, would continue the journey back to Barrayar with most of their little entourage: Ekaterin's personal maid, Miss Pym, and, to Miles's greater regret, both of Roic's relief arms-men. It occurred to him belatedly, as he and Ekaterin fitted themselves into their new shared cabin, that he ought to have mentioned how cramped their quarters would be. He'd traveled on similar vessels so often during his own years in ImpSec, he took their limi-tations for granted—one of the few aspects of his former career where his undersized body had worked to his advantage.

So while he did spend the remainder of the day in bed with his wife after all, it was primarily due to the absence of other seating. They folded back the upper bunk for head space and sat up on opposite ends, Ekaterin to read quietly from a hand viewer, Miles to plunge into Gregor's promised Pandora's box of reports from the diplomatic front.

He wasn't five minutes into this study before he uttered a *Ha!*

Ekaterin indicated her willingness to be interrupted by looking up at him with a reciprocal *Hm?*

"I just figured out why Graf Station sounded familiar. We're headed for Quaddiespace, by God."

"Quaddiespace? Is that someplace you've been before?"

"Not personally, no." This was going to take more politic preparation than he'd anticipated. "Although I actually met a quaddie once. The quaddies are a race of bioengineered humans developed, oh, two or three hundred years ago. Before Barrayar was rediscovered. They were supposed to be permanent free fall dwell-ers. Whatever their creators' original plan for them was, it fell through when the new grav technologies came in, and they ended up as sort of economic refugees. After assorted travels and adventures, they finally settled as a group in what was at the time the far end of the wormhole nexus. They were wary of other people by then, so they deliberately picked a system with no habitable planets, but with considerable asteroid and cometary resources. Planning to keep themselves to themselves, I guess. Of course, the explored nexus has grown around them since then, so now they get some foreign exchange by servicing ships and providing transfer facilities. Which explains why our fleet came to be docked there, although not what happened afterwards. The, ah . . ." He hesitated. "The bioengineering included a lot of metabolic changes, but the most spectacular alteration was, they have a second set of arms where their legs should be. Which is really, um, handy in free fall. So to speak. I've often wished I'd had a couple of extra hands, when I was operating in vacuum."

He passed the viewer across and displayed the shot of a quaddie, dressed in bright yellow shorts and a singlet, handing himself along a gravity-less corridor with the speed and agility of a monkey navigating through treetops.

"*Oh*," gulped Ekaterin, then quickly regained control of her features. "How, uh . . . interesting." After a moment she added, "It does look quite practical, for their environment."

Miles relaxed a trifle. Whatever her buried Barrayaran reflexes were regarding visible mutations, they would be trumped by her iron grip on good manners.

The same, unfortunately, did not appear to be true of their fellow members of the Imperium now stranded in the quaddies' system. The difference between deleterious mutation and benign or advantageous modification was not readily grasped by Barrayarans from the backcountry. Given that one officer referred to them as *horrible spider mutants* right in his report, it was clear that Miles could add racial tensions to the mix of complications they were now racing toward.

"You get used to them pretty quickly," he reassured her.

"Where did you meet one, if they keep to themselves?"

"Um . . ." Some quick internal editing, here . . . "It was on an ImpSec mission. I can't talk about it. But she was a musician, of all things. Played the hammer dulcimer with all four arms." His attempt to mime this remarkable sight resulted in his banging his elbow painfully on the cabin wall. "Her name was Nicol. You would have liked her. We got her out of a tight spot. I wonder if she ever made it home?" He rubbed his elbow and added hopefully, "I'll bet the quaddies' free fall gardening techniques would interest you."

Ekaterin brightened. "Yes, indeed."

Miles returned to his reports with the uncomfortable certainty that this was not going to be a good task to plunge into underprepared. He mentally added a review of quaddie history to his list of studies for the next few days.

CHAPTER TWO

"Is my collar straight?"

Ekaterin's cool fingers made businesslike work upon the back of Miles's neck; he concealed the shiver down his spine. "Now it is," she said.

"Clothes make the Auditor," he muttered. The little cabin lacked such amenities as a full-length mirror; he had to use his wife's eyes instead. This did not seem a disadvantage. She stepped back as far as she could, a half-pace to the bulkhead, and looked him up and down to check the effect of his Vorkosigan House uniform: brown tunic with his family crest in silver thread upon the high collar, silver-embroidered cuffs, brown trousers with silver side piping, tall brown riding boots. The Vor class had been cavalry soldiers, in their heyday. No horse within God knew how many light-years now, that was certain.

He touched his wrist com, mate in function to the one she wore, though hers was made Vor-lady-like with a decorative silver bracelet. "I'll give you a heads-up when I'm ready to come back and change." He nodded toward the plain gray suit she'd already laid out on the bunk. A uniform for the military-minded, civvies for the civilians. And let the weight of Barrayaran history, eleven generations of Counts Vorkosigan at his back, make up for his lack of height, his faintly hunched stance. His less visible defects, he didn't need to mention.

"What should I wear?"

"Since you'll have to play the whole entourage, something effective." He smiled crookedly. "That red silk thing ought to be distractingly civilian enough for our Stationer hosts."

"Only the male half, love," she pointed out. "Suppose their security chief is a female quaddie? Are quaddies even attracted to downsiders?"

"One was, apparently," he sighed. "Hence this mess. . . . Parts of Graf Station are null-gee, so you'll likely want trousers or leggings instead of Barrayaran-style skirts. Something you can move in."

"Oh. Yes, I see."

A knock sounded at the cabin door, and Armsman Roic's diffident voice, "My lord?"

"On my way, Roic." Miles and Ekaterin exchanged places—finding himself at her chest height, he stole a pleasantly resilient hug in passing—and he exited to the courier ship's narrow corridor.

Roic wore a slightly plainer version of Miles's Vorkosigan House uniform, as befitted his liege-sworn armsman's status. "Do you want me to pack up your things now for transfer to the Barrayaran flagship, m'lord?" he asked.

"No. We're going to stay aboard the courier."

Roic almost managed to conceal his wince. He was a young man of imposing height and intimidating breadth of shoulder, and had described his bunk above the courier ship's engineer as *Sort of like sleeping in a coffin, m'lord, except for the snoring.*

Miles added, "I don't care to hand off control of my movements, not to mention my air supply, to either side in this squabble just yet. The flagship's bunks aren't much bigger anyway, I assure you, Armsman."

Roic smiled ruefully, and shrugged. "I'm afraid you should've brought Jankowski, sir."

"What, because he's shorter?"

"No, m'lord!" Roic looked faintly indignant. "Because he's a real veteran."

A Count of Barrayar was limited by law to a bodyguard of a score of sworn men; the Vorkosigans had by tradition recruited most of their armsmen from retiring twenty-year veterans of the Imperial Service. By political need, in the last decades they'd mostly been former ImpSec men. They were a keen but graying bunch. Roic was an interesting new exception.

"When did that become a concern?" Miles's father's cadre of armsmen treated Roic as a junior because he was, but if they were treating him as a second-class citizen . . .

"Eh . . ." Roic waved somewhat inarticulately around the courier ship, by which Miles construed that the problem lay in more recent encounters.

Miles, about to lead off down the short corridor, instead leaned against the wall and folded his arms. "Look, Roic—there's scarcely a man in the Imperial Service your age or younger who's faced as much live fire in the Emperor's employ as you have in the Hassadar Municipal Guard. Don't let the damned green uniforms spook you. It's empty swagger. Half of 'em would fall over in a faint if they were asked to take down someone like that murderous lunatic who shot up Hassadar Square."

"I was already halfway across the plaza, m'lord. It would've been like swimming halfway across a river, deciding you couldn't make it, and turning around to swim back. It was *safer* to jump him than to turn and run. He'd 'a had the same amount of time to take aim at me either way."

"But not the time to take out another dozen or so bystanders. Auto-needler's a filthy weapon." Miles brooded briefly.

"That it is, m'lord."

For all his height, Roic tended to shyness when he felt himself to be socially outclassed, which unfortunately seemed to be much of the time in the Vorkosigans' service. Since the shyness showed on his surface mainly as a sort of dull stolidity, it tended to get overlooked.

"You're a Vorkosigan armsman," said Miles firmly. "The ghost of General Piotr is woven into that brown and silver. They'll be spooked by *you*, I promise you."

Roic's brief smile conveyed more gratitude than conviction. "Wish I could've met your grandfather, m'lord. From all the tales they told of him back in the District, he was quite something. My great-grandfather served with him in the mountains during the Cetagandan Occupation, m'mother says."

"Ah! Did she have any good stories about him?"

Roic shrugged. "He died of t' radiation after Vorkosigan Vashnoi was destroyed. M'grandmother would never talk about him much, so I don't know."

"Pity."

Lieutenant Smolyani poked his head around the corner. "We're locked on to the *Prince Xav* now, Lord Auditor Vorkosigan. Transfer tube's sealed and they're ready for you to board."

"Very good, Lieutenant."

Miles followed Roic, who had to duck his head

through the oval doorway, into the courier's cramped personnel hatch bay. Smolyani took up station by the hatch controls. The control pad twinkled and beeped; the door slid open onto the airlock and the flex tube, beyond it. Miles nodded to Roic, who took a visible breath and swung himself through. Smolyani braced to a salute; Miles returned him an acknowledging nod and a "Thank you, Lieutenant," and followed Roic.

A meter of stomach-lifting zero-gee in the flex tube ended at a similar hatchway. Miles grasped the handgrips and swung himself through and smoothly to his feet in the open airlock. He stepped from it into a very much more spacious hatch bay. On his left, Roic loomed formally, awaiting him. The flagship's door slid closed behind him.

Before him, three green-uniformed men and a civilian stood stiffly to attention. Not one of them changed expression at Miles's un-Barrayaran physique. Presumably Vorpatril, whom Miles barely recalled from a few passing encounters in Vorbarr Sultana's capital scene, remembered him more vividly, and had prudently briefed his staff on the mutoid appearance of Emperor Gregor's shortest, not to mention youngest and newest, Voice.

Admiral Eugin Vorpatril was of middle height, stocky, white-haired, and grim. He stepped forward and gave Miles a crisp and proper salute. "My Lord Auditor. Welcome aboard the *Prince Xav.*"

"Thank you, Admiral." He did not add *Happy to be here*; no one in this group could be happy to see him, under the circumstances.

Vorpatril continued, "May I introduce my Fleet Security commander, Captain Brun."

The lean, tense man, possibly even grimmer than his admiral, nodded curtly. Brun had been in operational charge of the ill-fated patrol whose hair-trigger

exploits had blown the situation from minor legal
brangle to major diplomatic incident. No, not happy
at all.

"Senior Cargomaster Molino of the Komarran fleet
consortium."

Molino too was middle-aged, and quite as dyspeptic-
looking as the Barrayarans, though dressed in neat
dark Komarran-style tunic and trousers. A senior
cargomaster was the ranking executive and financial
officer of the limited-term corporate entity that was
a commercial convoy, and as such bore most of the
responsibilities of a fleet admiral with a fraction of
the powers. He also had the unenviable task of being
the designated interface between a potentially very dis-
parate bunch of commercial interests, and their
Barrayaran military protectors, which was usually
enough to account for dyspepsia even without a crisis. He murmured a polite, "My Lord Vorkosigan."

Vorpatril's tone took on a slightly gritty quality. "My
fleet legal officer, Ensign Deslaurier."

Tall Deslaurier, pale and wan beneath a lingering
touch of adolescent acne, managed a nod.

Miles blinked in surprise. When, under his old
covert ops identity, he had run a supposedly independent mercenary fleet for ImpSec's galactic operations,
Fleet Legal had been a major department; just negotiating the peaceful passage of armed ships through all
the varied local space legal jurisdictions had been a full-
time job of nightmarish complexity. "Ensign." Miles
returned the nod, and chose his wording carefully. "You,
ah . . . would seem to have a considerable responsibility,
for your rank and age."

Deslaurier cleared his throat, and said in a nearly
inaudible voice, "Our department chief was sent home
earlier in the voyage, my Lord Auditor. Compassionate
leave. His mother'd died."

I think I'm getting the drift of this already. "This your first galactic voyage, by chance?"

"Yes, my lord."

Vorpatril put in, possibly mercifully, "I and my staff are entirely at your disposal, my Lord Auditor, and are ready with our reports as you requested. Would you care to follow me to our briefing room?"

"Yes, thank you, Admiral."

Some shuffling and ducking through the corridors brought the party to a standard military briefing room: bolted-down holovid-equipped table and station chairs, friction matting underfoot harboring the faint musty odor of a sealed and gloomy chamber that never enjoyed sunlight or fresh air. The place *smelled* military. Miles suppressed the urge to take a long, nostalgic inhalation, for old times' sake. At his hand signal, Roic took up an impassive guard's stance just inside the door. The rest waited for him to seat himself, then disposed themselves around the table, Vorpatril on his left, Deslaurier as far away as possible.

Vorpatril, displaying a clear understanding of the etiquette of the situation, or at least some sense of self-preservation, began, "So. How may we serve you, my Lord Auditor?"

Miles tented his hands on the table. "I am an Auditor; my first task is to listen. If you please, Admiral Vorpatril, describe for me the course of events from your point of view. How did you arrive at this impasse?"

"From my point of view?" Vorpatril grimaced. "It started out seeming no more than the usual one damned thing after another. We were supposed to be in dock here at Graf Station for five days, for contracted cargo and passenger transfers. Since there was no reason at that time to think that the quaddies were hostile, I granted as many station leaves as possible, which is standard procedure."

Miles nodded. The purposes of Barrayaran military escorts for Komarran ships ranged from overt to subtle to never-spoken. Overtly, escorts rode along to repel hijackers from the cargo vessels and supply the military part of the fleet with maneuvering experience scarcely less valuable than war games. More subtly, the ventures provided opportunity for all sorts of intelligence gathering—economic, political, and social, as well as military. And it provided cadres of young provincial Barrayaran men, future officers and future civilians, with seasoning contact with the wider galactic culture. On the never-spoken side were the lingering tensions between Barrayarans and Komarrans, legacy of the, in Miles's view, fully justified conquest of the latter by the former a generation ago. It was the Emperor's express policy to move from a stance of occupation to one of full political and social assimilation between the two planets. That process was proving slow and rocky.

Vorpatril continued, "The Toscane Corporation's ship *Idris* put into dock for jump drive adjustments, and ran into unexpected complications when they pulled things apart. Repaired parts failed to pass calibration tests when reinstalled and were sent back to the Station shops for refabrication. Five days became ten, while that bickering was going back and forth. Then Lieutenant Solian turned up missing."

"Do I understand correctly that the lieutenant was the Barrayaran security liaison officer aboard the *Idris*?" Miles said. Fleet beat cop, charged with maintaining peace and order among crew and passengers, keeping an eye out for any illegal or threatening activities or suspicious persons—not a few historic hijackings were inside jobs—and being first line of defense in counterintelligence. More quietly, keeping an ear out for potential disaffection among the Emperor's Komarran subjects. Obliged to render all possible assistance to the ship in physical emergencies, coordinating evacuation or rescue with the military escort. Liaison officer was a job that could shift from yawningly boring to lethally demanding in an eyeblink.

Captain Brun spoke for the first time. "Yes, my lord."

Miles turned to him. "One of your people, was he? How would you describe Lieutenant Solian?"

"He was newly assigned," Brun answered, then hesitated. "I did not have a close personal acquaintance with him, but all his prior personnel evaluations gave him high marks."

Miles glanced at the cargomaster. "Did you know him, sir?"

"We met a few times," said Molino. "I mostly stayed aboard the *Rudra*, but my impression of him was that he was friendly and competent. He seemed to get along well with crew and passengers. Quite the walking advertisement for assimilation."

"Excuse me?"

Vorpatril cleared his throat. "Solian was Komarran, my lord."

"Ah." *Argh*. The reports hadn't mentioned this wrinkle. Komarrans were but lately permitted admittance into the Barrayaran Imperial Service; the first generation of such officers was handpicked, and on their marks to prove their loyalty and competence. *The Emperor's pets*, Miles had heard at least one Barrayaran fellow-officer describe them in covert disgruntlement. The success of this integration was a high personal priority of Gregor's. Admiral Vorpatril certainly knew it, too. Miles moved the mysterious fate of Solian up a few notches in his mental list of most-urgent priorities.

"What were the circumstances of his original disappearance?"

Brun answered, "Very quiet, my lord. He signed off-shift in the usual manner, and never showed up for his next watch. When his cabin was finally checked, it seemed that some of his personal effects and a valise were missing, although most of his uniforms were left. There was no record of his finally leaving the ship, but then . . . he'd know how to get out without being seen if anyone could. Which is why I posit desertion. The ship was very thoroughly searched after that. He has to have altered the records, or slipped out with the cargo, or *something*."

"Any sense that he was unhappy in his work or place?"

"Not—no, my lord. Nothing special."

"Anything not special?"

"Well, there was the usual chronic chaff about being a Komarran in this"—Brun gestured at himself—"uniform. I suppose, where he was placed, he was in position to get it from both sides."

We're trying to all be one side, now. Miles decided this was not the time or place to pursue the unconscious assumptions behind Brun's word-choice. "Cargo-master Molino—do you have any sidelights on this? Was Solian subject to, ah, reproof from his fellow Komarrans?"

Molino shook his head. "The man seemed to be well liked by the crew of the *Idris* as far as I could tell. Stuck to business, didn't get into arguments."

"Nevertheless, I gather that your first . . . impression, was that he had deserted?"

"It seemed possible," Brun admitted. "I'm not casting aspersions, but he *was* Komarran. Maybe he'd found it tougher than he thought it would be. Admiral Vorpatril disagreed," he added scrupulously.

Vorpatril waved a hand in a gesture of judicious balance. "The more reason not to think desertion. High command's been pretty careful of what Komarrans they admit to the Service. They don't want public failures."

"In any case," said Brun, "we put all our own security people on alert to search for him, and asked for help from the Graf Station authorities. Which they were not especially eager to offer. They just kept repeating they'd had no sign of him in either the gravity or null-gee sections, and no record of anyone of his description leaving the station on their local-space carriers."

"And then what happened?"

Admiral Vorpatril answered, "Time ran on. Repairs on the *Idris* were completed and signed off. Pressure," he eyed Molino without favor, "grew to leave Graf Station and continue on the planned route. Me—I don't leave my men behind if I can help it."

Molino said, rather through his teeth, "It made no economic sense to tie up the entire fleet over one man. You might have left one light vessel or even a small team of investigators to pursue the matter, to follow on when they were concluded, and let the rest continue."

"I also have standing orders not to split the fleet," said Vorpatril, his jaw tightening.

"But we haven't suffered a hijacking attempt in this sector for decades," argued Molino. Miles felt he was witnessing round n-plus-one of an ongoing debate.

"Not since Barrayar began providing you with free military escorts," said Vorpatril, with false cordiality. "Odd coincidence, that." His voice grew firmer. "I don't leave my men. I swore *that* at the Escobar debacle, back when *I* was a milk-faced ensign." He glanced at Miles. "Under your father's command, as it happened."

Uh-oh. This could be trouble. . . . Miles let his brows climb in curiosity. "What was your experience there, sir?"

Vorpatril snorted reminiscently. "I was a junior pilot on a combat drop shuttle, orphaned when our mothership was blown to hell by the Escos in high orbit. I suppose if we'd made it back during the retreat, we'd have been blown up with her, but still. Nowhere to dock, nowhere to run, even the few surviving ships that had an open docking cradle not pausing for us, a couple of hundred men on board including wounded—it was a right nightmare, let me tell you."

Miles felt the admiral had barely clipped off a "son," at the end of that last sentence.

Miles said cautiously, "I'm not sure Admiral Vorkosigan had much choice left, by the time he inherited command of the invasion after the death of Prince Serg."

"Oh, none at all," Vorpatril agreed, with another wave of his hand. "I'm not saying the man didn't do all he could with what he had. But he couldn't do it all, and I was among those sacrificed. Spent almost a year in an Escobaran prison camp, before the negotiators finally got me mustered home. The Escobarans didn't make it a holiday for us, I can tell you that."

It could have been worse. You might have been a female Escobaran prisoner of war in one of our *camps.* Miles decided not to suggest this exercise of the imagination to the admiral just now. "I would expect not."

"All I'm saying is, I know what it is to be abandoned, and I won't do it to men of mine for any trivial reason." His narrow glance at the cargomaster made it clear that evaporating Komarran corporate profits did not qualify as a weighty enough reason for this violation of principle. "Events proved—" He hesitated, and rephrased himself. "For a time, I thought events had proved me right."

"For a time," Miles echoed. "Not any more?"

"Now . . . well . . . what happened next was pretty . . .

pretty disturbing. There was an unauthorized cycling of a personnel airlock in the Graf Station cargo bay next to where the *Idris* was locked on. No ship or personnel pod was sighted at it, however—the tube seals weren't activated. By the time the Station security guard got there, the bay was empty. But there was a quantity of blood on the floor, and signs of something dragged to the lock. The blood came up on testing as Solian's. It looked like he was trying to make it back to the *Idris*, and someone jumped him."

"Someone who didn't leave footprints," added Brun darkly.

At Miles's inquiring look, Vorpatril explained, "In the gravitational areas where the downsiders stay, the quaddies buzz around in these little personal floaters. They operate 'em with their lower hands, leaving their upper arms free. No footprints. No feet, for that matter."

"Ah, yes. I understand," said Miles. "Blood, but no body—has a body been found?"

"Not yet," said Brun.

"Searched for?"

"Oh, yes. In all the possible trajectories."

"I suppose it's occurred to you that a deserter might try to fake his own murder or suicide, to free himself from pursuit."

"I might have thought that," said Brun, "but I saw the loading bay floor. No one could lose that much blood and live. There must have been three or four liters at least."

Miles shrugged. "The first step in emergency cryonic prep is to exsanguinate the patient and replace his blood with cryo-fluid. That can easily leave several liters of blood on the floor, and the victim—well, potentially alive." He'd had close personal experience of the process, or so Elli Quinn and Bel Thorne had told him afterward, on that Dendarii Free Mercenary mission that had gone so disastrously wrong. Granted, he didn't remember that part, except through Bel's extremely vivid description.

Brun's brows flicked up. "I hadn't thought of that."

"It rather sprang to my mind," said Miles apologetically. *I could show you the scars.*

Brun frowned, then shook his head. "I don't think there would have been time before Station security arrived on the scene."

"Even if a portable cryochamber was standing ready?"

Brun opened his mouth, then closed it again. He finally said, "It's a complicated scenario, my lord."

"I don't insist on it," said Miles easily. He considered the other end of the cryo-revival process. "Except that I'd also point out that there are other sources of several liters of nice fresh one's-own-personal blood besides a victim's body. Such as a revival lab's or hospital's synthesizer. The product would certainly light up a cursory DNA scan. You couldn't even call it a false positive, exactly. A bio-forensics lab could tell the difference, though. Traces of cryo-fluid would be obvious, too, if only someone thought to look for them." He added wistfully, "I hate circumstantial evidence. Who ran the identification check on the blood?"

Brun shifted uncomfortably. "The quaddies. We'd downloaded Solian's DNA scan to them when he first went missing. But the security liaison officer from the *Rudra* had gone over by then—he was right there in the bay watching their tech. He reported the match to me as soon as the analyzer beeped. That's when I podded across to look at it all myself."

"Did he collect another sample to cross-check?"

"I . . . believe so. I can ask the fleet surgeon if he received one before, um, other events overtook us."

Admiral Vorpatril sat looking unpleasantly stunned. "I thought certainly poor Solian was murdered. By some—" He fell silent.

"It doesn't sound as though that hypothesis is ruled out either, yet," Miles consoled him. "In any case, you honestly believed it at the time. Have your fleet surgeon examine his samples more thoroughly, please, and report to me."

"And to Graf Station Security, too?"

"Ah . . . maybe not them yet." Even if the results were negative, the query would only serve to stir up more quaddie suspicions about Barrayarans. And if they were positive . . . Miles wanted to think about that first. "At any rate, what happened next?"

"That Solian was himself Fleet Security made his murder—apparent murder—seem especially sinister," Vorpatril admitted. "Had he been trying to get back with some warning? We couldn't tell. So I canceled all leaves, went to alert status, and ordered all ships to detach from dockside."

"With no explanation of *why*," put in Molino.

Vorpatril glowered at him. "During an alert, a commander does not stop to explain orders. He expects to be instantly obeyed. Besides, the way you people had been champing at the bit, complaining about the delays, I hardly thought I'd *need* to repeat myself." A muscle jumped in his jaw; he inhaled and returned to his narrative. "At this point, we suffered something of a communications breakdown."

Here comes the smokescreen, at last.

"*Our* understanding was that a two-man security patrol, sent to retrieve an officer who was late reporting in—"

"That would be Ensign Corbeau?"

"Yes. Corbeau. As we understood it at the time, the patrol and the ensign were attacked, disarmed, and

detained by quaddies. The real story as it emerged later
was more complex, but that was what I had to go on
as I was trying to clear Graf Station of all our personnel
and stand off for any contingency up to immediate
evacuation from local space."

Miles leaned forward. "Did you believe it to be
random quaddies who had seized your men, or did you
understand it to have been Graf Station Security?"

Vorpatril didn't quite grind his teeth, but almost. He
answered nonetheless, "Yes, we knew it was their
security."

"Did you ask your legal officer to advise you?"

"No."

"Did Ensign Deslaurier volunteer advice?"

"No, my lord," Deslaurier managed to whisper.

"I see. Go on."

"I ordered Captain Brun to send a strike patrol in
to retrieve, now, three men from a situation that I
believed had just proved lethally dangerous to Barrayaran personnel."

"Armed with rather more than stunners, I understand?"

"I couldn't ask my men to go up against those
numbers with only stunners, my lord," said Brun.
"There are a *million* of those mutants out there!"

Miles let his brows climb. "On Graf Station? I
thought its resident population was around fifty thousand. Civilians."

Brun made an impatient gesture. "A million to twelve,
fifty thousand to twelve—regardless, they needed weapons with authority. My rescue party needed to get in and
out as quickly as possible, having to deal with as little
argument or resistance as possible. Stunners are useless as weapons of intimidation."

"I am familiar with the argument." Miles leaned back
and rubbed his lips. "Go on."

"My patrol reached the place our men were being held—"

"Graf Station Security Post Number Three, was it not?" Miles put in.

"Yes."

"Tell me—in all the time since the fleet has been here, hadn't any of your men on leave had close encounters with Station Security? No drunk and disorderlies, no safety violations, nothing?"

Brun, looking as though the words were being pulled from his mouth with dental pliers, said, "Three men were arrested by Graf Station Security last week for racing float chairs in an unsafe manner while inebriated."

"And what happened to them? How did your fleet legal advisor handle it?"

Ensign Deslaurier muttered, "They spent a few hours in lock-up, then I went down and saw that their fines were paid, and pledged to the stationer adjudicator that they would be confined to quarters for the duration of our stay."

"So you were all by then familiar with standard procedures for retrieving men from contretemps with Station authorities?"

"These were not drunk and disorderlies this time. These were our own security forces carrying out their duties," said Vorpatril.

"Go on," sighed Miles. "What happened with your patrol?"

"I still don't have their own firsthand reports, my lord," said Brun stiffly. "The quaddies have only let one unarmed medical officer visit them in their current place of confinement. Shots were exchanged, both stunner and plasma fire, inside Security Post Three. Quaddies swarmed the place, and our men were overwhelmed and taken prisoner."

The "swarming" quaddies had included, not unnaturally in Miles's view, most of the Graf Station professional and volunteer fire brigades. *Plasma fire. In a civilian space station. Oh, my aching head.*

"So," said Miles gently, "after we shot up the police station and set the habitat on fire, what did we do for an encore?"

Admiral Vorpatril's teeth set, briefly. "I am afraid that, when the Komarran ships in dock failed to obey my urgent orders to cast off and instead allowed themselves to be locked down, I lost the initiative in the situation. Too many hostages had passed into quaddie control by then, the Komarran independent captain-owners were entirely laggard in obeying my position orders, and the quaddies' own militia, such as it is, was allowed to move into position around us. We froze in a standoff for almost two full days. Then we were ordered to stand down and wait your arrival."

Thank all the gods for that. Military intelligence was as nothing to military stupidity. But to slide halfway to stupid and *stop* was rare indeed. Vorpatril deserved some credit for that, at least.

Brun put in glumly, "Not much choice at that point. It's not as though we could threaten to blow up the station with our own ships in dock."

"You couldn't blow up the station in any case," Miles pointed out mildly. "It would be mass murder. Not to mention a criminal order. The Emperor would have you shot."

Brun flinched and subsided.

Vorpatril's lips thinned. "The Emperor, or you?"

"Gregor and I would flip a coin to see who got to go first."

A little silence fell.

"Fortunately," Miles continued, "it appears heads have cooled all round. For that, Admiral Vorpatril, I do thank you. I might add, the fates of your respective careers are a matter between you and your Ops command." *Unless you manage to make me late for the births of my very first children, in which case you'd better start looking for a deep, deep hole.* "*My* job is to talk out as many of the Emperor's subjects from quaddie hands, at the lowest prices, as I can. If I'm really lucky, when I'm done our trade fleets may be able to dock here again someday. You have not given me an especially strong hand of cards to play, here, unfortunately. Nonetheless, I'll see what I can do. I want copies of all raw transcripts pertaining to these late events provided for my review, please."

"Yes, my lord," growled Vorpatril. "But," his voice grew almost anguished, "that still doesn't tell me what happened to Lieutenant Solian!"

"I will undertake to give that question my keenest attention as well, Admiral." Miles met his eyes. "I promise you."

Vorpatril nodded shortly.

"But, Lord Auditor Vorkosigan!" Cargomaster Molino put in urgently. "Graf Station authorities are trying to fine our *Komarran* vessels for the damage done by *Barrayaran* troops. It must be made plain to them that the military stands alone in this . . . criminal activity."

Miles hesitated a long moment. "How fortunate for you, Cargomaster," he said at last, "that in the event of a genuine attack, the reverse would not be true." He tapped the table and rose to his feet.

CHAPTER THREE

Miles stood on tiptoe to peer through the little port beside the *Kestrel*'s personnel hatch as the ship maneuvered toward its assigned docking cradle. Graf Station was a vast jumbled aggregation, an apparent chaos of design not surprising in an installation in its third century of expansion. Somewhere buried in the core of the sprawling, bristling structure was a small metallic asteroid, honeycombed for both space and the material used in building this very oldest of the quaddies' many habitats. Also somewhere in its innermost sections could still be seen, according to the guidevids, actual elements from the broken-apart and reconfigured jumpship in which the initial band of hardy quaddie pioneers had made their historic voyage to this refuge.

Miles stepped back and gestured Ekaterin to the port for a look. He reflected on the political astrography of Quaddiespace, or rather, as it was formally designated, the Union of Free Habitats. From this initial point, quaddie groups had leapfrogged out to build daughter colonies in both directions along the inner of the two rings of asteroids that had made this system so attractive to their ancestors. Several generations and a million strong later, the quaddies were in no danger whatsoever of running out of space, energy, or materials. Their population could expand as fast as it chose to build.

Only a handful of their many scattered habitats maintained areas supplied with artificial gravity for legged humans, either visitor or resident, or even dealt with outsiders. Graf Station was one that did accept galactics and their trade, as did the orbital arcologies dubbed Metropolitan, Sanctuary, Minchenko, and Union Station. This last was the seat of Quaddie government, such as it was; a variant of bottom-up representative democracy based, Miles was given to understand, on the work gang as its primary unit. He hoped to God he wasn't going to end up negotiating with a committee.

Ekaterin glanced around and, with an excited smile, motioned Roic to take a turn. He ducked his head and nearly pressed his nose to the port, staring in open curiosity. This was Ekaterin's first trip outside the Barrayaran Empire, and Roic's first venture off Barrayar ever. Miles paused to thank his habits of mild paranoia that before he'd dragged them off world he'd troubled to send them both through a short intensive course in space and free fall procedures and safety. He'd pulled rank and strings to get access to the military academy facilities, albeit on a free week between scheduled classes, for a tailored version of the longer course that Roic's older armsmen colleagues had received routinely in their former Imperial Service training.

Ekaterin had been extremely startled when Miles had invited—persuaded—well, hustled—her to join the bodyguard in the orbital school: daunted at first, exhausted and close to mutiny partway through, proud and elated at the finish. For passenger liners in pressurization trouble, it was the usual method to stuff their paying customers into simple bubbles called bod pods to passively await rescue. Miles had been stuck in a bod pod a time or two himself. He'd sworn that no man, and most especially no wife, of his would ever be rendered so artificially helpless in an emergency. His whole party had traveled with their own personally tailored quick-donning suits at hand. Regretfully, Miles had left his old customized battle armor in storage. . . .

Roic unbent from the port, looking especially stoic, faint vertical lines of worry between his eyebrows.

Miles asked, "Has everyone had their antinausea pills?"

Roic nodded earnestly.

Ekaterin said, "Have you had *yours*?"

"Oh, yes." He glanced down his plain gray civilian tunic and trousers. "I used to have this nifty bio-chip on my vagus nerve that kept me from losing my lunch in free fall, but it got blown out with the rest of my guts in that unpleasant encounter with the needle-grenade. I should get it replaced one of these days. . . ." Miles stepped forward and took one more glance outside. The station had grown to occlude most of the view. "So, Roic. If some quaddies visiting Hassadar made themselves obnoxious enough to win a visit to the Municipal Guard's gaol, and then a bunch more quaddies popped up and tried to bust them out with military-grade weapons, and shot up the place and torched it and burned some of your comrades, just how would you feel about quaddies at that point?"

"Um . . . not too friendly, m'lord." Roic paused. "Pretty pissed, actually."

"That's what I figured." Miles sighed. "Ah. Here we go."

Clanks and thumps sounded as the *Kestrel* came gently to rest and the docking clamps felt their way to a firm grip. The flex tube whined, seeking its seal, guided by the *Kestrel*'s engineer at the hatch controls, and then seated itself with an audible chink. "All tight, sir," the engineer reported.

"All right, troops, we're on parade," Miles murmured, and waved Roic on.

The bodyguard nodded and slipped through the hatch; after a moment he called back, "Ready, m'lord."

All was, if not well, good enough. Miles followed through the flex tube, Ekaterin close behind him. He stole a glance over his shoulder as he floated forward. She was svelte and arresting in the red tunic and black leggings, her hair in a sophisticated braid around her head. Zero gee had a charming effect on well-developed female anatomy that he decided he had probably better not point out to her. As an opening move, setting this first meeting in the null-gee section of Graf Station was clearly calculated to put the visitors off balance, to emphasize just whose space this was. If they'd wanted to be polite, the quaddies would have received them in one of the grav sections.

The station-side airlock opened into a spacious cylindrical bay, its radial symmetry airily dispensing with the concepts of "up" and "down." Roic floated with one hand on the grip by the hatch, the other kept carefully away from his stunner holster. Miles craned his neck to take in the array of half a dozen quaddies, males and females, in paramilitary grade half-armor, floating in cross-fire positions around the bay. Their weapons were out but shouldered, formality masking threat. Lower arms, thicker and more muscular than their uppers, emerged from their hips. Both sets of arms were protected by plasma-deflecting vambraces. Miles couldn't help reflecting that here were people who actually could shoot and reload at the same time. Interestingly, though two bore the insignia of Graf Station Security, the rest were in the colors and badges of the Union Militia.

Impressive window dressing, but these were not the people he needed to be attending to. His gaze swept on to the three quaddies and the legged downsider waiting directly across from the hatch. Faintly startled expressions, as they in turn took in his own nonstandard appearance, were quickly suppressed on three out of four faces.

The senior Graf Station Security officer was instantly recognizable by his uniform, weapons, and glower. Another middle-aged quaddie male also wore some sort of Stationer uniform, slate blue, in a conservative style designed to reassure the public. A white-haired female quaddie was more elaborately dressed in a maroon velvet doublet with slashed upper sleeves, silky silver fabric puffing from the slits, with matching puffy shorts and tight lower sleeves. The legged downsider also wore the slate-blue uniform, except with trousers and friction boots. Short, graying brown hair floated around the head that turned toward Miles. Miles choked, trying not to swear aloud in shock.

My God. It's Bel Thorne. What the devil was the ex-mercenary Betan hermaphrodite doing *here*? The question answered itself as soon as it formed. *So. Now I know who our ImpSec observer on Graf Station is.* Which, abruptly, raised the reliability of *those* reports to a vastly higher level . . . or did it? Miles's smile froze, concealing, he hoped, his sudden mental disarray.

The white-haired woman was speaking, in a very chilly tone—some automatic part of Miles's mind pegged her as senior, as well as oldest, present. "Good afternoon, Lord Auditor Vorkosigan. Welcome to the Union of Free Habitats."

Miles, one hand still guiding a blinking Ekaterin into the bay, managed a polite return nod. He left the second handhold flanking the hatch to her for an anchor, and managed to set himself in air, without imparting an unwanted spin, right side up with relation to the senior quaddie woman. "Thank you," he returned neutrally. *Bel, what the hell . . . ? Give me a sign, dammit.* The hermaphrodite returned his brief wide-eyed stare with cool disinterest, and, as if casually, raised a hand to scratch the side of its nose, signaling, perhaps, *Wait for it. . . .*

"I am Senior Sealer Greenlaw," the quaddie woman continued, "and I have been assigned by my government to meet with you and provide arbitration between you and your victims on Graf Station. This is Crew Chief Venn of Graf Station Security, Boss Watts, who is supervisor of Graf Station Downsider Relations, and Assistant Portmaster Bel Thorne."

"How do you do, madam, gentlemen, honorable herm," Miles's mouth continued on autopilot. He was too shaken by the sight of Bel to take exception to that *your victims*, for now. "Permit me to introduce my wife, Lady Ekaterin Vorkosigan, and my personal assistant, Armsman Roic."

All the quaddies frowned disapprovingly at Roic. But now it was the turn for Bel's eyes to widen, staring with sudden attention at Ekaterin. A purely personal aspect of it all blazed across Miles's mind then, as he realized that he was shortly, very probably, going to be in the unsettling position of having to introduce his new wife to his old flame. Not that Bel's oft-expressed crush on him had ever been *consummated*, exactly, to his retrospective sometimes-regret. . . .

"Portmaster Thorne, ah . . ." Miles felt himself

scrambling for firm footing in more ways than one. His voice went brightly inquiring. "Have we met?"

"I don't believe we've ever met, *Lord Auditor Vorkosigan*, no," returned Bel; Miles hoped his was the only ear that detected the slight emphasis on his Barrayaran name and title in that familiar alto drawl.

"Ah." Miles hesitated. *Throw out a lure, a line, something . . .* "My mother was Betan, you know."

"What a coincidence," Bel said blandly. "So was mine."

Bel, goddammit! "I have had the pleasure of visiting Beta Colony several times."

"I haven't been back but once in decades." The faint light of Bel's notably vile sense of humor faded in the brown eyes, and the herm relented as far as, "I'd like to hear about the old sandbox."

"It would be my pleasure to discuss it," Miles responded, praying this exchange sounded diplomatic and not cryptic. *Soon, soon, bloody soon.* Bel returned him a cordial, acknowledging nod.

The white-haired quaddie woman gestured toward the end of the bay with her upper right hand. "If you would please accompany us to the conference chamber, Lord and Lady Vorkosigan, Armsman Roic."

"Certainly, Sealer Greenlaw." Miles favored her with an *after you, ma'am* half-bow in air, then uncurled to get a foot to the wall to push off after her. Ekaterin and Roic followed. Ekaterin arrived and braked at the round airseal door with reasonable grace, though Roic landed crookedly with an audible thump. He'd used too much power pushing off, but Miles couldn't stop to coach him on the fine points here. He'd come to the right of it soon enough, or break an arm. The next series of corridors featured a sufficiency of handgrips. The downsiders kept up with the quaddies, who both preceded and followed; to Miles's secret satisfaction, none of the guards had to pause and collect any out-of-control spinning or helplessly becalmed Barrayarans.

They came at length to a chamber with a window-wall offering a panoramic view out across one arm of the station and into the deep, star-dusted void beyond. Any downsider suffering from a touch of agoraphobia or pressurization paranoia would doubtless prefer to cling to the wall on the opposite side. Miles floated gently up to the transparent barrier, stopping himself with two delicately extended fingers, and surveyed the spacescape; his mouth crooked up, unwilled. "This is very fine," he said honestly.

He glanced around. Roic had found a wall grip near the door, awkwardly shared with the lower hand of a quaddie guard, who glowered at him as they both shifted fingers trying not to touch the other. The majority of the honor guard had been shed in the adjoining corridor, and only two, one Graf Station and one Union, now hovered, albeit alertly. The chamber end-walls featured decorative plants growing out of illuminated spiraling tubes that held their roots in a hydroponic mist. Ekaterin paused by one, examining the multicolored leaves closely. She tore her attention away, and her brief smile faded, watching Miles, watching their quaddie hosts, watching for cues. Her eye fell curiously on Bel, who was surveying Miles in turn, the herm's expression—well, anyone else would see it as bland, probably. Miles suspected it was deeply ironic.

The quaddies took up position in a hemispherical arrangement around a central vid plate, Bel hovering near its comrade-in-slate-blue, Boss Watts. Arching posts of different heights featured the sort of com link control boards usually found on station-chair arms, looking a bit like flowers on stalks, which provided suitably spaced tethering points. Miles picked a post with his back to open space. Ekaterin floated over and took up a spot a little behind him. She'd gone into her silent, highly reserved mode, which Miles had to school himself not to read as unhappy; it might just mean that she was processing too hard to remember to be animated. Fortunately, the ivory-carved expression also simulated aristocratic poise.

A pair of younger quaddies, whose green shirt-and-shorts garb Miles's eye decoded as *servitor*, offered drink bulbs all around; Miles selected something billed to be tea, Ekaterin took fruit juice, and Roic, with a glance at his quaddie opposite numbers who were offered none, declined. A quaddie could grip a handhold and a drink bulb, and still have two hands left to draw and aim a weapon. It hardly seemed fair.

"Senior Sealer Greenlaw," Miles began. "My credentials, you should have received." She nodded, her short, fine hair floating in a wispy halo with the motion. He continued, "I am, unfortunately, not wholly familiar with the cultural context and meaning of your title. Who do you speak for, and do your words bind them in honor? That is to say, do you represent Graf Station, a department within the Union of Free Habitats, or some larger entity still? And who reviews your recommendations or sanctions your agreements?" *And how long does it usually take them?*

She hesitated, and he wondered if she was studying him with the same intensity that he studied her. Quaddies were even longer-lived than Betans, who routinely made it to one-hundred-and-twenty standard, and might expect to see a century and a half; how old was this woman?

"I am a Sealer for the Union's Department of Downsider Relations; I believe some downsider cultures would term this a minister plenipotentiary for their state department, or whatever body administers their embassies. I've served the department for the past forty years, including tours as junior and senior counsel for the Union in both our bordering systems."

The near neighbors to Quaddiespace, a few jumps away on heavily used routes; she was saying she'd spent time on planets. *And, incidentally, that she's been doing this job since before I was born.* If only she wasn't one of those people who figured that if you'd seen one planet, you'd seen 'em all, this sounded promising. Miles nodded.

"My recommendations and agreements will be reviewed by my work gang on Union Station—which is the Board of Directors of the Union of Free Habitats."

Well, so there was a committee, but happily, they weren't here. Miles pegged her as being roughly the equivalent of a senior Barrayaran minister in the Council of Ministers, well up to his own weight as an Imperial Auditor. Granted, the quaddies had nothing in their governmental structure equivalent to a Barrayaran Count, though they seemed none the worse for the deprivation—Miles suppressed a dry snort. One layer from the top, Greenlaw had a finite number of persons to please or persuade. He permitted himself his first faint hope for a reasonably supple negotiation.

Her white brows drew in. "They called you the Emperor's Voice. Do Barrayarans *really* believe their emperor's voice comes from your mouth, across all those light-years?"

Miles regretted his inability to lean back in a chair; he straightened his spine a trifle instead. "The name is a legal fiction, not a superstition, if that's what you're asking. Actually, Emperor's Voice is a nickname for my job. My real title is Imperial Auditor—a reminder that always my first task is to listen. I answer to—and for— Emperor Gregor alone." This seemed a good place to leave out such complications as potential impeachment by the Council of Counts, and other Barrayaran-style checks and balances. *Such as assassination.*

The security officer, Venn, spoke up. "So do you, or do you not, control the Barrayaran military forces here in Union space?" He'd evidently acquired enough experience of Barrayaran soldiers by now to have a little trouble picturing the slightly crooked runt floating before him dominating the bluff Vorpatril, or his no-doubt large and healthy troopers.

Yeah, but you should see my Da . . . Miles cleared his throat. "As the Emperor is commander-in-chief of the Barrayaran military, his Voice is automatically the ranking officer of any Barrayaran force in his vicinity, yes. If the emergency so demands it."

"So are you saying that if you ordered it, those thugs out there would shoot?" said Venn sourly.

Miles managed a slight bow in his direction, not easy in free fall. "Sir, if an Emperor's Voice so ordered it, they'd shoot *themselves.*"

This was pure swagger—well, part swagger—but Venn didn't need to know it. Bel remained straight-faced, somehow, thank whatever gods hovered here, though Miles could almost see the laugh getting choked back. *Don't pop your eardrums, Bel.* The Sealer's white eyebrows took a moment to climb back down to horizontal again.

Miles continued, "Nevertheless, while it's not hard to get any group of persons excited enough to shoot at things, one purpose of military discipline is to ensure they also *stop* shooting on command. This is not a time for shooting, but for talking—and listening. I am listening." He tented his fingers in front of what would be his lap, if he were sitting. "From your point of view, what was the sequence of events that led to this unfortunate incident?"

Greenlaw and Venn both started to speak at once; the quaddie woman opened an upper hand in a gesture of invitation to the security officer.

Venn nodded and continued, "It *started* when my department received an emergency call to apprehend a pair of your men who had assaulted a quaddie woman."

Here was a new player on stage. Miles kept his expression neutral. "Assaulted in what sense?"

"Broke into her living quarters, roughed her up, threw her around, broke one of her arms. They evidently had been sent in pursuit of a certain Barrayaran officer who had failed to report for duty—"

"Ah. Would that be Ensign Corbeau?"

"Yes."

"And was he in her living quarters?"

"Yes—"

"By her invitation?"

"Yes." Venn grimaced. "They had apparently, um, become friends. Garnet Five is a premier dancer in the Minchenko Memorial Troupe, which performs live zero-gee ballet for residents of the Station and for downsider visitors." Venn inhaled. "It is not entirely clear who went to whose defense when the Barrayaran patrol came to remove their tardy officer, but it degenerated into a noisy brawl. We arrested all the downsiders and took them to Security Post Three to sort out."

"By the way," Sealer Greenlaw broke in, "your Ensign Corbeau has lately requested political asylum in the Union."

This was new, too. "How lately?"

"This morning. When he learned you were coming."

Miles hesitated. He could imagine a dozen scenarios to account for this, ranging from the sinister to the foolish; he couldn't help it that his mind leapt to the sinister. "Are you likely to grant it?" he asked finally.

She glanced at Boss Watts, who made a little non-committal gesture with a lower hand and said, "My department has taken it under advisement."

"If you want my advice, you'll bounce it off the far wall," growled Venn. "We don't need that sort here."

"I should like to interview Ensign Corbeau at the earliest convenience," said Miles.

"Well, he evidently doesn't want to talk to *you*," said Venn.

"Nevertheless. I consider firsthand observation and eyewitness testimony critical for my correct understanding of this complex chain of events. I'll also need to speak with the other Barrayaran—" he clipped the word *hostages*, and substituted, "detainees, for the same reason."

"It's not that complex," said Venn. "A bunch of armed thugs came charging onto my station, violated customs, stunned dozens of innocent bystanders and a number of Station Security officers attempting to carry out their duties, tried to effect what can only be called a jailbreak, and vandalized property. Charges against them for their crimes—documented on vid!—range from the discharge of illegal weapons to resisting arrest to arson in an inhabited area. It's a miracle that no one was killed."

"*That*, unfortunately, has yet to be demonstrated," Miles countered instantly. "The trouble is that from our point of view, the arrest of Ensign Corbeau was *not* the beginning of the sequence of events. Admiral Vorpatril had reported a man missing well before that—Lieutenant Solian. According to both your witnesses and ours, a quantity of his blood tantamount to a body part was found on the floor of a Graf Station loading bay. Military loyalty runs two ways—Barrayarans do not abandon our own. Dead or alive, *where* is the rest of him?"

Venn nearly ground his teeth. "We looked for the man. He is not on Graf Station. His body is not in space in any reasonable trajectory *from* Graf Station. We checked. We've told Vorpatril that, repeatedly."

"How hard—or easy—is it for a downsider to disappear in Quaddiespace?"

"If I may answer that," Bel Thorne broke in smoothly, "as that incident impinges on my department."

Greenlaw motioned assent with a lower hand, while simultaneously rubbing the bridge of her nose with an upper.

"Boarding to and from galactic ships here is fully controlled, not only from Graf Station, but from our other nexus trade depots as well. It is, if not impossible, at least difficult to pass through customs and immigration areas without leaving some sort of record, including general vid monitors of the areas. Your Lieutenant Solian does not show up anywhere in our computer or visual records for that day."

"Truly?" Miles gave Bel a look, *Is this the straight story?*

Bel returned a brief nod, *Yes.* "Truly. Now, in-system travel is much less strictly controlled. It is more . . . feasible, for someone to pass out of Graf Station to another Union habitat without notice. *If* that person is a quaddie. Any downsider, however, would stand out in the crowd. Standard missing-person procedures were followed in this case, including notifications of other habitat security departments. Solian has simply not been seen, on Graf Station or any other Union habitat."

"How do you account for his blood in the loading bay?"

"The loading bay is on the outboard side of the station access control points. It is my opinion that whoever created that scene came from and returned to one of the ships in that docks-and-locks sector."

Miles silently noted Bel's word choice, *whoever created that scene*, not *whoever murdered Solian*. Of course, Bel had been present at a certain spectacular emergency cryo-prep, too. . . .

Venn put in irritably, "All of which were ships from *your* fleet, at the time. In other words, you brought your own troubles with you. We are a peaceful people here!"

Miles frowned thoughtfully at Bel, and mentally reshuffled his plan of attack. "Is the loading bay in question very far from here?"

"It's on the other side of the station," said Watts.

"I think I would like to see it, and its associated areas, first, before I interview Ensign Corbeau and the other Barrayarans. Perhaps Portmaster Thorne would be so good as to conduct me on a tour of the facility?"

Bel glanced at Boss Watts and got an approving low sign.

"I should be very pleased to do so, Lord Vorkosigan," said Bel.

"Next, perhaps? We could take my ship around."

"That would be very efficient, yes," replied Bel, eyes brightening with appreciation. "I could accompany you."

"Thank you." *Good catch.* "That would be most satisfactory."

Wild as Miles now was to get away and shake Bel down in private, he had to smile his way through further formalities, including the official presentation of the list of charges, costs, fines, and punitive fines Vorpatril's strike force had garnered. He plucked the data disk Boss Watts spun to him delicately out of the air and intoned, "Note, please, I do not *accept* these charges. I will, however, undertake to review them fully at the earliest possible moment."

A lot of unsmiling faces greeted this pronouncement.

Quaddie body language was a study in its own right. Talking with one's hands was fraught with so many more possibilities, here. Greenlaw's hands were very controlled, both uppers and lowers. Venn clenched his lower fists a lot, but then, Venn had helped carry out his burned comrades after the fire.

The conference drew to an end without achieving anything resembling closure, which Miles counted as a small victory for his side. He was getting away without committing himself or Gregor to anything much, so far. He didn't yet see how to twist this unpromising tangle his way. He needed more data, subliminals, people, some handle or lever he hadn't spotted yet. *I need to talk to Bel.*

That wish, at least, looked to be granted. At Greenlaw's word, the meeting broke up, and the honor guard escorted the Barrayarans back through the corridors to the bay where the *Kestrel* waited.

CHAPTER FOUR

At the *Kestrel*'s lock, Boss Watts took Bel aside for a low-voiced conversation with some anxious hand waving. Bel shook its head, made *calm down* gestures, and finally turned to follow Miles, Ekaterin, and Roic through the flex tube and into the *Kestrel*'s tiny and now crowded personnel hatch deck. Roic stumbled and looked a trifle dizzied, readjusting to the grav field, but then found his balance again. He frowned warily at the Betan hermaphrodite in the quaddie uniform. Ekaterin flashed a covertly curious glance.

"What was that all about?" Miles asked Bel as the airlock door slid shut.

"Watts wanted me to take a bodyguard or three. To protect me from the brutal Barrayarans. I told him there wouldn't be room aboard, and besides, you were a diplomat—not a soldier." Bel, head cocked, gave him an indecipherable look. "Is that so?"

"It is now. Uh . . ." Miles turned to Lieutenant Smolyani, manning the hatch controls. "Lieutenant, we're going to take the *Kestrel* around to the other side of Graf Station to another docking cradle. Their traffic control will direct you. Go as slowly as you can without looking odd. Take two or three tries to align with the docking clamps, or something."

"My lord!" said Smolyani indignantly. ImpSec fast courier pilots made a religion out of fast, tight maneuvering and swift, perfect dockings. "In front of *these* people?"

"Well, do it however you wish, but buy me some time. I need to talk with this herm. Go, go." He waved Smolyani out. He drew breath, and added to Roic and Ekaterin, "We'll take over the wardroom. Excuse us, please." Thus consigning her and Roic to their cramped cabins to wait. He gripped Ekaterin's hand in brief apology. He dared not say more until he'd decanted Bel in private. There were security angles, political angles, personal angles—how many angles could dance on the head of a pin?—and, as the first thrill of seeing that familiar face alive and well wore off, the nagging memory that the last time they'd met, the purpose had been to strip Bel of command and discharge it from the mercenary fleet for its unfortunate role in the bloody Jackson's Whole debacle. He *wanted* to trust Bel. Dare he?

Roic was too well trained to ask, *Are you sure you don't want me to come with you, m'lord?* out loud, but from the expression on his face he was doing his best to send it telepathically.

"I'll explain it all later," Miles promised Roic in an under-voice, and sent him on his way with what he hoped was a reassuring half-salute.

He led Bel the few steps to the tiny chamber that doubled as the *Kestrel*'s wardroom, dining room, and briefing room, shut both its doors, and activated the security cone. A faint hum from the projector on the ceiling and a shimmer in the air surrounding the wardroom's circular dining/vid conference table assured him it was working. He turned to find Bel watching him, head a little to one side, eyes quizzical, lips quirked. He hesitated a moment. Then, simultaneously, they both burst into laughter. They fell on each other in a hug; Bel pounded him on the back, saying in a tight voice, "Damn, damn, damn, you sawed-off little half-breed maniac..."

Miles fell back, breathless. "Bel, by God. You look good."

"Older, surely?"

"That, too. But I don't think I'm the one to talk."

"*You* look terrific. Healthy. Solid. I take it that woman's been feeding you right? Or doing something right, anyway."

"Not *fat*, though?" Miles said anxiously.

"No, no. But the last time I saw you, right after they thawed you out of cryo-freeze, you looked like a skull on a stick. You had us all worried."

Bel remembered that last meeting with the same clarity as he did, evidently. More, perhaps.

"I worried about you, too. Have you ... been all right? How the devil did you end up *here*?" Was that a delicate enough inquiry?

Bel's brows rose a trifle, reading who-knew-what expression on Miles's face. "I suppose I was a little disoriented at first, after I parted company with the Dendarii Mercenaries. Between Oser and you as commanders, I'd served there almost twenty-five years."

"I was sorry as hell about it."

"I'd say, not half as sorry as I was, but *you* were the one who did the dying." Bel looked away briefly. "Among other people. It wasn't as if either of us had a choice, at that point. I couldn't have gone on. And— in the long run—it was a good thing. I'd got in a rut without knowing it, I think. I needed something to kick me out of it. I was ready for a change. Well, not *ready*, but . . ."

Miles, hanging on Bel's words, was reminded of their place. "Sit, sit." He gestured to the little table; they took seats next to each other. Miles rested his arm on the dark surface and leaned closer to listen.

Bel continued, "I even went home for a little while. But I found that a quarter of a century kicking around the nexus as a free herm had put me out of step with Beta Colony. I took a few spacer jobs, some at the suggestion of our mutual employer. Then I drifted in here." Bel tucked its gray-brown bangs up off its forehead with spread fingers, a familiar gesture; they promptly fell back again, even more heart-catching.

"ImpSec's not my employer any more, exactly," Miles said.

"Oh? So what are they, exactly?"

Miles hesitated over this one. "My . . . intelligence utility," he chose at last. "By virtue of my new job."

Bel's eyebrows went up farther, this time. "This Imperial Auditor thing isn't a cover for the latest covert ops scam, then."

"No. It's the real thing. I'm done with scam."

Bel's lips twitched. "What, with that funny accent?"

"This is my real voice. The Betan accent I affected for Admiral Naismith was the put-on. Sort of. Not that I didn't learn it at my mother's knee."

"When Watts told me the name of the supposedly-hot-shot envoy the Barrayarans were sending out, I thought it had to be you. That's why I made sure to get myself onto the welcoming committee. But this Emperor's Voice thing sounded like something out of a fairy tale, to me. Until I got to the fine print. Then it sounded like something out of a really *gruesome* fairy tale."

"Oh, did you look up my job description?"

"Yeah, it's pretty amazing what's in the historical databases here. Quaddiespace is fully plugged in to the galactic information exchange, I've found. They're almost as good as Beta, despite having only a fraction of the population. Imperial Auditor's a pretty stunning promotion—whoever handed you that much unsupervised power on a platter has to be almost as much of a lunatic as you are. I want to hear your explanation of that."

"Yes, it can take some explaining, to non-Barrayarans." Miles took a breath. "You know, that cryo-revival of mine was a little dicey. Do you remember the seizures I was having, right after?"

"Yes . . ." said Bel cautiously.

"They turned out to be a permanent side effect, unfortunately. Too much for even ImpSec's version of the military to tolerate in a field officer. As I managed to demonstrate in a particularly spectacular manner, but that's another story. It was a medical discharge, officially. So that was the end of my galactic covert ops career." Miles's smile twisted. "I had to get an honest job. Fortunately, Emperor Gregor gave me one. Everyone assumes my appointment was high Vor nepotism at work, for my father's sake. Over time, I trust I'll prove them wrong."

Bel was silent for a moment, face set. "So. It seems I killed Admiral Naismith after all."

"Don't hog the blame. You had lots of help," Miles said dryly. "Including mine." He was reminded that this slice of privacy was precious and limited. "It's all blood over the dam now anyway, for you and me both. We have other crises on our plate today. Quickly, from the top—I've been assigned to straighten out this mess, to Barrayar's, if not benefit, least-cost. If you're our ImpSec informer here—are you?"

Bel nodded.

After Bel had handed in its resignation from the Dendarii Free Mercenaries, Miles had seen to it that the hermaphrodite had gone on ImpSec's payroll as a civilian informer. In part it was payback for all Bel had done for Barrayar before the ill-conceived disaster that had ended Bel's career directly and Miles's indirectly, but mostly it had been to keep ImpSec from getting lethally excited about Bel wandering the wormhole nexus with a head full of hot Barrayaran secrets. Aging, tepid secrets now, for the most part. Miles had figured the illusion that they held Bel's string would prove reassuring to ImpSec, and so it had apparently proved. "Portmaster, eh? What a superb job for an intelligence observer. Data on everyone and everything that passes in and out of Graf Station at your fingertips. Did ImpSec place you here?"

"No, I found this job on my own. Sector Five was happy, though. Which, at the time, seemed an added bonus."

"I'd think they damned well should be happy."

"The quaddies like me, too. It seems I'm good at handling all sorts of upset downsiders, without losing my equilibrium. I don't explain to them that after years of trailing around after *you*, my definition of an emergency is seriously divergent from theirs."

Miles grinned and made calculations in his head. "Then your most recent reports are probably still somewhere in transit between here and Sector Five headquarters."

"Yeah, that's what I figure."

"What are the most important things I need to know?"

"Well, for one, we *really* haven't seen your Lieutenant Solian. Or his body. Really. Union Security hasn't stinted on the search for him. Vorpatril—is he any relation to your cousin Ivan, by the way?"

"Yes, a distant one."

"I thought I sensed a family resemblance. In more ways than one. Anyway, he thinks we're lying. But we're not. Also, your people are idiots."

"Yes. I know. But they're *my* idiots. Tell me something new."

"All right, here's a good one. Graf Station Security has pulled all the passengers and crew off the Komarran ships impounded in dock and lodged 'em in station-side hostels, to prevent ill-considered actions and to put pressure on Vorpatril and Molino. Naturally, they're none too happy. The supercargo—non-Komarrans who just took passage for a few jumps—are wild to get away. Half a dozen have tried to bribe me to let them take their goods off the *Idris* or the *Rudra*, and transfer off Graf Station on somebody else's ships."

"Have any, ah, succeeded?"

"Not yet." Bel smirked. "Although if the price keeps going up at the current rate, even I could be tempted. Anyway, several of the most anxious ones struck me as . . . potentially interesting."

"Check. Have you reported this to your Graf Station employers?"

"I made a remark or two. But it's only suspicion. The individuals are all well behaved, so far—especially compared to Barrayarans—it's not like we have any pretext for fast-penta interrogations."

"Attempting to bribe an official," Miles suggested.

"I hadn't actually mentioned that last part to Watts yet." At Miles's raised eyebrows, Bel added, "Did you *want* more legal complications?"

"Ah—no."

Bel snorted. "Didn't think so." The herm paused a moment, as if marshaling its thoughts. "Anyway, back to the idiots. Your Ensign Corbeau, to wit."

"Yes. That political asylum request of his has got all

my antennae quivering. Granted, he was in some trouble for being late reporting in, but why is he suddenly trying to desert? What connection does he have to Solian's disappearance?"

"Not any, as far as I've been able to make out. I actually met the fellow, before all this blew up."

"Oh? How and where?"

"Socially, as it happens. What is it about you people who run sexually segregated fleets that makes you all disembark insane? No, don't bother answering that, I think we all know. But the all-male military organizations who have that custom for religious or cultural reasons all come onto station leave like some horrible combination of kids let out of school and convicts let out of prison. The worst of both, actually—the judgment of children combined with the sexual deprivation of—never mind. The quaddies cringe when they see you coming. If you didn't spend money with such wild abandon, I think the commercial stations in the Union would all vote to quarantine you aboard your own ships and let you die of blue balls."

Miles rubbed his forehead. "Let's get back to Ensign Corbeau, shall we?"

Bel grinned. "We hadn't left. So, this backwoods Barrayaran boy on his first-ever trip into the glittering galaxy tumbles off his ship and, being under instructions, as I understand it, to enhance his cultural horizons—"

"That is actually correct."

"Goes off to see the Minchenko Ballet. Which is something to behold in any case. You should take it in while you're station-side."

"What, it isn't just, uh, exotic dancers?"

"Not in the advertising-for-the-sex-workers sense. Or even in the Betan Orb ultra-classy sexual smorgasbord and training academy sense."

Miles considered, then reconsidered, mentioning his and Ekaterin's honeymoon layover at the Orb of Unearthly Delights, possibly the most peculiarly *useful* stop on their itinerary . . . *Focus, my Lord Auditor.*

"It's exotic, and it's dancers, but it's real art, the real thing—it goes way beyond craft. A two-hundred-year-old tradition, a jewel of this culture. The fool boy *ought* to have fallen in love at first sight. It was his subsequent pursuit with all guns blazing—in the metaphorical sense, this time—that was a little out of line. Soldier on leave falls madly in lust with local girl is not precisely a new scenario, but what I *really* don't understand is what Garnet Five saw in him. I mean, he's a nice enough looking young male, but still . . . !" Bel smiled slyly. "Too tall for my taste. Not to mention too young."

"Garnet Five is this quaddie dancer, yes?"

"Yes."

Remarkable enough, for a Barrayaran to be attracted to a quaddie; the deeply ingrained cultural prejudice against anything that smacked of mutation would seem to work against it. Had Corbeau received less than the usual indulgent understanding from his fellows and superiors that a young officer in such a plight might ordinarily expect?

"And your connection with all this is—what?"

Did Bel take an apprehensive breath? "Nicol plays harp and hammer dulcimer in the Minchenko Ballet orchestra. You do remember Nicol, the quaddie musician we rescued during that personnel pickup that almost went down the disposer?"

"I remember Nicol vividly." And so, apparently, had Bel. "I gather she made it home safely after all."

"Yes." Bel's smile grew tenser. "Not surprisingly, she also remembers *you* vividly—Admiral Naismith."

Miles went still for a moment. At last he said cautiously, "Do, ah . . . you know her well? Can you command, or persuade, her discretion?"

"I live with her," said Bel briefly. "No one needs to command anything. She *is* discreet."

Oh. Much becomes clear . . .

"But she's a personal friend of Garnet Five's. Who is in a tearing panic over all of this. She's convinced, among other things, that the Barrayaran command wants to shoot her boyfriend out of hand. The pair of thugs that Vorpatril sent to pick up your stray evidently—well, it went beyond rude. They were insulting and brutal, for starters, and it slid downhill from there. I've heard the unabridged version."

Miles grimaced. "I know my countrymen. You can take the ugly details as read, thanks."

"Nicol has asked me to do what I can for her friend and her friend's friend. I promised I'd put in a word. This is it."

"I understand." Miles sighed. "I can't make any promises yet. Except to listen to everyone."

Bel nodded and looked away. It said after a moment, "This Imperial Auditor gig of yours—you're a big wheel in the Barrayaran machine now, huh?"

"Something like that," said Miles.

"The Emperor's Voice sounds like it would be pretty loud. People listen, do they?"

"Well, Barrayarans do. The rest of the galaxy"—one side of Miles's mouth turned up—"tend to think it's some kind of fairy tale."

Bel shrugged apologetically. "ImpSec is Barrayarans. So. The thing is, I've come to like this place—Graf Station, Quaddiespace. And these people. I like them a lot. I believe you'll see why, if I get much chance to show you around. I'm thinking of settling here permanently."

"That's . . . nice," said Miles. *Where are you taking me, Bel?*

"But if I *do* take an oath of citizenship here—and I've been thinking hard about it for a while—I want to take it honestly. I can't offer them a false oath, or divided loyalties."

"Your Betan citizenship never interfered with your career in the Dendarii Mercenaries," Miles pointed out.

"You never asked me to operate on Beta Colony," said Bel.

"And if I had?"

"I . . . would have faced a dilemma." Bel's hand stretched in urgent entreaty. "I want a clean start, with no secret strings attached. You claim ImpSec is your personal utility now. Miles—can you please fire me again?"

Miles sat back and chewed on his knuckle. "Cut you loose from ImpSec, you mean?"

"Yes. From all old obligations."

He blew out his breath. *But you're so valuable to us here!* "I . . . don't know."

"Don't know if you have the power? Or don't know if you want to use it?"

Miles temporized, "This power business has proved a lot stranger than I anticipated. You'd think more power would bring one more freedom, but I've found it's brought me less. Every word that comes out of my mouth has this *weight* that it never had before, when I was babbling Mad Miles, hustler of the Dendarii. I never had to watch my mass like this. It's . . . damned uncomfortable, sometimes."

"I'd have thought *you'd* love it."

"I'd have thought that too."

Bel leaned back, easing off. It would not make the request again, not soon, anyway.

Miles drummed his fingers on the cool, reflective

surface of the table. "If there is anything more behind this mess than overexcitement and bad judgment—not that that isn't enough—it hinges on the evaporation of that Komarran fleet security fellow, Solian—"

Miles wrist com chimed, and he raised it to his lips. "Yes?"

"M'lord," came Roic's apologetic voice. "We're in dock again now."

"Right. Thanks. We'll be out directly." He rose from the table, saying, "You must meet Ekaterin properly, before we go back out there and have to play dumb again. She and Roic have full Barrayaran security clearances, by the way—they have to, to live this close to me. They both need to know who you are, and that they can trust you."

Bel hesitated. "Do they really need to know I'm ImpSec? Here?"

"They might, in an emergency."

"I would particularly like the quaddies not to know I've been selling intelligence to downsiders, you see. Maybe it would be safer if you and I were mere acquaintances."

Miles stared. "But Bel, she knows perfectly well who you are. Or were, anyway."

"What, have you been telling covert ops war stories to your wife?" Clearly disconcerted, Bel frowned. "Those rules always applied to someone else, didn't they?"

"Her clearance was earned, not just granted," Miles said a little stiffly. "But Bel, we sent you a wedding invitation! Or . . . did you get it? ImpSec notified me it was delivered—"

"Oh," said Bel, looking confused. "That. Yes. I did get it."

"Was it delivered too late? It should have included

a travel voucher—if someone pocketed that, I'll have his hide—"

"No, the voucher came through all right. About a year and a half ago, yes? I could have made it, if I'd scrambled a bit. It just arrived at an awkward period for me. Kind of a low point. I'd just left Beta for the last time, and I was in the middle of a little job I was doing for ImpSec. Arranging a substitute would have been difficult. It was just effort, at a time when more effort . . . I wished you well, though, and hoped you'd finally got lucky." A wry grin flashed. "Again."

"Finding the right Lady Vorkosigan . . . was a bigger, rarer kind of luck than any I'd had before." Miles sighed. "Elli Quinn didn't come either. Though she sent a present and a letter." Neither especially demure.

"Hm," said Bel, smiling a little. And added rather slyly, "And Sergeant Taura?"

"*She* attended." Miles's lips curled up, unwilled. "Spectacularly. I had a burst of genius, and put my Aunt Alys in charge of getting her dressed civilian-style. It kept them both happily occupied. The old Dendarii contingent all missed you. Elena and Baz were there—with their new baby girl, if you can imagine it—and Arde Mayhew, too. So the very beginning of it all was fully represented. It was as well that the wedding was small. A hundred and twenty people is small, yes? It was Ekaterin's second, you see—she was a widow." And profoundly stressed thereby. Her tense, distraught state the night before the wedding had reminded Miles forcibly of a particular species of precombat nerves he'd seen in troops facing, not their first, but their second battle. The night after the wedding, now—that had gone much better, thank God.

Longing and regret had shadowed Bel's face during this recitation of old friends lifting a glass to new beginnings. Then the herm's expression sharpened. "Baz

Jesek, back on Barrayar?" said Bel. "Someone must have worked out his little problems with the Barrayaran military authorities, eh?"

And if Someone could arrange Baz's relationship with ImpSec, maybe that same Someone might arrange Bel's? Bel didn't even need to make the point out loud. Miles said, "The old desertion charges made too good a cover when Baz was active in ops to allow them to be rescinded, but the need had become obsolete. Baz and Elena are both out of the Dendarii too, now. Hadn't you heard? We're all getting to be history." *All of us who made it out alive, anyway.*

"Yes," sighed Bel. "There is a deal of sanity to be saved in letting the past go, and moving on." The herm glanced up. "If the past will let you go too, that is. So let's keep this as simple as possible with your people, please?"

"All right," Miles agreed reluctantly. "For now, we'll mention the past, but not the present. Don't worry—they'll be, ah—discreet." He deactivated the security cone above the little conference table and unlocked the doors. Raising his wrist com to his lips, he murmured, "Ekaterin, Roic, could you step over to the wardroom, please."

When they had both arrived, Ekaterin smiling expectantly, Miles said, "We've had a piece of undeserved good fortune. Although Portmaster Thorne works for the quaddies now, the herm's an old friend of mine from an organization I worked with in my ImpSec days. You can rely on what Bel has to say."

Ekaterin held out her hand. "I'm so glad to meet you at last, Captain Thorne. My husband and his old friends have spoken highly of you. I believe you were much missed from their company."

Looking decidedly bemused, but rising to the challenge, Bel shook her hand. "Thank you, Lady Vorkosigan.

But I don't go by that old rank here. Portmaster Thorne, or just call me Bel."

Ekaterin nodded. "And please call me Ekaterin. Oh—in private, I suppose." She looked a silent inquiry at Miles.

"Ah, right," said Miles. His gesture took in Roic, who looked attentive. "Bel knew me under another identity then. As far as Graf Station is concerned, we've just met. But we've hit it off splendidly, and Bel's talent for dealing with difficult downsiders is paying off for them."

Roic nodded. "Got it, m'lord."

Miles shepherded them into the hatch bay where the *Kestrel's* engineer waited to pipe them back aboard Graf Station. He reflected that yet another reason Ekaterin's security clearance needed to be as high as his own was that, according to several persons' historical reports and her own witness, he talked in his sleep. Until Bel grew less nervy over the situation, he decided he'd probably better not mention this.

Two quaddie Station Security men waited for them in the freight loading bay. This being the section of Graf Station supplied with artificially generated gravitational fields for the comfort and health of its downsider visitors and residents, the pair hovered in personal float chairs with Station Security markings emblazoned on the sides. The floaters were stubby cylinders, barely larger in diameter than a man's shoulders, and the general effect was of people riding in levitating washtubs, or maybe the Baba Yaga's magic flying mortar from Barrayaran folklore. Bel gave the quaddie sergeant a nod and a murmured greeting as they emerged into the echoing cavern of the loading bay. The sergeant returned the nod, evidently reassured, and turned his close attention to the

dangerous Barrayarans. Since the dangerous Barrayarans were frankly gawking like tourists, Miles hoped
the tough-looking fellow would soon grow less twitchy.

"This personnel lock here," Bel pointed back to the
one by which they'd just entered, "was the one that
was opened by the unauthorized person. The blood trail
ended in it, in a smeary smudge. It started," Bel walked
across the bay toward the wall to the right, "a few
meters away, not far from the door to the next bay.
This is where the large pool of blood was found."

Miles walked after Bel, studying the deck. It had
been cleaned up in the several days since the incident.
"Did you see this yourself, Portmaster Thorne?"

"Yes, about an hour after it was first found. The mob
had arrived by then, but Security had been pretty good
about keeping the area uncontaminated."

Miles had Bel walk him around the bay, detailing
all exits. It was a standard sort of place, utilitarian,
undecorated, efficient; a few pieces of freight-handling
equipment stood silently in the opposite end, near a
darkened, airsealed control booth. Miles had Bel
unlock it and give him a look inside. Ekaterin too
walked about, clearly glad to have room to stretch
her legs after several days cooped up in the *Kestrel*.
Her expression, gazing about the cool, echoing space,
was thoughtfully reminiscent, and Miles smiled in
appreciation.

They returned to the spot where the blood implied
Lieutenant Solian's throat had been cut, and discussed
the details of the spatter marks and smears. Roic
observed with keen professional interest. Miles had
one of the quaddie guards give up his float tub;
scooped out of his shell, he sat up on the deck on
his haunches and lower arms, looking a bit like a
large, disgruntled frog. Quaddie locomotion in a gravity field without a floater was rather disturbing to

watch. They either went on all fours, only slightly more mobile than a person on hands and knees, or managed a sort of forward-leaning, elbows-out, upright chicken-walk on their lower hands. Either mode looked very wrong and ungainly, compared to their grace and agility in zero gee.

With Bel, whom Miles judged to be about the right size for a Komarran, cooperatively playing the part of the corpse, they experimented with the problem of a person in a float chair shifting seventy or so kilos of inert meat the several meters to the airlock. Bel wasn't as slim and athletic as formerly, either; the added, ah, masses made it harder for Miles to fall back into his old subconscious default habit of thinking of Bel as male. Probably just as well. Miles found it extremely difficult, legs folded awkwardly in a seat not designed for them, trying to keep one hand on the float chair controls at roughly crotch level and also maintain a grip on Bel's clothing. Bel tried trailing either an arm or a leg artistically over the side; Miles stopped short of pouring water down Bel's sleeve to try to duplicate the smears. Ekaterin did little better than he did, and Roic, surprisingly, worse. His superior strength was counteracted by the awkwardness of squeezing his greater size into the cup-like space, his knees sticking up, and trying to work the hand controls in the constricted clearances. The quaddie sergeant managed it handily, but glowered at Miles afterwards.

Floaters, Bel explained, were not hard to come by, being considered shared public property, although quaddies who spent a lot of time on the grav side sometimes owned their own personalized models. The quaddies kept racks of floaters by the access ports between the grav and the free fall sections of the station, for any quaddie to grab and use, and drop off again upon returning. They were numbered for

maintenance record purposes, but not tracked otherwise. Anyone could obtain one by simply walking up
and getting in, apparently, even drunken Barrayaran
soldiers on leave.

"When we came into that first docking cradle around
on the other side, I noticed a lot of personal craft
puttering around the outside of the station—pushers,
personnel pods, in-system flitters," Miles said to Bel.
"It occurs to me that someone could have picked up
Solian's body within a short time of its being ejected
from the airlock, and removed it damned near trace-
lessly. It could be anywhere by now, including still
stored in a pod airlock or put through a disposer in
one-kilo lumps or tucked away to mummify in some
random asteroid crevice. Which offers an alternate
explanation of why it hasn't been found floating out
there. But that scenario requires either two persons,
with prior planning, or one spontaneous murderer who
moved very quickly. How much time would a single
person have had between the throat-cutting and the
pickup?"

Bel, straightening uniform and hair after the last
drag across the loading bay, pursed its lips. "There were
maybe five or ten minutes between the time the lock
cycled, and the time the security guard arrived to check
it. Maybe twenty minutes max after that before all sorts
of people were looking around outside. In thirty
minutes . . . yes, one person could just about have
dumped the body, run to another bay and jumped in
a small craft, zipped around, and collected it again."

"Good. Get me a list of everything that went out
a lock in that period." For the sake of the listening
quaddie guards he remembered to add a formal, "If
you please, Portmaster Thorne."

"Certainly, Lord Auditor Vorkosigan."

"Seems damned odd to go to all that trouble to

remove the body but leave the blood, though. Timing? Tried to get back to clean up, but it was too late? Something very, very strange to hide about the body?"

Maybe just blind panic, if the murder had not been planned in advance. Miles could imagine someone who was not a spacer shoving a body out an airlock, and only then realizing what poor concealment it really was. That didn't exactly jibe with a subsequent swift and handy outside pickup, though. And no quaddie qualified as not-a-spacer.

He sighed. "This is not getting us much forwarder. Let's go talk to my idiots."

CHAPTER FIVE

Graf Station Security Post Three lay on the border between the free fall and the grav sides of the station, with access to both. Construction quaddies in yellow shirts and shorts, and a few legged downsiders similarly dressed, were at work on repairs around the main grav-side entrance. Miles, Ekaterin, and Roic were escorted through by Bel and one of their quaddie outriders, the other having been left on dour guard at the *Kestrel's* docking hatch. The workers turned their heads to stare, frowning, as the Barrayarans passed.

They wound via a couple of corridors down one level, where they found the control booth at the portal to the grav-side detention block. A quaddie and a downsider were just collaborating on raising a new, possibly more plasma-fire-resistant, window into place in its frame; beyond, another yellow-clad quaddie could be seen putting the finishing touches on a monitor array while a uniformed quaddie in a Security floater, upper arms crossed, watched glumly.

In the tool-cluttered staging area in front of the

booth they found Sealer Greenlaw and Chief Venn, now supplied with floaters, awaiting them. Venn immediately made sure to point out to Miles all the repairs completed and still in progress, in detail, with approximate costs, with a chronicle appended of all the quaddies who had been injured in the imbroglio, including names, ranks, prognoses, and the distress suffered by their family members. Miles made acknowledging yet neutral noises, and went into a short counter-riff on the missing Solian and the sinister testimony of the blood on the loading bay deck, with a brief dissertation on the logistics of his ejected body being spirited away by a possible outboard coconspirator. This last gave Venn pause, at least temporarily; his face twinged, like a man in stomach pain.

While Venn went to arrange Miles's entry to the cell block with the guard in the control booth, Miles glanced at Ekaterin, and a little doubtfully around the less-than-inviting staging area. "Do you want to wait here, or sit in?"

"Do you want me to sit in?" she asked, with a lack of enthusiasm in her voice that even Miles could sense. "Not that you don't draft anyone in sight, as needed, but surely I'm not needed for this."

"Well, perhaps not. But it looks like it might be a trifle boring out here."

"I don't have quite your allergic response to boredom, love, but to tell the truth, I was rather hoping I could get more of a look around the station while you were tied up here this afternoon. The glimpses we saw on the way in seemed quite enticing."

"But I want Roic." He hesitated, the security triage problem turning in his head.

She glanced across in friendly speculation at Bel, listening. "I admit I would be glad for a guide, but do you really think I need a bodyguard here?"

Insult seemed possible, though only from quaddies who knew whose wife she was, but assault, Miles had to admit, seemed unlikely. "No, but . . ."

Bel smiled cordially back at her. "If you would accept my escort, Lady Vorkosigan, I would be pleased to show you around Graf Station while the Lord Auditor conducts his interviews."

Ekaterin brightened still further. "I would like that very much, yes, thank you, Portmaster Thorne. If things go well, as we must hope they do, we might not be here very long. I feel I should seize my opportunities."

Bel was more experienced than Roic in everything from hand-to-hand combat to fleet maneuvers, and vastly less likely to blunder into trouble here through ignorance. "Well . . . all right, why not? Enjoy." Miles touched his wrist com. "I'll call when I'm about finished. Maybe you can go shopping." He waved them off, smiling. "Just don't haul home any severed heads." He glanced up to find Venn and Greenlaw both staring at him in some dismay. "Ah—family joke," he explained weakly. The dismay did not abate.

Ekaterin smiled back, and sailed out on Bel's cheerfully proffered arm. It occurred to Miles belatedly that Bel was notably universal in its sexual tastes, and that maybe he ought to have warned Ekaterin that she needn't be especially delicate in redirecting Bel's attentions, should any be offered. But surely Bel wouldn't . . . on the other hand, maybe they'd just take turns trying things on.

Reluctantly, he turned back to business.

The Barrayaran prisoners were stacked three to a cell in chambers meant for two occupants, a circumstance about which Venn half complained, half apologized. Security Post Three, he gave Miles to understand, had been unprepared for such an abnormal influx of recalcitrant downsiders. Miles murmured comprehension, if not necessarily sympathy, and refrained from observing that the quaddies' cells were larger than the sleeping cabins housing four aboard the *Prince Xav*.

Miles began by interviewing Brun's squad commander. The man was shocked to find his exploits receiving the high-powered attention of an actual Imperial Auditor, and as a result defaulted to a thick MilSpeak in his account of events. The picture Miles unpacked behind such formal phrases as *penetrated the perimeter* and *enemy forces amassed* still made him wince. But allowing for the changed point of view, his testimony did not materially contradict the Stationer version of the events. Alas.

Miles spot-checked the squad commander's story with another cell full of fellows, who added details unfortunate but not surprising. As the squad had been attached to the *Prince Xav*, none of them were personally acquainted with Lieutenant Solian, posted on the *Idris*.

Miles emerged and tested an argument on the hovering Sealer Greenlaw. "It is quite improper for you to continue holding these men. The orders they were following, though perhaps ill thought out, were not in fact illegal in Barrayaran military definition. If their orders had been to plunder, rape, or massacre civilian quaddies, they would have been under a legal military obligation to resist them, but in fact they were specifically ordered not to kill. If they had disobeyed Brun, they could have faced court-martial. It's double jeopardy, and seriously unfair to them."

"I will consider this contention," said Greenlaw dryly, with the *For about ten seconds, after which I shall toss it out the nearest airlock* hanging unspoken.

"And, looking ahead," added Miles, "you can't wish

to be stuck housing these men indefinitely. Surely it would be preferable for us to take them," he just managed to convert *off your hands* to, "with us when we leave."

Greenlaw looked even dryer; Venn grunted disconsolately. Miles gathered Venn would be just as glad for the Imperial Auditor to take them away *now*, except for the politics of the larger situation. Miles didn't push the point, but stored it up for near-future reference. He entertained a brief, wistful fantasy of trading Brun for his men, and leaving Brun here, to the net benefit of the Emperor's Service, but did not air it aloud.

His interview with the two service security men who'd initially been sent to pick up Corbeau was, in its way, even more wince-worthy. They were sufficiently intimidated by his Auditor's rank to give full and honest, if muttered, accounts of the contretemps. But such infelicitous phraseology as *I wasn't trying to break her arm, I was trying to bounce the mutie bitch off the wall*, and *All those clutching hands gave me the creeps—it was like having snakes wrapping around my boot*, convinced Miles that here were two men he wouldn't care to have testify in public, at least not in public in Quaddiespace. However, he was able to establish the significant point that at the time of the clash they, too, had been under the impression that Lieutenant Solian had just been murdered by an unknown quaddie.

He emerged from this interrogation to say to Venn, "I think I'd better speak privately to Ensign Corbeau. Can you find us a space?"

"Corbeau already has his own cell," Venn informed him coolly. "As a result of his being threatened by his comrades."

"Ah. Take me to him, then, if you please."

～　～　～

The cell door slid aside to reveal a tall young man sitting silently on a bunk, elbows on knees, his face propped in his hands. The metallic contact circles of a jump pilot's neural implant gleamed at his temples and mid-forehead, and Miles mentally tripled the young officer's recent training costs to the Imperium. He looked up and frowned in confusion at Miles.

He was a typical enough Barrayaran: dark haired, brown eyed, with an olive complexion made pale by his months in space. His regular features reminded Miles a bit of his cousin Ivan at the same feckless age. An extensive bruise around one eye was fading, turning yellowish green. His uniform shirt was open at the throat, sleeves rolled up. Some paling, irregular pink scars zigzagged over his exposed skin, marking him as a victim of the Sergyaran worm plague of some years back; he had evidently grown up, or at least been resident, on Barrayar's new colony planet during that difficult period before the oral vermicides had been perfected.

Venn said, "Ensign Corbeau, this is the Barrayaran Imperial Auditor, Lord Vorkosigan. Your emperor sent him out as the official diplomatic envoy to represent your side in negotiations with the Union. He wishes to interview you."

Corbeau's lips parted in alarm, and he scrambled to his feet and bobbed his head nervously at Miles. It made their height differential rather spring to the eye, and Corbeau's brow wrinkled in increased confusion.

Venn added, not so much kindly as punctiliously, "Due to the charges lodged against you, as well as your petition for asylum still pending for review, Sealer Greenlaw will *not* permit him to remove you from our custody at this time."

Corbeau exhaled a little, but still stared at Miles with

the expression of a man introduced to a poisonous snake.

Venn added, a sardonic edge in his voice, "He has undertaken not to order you to shoot yourself, either."

"Thank you, Chief Venn," said Miles. "I'll take it from here, if you don't mind."

Venn took the hint, and his leave. Roic took up his silent guard stance by the cell door, which hissed closed.

Miles gestured at the bunk. "Sit down, Ensign." He seated himself on the bunk across from the young man and cocked his head in brief study as Corbeau refolded himself. "Stop hyperventilating," he added.

Corbeau gulped, and managed a wary, "My lord."

Miles laced his fingers together. "Sergyaran, are you?"

Corbeau glanced down at his arms and made an abortive move to roll down his sleeves. "Not born there, my lord. My parents emigrated when I was about five years old." He glanced at the silent Roic in his brown-and-silver uniform, and added, "Are you—" then swallowed whatever he'd been about to say.

Miles could fill in the blank. "I'm Viceroy and Vicereine Vorkosigan's son, yes. One of them."

Corbeau managed an unvoiced *Oh*. His look of suppressed terror did not diminish.

"I have just interviewed the two fleet patrollers sent to retrieve you from your station leave. In a moment, I'd like to hear your version of that event. But first— did you know Lieutenant Solian, the Komarran fleet security officer aboard the *Idris*?"

The pilot's thoughts were so clearly focused on his own affairs that it took him a moment to parse this. "I met him once or twice at some of our prior stops, my lord. I can't say as I knew him. I never went aboard the *Idris*."

"Do you have any thoughts or theories about his disappearance?"

"Not . . . not really."

"Captain Brun thinks he might have deserted."

Corbeau grimaced. "Brun would."

"Why Brun especially?"

Corbeau's lips moved, halted; he looked still more miserable. "It would not be appropriate for me to criticize my superiors, my lord, or to comment on their personal opinions."

"Brun is prejudiced against Komarrans."

"I didn't say that!"

"That was *my* observation, Ensign."

"Oh."

"Well, let's leave that for the moment. Back to your troubles. Why didn't you answer your wrist com recall order?"

Corbeau touched his bare left wrist; the Barrayarans' com links had all been confiscated by their quaddie captors. "I'd taken it off and left it in another room. I must have slept through the beep. The first I knew of the recall order was when those two, two . . ." he struggled for a moment, then continued bitterly, "*thugs* came pounding at Garnet Five's door. They just pushed her aside—"

"Did they identify themselves properly, and relay your orders clearly?"

Corbeau paused, his glance at Miles sharpening. "I admit, my lord," he said slowly, "Sergeant Touchev announcing, 'All right, mutie-lover, this show's over,' did not exactly convey 'Admiral Vorpatril has ordered all Barrayaran personnel back to their ships' to *my* mind. Not right away, anyway. I'd just woken up, you see."

"Did they identify themselves?"

"Not—not verbally."

"Show any ID?"

"Well . . . they were in uniform, with their patrol armbands."

"Did you recognize them as fleet security, or did you think this was a private visit—a couple of comrades taking out their racial offense on their own time?"

"It . . . um . . . well—the two aren't exactly mutually exclusive, my lord. In my experience."

The kid has that one straight, unfortunately. Miles took a breath. "Ah."

"I was slow, still half asleep. When they shoved me around, Garnet Five thought they were attacking me. I wish she hadn't tried to . . . I didn't slug Touchev till he dumped her out of her float chair. At that point . . . everything sort of went down the disposer." Corbeau glowered at his feet, encased in prison-issue friction slippers.

Miles sat back. *Throw this boy a line. He's drowning.* He said mildly, "You know, your career is not necessarily cooked yet. You aren't, technically, AWOL as long as you are involuntarily confined by the Graf Station authorities, any more than Brun's strike patrol here is. For a little while yet, you're in a legal limbo. Your jump pilot's training and surgery would make you a costly loss, from command's viewpoint. If you make the right moves, you could still get out of this pretty cleanly."

Corbeau's face screwed up. "I don't . . ." He trailed off.

Miles made an encouraging noise.

Corbeau burst out, "I don't want my damned career any more. I don't want to be part of"—he waved around inarticulately—"*this*. This . . . idiocy."

Suppressing a certain sympathy, Miles asked, "What's your present status—how far along are you in your enlistment?"

"I signed up for one of the new five-year hitches, with the option to reenlist or go to reserve status for the next five. I've been in three years, two still to go."

At age twenty-three, Miles reminded himself, two years still seemed a long time. Corbeau could be barely more than an apprentice junior pilot at this stage of his career, although his assignment to the *Prince Xav* implied a superior rating.

Corbeau shook his head. "I see things differently these days, somehow. Attitudes I used to take for granted, jokes, remarks, just the way things are done—they bother me now. They grate. People like Sergeant Touchev, Captain Brun—God. Were we always this awful?"

"No," said Miles. "We used to be much worse. I can personally testify to that one."

Corbeau stared searchingly at him.

"But if all the progressive-minded men had opted out then, as you are proposing to do now, none of the changes I've seen in my lifetime could have happened. We've changed. We can change some more. Not instantly, no. But if all the decent folks quit and only the idiots are left to run the show, it won't be good for the future of Barrayar. About which I do care." It startled him to realize how passionately true that statement had become, of late. He thought of the two replicators in that guarded room in Vorkosigan House. *I always thought my parents could fix anything. Now it's my turn. Dear God, how did this happen?*

"I never imagined a place like this." Corbeau's jerky wave around, Miles construed, now meant Quaddie-space. "I never imagined a woman like Garnet Five. I want to stay here."

Miles had a bad sense of a desperate young man making permanent decisions for the sake of temporary stimuli. Graf Station was attractive at first glance, certainly, but Corbeau had grown up in open country with real gravity, real air—would he adapt, or would the techno-claustrophobia creep up on him? And the young woman for whom he proposed to throw his life over, was she worthy, or would Corbeau prove a passing amusement to her? Or, over time, a bad mistake? Hell, they'd known each other bare weeks—no one could know, least of all Corbeau and Garnet Five.

"I want out," said Corbeau. "I can't stand it any more."

Miles tried again. "If you withdraw your request for political asylum in the Union before the quaddies reject it, it might still be folded into your present legal ambiguity and made to disappear, without further prejudice to your career. If you don't withdraw it first, the desertion charge will certainly stick, and do you vast damage."

Corbeau looked up and said anxiously, "Doesn't this firefight that Brun's patrol had with the quaddie security here make it in the heat? The *Prince Xav's* surgeon said it probably did."

In the heat, desertion in the face of the enemy, was punishable by death in the Barrayaran military code. Desertion in peacetime was punishable by long stretches of time in some extremely unpleasant stockades. Either seemed excessively wasteful, all things considered. "I think it would require some pretty convoluted legal twisting to call this episode a battle. For one thing, defining it so runs directly counter to the Emperor's stated desire to maintain peaceful relations with this important trade depot. Still . . . given a sufficiently hostile court and ham-handed defense counsel . . . I shouldn't call court-martial a wise risk, if it can possibly be avoided." Miles rubbed his lips. "Were you drunk, by chance, when Sergeant Touchev came to pick you up?"

"No!"

"Hm. Pity. Drunk is a wonderfully safe defense. Not politically or socially radical, y'see. I don't suppose . . . ?"

Corbeau's mouth tightened in indignation. Suggesting Corbeau lie about his chemical state would not go over well, Miles sensed. Which gave him a higher opinion of the young officer, true. But it didn't make Miles's life any easier.

"I still want out," Corbeau repeated stubbornly.

"The quaddies don't much like Barrayarans this week, I'm afraid. Relying on them granting your asylum to pluck you out of your dilemma seems to me to be a grave mistake. There must be half a dozen better ways to solve your problems, if you'd open your mind to wider tactical possibilities. In fact, almost any other way would be better than this."

Corbeau shook his head, mute.

"Well, think about it, Ensign. I suspect the situation will remain murky until I find out what happened to Lieutenant Solian. At that point, I hope to unravel this tangle quickly, and the chance to change your mind about really bad ideas could run out abruptly."

He climbed wearily to his feet. Corbeau, after a moment of uncertainty, rose and saluted. Miles returned an acknowledging nod and motioned to Roic, who spoke into the cell's intercom and obtained their release.

He exited, frowning thoughtfully, to encounter the hovering Chief Venn. "I want *Solian*, dammit," Miles said grouchily to him. "This remarkable evaporation of his doesn't reflect any better on the competence of your security than it does on ours, y'know."

Venn glowered at him. But he didn't contradict this remark.

Miles sighed and raised his wrist com to his lips to call Ekaterin.

~   ~   ~

She insisted on having him rendezvous with her back at the *Kestrel*. Miles was just as glad for the excuse to escape the depressing atmosphere of Security Post Three. He couldn't call it moral ambiguity, alas. Worse, he couldn't call it legal ambiguity. It was quite clear which side was in the right; it just wasn't his side, dammit.

He found her in their little cabin, just hanging his brown-and-silver House uniform out on a hook. She turned and embraced him, and he tilted his head back for a long, luxurious kiss.

"So, how did your venture into Quaddiespace with Bel go?" he inquired, when he had breath to spare again.

"Very well, I thought. If Bel ever wants a change from being a portmaster, I believe it could go into Union public relations. I think I saw all the best parts of Graf Station that could be squeezed into the time we had. Splendid views, good food, history—Bel took me deep down into the free fall sector to see the preserved parts of the old jumpship that first brought the quaddies to this system. They have it set up as a museum—when we arrived it was full of quaddie schoolchildren, bouncing off the walls. Literally. They were incredibly cute. It almost reminded me of a Barrayaran ancestor-shrine." She released him and indicated a large box decorated with shiny, colorful pictures and schematics, occupying half the lower bunk. "I found this for Nikki in the museum shop. It's a scale model of the D-620 Superjumper, modified with the orbital habitat configured on, that the quaddies' fore-bears escaped in."

"Oh, he'll like *that*." Nikki, at eleven, had not yet outgrown a passion for spaceships of every kind, but especially jumpships. It was still too early to guess whether the enthusiasm would turn into an adult avocation or fall by the wayside, but it certainly hadn't flagged yet. Miles peered more closely at the picture. The ancient D-620 had been an amazingly ungainly looking beast of a ship, appearing in this artist's rendition rather like an enormous metallic squid clutching a collection of cans. "Large-scale replica, I take it?"

She glanced rather doubtfully at it. "Not especially. It was a huge ship. I wonder if I should have chosen the smaller version? But it didn't come apart like this one. Now that I have it back here I'm not quite sure where to put it."

Ekaterin in maternal mode was quite capable of sharing her bunk with the thing all the way home, for Nikki's sake. "Lieutenant Smolyani will be happy to find a place to stow it."

"Really?"

"You have my personal guarantee." He favored her with a half-bow, hand over his heart. He wondered briefly if he ought to snag a couple more for little Aral Alexander and Helen Natalia while they were here, but the conversation with Ekaterin about *age-appropriate toys*, several times repeated during their sojourn on Earth, probably did not need another rehearsal. "What did you and Bel find to talk about?"

She smirked. "You, mostly."

Belated panic came out as nothing more self-incriminating than a brightly inquiring, "Oh?"

"Bel was wildly curious as to how we'd met, and obviously racking its brains to figure out how to ask without being rude. I took pity and told a little about meeting you on Komarr, and after. With all the classified parts left out, our courtship sounds awfully odd, do you know?"

He acknowledged this with a rueful shrug. "I've noticed. Can't be helped."

"Is it really true that the first time you met, you shot Bel with a stunner?"

The curiosity hadn't all run one way, evidently. "Well, yes. It's a long story. From a long time ago."

Her blue eyes crinkled with amusement. "So I understand. You were an absolute lunatic when you were younger, by all accounts. I'm not sure, if I'd met you back then, whether I'd have been impressed, or horrified."

Miles thought it over. "I'm not sure, either."

Her lips curled up again, and she stepped around him to lift a garment bag from the bunk. She drew from it a heavy fall of fabric in a blue-gray hue matching her eyes. It resolved itself into a jumpsuit of some swinging velvety stuff gathered to long, buttoned cuffs at the wrists and ankles, which gave the trouser legs a subtly sleeve-like look. She held it up to herself.

"*That's* new," he said approvingly.

"Yes, I can be both fashionable in gravity and demure in free fall." She laid the garment back down and stroked its silky nap.

"I take it Bel blocked any unpleasantness due to your being Barrayaran, when you two were out and about?"

She straightened. "Well, *I* didn't have any problems. Bel was accosted by one odd-looking fellow—he had the longest, narrowest hands and feet. Something funny about his chest, too, rather oversized. I wondered if he was genetically engineered for anything special, or if it was some sort of surgical modification. I suppose one meets all kinds, out here on the edge of the nexus. He badgered Bel to tell how soon the passengers were to be let back aboard, and said there was a rumor someone had been allowed to take off their cargo, but Bel assured him—firmly!—that no one had been let on the ships since they were impounded. One of the passengers from the *Rudra*, worrying about his goods, I gather. He implied the seized cargoes were subject to rifling and theft by the quaddie dockhands, which didn't go over too well with Bel."

"I can imagine."

"Then he wanted to know what you were doing, and how the Barrayarans were going to respond. Naturally, Bel didn't say who I was. Bel said if he wanted to know what Barrayarans were doing, he'd do better to ask one directly, and to get in line to make an appointment with you through Sealer Greenlaw like everyone else. The fellow wasn't too happy, but Bel threatened to have him escorted back to his hostel by Station Security and confined there if he didn't give over pestering, so he shut up and went scurrying to find Greenlaw."

"Good for Bel." He sighed, and hitched his tight shoulders. "I suppose I'd better deal with Greenlaw again next."

"No, you shouldn't," Ekaterin said firmly. "You've done nothing but talk with committees of upset people since the first thing this morning. The answer, I expect, is no. The question is, did you ever stop to eat lunch, or take any sort of break?"

"Um . . . well, no. How did you guess?"

She merely smiled. "Then the next item on your schedule, my Lord Auditor, is a nice dinner with your wife and your old friends. Bel and Nicol are taking us out. And after that, we're going to the quaddie ballet."

"We are?"

"Yes."

"Why? I mean, I have to eat sometime, I suppose, but my wandering off in the middle of the case to, um, disport myself, won't thrill anyone who's waiting on me to solve this mess. Starting with Admiral Vorpatril and his staff, I daresay."

"It will thrill the quaddies. They're vastly proud of the Minchenko Ballet, and being seen to show an interest in their culture can do you nothing but good with them. The troupe only performs once or twice a week, depending on the passenger traffic in port and the season—do they have seasons here? time of year, anyway—so we might not get another chance." Her smile grew sly. "It was a sold-out show, but Bel had Garnet Five pull strings and get us a box. She'll be joining us there."

Miles blinked. "She wants to pitch her case to me about Corbeau, does she?"

"That's what I'd guess." At his dubiously wrinkled nose, she added, "I found out more about her today. She's a famous person on Graf Station, a local celebrity. The Barrayaran patrol's assault on her was news; because she's a performing artist, breaking her arm like that has put her out of work for a time, as well as being an awful thing in its own right—it was extra culturally offensive, in quaddie eyes."

"Oh, terrific." Miles rubbed the bridge of his nose. It wasn't just his imagination; he did have a headache.

"Yes. So the sight of Garnet Five at the ballet, chatting cordially with the Barrayaran envoy, all forgiven and amicable, is worth what to you, in propaganda points?"

"Ah ha!" He hesitated. "As long as she doesn't end up flouncing out of my presence in a public rage because I can't promise her anything yet about Corbeau. Tricky situation, that one, and the boy's not being as smart as he could about it."

"She's apparently a person of strong emotions, but not stupid, or so I gather from Bel. I don't *think* Bel would have coaxed me to let it arrange this in order to engineer a public disaster . . . but perhaps you have reason to think otherwise?"

"No . . ."

"Anyway, I'm sure you'll be able to handle Garnet Five. Just be your usual charming self."

Ekaterin's vision of him, he reminded himself, was not exactly objective. Thank God. "I've been trying to charm quaddies all day, with no noticeable success."

"If you make it plain you like people, it's hard for them to resist liking you back. And Nicol will be playing in the orchestra tonight."

"Oh." He perked up. "*That* will be worth hearing." Ekaterin was shrewdly observant; he had no doubt she had spent the afternoon picking up cultural vibrations that went well beyond local fashions. The quaddie ballet it was. "Will you wear your fancy new outfit?"

"That's why I bought it. We honor the artists by dressing up for them. Now, skin back into your House uniform. Bel will be along to collect us soon."

"I'd better stick to my dull grays. I have a feeling that parading Barrayaran uniforms in front of the quaddies just now is a bad idea, diplomatically speaking."

"In Security Post Three, probably. But there's no point in being seen enjoying their art if we just look like any other anonymous downsiders. Tonight, I think we should both look as Barrayaran as possible."

His being seen with *Ekaterin* was good for a few points, too, he rather fancied, although not so much propaganda as pure swaggering one-upsmanship. He tapped his trouser seam, where no sword hung. "Right."

CHAPTER SIX

Bel arrived promptly at the *Kestrel's* hatch, having changed from its staid work uniform into a startling but cheerful orange doublet with glinting, star-decorated blue sleeves, slashed trousers bloused into cuffs at the knee, and color-coordinated midnight-blue hose and friction boots. Variations of the style seemed to be the local high fashion for both males and females, whether with or without legs, judging by Greenlaw's less blinding outfit.

The herm conducted them to a hushed and serene restaurant on the grav side of the station with the usual transparent window-wall overlooking station and starscape. An occasional tug or pod zipped silently past outside, adding interest to the scene. Despite the gravitation, which at least kept food on open plates, the place bowed to quaddie architectural ideals by having tables set on their own private pillars at varying heights, using all three dimensions of the room. Servers flitted back and forth and up and down in floaters. The design pleased everyone but Roic, who cranked his neck around in dismay, watching for trouble in 3-D. But Bel, ever thoughtful, as well as trained in security protocols, had provided Roic with his own perch above theirs, with an overview of the whole room; Roic mounted to his eyrie looking more reconciled.

Nicol was waiting for them at their table, which commanded a superior view out the window-wall. Her garments ran to form-fitting black knits and filmy rainbow scarves; otherwise, her appearance was not much changed from when Miles had first met her so many years and wormhole jumps ago. She was still slim, graceful of movement even in her floater, with pure ivory skin and short-clipped ebony hair, and her eyes still danced. She and Ekaterin regarded each other with great interest, and fell at once into conversation with very little prompting from Bel or Miles.

The talk ranged widely as exquisite food appeared in a smooth stream, presented by the place's well-trained and unobtrusive staff. Music, gardening, and station bio-recycling techniques led to discussion of quaddie population dynamics and the methods—technical, economic, and political—for seeding new habitats in the growing necklace along the asteroid belt. Only old war stories, by a silent, mutual agreement, failed to trickle into the conversational flow.

When Bel guided Ekaterin off to the lavatory between the last course and dessert, Nicol watched her out of earshot, then leaned over and murmured to Miles, "I am glad for you, Admiral Naismith."

He touched a finger briefly to his lips. "Be glad for Miles Vorkosigan. I certainly am." He hesitated, then asked, "Should I be equally glad for Bel?"

Her smile crimped a little. "Only Bel knows. I'm done with traveling the nexus. I've found my place, home at last. Bel seems happy here too, most of the time, but—well, Bel is a downsider. They get *itchy feet*, I'm told. Bel talks about making a commitment to the Union, yet . . . somehow, never gets around to applying."

"I'm sure Bel's interested in doing so," Miles offered.

She shrugged, and drained the last of her lemon drink; anticipating her performance later, she had forgone the wine. "Maybe the secret of happiness is to live for today, to never look ahead. Or maybe that's just a habit of mind Bel got into in its former life. All that risk, all that danger—it takes a certain sort to thrive on it. I'm not sure Bel can change its nature, or how much it would hurt to try. Maybe too much."

"Mm," said Miles. *I can't offer them a false oath, or divided loyalties*, Bel had said. Even Nicol, apparently, was not aware of Bel's second source of income—and hazard. "I do note, Bel could have found a portmaster's berth in quite a few places. It traveled a very long way to get one here, instead."

Nicol's smile softened. "That's so." She added, "Do you know, when Bel arrived at Graf Station, it still had that Betan dollar I'd paid you on Jackson's Whole tucked in its wallet?"

Miles managed to stop the logical query, *Are you sure it was the same one?* on his lips before it fell out of his mouth leaving room for his downsider foot. One Betan dollar looked like any other. If Bel had claimed it for the same one, when making Nicol's reacquaintance, who was Miles to suggest otherwise? Not that much of a spoilsport, for damn sure.

After dinner they made their way under Bel and Nicol's guidance to the bubble-car system, its arteries of transit recently retrofitted into the three-dimensional maze Graf Station had grown to be. Nicol left her floater in a common rack on the passenger platform.

It took their car about ten minutes to wend through the branching tubes to their destination; Miles's stomach lifted when they crossed into the free fall side, and he made haste to slip his antinausea meds from his pocket, swallow one, and offer them discreetly to Ekaterin and Roic.

The entrance to the Madame Minchenko Memorial Auditorium was neither large nor imposing, being just one of several accessible airseal doorways on different levels of the station here. Nicol kissed Bel and flitted off. No crowds yet clogged the cylindrical corridors, as they'd come early to give Nicol time to make her way backstage and change. Miles was therefore unprepared for the vast chamber into which they floated.

It was an enormous sphere. Nearly a third of its interior surface was a round, transparent window-wall, the universe itself turned into backdrop, thick with bright stars on this shaded side of the station. Ekaterin grabbed his hand rather abruptly, and Roic made a small choked noise. Miles had the sense of having swum inside a giant beehive, for the rest of the wall was lined with hexagonal cells like a silver-edged honeycomb filled with rainbow jewels. As they floated out toward the middle the cells resolved into velvet-lined boxes for the audience, varying in size from cozy niches for one patron to units spacious enough for parties of ten, if the ten were quaddies, not trailing long useless legs. Other sectors, interspersed, seemed to be dark, flat panels of various shapes, or to contain other exits. He tried at first to impose a sense of up and down upon the space, but then he blinked, and the chamber seemed to rotate around the window, and then he wasn't sure if he was looking up, down, or sideways through it. Down was a particularly disturbing mental construction, as it gave the dizzy impression of falling into a vast well of stars.

A quaddie usher wearing an air-jet belt took them in tow, after they had gawked their fill, and steered them gently wall-ward to their assigned hexagon. It was lined with some dark, soft, sound-baffling padding and convenient handgrips, and included its own lighting, the colored jewels seen from afar.

A dark shape and a gleam of motion in their generously sized box resolved itself, as they approached, as a quaddie woman. She was slim and long-limbed, with fine white-blond hair cut finger length and waving in an aureole around her head. It made Miles think of mermaids of legend. Cheekbones to inspire men to duel with each other, or perhaps scribble bad poetry, or drown in drink. Or worse, desert their brigade. She was clothed in close-fitting black velvet with a little white lace ruff at her throat. The cuff on the lower right elbow of her softly pleated black velvet pants . . . sleeve, Miles decided, not leg, had been left unfastened to make room for a medical air-filled arm immobilizer of a sort painfully familiar to Miles from his fragile-boned youth. It was the only stiff, ungraceful thing about her, a crude insult to the rest of the ensemble.

No mistaking her for anyone other than Garnet Five, but he waited for Bel to introduce them all properly, which Bel promptly did. They shook hands all around; Miles found her grip athlete-firm.

"Thank you for obtaining these—" *seats* did not apply, "this space for us on such short notice," Miles said, releasing her slim upper hand. "I understand we are to be privileged to view some very fine work." *Work* was a word with extra resonance in Quaddiespace, he had already gathered, like *honor* on Barrayar.

"My pleasure, Lord Vorkosigan." Her voice was melodious; her expression seemed cool, almost ironic, but an underlying anxiety glowed in her leaf-green eyes.

Miles opened his hand to indicate her broken lower

right arm. "May I convey my personal apologies for the poor behavior of some of our men. They will be disciplined for it, when we get them back. Please do not judge all Barrayarans by our worst examples." *Well, she can't; we actually don't ship out our worst, Gregor be praised.*

She smiled briefly. "I do not, for I've also met your best." The urgency in her eyes tinged her voice. "Dmitri—what will happen to him?"

"Well, that depends to a great extent on Dmitri." Pitches, Miles suddenly realized, could run two ways, here. "It could range, when he is released and returns to duty, from a minor black mark on his record—he wasn't supposed to remove his wrist com while on station leave, you know, for just the sort of reason you unfortunately discovered—to a very serious charge of attempted desertion, if he fails to withdraw his request for political asylum before it is denied."

Her jaw set a trifle. "Perhaps it won't be denied."

"Even if granted, the long-term consequences could be more complex than you perhaps anticipate. He would at that point be plainly guilty of desertion. He would be permanently exiled from his home, never able to return or see his family. Barrayar might seem a world well lost now, in the first flush of . . . emotion, but I think—I'm sure—it's something he could come to deeply regret later." He thought of melancholy Baz Jesek, exiled for years over an even more badly managed conflict. "There are other, if less speedy, ways Ensign Corbeau might yet end up back here, if his desire to do so is true will and not temporary whim. It would take a little more time, but be infinitely less damaging—he's playing for the rest of his life with this, after all."

She frowned. "Won't the Barrayaran military have him shot, or horribly butchered, or—or assassinated?"

"We are not at war with the Union." *Yet, anyway.* It would take more heroic blundering than this to make that happen, but he ought not to underestimate his fellow Barrayarans, he supposed. And he didn't think Corbeau was politically important enough to assassinate. *So let's try to make sure he doesn't become so, eh?* "He wouldn't be executed. But twenty years in jail is hardly better, from your point of view. You don't serve him *or* yourself by encouraging him to this desertion. Let him return to duty, serve out his hitch, get passage back. If you're both still of the same mind then, continue your relationship without his unresolved legal status poisoning your future together."

Her expression had grown still more grimly stubborn. He felt horribly like some stodgy parent lecturing his angst-ridden teenager, but she was no child. He'd have to ask Bel her age. Her grace and authority of motion might be the results of her dancer's training. He remembered that they were supposed to be looking cordial, so tried to soften his words with a belated smile.

She said, "We wish to become partners. Permanently."

After only two weeks of acquaintance, are you so sure? He strangled this comment in his throat as Ekaterin's sideways glance at him put him in mind of just how many days—or was it hours?—it had taken him to fall in love with her. Granted, the *permanently* part had taken longer. "I can certainly see why Corbeau would wish that." The reverse was more puzzling, of course. In both cases. He himself did not find Corbeau lovable—his strongest emotion so far was a deep desire to whack the ensign on the side of the head—but this woman clearly didn't see him that way.

"Permanently?" said Ekaterin doubtfully. "But . . . don't you think you might wish to have children someday? Or might he?"

Garnet Five's expression grew hopeful. "We've talked about having children together. We're both interested."

"Um, er," said Miles. "Quaddies are not interfertile with downsiders, surely?"

"Well, one has to make choices, before they go into the replicators, just as a herm crossing with a mono-sexual has to choose whether to have the genetics adjusted to produce a boy or a girl or a herm. Some quaddie-downsider partnerships have quaddie children, some have downsiders, some have some of each—Bel, show Lord Vorkosigan your baby pictures!"

Miles's head swiveled around. "What?"

Bel blushed and dug in its trouser pocket. "Nicol and I . . . when we went to the geneticist for counseling, they ran a projection of all the possible combinations, to help us choose." The herm held up a holocube and turned it on. Six full-length still shots of children sprang into being above its hand. They were all frozen in their early teens, with the sense of adult features just starting to emerge from childhood's roundness. They had Bel's eyes, Nicol's jawline, hair a brownish black with that famil-iar swipe of a forelock. A boy, a girl, and a herm with legs; a boy, a girl, and a herm quaddie.

"Oh," said Ekaterin, reaching for it. "How *interest-ing.*"

"The facial features are just an electronic blend of Nicol's and mine, not a genuine genetic projection," Bel explained, willingly giving the cube to her. "For that, they'd need an actual cell from a real conceptus, which, of course, they can't have till a real one is made for the genetic modifications."

Ekaterin turned the array back and forth, examin-ing the portraits from all angles. Miles, looking over her shoulder, told himself firmly that it was probably just as well that his holovid of the blandly blastular Aral Alexander and Helen Natalia was still in his luggage back aboard the *Kestrel*. But maybe later he would have a chance to show Bel—

"Have you two finally decided what you want?" asked Garnet Five.

"A little quaddie girl, to start. Like Nicol." Bel's face softened, then, abruptly, recovered its habitual ironic smile. "Assuming I take the plunge and apply for my Union citizenship."

Miles imagined Garnet Five and Dmitri Corbeau with a string of handsome, athletic quaddie children. Or Bel and Nicol, with a clutch of smart, musical ones. It made his head spin. Roic, looking quietly boggled, shook his head at Ekaterin's proferment of a closer examination of the holo-array.

"Ah," said Bel. "The show's about to start." The herm retrieved the holocube and switched it off, and plunged it back safely deep in the pocket of its baggy blue knee breeches, carefully fastening the flap.

The auditorium had filled to capacity while they spoke, the honeycomb of cells now harboring an attentive crowd including a fair smattering of other downsiders, though whether Union citizen or galactic visitor Miles could not always tell. No green Barrayaran uniforms tonight, in any case. The lights dimmed; the hubbub quieted, and a few last quaddies sped across to their boxes and settled in. A couple of downsiders who had misjudged their momentum and were stranded in the middle were rescued by the ushers and towed to their box, earning a quiet snicker from the quaddies who noticed. An electric tension filled the air, the odd blend of hope and fear that any live performance bore, with its risk of imperfection, chance of greatness. The lights dimmed further, till only the blue-white starshine glinted off the chamber's array of now-crowded cells.

Lights flared, an exuberant fountain of red and

orange and gold, and from all sides, the performers flowed in. *Thundered* in. Quaddie males, athletic and vastly enthusiastic, in skin-fitting ship knits made splendid with glitter. *Drumming.*

I wasn't expecting hand drums. Other free fall performances Miles had seen, whether dance or gymnastic, had been eerily silent except for the music and sound effects. Quaddies made their own noise, and still had hands left to play hands-across; the drummers met in the middle, clasped, gripped, exchanged momentum, turned, and doubled back in a shifting pattern. Two dozen men in free fall took up perfect station in the center of the spherical auditorium, their motion so controlled as to permit no sideways drift as the energy of their spins and duckings, twistings and turnings, flowed through their bodies one to another and on around again. The air pulsed with the rhythm of their drumming: drums of all sizes, round, oblong, two-headed; not only played by each holder, but some batted back and forth among them in an eye-and-ear-stunning cross between music and juggling, never missing a beat or a blow. The lights danced. Reflections spattered on the walls, picking out flashes from the boxes of upraised hands, arms, bright cloth, jewelry, entranced faces.

Then, from another entrance, a dozen female quaddies all in blues and greens geysered up into the growing, geodesic pattern and joined the dance. All Miles could think was, *Whoever first brought castanets to Quaddiespace has much to answer for.* They added a laughing descant note to the percussive braid of sound: hand drums and castanets, no other instruments. None needed. The round chamber reverberated, fairly rocked. He stole a glance sideways; Ekaterin's lips were parted, her eyes wide and shining, drinking in all this booming splendor without reserve.

Miles considered Barrayaran marching bands. It wasn't enough that humans did something so difficult as learning to play a musical instrument. Then they had to do it in *groups*. While *walking around*. In *complicated patterns*. And then they competed with one another to do it even *better*. Excellence, this kind of excellence, could never have any sane economic justification. It had to be done for the honor of one's country, or one's people, or the glory of God. For the joy of being human.

The piece ran for twenty minutes, until the players were gasping and sweat spun off them in tiny drops to speed in sparking streaks into the darkness, and still they whirled and thundered. Miles had to stop himself from hyperventilating in sympathy, heartbeat synchronized with their rhythms. Then, one last grand blast of joyous noise—and somehow the shifting net of four-armed men and women resolved itself into two chains, which flowed away into the exits from which they had emerged a revelation ago.

Darkness again. The silence was like a blow; behind him, Miles heard Roic exhale reverently, longingly, like a man home from war easing himself into his own bed for the first time.

The applause—hand-clapping, of course—rocked the room. No one in the Barrayaran party, Miles thought, had to *pretend* enthusiasm for quaddie culture now.

The chamber hushed again as the orchestra emerged from four points and filtered into positions all around the great window. The half-a-hundred quaddies bore a more standard array of instruments—all acoustic, Ekaterin observed to him in a fascinated whisper. They spotted Nicol, assisted by two more quaddies who helped manage and secure her harp, which was nearly the usual shape for a harp, and her double-sided hammer dulcimer, appearing to be a dull oblong box from this angle. But the piece that followed included a solo section for her with the dulcimer, her ivory face picked out in spotlights, and the music that poured forth between her four flashing hands was anything but dull. Radiantly ethereal; heartbreaking; electrifying.

Bel must have seen this dozens of times, Miles guessed, but the herm was surely as entranced as any newcomer. It wasn't just a lover's smile that illuminated Bel's eyes. *Yes. You would not be loving her properly if you did not also love her improvident, lavish, spendthrift excellence.* No jealous lover, greedy and selfish, could hoard it all; it had to be poured forth upon the world, or burst its wellspring. He glanced at Ekaterin and thought of her glorious gardens, much missed back on Barrayar. *I shall not keep you away from them much longer, love, I promise.*

There was a brief pause, while quaddie stagehands arranged a few mysterious poles and bars sticking in at odd angles around the interior of the sphere. Garnet Five, floating sideways with respect to Miles, murmured over her shoulder, "Coming up is the piece I usually dance. It's an excerpt from a larger work, Aljean's classic ballet *The Crossing*, which tells the story of our people's migration through the nexus to Quaddie-space. It's the love duet between Leo and Silver. I dance Silver. I hope my understudy doesn't muck it up . . ." She trailed off as the overture swelled.

Two figures, a downsider male and a blond quaddie woman, floated in from opposite sides of the space, picked up momentum with hand-spins around a couple of the poles, and met in the middle. No drums this time, just sweet, liquid sound from the orchestra. The Leo character's legs trailed uselessly, and it took Miles a moment to realize that he was being played by a quaddie dancer with dummy legs. The woman's use of

angular momentum, drawing in or extending various arms as she twirled or spun, was brilliantly controlled, her changes of trajectory around the various
poles precise. Only a few indrawn breaths and critical mutters from Garnet Five suggested anything less
than perfection to Miles's perceptions. The false-legged
fellow was deliberately clumsy, earning a chuckle from
the quaddie audience. Miles shifted uncomfortably,
realizing he was watching a near-parody of how downsiders looked to quaddie eyes. But the woman's charming gestures of assistance made it seem more endearing
than cruel. Bel, grinning, leaned over to murmur in
Miles's ear, "It's all right. Leo Graf's supposed to dance
like an engineer. He was."

The love angle of it all was clear enough. Affairs
between quaddies and downsiders apparently had a
long and honorable history. It occurred to Miles that
certain aspects of his youth might have been rendered
much easier if Barrayar had possessed a repertoire of
romantic tales starring short, crippled heroes, instead
of mutie villains. If this was a fair sample, it was clear
that Garnet Five was culturally primed to play Juliet
to her Barrayaran Romeo. *But let's not enact a tragedy
this time, eh?*

The enchanting piece drew to a climax, and the two
dancers saluted the enthusiastically clapping audience
before making their way out. The lights came up; break
time. Performance art was fundamentally constrained,
Miles realized, by biology, in this case the capacity of
the human bladder, whether downsider or quaddie.

When they all rendezvoused again in their box, he
found Garnet Five explaining quaddie naming conven-
tions to Ekaterin.

"No, it's not a surname," said Garnet Five. "When
quaddies were first made by the GalacTech Corporation, there were only one thousand of us. Each had

just one given name, plus a numerical designation, and with so few, each name was unique. When our ancestors fled to their freedom, they altered what the numbers coded, but kept the system of single, unique names, tracked in a register. With all of old Earth's languages to draw on, it was several generations before the system really began to be strained. The waiting lists for the really popular names were insanely long. So they voted to allow duplication, but only if the name had a numerical suffix, so we could always tell every Leo from every other Leo. When you die, your name-number goes back in the registry to be drawn again."

"I have a Leo Ninety-nine in my Docks and Locks crew," said Bel. "It's the highest number I've run across yet. Lower numbers, or none, seem to be preferred."

"I've never run across any of the other Garnets," said Garnet Five. "There were eight altogether somewhere in the Union, last time I looked it up."

"I'll bet there will be more," said Bel. "And it'll be your fault."

Garnet Five laughed. "I can wish!"

The second half of the show was as impressive as the first. During one of the musical interludes, Nicol had an exquisite harp part. There were two more large group dances, one abstract and mathematical, the other narrative, apparently based on a tragic pressurization disaster of a prior generation. The finale put everyone out in the middle, for a last vigorous, dizzying whirl, with drummers, castanet players, and orchestra combining in musical support that could only be described as massive.

It felt to Miles as though the performance ended all too soon, but his chrono told him four hours had passed in this dream. He bade a grateful but noncommittal farewell to Garnet Five. As Bel and Nicol escorted the three Barrayarans back to the *Kestrel* in the bubble car, he reflected on how cultures told their stories to themselves, and so defined themselves. Above all, the ballet celebrated the quaddie body. Surely no downsider could walk out of the quaddie ballet still imagining the four-armed people as mutated, crippled, or otherwise disadvantaged or inferior. One might even—as Corbeau had demonstrated—walk out having free-fallen in love.

Not that all crippling damage was visible to the eye. All this exuberant athleticism reminded him to check his brain chemical levels before bed, and see how soon his next seizure was likely to be.

CHAPTER SEVEN

Miles woke from a sound sleep to tapping on his cabin door.

"M'lord?" came Roic's hushed voice. "Admiral Vorpatril wants to talk with you. He's on the secured comconsole in the wardroom."

Whatever inspiration his backbrain might have floated up to his consciousness in the drowsy interlude between sleep and waking flitted away beyond recall. Miles groaned and swung out of his bunk. Ekaterin's hand extended from the top bunk, and she peeked over blearily at him; he touched it and whispered, "Go back to sleep, love." She snuffled agreeably and rolled over.

Miles ran his hands through his hair, grabbed his gray jacket, shrugged it on over his underwear, and padded out barefoot into the corridor. As the airseal door hissed closed behind him, he checked his chrono. Since Quaddiespace didn't have to deal with inconvenient planetary rotations, they kept a single time zone throughout local space, to which Miles and Ekaterin had supposedly adjusted on the trip in. All right, so it wasn't the middle of the night, it was early morning.

Miles sat at the wardroom table, straightened his jacket and fastened it to the neck, and touched the control on his station chair. Admiral Vorpatril's face and torso appeared over the vid plate. He was awake, dressed, shaved, and had a coffee cup at his right hand, the rat-bastard.

Vorpatril shook his head, lips tight. "How the hell did you know?" he demanded.

Miles squinted. "I beg your pardon?"

"I just got back the report on Solian's blood sample from my chief surgeon. It *was* manufactured, probably within twenty-four hours of its being spilled on the deck."

"Oh." *Hell and damnation.* "That's . . . unfortunate."

"But what does it mean? Is the man still alive somewhere? I'd have sworn he wasn't a deserter, but maybe Brun was right."

Like the stopped clock, even idiots could be correct sometimes. "I'll have to think about this. It doesn't actually prove if Solian's alive or dead, either way. It doesn't even, necessarily, prove that he wasn't killed *there*, just not by getting his throat cut."

Armsman Roic, God bless and keep him forever, set a cup of steaming coffee down by Miles's elbow and withdrew to his station by the door. Miles cleared his mouth, if not his mind, with the first sluicing swallow, and took a second sip to buy a moment to think.

Vorpatril had a head start on both coffee and calculation. "Should we report this to Chief Venn? Or . . . not?"

Miles made a dubious noise in his throat. His one diplomatic edge, the only thing that had given him, so to speak, a leg to stand on here, had been the possibility that Solian had been murdered by an unknown quaddie. This was now rendered even more problematic, it seemed. "The blood had to have been manufactured somewhere. If you have the right equipment, it's easy, and if you don't, it's impossible. Find all such equipment on station—or aboard ships in dock—and the place it was done has to be one of 'em. The place plus the time should lead to the people. Process of elimination. It's the sort of footwork . . ." Miles hesitated, but went on, "that the local police are better equipped to carry out than we are. If they can be trusted."

"Trust the quaddies? Hardly!"

"What motivation do they have to lie or misdirect us? *What, indeed?* "I have to work through Greenlaw and Venn. I have no authority on Graf Station in my own right." Well, there was Bel, but he had to use Bel sparingly or risk the herm's cover.

He wanted the truth. Ruefully, he recognized that he also would prefer to have a monopoly on it, at least until he had time to figure out how best to play for Barrayar's interests. *Yet if the truth doesn't serve us, what does that say about us, eh?* He rubbed his stubbled chin. "It does clearly prove that whatever happened in that freight bay, whether murder or cover-up, was carefully planned, and not spontaneous. I'll undertake to speak with Greenlaw and Venn about it. Talking to the quaddies is my job now, anyway." *For my sins, presumably. What god did I piss off this time?* "Thank you, Admiral, and thank your fleet surgeon from me for a good job."

Vorpatril gave a grudgingly pleased nod at this acknowledgment, and Miles cut the com.

"Dammit," he muttered querulously, frowning into the blank space. "Why didn't anyone pick up this information on the first pass? It's not *my* job to be a bloody forensic pathologist."

"I expect," began Armsman Roic, and stopped. "Uh . . . was that a question, m'lord?"

Miles swung around in his station chair. "A rhetorical one, but do you have an answer?"

"Well, m'lord," said Roic diffidently. "It's about the size of things here. Graf Station is a pretty big space habitat, but it's really a kind of a small city, by Barrayaran standards. And all these spacer types tend to be pretty law-abiding, in certain ways. All those safety rules. I don't imagine they *get* many murders here."

"How many did you get in Hassadar?" Graf Station boasted fifty thousand or so residents; the Vorkosigans' District capital's population was approaching half a million, these days.

"Maybe one or two a month, on average. They didn't come in smoothly. Seems there'd be a run of 'em, then a quiet period. More in the summer than the winter, except around Winterfair. Got a lot of multiples then. Most of 'em weren't *mysteries*, of course. But even in Hassadar there weren't enough really odd ones to keep our forensics folks in practice, y'see. Our medical people were part-timers from the District University, mostly, on call. If we ever got anything really strange, we'd call in one of Lord Vorbohn's homicide investigators from Vorbarr Sultana. They must get a murder every day or so up there—all sorts, lots of experience. I'll bet Chief Venn doesn't even have a forensics department, just some quaddie doctors he taps once in a while. So I wouldn't *expect* them to be, um, up to ImpSec standards like what you're used to. M'lord."

"That's . . . an interesting point, Armsman. Thank you." Miles took another swallow of his coffee. "Solian . . ." he said thoughtfully. "I don't know enough about Solian yet. Did he have enemies? Damn it, didn't the man have even one friend? Or a lover? If he *was* killed, was it for personal or for professional reasons? It makes a huge difference."

Miles had glanced through Solian's military record on the inbound leg, and found it unexceptionable. If the man had ever been to Quaddiespace before, it wasn't since he'd joined the Imperial service six years previously. He'd had two prior voyages, with different fleet consortiums and different military escorts; his experiences had apparently included nothing more exciting than handling an occasional inebriated crewman or belligerent passenger.

On average, more than half the military personnel on any tour of nexus escort duty would be new to each other. If Solian had made friends—or enemies—in the weeks since this fleet had departed Komarr, they almost had to have been on the *Idris*. If his disappearance had been closer to the time of the fleet's arrival in Quaddiespace, Miles would have pegged the professional possibilities to the *Idris* as well, but the ten days in dock was plenty of time for a nosy security man to find trouble stationside, too.

He drained his cup and punched up Chief Venn's number on the station-chair console. The quaddie security commander had also arrived early to work, apparently. His personal office was evidently on the free fall side of things. He appeared floating sideways to Miles in the vid view, a coffee bulb clutched in his upper right hand. He murmured a polite, "Good morning, Lord Auditor Vorkosigan," but undercut the verbal courtesy by not righting himself with respect to Miles, who had to exert a conscious effort to keep from tilting out of his chair. "What can I do for you?"

"Several things, but first, a question. When was the last murder on Graf Station?"

Venn's brows twitched. "There was one about seven years ago."

"And, ah, before that?"

"Three years before, I believe."

A veritable crime wave. "Did you have charge of those investigations?"

"Well, they were before my time—I became security chief for Graf Station about five years back. But there wasn't that much to investigate. Both suspects were downsider transients—one killed another downsider, the other murdered a quaddie he'd got into some stupid dispute over a payment with. Guilt confirmed by witnesses and fast-penta interrogation. It's almost always downsiders in these affairs, I notice."

"Have you *ever* investigated a mysterious killing before?"

Venn righted himself, apparently in order to frown more effectively at Miles. "I and my people are fully trained in the appropriate procedures, I assure you."

"I'm afraid I must reserve judgment on that point, Chief Venn. I have some rather curious news. I had the Barrayaran fleet surgeon reexamine Solian's blood sample. It appears that the blood in question was artificially produced, presumably using an initial specimen or template of Solian's real blood or tissue. You may wish to have your forensics people—whoever they are—retest your own archived evidence from the freight bay and confirm this."

Venn's frown deepened. "Then . . . he *was* a deserter—not murdered after all! No wonder we couldn't find a body!"

"You run—you hurry ahead, I believe. I grant you the scenario has grown extremely murky. My request, then, is that you locate all possible facilities on Graf Station where such a tissue synthesis could be carried out, and see if there is any record of such a batch being run off, and who for. Or if it could have been slipped through off the record, for that matter. I think we can safely assume that whoever had it done, Solian or some unknown, was keenly interested in concealment. The surgeon reports the blood likely was generated not much more than a day before it was spilled, but the inquiry had better be run back to the time the *Idris* first docked, to be sure."

"I . . . follow your logic, certainly." Venn held his coffee bulb to his mouth and squeezed, then transferred it absently to his lower left hand. "Yes, certainly," he echoed himself more faintly. "I'll see to it myself."

Miles felt satisfied that he'd rocked Venn off-balance to just the right degree to embarrass him into effective action, yet not freeze him into defensiveness. "Thank you."

Venn added, "I believe Sealer Greenlaw wished to speak with you this morning, also, Lord Vorkosigan."

"Very well. You may transfer my call to her, if you please."

Greenlaw was a morning person, it appeared, or else had drunk her coffee earlier. She appeared in the holovid dressed in a different elaborate doublet, looking stern and fully awake. Perhaps more by diplomatic habit than any desire to please, she twitched herself around right-side-up to Miles.

"Good morning, Lord Auditor Vorkosigan. In response to their petitions, I have arranged you an appointment with the Komarran fleet's stranded passengers at ten-hundred. You may meet with them to answer their questions at the larger of the two hostels where they are presently housed. Portmaster Thorne will meet you at your ship and conduct you there."

Miles's head jerked back at this cavalier arrangement of his time and attention. Not to mention blatant pressure move. On the other hand . . . this delivered him a room *full* of suspects, just the people he wished to study. He split the difference between irritation and eagerness by remarking blandly, "Nice of you to let me know. Just what is it that you imagine I will be able to tell them?"

"That, I must leave to you. These people came in with you Barrayarans; they are your responsibility."

"Madam, if that were so, they would all be on their way already. There can be no responsibility without power. It is the Union authorities who have placed them under this house arrest, and therefore the Union authorities who must free them."

"When you finish settling the fines, costs, and charges your people have incurred here, we will be only too happy to do so."

Miles smiled thinly, and laced his hands together on the tabletop. He wished the only new card he had to play this morning were less ambiguous. Nevertheless, he repeated to her the news about Solian's manufactured blood sample, well-larded with complaint about quaddie Security not having determined this peculiar fact earlier. She bounced it back instantly, as Venn had, as evidence more supporting of desertion than murder.

"Fine," said Miles. "Then have Union Security produce the man. A foreign downsider wandering about in Quaddiespace can't be that hard for a *competent* police force to locate. Assuming they're actually trying."

"Quaddiespace," she sniffed back, "is not a *totalitarian* polity. As your Lieutenant Solian may perhaps have observed. Our guarantees of freedom of movement and personal privacy could well have been what attracted him to separate himself here from his former comrades."

"So why hasn't he asked for asylum like Ensign Corbeau? No. I greatly fear what we have here is not a missing man, but a missing corpse. The dead cannot cry out for justice; it is a duty of the living to do so for them. And that *is* a responsibility of mine for mine, madam."

They closed the conversation on that note; Miles could only hope he'd made her morning as aggravating as she'd made his. He cut the com and rubbed the back of his neck. "Gah. That ties *me* down for the rest of the day, I'll bet." He glanced up at Roic, whose guard stance by the door had segued into at ease, his shoulders propped against the wall. "Roic."

Roic quickly drew himself upright. "My lord?"

"Have *you* ever conducted a criminal investigation?"

"Well . . . I was just a street guard, mostly. But I got to go along and help the senior officers on a few fraud and assault cases. And one kidnapping. We got her back alive. Several missing persons. Oh, and about a dozen murders, though like I said, they weren't hardly mysteries. And the series of arsons that time that—"

"Right." Miles waved a hand to stem this gentle tide of reminiscence. "I want you to do the detail work for me on Solian. First, the timetable. I want you to find out every documented thing the man did. His watch reports, where he was, what he ate, when he slept— and who with, if anyone—minute by minute, or as nearly as you can come to it, from the time of his disappearance right on back as far as you can take it. Especially any movements off the ship, and missing time. And then I want the personal slant—talk to the crew and captain of the *Idris*, try to find out anything you can about the fellow. I take it I don't need to give you the lecture on the difference between fact, conjecture, and hearsay?"

"No, m'lord. But . . ."

"Vorpatril and Brun will give you full cooperation and access, I promise you. Or if they don't, let me know." Miles smiled a bit grimly.

"It's not that, m'lord. Who'll run your personal security on Graf Station if I'm off poking around Admiral Vorpatril's fleet?"

Miles managed to swallow his airy, *I won't need a bodyguard*, upon the reflection that by his own pet theory, a desperate murderer might be floating around, possibly literally, on the station. "I'll have Captain Thorne with me."

Roic looked dubious. "I can't approve, m'lord. He's—it's—not even Barrayaran. What do you really know about, um, the portmaster?"

"Lots," Miles assured him. *Well, I used to, anyway.* He placed his hands on the table and pushed to his feet. "Solian, Roic. Find me Solian. Or his trail of breadcrumbs, or *something*."

"I'll try, m'lord."

Back in what he was starting to think of as their cabinet, Miles encountered Ekaterin returning from the shower, dressed again in her red tunic and leggings. They maneuvered for a kiss, and he said, "I've acquired an involuntary appointment. I have to go stationside almost immediately."

"You *will* remember to put on pants?"

He glanced down at his bare legs. "Planned to, yeah."

Her eyes danced. "You looked abstracted. I thought it would be safer to ask."

He grinned. "I wonder how strangely I *could* behave before the quaddies would say anything?"

"Judging by some of the stories my Uncle Vorthys tells me of the Imperial Auditors of past generations, a lot stranger than that."

"No, I'm afraid it would only be our loyal Barrayarans who'd have to bite their tongues." He captured
her hand and rubbed it enticingly. "Want to come along
with me?"

"Doing what?" she asked, with commendable
suspicion.

"Telling the trade fleet's galactic passengers I
can't do a damned thing for them, they're stuck till
Greenlaw shifts, thank you very much, have a pleasant day."

"That sounds . . . really unrewarding."

"That would be my best guess."

"A Countess is by law and tradition something of
an assistant Count. An Auditor's wife, however, is not
an assistant Auditor," she said in a firm tone, reminiscent to Miles's ear of her aunt—Professora Vorthys was
herself an Auditor's spouse of some experience. "Nicol
and Garnet Five made arrangements to take me out
this morning and show me quaddie horticulture. If you
don't mind, I think I'll stick to my original plan." She
softened this sensible refusal with another kiss.

A flash of guilt made him grimace. "Graf Station is
not exactly what we had in mind for a honeymoon
diversion, I'm afraid."

"Oh, I'm having a good time. *You're* the one who
has to deal with all the difficult people." She made a
face, and he was reminded again of her tendency
to default to extreme reserve when painfully overwhelmed. He did fancy that it happened less often,
these days. Her growing confidence and ease with the
role of Lady Vorkosigan had been his secret delight
to watch develop, this past year and a half. "Maybe,
if you're free by lunch, we can rendezvous and you can
vent at me," she added, rather in the tone of one
offering a trade of hostages. "But not if I have to
remind you to chew and swallow."

"Only the carpet." This won a snicker; a good-bye kiss, as he headed off to the shower, eased his heart in advance. He reflected that while he might feel lucky that she'd agreed to come with him to Quaddiespace, everyone on Graf Station from Vorpatril and Greenlaw on down was *much luckier*.

The crews of all four Komarran ships now locked into their docking cradles had been herded into one hostel, and held there under close arrest. The quaddie authorities had feigned not to charge the passengers, an odd lot of galactic businesspeople who, with their goods, had joined the convoy for various segments of its route as the most economical transport going their way. But of course, they could not be left aboard unmanned vessels, and so perforce had been removed to two other, more luxurious, hostels.

In theory, the erstwhile passengers were made free of the station with no more onerous requirement than to sign in and out with a couple of quaddie Security guards—armed with stunners only, Miles noted in passing—watching the hostel doors. It wasn't even that the passengers couldn't legally leave Quaddiespace— except that the cargoes most had been shepherding were still impounded aboard their respective ships. And so they were held on the principle of the monkey with its hand trapped in the jar of nuts, unwilling to let go of what they could not withdraw. The "luxury" of the hostel translated into another quaddie punishment, since the mandatory stay was being charged to the Komarran fleet corporation.

The hostel's lobby was faux-grandiose, to Miles's eye, with a high domed ceiling simulating a morning sky with drifting clouds that probably cycled through sunrise, sunset, and night with the day-cycle. Miles wondered which planet's constellations were displayed, or if they could be varied to flatter the transients du jour. The large open space was circled by a second-story balcony given over to a lounge, restaurant, and bar where patrons could meet, greet, and eat. In the center an array of drum-shaped fluted marble pillars, waist-high, supported a long double-curved sheet of thick glass that in turn held a large and complex live floral display. Where did they grow such flowers on Graf Station? Was Ekaterin viewing the source of them even now?

In addition to the usual lift tubes, a wide curving staircase led from the lobby down to the conference level. Bel guided Miles down it to a more utilitarian meeting room in the level below.

They found the chamber crammed with about eighty irate individuals of what seemed every race, dress, planetary origin, and gender in the nexus. Galactic traders with a keenly honed sense of the value of their time, and no Barrayaran cultural inhibitions about Imperial Auditors, they unleashed several days of accumulated frustrations upon Miles the moment he stepped to the front and turned to face them. Fourteen languages were handled by nineteen different brands of auto-translators, several of which, Miles decided, must have been purchased at close-out prices from makers going deservedly belly-up. Not that his answers to their barrage of questions were any special tax on the translators—what seemed ninety percent of them came up either, "I don't know yet," or "Ask Sealer Greenlaw." The fourth iteration of this latter litany was finally met with a heartrending wail, in chorus, from the back of the room of, "But Greenlaw said to ask *you*!", except for the translation device that came up a beat later with, "Lawn rule sea-hunter inquiring altitude unit!"

Miles did get Bel to quietly point out to him the

men who had attempted to bribe the portmaster into releasing their wares. Then he asked all passengers from the *Idris* who had ever met Lieutenant Solian to stay and debrief their experiences to him. This actually seemed to foster some illusion of Authority Doing Something, and the rest shuffled out merely grumbling.

An exception was an individual Miles's eye placed, after an uncertain pause, as a Betan hermaphrodite. Tall for a herm, the age suggested by its silver hair and eyebrows was belied by its firm posture and fluid movements. If a Barrayaran, Miles would have pegged the individual as a healthy and athletic sixty—which probably meant it had achieved its Betan century. A long sarong in a dark, conservative print, a high-necked shirt and long-sleeved jacket against what a Betan would doubtless interpret as the station chill, and fine leather sandals completed an expensive-looking ensemble in the Betan style. The handsome features were aquiline, the eyes dark, liquid, and sharply observant. Such extraordinary elegance seemed something Miles should remember, but he could not bring his dim sense of familiarity into focus. Damn cryo-freeze—he couldn't guess if it was a true memory, smudged as too many had been by the neural traumas of the revival process, or a false one, even more distorted.

"Portmaster Thorne?" said the herm in a soft alto.

"Yes?" Bel too, unsurprisingly, studied a fellow-Betan with special interest. Despite the herm's dignified age, its beauty drew admiration, and Miles was amused to note Bel's glance go to the customary Betan earring hanging in its left lobe. Disappointingly, it was of the style that coded, *Romantically attached, not looking.*

"I'm afraid I have a special problem with my cargo."

Bel's expression returned to bland, preparing no

doubt to hear yet another woeful story, with or without bribes.

"I am a passenger on the *Idris*. I'm transporting several hundred genetically engineered animal fetuses in uterine replicators, which require periodic servicing. The servicing is due again. I really cannot put it off much longer. If they are not cared for, my creatures may be damaged or even die." One long-fingered hand pulled on the other, nervously. "Worse, they are nearing term. I really didn't expect such a long delay in my travels. If I am held here very much longer, they will have to be decanted or destroyed, and I will lose all the value of my cargo and of my time."

"What kind of animals?" Miles asked curiously.

The tall herm glanced down at him. "Sheep and goats, mostly. Some other specialty items."

"Mm. I suppose you could threaten to turn them loose on the station, and force the quaddies to deal with 'em. Several hundred custom-colored baby lambs running around the loading bays . . ." This earned an extremely dry look from Portmaster Thorne, and Miles continued smoothly, "But I trust it won't come to that."

"I'll submit your petition to Boss Watts," said Bel. "Your name, honorable herm?"

"Ker Dubauer."

Bel bowed slightly. "Wait here. I'll return shortly."

As Bel moved off to make a vid call in private, Dubauer, smiling faintly, murmured, "Thank you so much for assisting me, Lord Vorkosigan."

"No trouble." Brow wrinkling, Miles added, "Have we ever met?"

"No, my lord."

"Hm. Oh, well. When you were aboard the *Idris*, did you encounter Lieutenant Solian?"

"The poor young male everyone thought had deserted, but now it seems not? I saw him going about his duties. I never spoke with him at any length, to my regret."

Miles considered imparting his news about the synthetic blood, then decided to hold that close for a little while. There might yet prove some better, cleverer thing to do with it than unleash it with the rest of the rumors. Some half dozen other passengers from the *Idris* had shuffled forward during this conversation, waiting to volunteer their own experiences of the missing lieutenant.

The brief interviews were of dubious value. A bold murderer would surely lie, but a smart one might simply not come forward at all. Three of the passengers were wary and curt, but dutifully precise. The others were eager and full of theories to share, none consonant with the blood on the docking bay deck being a plant. Miles wistfully considered the charms of a wholesale fast-penta interview of every passenger and crew person aboard the *Idris*. Another task Venn, or Vorpatril, or both together should have done already, dammit. Alas, the quaddies had tedious rules about such invasive methods. These transients on Graf Station were off-limits to the more abrupt Barrayaran interrogation techniques; and the Barrayaran military personnel, with whose minds Miles might make free, were much farther down his current list of suspects. The Komarran civilian crew was a more ambiguous case, Barrayaran subjects now on quaddie—well, not soil—and under quaddie custody.

While this was going forth, Bel returned to Dubauer, waiting quietly by the side of the room with its hands folded, and murmured, "I can personally escort you aboard the *Idris* to service your cargo as soon as the Lord Auditor is finished here."

Miles cut short the last crime-theory enthusiast and sent him on his way. "I'm done," he announced. He glanced at the chrono in his wrist com. Could he catch up with Ekaterin for lunch? It seemed doubtful, by this hour, but on the other hand, she could spend unimaginable amounts of time looking at vegetation, so maybe there was still a chance.

The three exited the conference chamber together and mounted the broad stairs to the spacious lobby. Neither Miles nor, he supposed, Bel ever entered a room without running a visual sweep of every possible vantage for aim, a legacy of years of unpleasant shared learning experiences. Thus it was that they spotted, simultaneously, the figure on the balcony opposite hoisting a strange oblong box onto the railing. Dubauer followed his glance, eyes widening in astonishment.

Miles had a flashing impression of dark eyes in a milky face beneath a mop of brass-blond curls, staring down intently at him. He and Bel, on either side of Dubauer, reached spontaneously and together for the startled Betan's arms and flung themselves forward. Bright bursts from the box chattered with a loud, echoing, tapping noise. Blood spattered from Dubauer's cheek as the herm was yanked along; something like a swarm of angry bees seemed to pass directly over Miles's head. Then they were, all three, sliding on their stomachs to cover behind the wide marble drums holding the flowers. The bees seemed to follow them; pellets of safety glass exploded in all directions, and chips of marble fountained in a wide spray. A vast vibrato filled the room, shook the air, the thunderous thrumming noise sliced with screams and cries.

Miles, trying to raise his head for a quick glance, was crushed down again by Bel diving over the intervening Betan and landing on him in a smothering clutch. He could only hear the aftermath: more yells, the sudden cessation of the hammering, a heavy *clunk.* A woman's voice sobbed and hiccoughed in the startling silence, then choked down to a spasmodic gulping. His hand jerked at a soft, cool kiss, but it was only a few last shredded leaves and flower petals sifting gently down out of the air to settle all around them.

CHAPTER EIGHT

Miles said in a muffled voice, "Bel, will you please get off my head?

There was a brief pause. Then Bel rolled away and, cautiously, sat up, head hunched into collar. "Sorry," said Bel gruffly. "Thought for a moment there I was about to lose you. Again."

"Don't apologize." Miles, his heart still racing and his mouth very dry, pushed up and sat, his back pressed to a now-shorter marble drum. He spread his fingers to touch the cool synthetic stone of the floor. A little beyond the narrow, irregular arc of space shielded by the table pillars, dozens of deep gouges scored the pavement. Something small and bright and brassy rolled past, and Miles's hand reached for it, then sprang back at its branding heat.

The elderly herm, Dubauer, also sat up, hand going to pat its face where blood trickled. Miles's glance took quick inventory: no other hits, apparently. He shifted and drew his Vorkosigan-monogrammed handkerchief from his trouser pocket, folded it, and silently handed it across to the bleeding Betan. Dubauer swallowed, took it, and mopped at the minor wound. It held the pad out a moment to stare at its own blood as if in surprise, then pressed the cloth back to its hairless cheek.

In a way, Miles thought shakily, it was all rather flattering. At least *someone* figured he was competent and effective enough to be dangerous. *Or maybe I'm onto something. I wonder what the hell it is?*

Bel placed its hands upon the shattered drum top, peered cautiously over, then slowly pulled itself to its feet. A downsider in the uniform of the hostel staff scurried, a little bent over, around the ex-centerpiece and asked in a choked voice, "Are you people all right?"

"I think so," said Bel, glancing around. "What *was* that?"

"It came from the balcony, sir. The, the person up there dropped it over the side and fled. The door guard went after him."

Bel didn't bother to correct the gender of the honorific, a sure sign of distraction. Miles rose too, and nearly passed out. Still hyperventilating, he crunched around their bulwark through the broken glass pellets, marble chips, half-melted brass slugs, and flower salad. Bel followed in his path. On the far side of the lobby, the oblong box lay on its side, notably dented. They both knelt to stare.

"Automated hot riveter," said Bel after a moment. "He must have disconnected . . . quite a few safety devices, to make it do that."

A slight understatement, Miles felt. But it did explain their assailant's uncertain aim. The device had been designed to throw its slugs with vast precision a matter of millimeters, not meters. Still . . . if the would-be assassin had succeeded in framing Miles's head for even a short burst—he glanced again at the shattered marble—no cryo-revival ever invented could have brought him back this time.

Ye gods—what if he hadn't missed? What would Ekaterin have done, this far from home and help, a messily decapitated husband on her hands before her honeymoon trip was even over, with no immediate support but the inexperienced Roic— *If they're shooting at me, how much danger is she in?*

In belated panic, he slapped his wristcom. "Roic! Roic, answer me!"

It was at least three agonizing seconds before Roic's drawl responded, "My lord?"

"Where are—never mind. Drop whatever you're doing and go at once to Lady Vorkosigan, and stay with her. Get her back aboard—" he clipped off the *Kestrel*. Would she be safer there? By now, any number of people knew that was where to look for Vorkosigans. Maybe aboard the *Prince Xav*, standing off a good safe distance from the station, surrounded by troops— *Barrayar's finest, God help us all*—"Just stay with her, till I call again."

"My lord, what's happening?"

"Someone just tried to rivet me to the wall. No, don't come here," he overrode Roic's beginning protest. "The fellow ran off, and anyway, quaddie security is beginning to arrive." Two uniformed quaddies in floaters were entering the lobby even as he spoke. At a hostel employee's gesticulations, one rose smoothly up over the balcony; the other approached Miles and his party. "I have to deal with these people now. I'm all right. Don't alarm Ekaterin. Don't let her out of your sight. Out."

He glanced up to see Dubauer unbend from examining a rivet-chewed marble drum, face very strained.

The herm, hand still pressed to cheek, was visibly shaken as it walked over to glance at the riveter. Miles rose smoothly to his feet.

"My apologies, honorable herm. I should have warned you never to stand too close to me."

Dubauer stared at Miles. Its lips parted in momentary bewilderment, then made a small circle, *Oh*. "I believe you two gentlepersons saved my life. I . . . I'm afraid I didn't see anything. Until that thing—what was it?—hit me."

Miles bent and picked up a loose rivet, one of hundreds, now cooled. "One of these. Have you stopped bleeding?"

The herm pulled the pad away from its cheek. "Yes, I think so."

"Here, keep it for a souvenir." He held out the gleaming brass slug. "Trade you for my handkerchief back." Ekaterin had embroidered it by hand, for a present.

"Oh—" Dubauer folded the pad over the bloodstain. "Oh, dear. Is it of value? I'll have it cleaned, and return it to you."

"Not necessary, honorable herm. My batman takes care of such things."

The elderly Betan looked distressed. "Oh, no—"

Miles ended the argument by reaching over and plucking the fine cloth from the clutching fingers, and stuffing it back in his pocket. The herm's hand jerked after it, and fell back. Miles had met diffident people, but never before one who apologized for bleeding. Dubauer, unused to personal violence on low-crime Beta Colony, was on the edge of distraught.

A quaddie security patrolwoman hovered anxiously in her floater. "What the hell happened here?" she demanded, snapping open a recorder.

Miles gestured to Bel, who took over describing the

incident into the recorder. Bel was as calm, logical, and detailed as at any Dendarii debriefing, which possibly took the woman more aback than the crowd of witnesses who clustered eagerly around trying to tell the tale in more excited terms. To Miles's intense relief, no one else had been hit except for a few minor clips from ricocheting marble chips. The fellow's aim might have been imperfect, but he apparently hadn't intended a general massacre.

Good for public safety on Graf Station, but not, upon reflection, so good for Miles. . . . His children might have been orphaned, just now, before they'd even had a chance to be born. His will was spot up to date, the size of an academic dissertation complete with bibliography and footnotes. It suddenly seemed entirely inadequate to the task.

"Was the suspect a downsider or a quaddie?" the patrolwoman asked Bel urgently.

Bel shook its head. "I couldn't see the lower half of his body below the balcony rail. I'm not even sure it was male, really."

A downsider transient and the quaddie waitress who'd been serving his drink on the lounge level chimed in with the news that the assailant had been a quaddie, and had fled down an adjoining corridor in his floater. The transient was sure he'd been male, although the waitress, now that the question was raised, grew less certain. Dubauer apologized for not having glimpsed the person at all.

Miles prodded the riveter with his toe, and asked Bel in an under-voice, "How hard would it be to carry something like that through Station Security checkpoints?"

"Easy," said Bel. "No one would even blink."

"Local manufacture?" It looked quite new.

"Yes, that's a Sanctuary Station brand. They make good tools."

"First job for Venn, then. Find out where the thing was sold, and when. And who to."

"Oh, yeah."

Miles was nearly dizzy with a weird combination of delight and dismay. The delight was partly adrenaline high, a familiar and dangerous old addiction, partly the realization that having been potshotted by a quaddie gave him a stick to beat back Greenlaw's relentless attack on his Barrayaran brutality. Quaddies were killers too, hah. They just weren't as *good* at it. . . . He remembered Solian, and took back that thought. *Yeah, and if Greenlaw didn't set me up for this herself.* Now *there* was a nice, paranoid theory. He set it aside to reexamine when his head had cooled. After all, a couple of hundred people, both quaddies and transients—including all of the fleet's galactic passengers—must have known he'd be coming here this morning.

A quaddie medical squad arrived, and on their heels—immediately after them, Chief Venn. The security chief was instantly deluged with excited descriptions of the spectacular attack on the Imperial Auditor. Only the erstwhile victim Miles was calm, standing in wait with a certain grim amusement.

Amusement was an emotion notably lacking in Venn's face. "Were you hit, Lord Auditor Vorkosigan?"

"No." *Time to put in a good word—we may need it later.* "Thanks to the quick reactions of Portmaster Thorne, here. But for this remarkable herm, you—and the Union of Free Habitats—would have one hell of a mess on your hands just now."

A babble of confirmation solidified this view, with a couple of people breathlessly describing Bel's selfless defense of the visiting dignitary with the shield of its own body. Bel's eye glinted briefly at Miles, though whether with gratitude or its opposite Miles was not just sure. The portmaster's modest protests served only to firmly affix the picture of this heroism in the eyewitnesses' minds, and Miles suppressed a grin.

One of the quaddie security patrollers who had gone in pursuit of the assailant now returned, floating back over the balcony to jerk to a halt before Chief Venn and report breathlessly, "Lost him, sir. We've put all duty personnel on alert, but we don't have much of a physical description."

Three or four people attempted to supplement this lack, in vivid and contradictory terms. Bel, listening, frowned more deeply.

Miles nudged the herm. "Hm?"

Bel shook its head and murmured back, "Thought for a moment he looked like someone I'd seen recently, but that was a downsider, so—no."

Miles considered his own brief impression. Bright-haired, light-skinned, a trifle bulky, of indeterminate age, probably male—this could cover some several hundred quaddies on Graf Station. Laboring under intense emotion, but by that time, Miles had been too. Seeing him once, at that distance, under such circumstances, Miles didn't think even he could reliably pick the fellow out of a group of similar physical types. Unfortunately, none of the transients had happened just then to be doing a vid scan of the lobby décor or each other to show the folks back home. The waitress and her patron weren't even quite sure when the fellow had arrived, though they thought he'd been in position for a few minutes, upper hands resting casually upon the balcony railing, as if waiting for some last straggler from the passengers' meeting to mount the stairs. *And so he was.*

The still-shaken Dubauer fended off the medtechs, insisting it could treat the clotted rivet-graze itself and, reiterating a lack of anything to add to the testimonies, begged to be let go back to its room to lie down.

Bel said to its fellow Betan, "Sorry about all this. I may be tied up for a while. If I can't get away myself, I'll have Boss Watts send another supervisor to escort you aboard the *Idris* to take care of your critters."

"Thank you, Portmaster. That would be very welcome. You'll call my room, yes? It really is most urgent." Dubauer withdrew hastily.

Miles couldn't blame Dubauer for fleeing, for the quaddie news services were arriving, in the persons of two eager reporters in floaters emblazoned with the logo of their journalistic work gang. An array of little vidcam floaters bobbed after them. The vidcams darted about, collecting scans. Sealer Greenlaw followed hurriedly in their wake, and wove her floater determinedly through the growing mob to Miles's side. *She* was flanked by two quaddie bodyguards in Union Militia garb, with serious weapons and armor. However useless against assassins, they at least had the salutary effect of making the babbling bystanders back off.

"Lord Auditor Vorkosigan, were you hurt?" she demanded at once.

Miles repeated to her the assurances he'd made to Venn. He kept one eye on the robot vidcams floating up to him and recording his words, and not just to be sure his good side was turned to them. But none appeared to be mini-weapons-platforms in disguise. He made sure to loudly mention Bel's heroics again, which had the useful effect of turning them in pursuit of the Betan portmaster, now on the other side of the lobby being grilled in more detail by Venn's security people.

Greenlaw said stiffly, "Lord Auditor Vorkosigan, may I convey my profound personal apologies for this untoward incident. I assure you, all of the Union's resources will be turned to tracking down what I am

certain must be an unbalanced individual and danger
to us all."

Danger to us all indeed. "I don't know what's
going on, here," said Miles. He let his voice sharpen.
"And clearly, *neither do you.* This is no diplomatic chess
game any more. Someone seems to be trying to start
a damned war in here. They nearly succeeded."

She took a deep breath. "I am certain the person
was acting alone."

Miles frowned thoughtfully. *The hotheads are always
with us, true.* He lowered his voice. "For what? Retali-
ation? Did any of the quaddies injured by Vorpatril's
strike force suddenly die last night?" He'd thought they
all were on the recovering list. It was hard to imagine a quaddie relative or lover or friend taking bloody
revenge for anything short of a fatality, but . . .

"No," said Greenlaw, her voice slowing as she considered this hypothesis. Regretfully, her voice firmed.
"No. I would have been told."

So, Greenlaw was wishing for a simple explanation,
too. But honest enough not to fool herself, at least.

His wrist com gave its high priority beep; he slapped
it. "Yes?"

"My Lord Vorkosigan?" It was Admiral Vorpatril's
voice, strained.

Not Ekaterin or Roic after all. Miles's heart climbed
back down out of his throat. He tried not to let his
voice go irritable. "Yes, Admiral?"

"Oh, thank God. We received a report that you were
attacked."

"All over now. They missed. Station Security is here
now."

There was a brief pause. Vorpatril's voice returned,
fraught with implication: "My Lord Auditor, my fleet
is on full alert, ready at your command."

Oh, crap. "Thank you, Admiral, but *stand down*,

please," Miles said hastily. "Really. It's under control. I'll get back to you in a few minutes. Do nothing without my direct, personal orders!"

"Very well, my lord," said Vorpatril stiffly, still in a very suspicious tone. Miles cut the channel.

Greenlaw was staring at him. He explained to her, "I'm Gregor's Voice. To the Barrayarans, it's as if that quaddie had fired on the Emperor, almost. When I said someone had nearly started a war, it wasn't a figure of speech, Sealer Greenlaw. At home, this place would be crawling with ImpSec's best by now."

She cocked her head, her frown sharpening. "And how would an attack on an ordinary Barrayaran subject be treated? More casually, I daresay?"

"Not more casually, but on a lower organizational level. It would be a matter for their Count's District guard."

"So on Barrayar, what kind of justice you receive depends on who you are? Interesting. I do not regret to inform you, Lord Vorkosigan, that on Graf Station you will be treated like any other victim— no better, no worse. Oddly enough, this is no loss for you."

"How salutary for me," said Miles dryly. "And while you're proving how unimpressed you are with my Imperial authority, a dangerous killer remains at large. What will it be to lovely, egalitarian Graf Station if he goes for a less personal method of disposing of me next time, such as a large bomb? Trust me—even on Barrayar, we all die the same. *Shall* we continue this discussion in private?" The vidcams, evidently finished with Bel, were zooming back toward him.

His head swiveled around at a breathless cry of, "Miles!" Also zooming toward him was Ekaterin, Roic lumbering at her shoulder. Nicol and Garnet Five followed in floaters. Pale of face and wide of eye,

Ekaterin strode across the detritus in the lobby, gripped his hands, and, at his crooked smile, hugged him fiercely. Fully conscious of the vidcams avidly circling, he hugged her back, making sure that no journalists alive, no matter how many arms or legs they possessed, could resist putting *this* one up front and center. A human-interest shot, yeah.

Roic said apologetically, "I tried to stop her, m'lord, but she insisted on coming here."

"It's all right," said Miles in a muffled voice.

Ekaterin murmured unhappily in his ear, "I thought this was a safe place. It *felt* safe. The quaddies seemed like such peaceful people."

"The majority of them undoubtedly are," Miles said. Reluctantly, he released her, though he still kept a firm grip on one hand. They stood back and regarded each other anxiously.

Across the lobby, Nicol flew to Bel with much the same look on her face as had been on Ekaterin's, and the vidcams flocked after her.

Miles asked Roic quietly, "How far did you get on Solian?"

"Not far, m'lord. I decided to start with the *Idris*, and got all the access codes from Brun and Molino all right, but the quaddies wouldn't permit me to board her. I was about to call you."

Miles grinned briefly. "Bet I can fix that now, by damn."

Greenlaw returned to invite the Barrayarans to step into the hostel management's meeting room, hastily cleared as a refuge.

Miles tucked Ekaterin's hand into his arm, and they followed; he shook his head regretfully at a reporter who flitted purposefully toward them, and one of Greenlaw's Union Militia guards made a stern warding motion. Thwarted, the quaddie journalist pounced on Garnet Five instead. With a performer's reflex, she welcomed him with a blinding smile.

"Did you have a nice morning?" Miles asked Ekaterin brightly as they picked their way over the mess on the floor.

She eyed him in some bemusement. "Yes, lovely. Quaddie hydroponics are extraordinary." Her voice went dry as she glanced around the battle zone. "And you?"

"Delightful. Well, not if we hadn't ducked. But if I can't figure out how to use this to break our deadlock, I should turn in my Auditor's chain." He stifled a fox's smile, contemplating Greenlaw's back.

"The things one learns on a honeymoon. Now I know how to coax you out of your glum moods. Just hire someone to shoot at you."

"Peps me right up," he agreed. "I figured out years ago that I was addicted to adrenaline. I also figured out that it was going to be toxic, eventually, if I didn't taper off."

"Indeed." She inhaled. The slight trembling in the hand tucked in the crook of his elbow was lessening, and its clamp on his biceps was growing less circulation-stopping. Her face was back to being deceptively serene.

Greenlaw led them through the office corridor behind the reception area to a cluttered workroom. Its small central vid table had been swept clean of ringed cups, flaccid drink bulbs, and plastic flimsies, now piled haphazardly on a credenza shoved to one wall. Miles saw Ekaterin into a station chair and sat next to her. Greenlaw positioned her floater at chair-height opposite. Roic and one of the quaddie guards jockeyed for position at the door, frowning at each other.

Miles reminded himself to be indignant and not

ecstatic. "Well." He let a distinct note of sarcasm creep into his voice. "That was a remarkable addition to my morning's speaking schedule."

Greenlaw began, "Lord Auditor, you have my apologies—"

"Your apologies are all very well, Madam Sealer, but I would happily trade them for your cooperation. Assuming *you* are not behind this incident," he overrode her indignant splutter, continuing smoothly, "and I don't see why you should be, despite the suggestive circumstances. Random violence does not seem to me to be in the usual quaddie style."

"It certainly is not!"

"Well, if it's not random, then it must be connected. The central mystery of this entire imbroglio remains the neglected disappearance of Lieutenant Solian."

"It was not neglected—"

"I disagree. The answer to it might—should!— have been put together days ago, except that Tab A seems to be on one side of an artificial divide from Slot B. If pursuing my quaddie assailant is the Union's task"—he paused and raised his eyebrows; she nodded grimly—"then pursuing Solian is surely mine. It's the one string I have in hand, and I intend to follow it up. And if the two investigations don't meet in the middle somewhere, I'll eat my Auditor's seal."

She blinked, seeming a little surprised by this turn of discourse. "Possibly . . ."

"Good. Then I want complete and unimpeded access for me, my assistant Armsman Roic, and anyone else I may designate to any and all areas and records pertinent to this search. Starting with the *Idris*, and starting immediately!"

"We cannot give downsiders license to roam at will over Station secure areas that—"

"Madam Sealer. You are here to promote and

protect Union interests, as I am to promote and protect Barrayaran interests. But if there is anything at
all about this mess that's good for either Quaddiespace
or the Imperium, it's not apparent to me! Is it to you?"

"No, but—"

"Then you agree, the sooner we dig to the center
of it, the better."

She tented her upper hands, regarding him through
narrowed eyes. Before she could marshal further
objections, Bel entered, having apparently escaped
Venn and the media at last. Nicol bobbed along
beside in her floater.

Greenlaw brightened, and seized on the one aus-
picious point for the quaddies in the chaos of the morning. "Portmaster Thorne. Welcome. I understand the
Union owes you a debt of thanks for your courage and
quick thinking."

Bel glanced at Miles—a trifle dryly, Miles thought—
and favored her with a self-deprecating half salute. "All
in a day's work, ma'am."

At one time, that would have been a statement of
plain fact, Miles couldn't help reflecting.

Greenlaw shook her head. "I trust not on Graf
Station, Portmaster!"

"Well, *I* certainly thank Portmaster Thorne!" said
Ekaterin warmly.

Nicol's hand crept into Bel's, and she shot a look
up from under her dark eyelashes for which a red-
blooded soldier of any gender would gladly have traded
medals, campaign ribbons, and combat bonuses all
three, high command's boring speeches thrown in gratis.
Bel began to look slightly more reconciled to being
designated Heroic Person of the Hour.

"To be sure," Miles agreed. "To say that I'm pleased
with the portmaster's liaison services is a profound
understatement. I would take it as a personal favor if

the herm might continue in this assignment for the duration of my stay."

Greenlaw caught Bel's eye, then nodded at Miles. "Certainly, Lord Auditor." Relieved, Miles gathered, to have something to hand to him that cost her no new concessions. A small smile moved her lips, a rare event. "Furthermore, I *shall* grant you and your designated assistants access to Graf Station records and secured areas—under the portmaster's direct supervision."

Miles pretended to consider this compromise, frowning artistically. "This places a substantial demand on Portmaster Thorne's time and attention."

Bel put in demurely, "I'll gladly accept the assignment, Madam Sealer, provided Boss Watts authorizes both all my overtime hours, and another supervisor to take over my routine duties."

"Not a problem, Portmaster. I'll direct Watts to add his increased departmental costs to the Komarran fleet's docking bill." Greenlaw delivered this promise with a glint of grim satisfaction.

Added to Bel's ImpSec stipend, this would put the herm on triple time, Miles estimated. Old Dendarii accounting tricks, hah. Well, Miles would see that the Imperium got its money's worth. "Very well," he conceded, endeavoring to appear stung. "Then I wish to proceed aboard the *Idris* immediately."

Ekaterin didn't crack a smile, but a faint light of appreciation glimmered in her eye.

And what if she had accepted his invitation to accompany him this morning? And had walked up those stairs next to him—his assailant's erratic aim would not have passed over *her* head. Picturing the probable results put an unpleasant knot in his stomach, and his lingering adrenaline high tasted suddenly very sour.

"Lady Vorkosigan,"—Miles swallowed—"I am going

to arrange for Lady Vorkosigan to stay aboard the *Prince Xav* until Graf Station Security apprehends the would-be killer and this mystery is resolved." He added in an apologetic murmur aside to her, "Sorry . . ."

She returned him a brief nod of understanding. "It's all right." Not happy, to be sure, but she possessed too much good Vor sense to argue about security issues.

He continued, "I therefore request special clearance for a Barrayaran personnel shuttle to dock and take her out." Or the *Kestrel*? No, he dared not lose access to his independent transport, bolthole, and secure communications station.

Greenlaw twitched. "Excuse me, Lord Vorkosigan, but that's how the last Barrayaran assault arrived stationside. We do not care to host another such influx." She glanced at Ekaterin and took a breath. "However, I appreciate your concern. I would be glad to offer one of our pods and pilots to Lady Vorkosigan as a courtesy transport."

Miles replied, "Madam Sealer, an unknown quaddie just tried to kill me. I'll grant I don't really think it was your secret policy, but the key word here is *unknown*. We don't yet know that it wasn't some quaddie—or group of quaddies—still in a position of trust. There are several experiments I'd be willing to run to find out, but this isn't one of them."

Bel sighed audibly. "If you wish, Lord Auditor Vorkosigan, I will undertake to personally pilot Lady Vorkosigan out to your flagship."

But I need you here!

Bel evidently read his look, for the herm added, "Or some pilot of my choosing?"

With an unfeigned reluctance, this time, Miles agreed. The next step was to call Admiral Vorpatril and inform him of his ship's new guest. Vorpatril, when his face appeared above the vid plate on the conference table, passed no comment at the news other than, "Certainly, my Lord Auditor. The *Prince Xav* will be honored." But Miles could read in the admiral's shrewd glance his estimation of the increased seriousness of the situation. Miles ascertained that no hysterical preliminary dispatches about the incident had yet been squirted on their several-day trip to HQ; news and reassurances would therefore arrive, thankfully, simultaneously. Aware of their quaddie listeners, Vorpatril made no other remark than a bland request that the Lord Auditor bring him up to date on developments at his earliest convenience—in other words, as soon as he could reach a private secured comconsole.

The meeting broke up. More of Greenlaw's Union Militia guards had arrived, and they all exited back into the hostel's lobby, well screened, belatedly, by armed outriders. Miles made sure to walk as far from Ekaterin as possible. In the shattered lobby, quaddie forensics techs, under Venn's direction, were taking vid scans and measurements. Miles frowned up at the balcony, considering trajectories; Bel, walking beside him and watching his glance, raised its eyebrows. Miles lowered his voice and said suddenly, "Bel, you don't suppose that loon could have been firing at *you*, could he?"

"Why me?"

"Well, just so. How many people does a portmaster usually piss off, in the normal course of business?" He glanced around; Nicol was out of earshot, floating beside Ekaterin and engaged in some low-voiced, animated exchange with her. "Or not-business? You haven't been, oh, sleeping with anyone's wife, have you? Or husband," he added conscientiously. "Or daughter, or whatever."

"No," said Bel firmly. "Nor with their household

pets, either. What a Barrayaran view of human motivations you do have, Miles."

Miles grinned. "Sorry. What about . . . *old* business?"

Bel sighed. "I thought I'd outrun or outlived all the old business." The herm eyed Miles sideways. "Almost." And added after a thoughtful moment, "You'd surely be way ahead of me in line for that one, too."

"Possibly." Miles frowned. And then there was Dubauer. *That* herm was certainly tall enough to be a target. Although how the devil could an elderly Betan dealer in designer animals, who'd spent most of its time on Graf Station locked in a hostel room anyway, have annoyed some quaddie enough to inspire him to try to blow its timid head off? *Too damned many possibles, here.* It was time to inject some hard data.

CHAPTER NINE

The quaddie pilot of Bel's selecting arrived and whisked Ekaterin off, together with a couple of stern-looking Union Militia guards. Miles watched her go in mild anguish. As she turned to look over her shoulder, walking out the hostel door, he tapped his wrist com meaningfully; she silently raised her left arm, com bracelet glinting, in return.

Since they were all on their way to the *Idris* anyway, Bel used the delay to call Dubauer down to the lobby again. Dubauer, smooth cheek now neatly sealed with a discreet dab of surgical glue, arrived promptly, and stared in some alarm at their new quaddie military escort. But the shy, graceful herm appeared to have regained most of its self-possession, and murmured sincere gratitude to Bel for recollecting its creatures' needs despite all the tumult.

The little party walked or floated, variously, trailing Portmaster Thorne via a notably un-public back way through the customs and security zone to the array of loading bays devoted to galactic shipping. The bay serving the *Idris,* clamped into its outboard docking cradle, was quiet and dim, unpeopled except for the two Graf Station security patrollers guarding the hatches.

Bel presented its authorization, and the two patrollers floated aside to allow Bel access to the hatch controls. The door to the big freight lock slid upward, and, leaving their Union Militia escort to help guard the entry, Miles, Roic, and Dubauer followed Bel aboard the freighter.

The *Idris,* like its sister ship the *Rudra,* was of a utilitarian design that dispensed with elegance. It was essentially a bundle of seven huge parallel cylinders: the central-most devoted to personnel, four of the outer six given to freight. The other two nacelles, opposite each other in the outer ring, housed the ship's Necklin rods that generated the field to fold it through jump points. Normal-space engines behind, mass shield generators in front. The ship rotated around its central axis to bring each outer cylinder to alignment with the stationside freight lock for automated loading or unloading of containers, or hand loading of more delicate goods. The design was not without added safety value, for in the event of a pressurization loss in one or more cylinders, any of the others could serve as a refuge while repairs were made or evacuation effected.

As they walked now through one freight nacelle, Miles glanced up and down its central access corridor, which receded into darkness. They passed through another lock into a small foyer in the forward section of the ship. In one direction lay passenger staterooms; in the other, personnel cabins and offices. Lift tubes and a pair of stairs led up to the level devoted to ship's mess, infirmary, and recreation facilities, and downward to life support, engineering, and other utility areas.

Roic glanced at his notes and nodded down the corridor. "This way to Solian's security office, m'lord."

"I'll escort Citizen Dubauer here to its flock," said Bel, "and catch up with you." Dubauer made an abortive little bow, and the two herms passed onward into the lock leading to one of the outboard freight sections.

Roic counted doorways past a second connecting foyer and tapped a code into a lock pad near the stern. The door slid aside and the light came up revealing a tiny, spare chamber housing scarcely more than a computer interface and two chairs, and some lockable wall cabinets. Miles fired up the interface while Roic ran a quick inventory of the cabinets' contents. All security-issue weapons and their power cartridges were present and accounted for, all safety equipment neatly packed in its places. The office was void of personal effects, no vid displays of the girl back home, no sly— or political—jokes or encouraging slogans pasted inside the cabinet doors. But Brun's investigators had been through here once already, after Solian had disappeared but before the ship had been evacuated by the quaddies following the clash with the Barrayarans; Miles made a note to inquire if Brun—or Venn, for that matter—had removed anything.

Roic's override codes promptly brought up all of Solian's records and logs. Miles started from Solian's final shift. The lieutenant's daily reports were laconic, repetitive, and disappointingly free of comments on potential assassins. Miles wondered if he was listening to a dead man's voice. By rights, there ought to be some psychic frisson. The eerie silence of the ship encouraged the imagination.

While the ship was in port, its security system did keep continuous vid records of everyone and everything that boarded or departed through the stationside or

other activated locks, as a routine antitheft, anti-
sabotage precaution. Slogging through the whole ten
days' worth of comings and goings before the ship had
been impounded, even on fast forward, was going to
be a time-consuming chore. The daunting possibility
of records having been altered or deleted, as Brun
suspected Solian had done to cover his desertion, would
also have to be explored.

Miles made copies of everything that seemed even
vaguely pertinent, for further examination, then he and
Roic paid a visit to Solian's cabin, just a few meters
down the same corridor. It too was small and spare
and unrevealing. No telling what personal items Solian
might have packed in the missing valise, but there
certainly weren't many left. The ship had left Komarr,
what, six weeks ago? With half a dozen ports of call
between. When the ship was in-port was the busiest
time for its security; perhaps Solian hadn't had much
time to shop for souvenirs.

Miles tried to make sense of what was left. Half a
dozen uniforms, a few civvies, a bulky jacket, some
shoes and boots . . . Solian's personally fitted pressure
suit. That seemed an expensive item one might want
for a long sojourn in Quaddiespace. Not very anonymous, though, with its Barrayaran military markings.

Finding nothing in the cabin to relieve them of the
chore of examining vid records, Miles and Roic
returned to Solian's office and began. If nothing else,
Miles encouraged himself, reviewing the security vids
would give him a mental picture of the potential
dramatis personae . . . buried somewhere in the mob
of persons who had nothing to do with anything, to
be sure. Looking at everything was a sure sign that he
didn't know what the hell he was doing yet, but it was
the only way he'd ever found to smoke out the non-
obvious clue that everyone else had overlooked. . . .

He glanced up, after a time, at a movement in the office door. Bel had returned, and leaned against the jamb.

"Finding anything yet?" the herm asked.

"Not so far." Miles paused the vid display. "Did your Betan friend get its problems taken care of?"

"Still working. Feeding the critters and shoveling manure, or at least, adding nutrient concentrate to the replicator reservoirs and removing the waste bags from the filtration units. I can see why Dubauer was upset at the delay. There must be a thousand animal fetuses in that hold. Major financial loss, if it becomes a loss."

"Huh. Most animal husbandry people ship frozen embryos," said Miles. "That's the way my grandfather used to import his fancy horse bloodstock from Earth. Implanted 'em in a grade mare upon arrival, to finish cooking. Cheaper, lighter, less maintenance—shipping delays not an issue, if it comes to that. Although I suppose this way uses the travel time for gestation."

"Dubauer did say time was of the essence." Bel hitched its shoulders, frowning uncomfortably. "What do the *Idris*'s logs have to say about Dubauer and its cargo, anyway?"

Miles called up the records. "Boarded when the fleet first assembled in Komarr orbit. Bound for Xerxes— the next stop after Graf Station, which must make this mess especially frustrating. Reservation made about . . . six weeks before the fleet departed, via a Komarran shipping agent." A legitimate company; Miles recognized the name. This record did not indicate where Dubauer-and-cargo had originated, nor if the herm had intended to connect with another commercial—or private—carrier at Xerxes for some further ultimate destination. He eyed Bel shrewdly. "Something got your hackles up?"

"I . . . don't know. There's something funny about Dubauer."

"In what way? Would I get the joke?"

"If I could say, it wouldn't bother me so much."

"It seems a fussy old herm . . . maybe something on the academic side?" University, or former university, bioengineering research and development would fit the oddly precise and polite style. So would personal shyness.

"That might account for it," said Bel, in an unconvinced tone.

"Funny. Right." Miles made a note to especially observe the herm's movements on and off the *Idris*, in his records search.

Bel, watching him, remarked, "Greenlaw was secretly impressed with you, by the way."

"Oh, yeah? She's certainly managed to keep it a secret from me."

Bel's grin sparked. "She told me you appeared very *task oriented*. That's a compliment, in Quaddiespace. I didn't explain to her that you considered getting shot at to be a normal part of your daily routine."

"Well, not *daily*. By preference." Miles grimaced. "Nor normally, in the new job. I'm supposed to be rear echelon, now. I'm getting old, Bel."

The grin twisted half-up in sardonic amusement. "Speaking from the vantage of one not quite twice your age, and in your fine old Barrayaran phrase of yore, horseshit, Miles."

Miles shrugged. "Maybe it's the impending fatherhood."

"Got you spooked, does it?" Bel's brows rose.

"No, of course not. Or—well, yes, but not in that way. My father was . . . I have a lot to live up to. And perhaps even a few things to do differently."

Bel tilted its head, but before it could speak again,

footsteps sounded down the corridor. Dubauer's light, cultured voice inquired, "Portmaster Thorne? Ah, there you are."

Bel moved within as the tall herm appeared in the doorway. Miles noted Roic's appraising eye flick, before the bodyguard pretended to return his attention to the vid display.

Dubauer pulled on its fingers anxiously and asked Bel, "Are you returning to the hostel soon?"

"No. That is, I'm not returning to the hostel at all."

"Oh. Ah." The herm hesitated. "You see, with strange quaddies flying around out there shooting at people, I didn't really want to go out on the station alone. Has anyone heard—he hasn't been apprehended yet, has he? No? I was hoping . . . can anyone go with me?"

Bel smiled sympathetically at this display of frazzled nerves. "I'll send one of the security guards with you. That all right?"

"I should be *extremely* grateful, yes."

"Are you all finished, now?"

Dubauer bit its lip. "Well, yes and no. That is, I have finished servicing my replicators, and done what little I can to slow the growth and metabolism of their contents. But if my cargo is to be held here very much longer, there'll not be time to get to my final destination before my creatures outgrow their containers. If I indeed have to destroy them, it will be a disastrous event."

"The Komarran fleet's insurance ought to make good on that, I'd think," said Bel.

"Or you could sue Graf Station," Miles suggested. "Better yet, do both, and collect twice." Bel spared him an exasperated glance.

Dubauer managed a pained smile. "That only addresses the immediate financial loss." After a longer pause, the herm continued, "To salvage the more important part, the proprietary bioengineering, I wish to take tissue samples and freeze them before disposal. I shall also require some equipment for complete biomatter breakdown. Or access to the ship's converters, if they won't become overloaded with the mass I must destroy. It's going to be a time-consuming and, I fear, extremely messy task. I was wondering, Portmaster Thorne—if you cannot obtain my cargo's release from quaddie impoundment, can you at least get me permission to stay aboard the *Idris* while I undertake its dispatch?"

Bel's brow wrinkled at the horrific picture the herm's soft words conjured. "Let's hope you're not forced to such extreme measures. How much time do you have, really?"

The herm hesitated. "Not very much more. And if I must dispose of my creatures—the sooner, the better. I'd prefer to get it over with."

"Understandable." Bel blew out its breath.

"There might be some alternate possibilities to stretch your time window," said Miles. "Hiring a smaller, faster ship to take you directly to your destination, for example."

The herm shook its head sadly. "And who would pay for this ship, my Lord Vorkosigan? The Barrayaran Imperium?"

Miles bit his tongue on either *Yeah, sure!* or alternate suggestions involving Greenlaw and the Union. He was supposed to be handling the big picture, not getting bogged down in all the human—or inhumane—details. He made a neutral gesture and let Bel shepherd the Betan out.

Miles spent a few more minutes failing to find anything exciting on the vid logs, then Bel returned.

Miles shut down the vid. "I think I'd like a look at that funny Betan's cargo."

"Can't help you there," said Bel. "I don't have the codes to the freight lockers. Only the passengers are supposed to have the access to the space they rent, by contract, and the quaddies haven't bothered to get a court order to make them disgorge 'em. Decreases Graf Station's liability for theft while the passengers aren't aboard, y'see. You'll have to get Dubauer to let you in."

"Dear Bel, I am an Imperial Auditor, and this is not only a Barrayaran-registered ship, it belongs to Empress Laisa's own family. I go where I will. Solian has to have a security override for every cranny of this ship. Roic?"

"Right here, m'lord." The armsman tapped his notation device.

"Very well, then, let's take a walk."

Bel and Roic followed him down the corridor and through the central lock to the adjoining freight section. The double-door to the second chamber down yielded to Roic's careful tapping on its lock pad. Miles poked his head through and brought up the lights.

It was an impressive sight. Gleaming replicator racks stood packed in tight rows, filling the space and leaving only narrow aisles between. Each rack sat bolted on its own float pallet, in four layers of five units—twenty to a rack, as high as Roic was tall. Beneath darkened display readouts on each, control panels twinkled with reassuringly green lights. For now.

Miles walked down the aisle formed by five pallets, around the end, and up the next, counting. More pallets lined the walls. Bel's estimate of a thousand seemed exactly right. "You'd think the placental chambers would be a larger size. These seem nearly identical to the ones at home." With which he'd grown intimately familiar, of late. These arrays were clearly meant for mass production. All twenty units stacked on a pallet economically shared reservoirs, pumps, filtration devices, and the control panel. He leaned closer. "I don't see a maker's mark." Or serial numbers or anything else that would reveal the planet of origin for what were clearly very finely made machines. He tapped a control to bring the monitor screen to life.

The glowing screen didn't contain manufacturing data or serial numbers either. Just a stylized scarlet screaming-bird pattern on a silver background. . . . His heart began to lump. What the hell was *this* doing *here* . . . ?

"Miles," said Bel's voice, seeming to come from a long way off, "if you're going to pass out, put your head down."

"Between my knees," choked Miles, "and kiss my ass good-bye. Bel, do you know what that sigil *is*?"

"No," said Bel, in a leery *now-what?* tone.

"Cetagandan Star Crèche. Not the military ghem-lords, not their cultivated—and I mean that in both senses—masters, the haut lords—not even the Imperial Celestial Garden. Higher still. The Star Crèche is the innermost core of the innermost ring of the whole damned giant genetic engineering project that is the Cetagandan Empire. The haut ladies' own gene bank. They design their emperors, there. Hell, they design the whole haut race, there. The haut ladies don't *work* in animal genes. They think it would be beneath them. They leave that to the ghem-ladies. Not, note, to the ghem-lords . . ."

Hand shaking slightly, he reached out to touch the monitor and bring up the next control level. General power and reservoir readouts, all in the green. The next level allowed individual monitoring of each fetus contained within one of the twenty separate placental chambers. Human blood temperature, baby mass, and if that weren't enough, tiny individual vid spy cameras built in, with lights, to view the replicators' inhabitants in real time, floating peacefully in their amniotic sacs. The one in the monitor twitched tiny fingers at the soft red glow, and seemed to scrunch up its big dark eyes. If not quite grown to term, it—no, she—was damned close to it, Miles guessed. He thought of Helen Natalia, and Aral Alexander.

Roic swung on his booted heel, lips parting in dismay, staring up the aisle of glittering devices. "D'you mean, m'lord, that all these things are full of *human* babies?"

"Well, now, that's a question. Actually, that's two questions. Are they full, and are they human? If they are haut infants, that latter is a most debatable point. For the first, we can at least look . . ." A dozen more pallet monitors, checked at random intervals around the room, revealed similar results. Miles was breathing rapidly by the time he gave it up for proven.

Roic said in a puzzled tone, "So what's a Betan herm doing with a bunch of Cetagandan replicators? And just because they're Cetagandan make, how d'you know it's Cetagandans inside 'em? Maybe the Betan bought the replicators used?"

Miles, lips drawn back on a grin, swung to Bel. "Betan? What do you think, Bel? How much did you two talk about the old sandbox while you were supervising this visit?"

"We didn't talk much at all." Bel shook its head. "But that doesn't prove anything. I'm not much for bringing up the subject of home myself, and even if I had, I'm too out of touch with Beta to spot inaccuracies in current events anyway. It wasn't Dubauer's *conversation* that was the trouble. There was just something . . . off, in its body language."

"Body language. Just so." Miles stepped to Bel,

reached up, and turned the herm's face to the light. Bel did not flinch at his nearness, but merely smiled. Fine hairs gleamed on cheek and chin. Miles's eyes narrowed as he carefully revisualized the cut on Dubauer's cheek.

"You have facial down, like women. All herms do, right?"

"Sure. Unless they're using a really thorough depilatory, I suppose. Some even cultivate beards."

"Dubauer doesn't." Miles made to pace down the aisle, stopped himself, turned back, and held still with an effort. "Nary a sprout in sight, except for the pretty silver eyebrows and hair, which I'd wager Betan dollars to sand are recent implants. Body language, hah. Dubauer's not double-sexed at all—what *were* your ancestors thinking?"

Bel smirked cheerily.

"But altogether sexless. *Truly* 'it.'"

"*It*, in Betan parlance," Bel began in the weary tone of one who has had to explain this far too often, "does not carry the connotation of an inanimate object that it does in other planetary cultures. I say this despite a certain ex-boss of my very distant past, who did a pretty fair imitation of the sort of large and awkward piece of furniture that one can neither get rid of nor decorate around—"

Miles waved this aside. "Don't tell *me*—I got that lecture at my mother's knee. But Dubauer's not a herm. Dubauer's a ba."

"A who what?"

"To the casual outside eye, the ba appear to be the bred servitors of the Celestial Garden, where the Cetagandan emperor dwells in serenity in surroundings of aesthetic perfection, or so the haut lords would have you believe. The ba seem the ultimate loyal servant race, human dogs. Beautiful, of course, because everything inside the Celestial Garden must be. I first ran into the ba about ten years back, when I was sent to Cetaganda—not as Admiral Naismith, but as Lieutenant Lord Vorkosigan—on a diplomatic errand. To attend the funeral of Emperor Fletchir Giaja's mother, as it happened, the old Dowager Empress Lisbet. I got to see a lot of ba up close. Those of a certain age—relics of Lisbet's youth a century ago, mainly—had all been made hairless. It was a fashion, which has since passed.

"But the ba aren't servants, or anyway, aren't *just* servants, of the Imperial haut. Remember what I said about the haut ladies of the Star Crèche only working in human genes? The ba are where the haut ladies test out prospective new gene complexes, improvements to the haut race, before they decide if they're good enough to add to this year's new model haut cohort. In a sense, the ba are the haut's siblings. Elder siblings, almost. Children, even, from a certain angle of view. The haut and the ba are two sides of one coin.

"A ba is every bit as smart and dangerous as a haut lord. But not as autonomous. The ba are as loyal as they are sexless, because they're made so, and for some of the same reasons of control. At least it explains why I kept thinking I'd met Dubauer someplace before. If that ba doesn't share most of its genes with Fletchir Giaja himself, I'll eat my, my, my—"

"Fingernails?" Bel suggested.

Miles hastily removed his hand from his mouth. He continued, "If Dubauer's a ba, and I'll swear it is, these replicators have to be full of Cetagandan . . . somethings. But why *here*? Why transport them covertly, and on a ship of a once-and-future enemy empire, at that? Well, I hope not future—the last three rounds of open warfare we had with our Cetagandan neighbors were surely enough. If this was something open and above-board, why not travel on a Cetagandan ship, with all the trimmings? I guarantee it's not for economy's sake. Deathly secret, this, but who from, and why? What the hell is the Star Crèche up to, anyway?" He swung in a circle, unable to keep still. "And what is so *hellish* secret that this ba would bring these live growing fetuses all this way, but then plan to *kill* them all to keep the secret rather than ask for help?"

"Oh," said Bel. "Yeah, that. That's . . . a bit unnerving, when you think about it."

Roic said indignantly, "That's *horrible*, m'lord!"

"Maybe Dubauer doesn't really intend to flush them," said Bel in an uncertain tone. "Maybe it just said that to get us to put more pressure on the quaddies to give it a break, let it take its cargo off the *Idris*."

"Ah . . ." said Miles. *There* was an attractive idea—wash his hands of this whole unholy mess . . . "Crap. No. Not yet, anyway. In fact, I want you to lock the *Idris* back down. Don't let Dubauer—don't let *anyone* back on board. For once in my life, I actually *want* to check with HQ before I jump. And as quickly as possible."

What was it that Gregor had said—had talked around, rather? *Something has stirred up the Ceta-gandans around Rho Ceta. Something* peculiar. *Oh, Sire, do we ever have peculiar here now.* Connections?

"*Miles*," said Bel in aggravation, "I just jumped through hoops persuading Watts and Greenlaw to let Dubauer back *on* the *Idris*. How am I going to explain the sudden reversal?" Bel hesitated. "If this cargo and its owner are dangerous to Quaddiespace, I should report it. D'you think that quaddie in the hostel might have been shooting at Dubauer, instead of at you or me?"

"The thought has crossed my mind, yes."

"Then it's . . . wrong, to blindside the station on what may be a safety issue."

Miles took a breath. "You are Graf Station's representative here; you know, therefore the station knows. That's enough. For now."

Bel frowned. "That argument's too disingenuous even for *me*."

"I'm only asking you to wait. Depending on what information I get back from home, I could damn well end up *buying* Dubauer a fast ship to take its cargo away on. One not of Barrayaran registry, preferably. Just stall. I know you can."

"Well . . . all right. For a little while."

"I want the secured comconsole in the *Kestrel*. We'll seal this hold and continue later. Wait. I want to have a look at Dubauer's cabin, first."

"Miles, have you ever heard of the concept of a *search warrant*?"

"Dear Bel, how fussy you have grown in your old age. This is a Barrayaran ship, and I am Gregor's Voice. I don't ask for search warrants, I *issue* them."

Miles took one last turn completely around the cargo hold before having Roic lock it back up. He didn't spot anything different, just, dauntingly, more of the same. Fifty pallets added up to a lot of uterine replicators. There were no decomposing dead bodies tucked in behind any of the replicator racks, anyway, worse luck.

Dubauer's accommodation, back in the personnel module, proved unenlightening. It was a small economy cabin, and whatever personal effects the . . . individual of unknown gender had possessed, it had evidently packed and taken them all along when the quaddies had transferred the passengers to the hostels. No bodies under the bed or in the cabinets here, either. Brun's people had surely searched it at least cursorily once, the day after Solian vanished. Miles made a mental note to try to arrange a more microscopically thorough forensics examination of both the cabin and the hold with the replicators. Although— by what organization? He didn't want to turn this over to Venn yet, but the Barrayaran fleet's medical people were mainly devoted to trauma. *I'll figure something out.* Never had he missed ImpSec more keenly.

"Do the Cetagandans have any agents here in Quaddiespace?" he asked Bel as they exited the cabin and locked up again. "Have you ever encountered your opposite numbers?"

Bel shook its head. "People from your region are pretty thinly spread out in this arm of the nexus. Barrayar doesn't even keep a full-time consul's office on Union Station, and neither does Cetaganda. All they have is some quaddie lawyer on retainer over there who keeps the paperwork for about a dozen minor planetary polities, if anyone should want it. Visas and entry permissions and such. Actually, as I recall, she handles *both* Barrayar and Cetaganda. If there are any Cetagandan agents on Graf, I haven't spotted them. I can only hope the reverse is also true. Though if the Cetagandans do keep any spies or agents or informers in Quaddiespace, they're most likely to be on Union. I'm only here on Graf for, um, personal reasons."

Before they exited the *Idris*, Roic insisted Bel call Venn for an update on the search for the murderous quaddie from the hostel lobby. Venn, clearly discommoded, rattled off reports of vigorous activity on the part of his patrollers—and no results. Roic was jumpy on the short walk from the *Idris*'s docking bay to the one where the *Kestrel* was locked on, eyeing their armed quaddie escort with almost as much suspicion as he eyed shadows and cross corridors. But they arrived without further incident.

"How hard would it be to get Greenlaw's permission to fast-penta Dubauer?" Miles asked Bel, as they made their way through the *Kestrel*'s airlock.

"Well, you'd need a court order. And an explanation that would convince a quaddie judge."

"Hm. Ambushing Dubauer with a hypospray aboard the *Idris* suggests itself to my mind as a simpler alternate possibility."

"It would." Bel sighed. "And it would cost me my job if Watts found out I'd helped you. If Dubauer's innocent of wrongdoing, it would certainly complain to the quaddie authorities, afterward."

"Dubauer's not innocent. At the very least, it's lied about its cargo."

"Not necessarily. Its manifest just reads, *Mammals, genetically altered, assorted*. You can't say they aren't mammals."

"Transporting minors for immoral purposes, then. Slave trading. Hell, I'll think of something." Miles waved Roic and Bel off to wait and took over the *Kestrel*'s wardroom again.

He seated himself, adjusted the security cone, and took a long breath, trying to round up his galloping thoughts. There was no faster way to get a tightbeam message, however coded, from Quaddiespace to Barrayar than via the commercial system of links. Message beams were squirted at the speed of light across local space systems between wormhole jump point stations. An hour's, or a day's, messages were collected at the stations and loaded on either dedicated communications ships, jumping back and forth on a regular schedule to squirt them across the next local space region, or, on less traveled routes, on whatever ship next jumped through. The round trip for a beamed message between Quaddiespace and the Imperium would take several days, at best.

He addressed the message triply, to Emperor Gregor, to ImpSec Chief Allegre, and to ImpSec galactic operations headquarters on Komarr. After a sketchy outline of the situation so far, including assurances of his assailant's bad aim, he described Dubauer, in as much detail as possible, and the startling cargo he'd found aboard the *Idris*. He requested full details on the new tensions with the Cetagandans that Gregor had alluded to so obliquely, and appended an urgent plea for information, if any, on known Cetagandan operatives and operations in Quaddiespace. He ran the results through the *Kestrel's* ImpSec encoder and squirted it on its way.

Now what? Wait for an answer that might be entirely inconclusive? Hardly . . .

He jumped in his chair when his wrist com buzzed. He gulped and slapped it. "Vorkosigan."

"Hello, Miles." It was Ekaterin's voice; his heart rate slowed. "Do you have a moment?"

"Not only that, I have the *Kestrel's* comconsole. A moment of privacy, if you can believe it."

"Oh! Just a second, then . . ." The wrist com channel closed. Shortly, Ekaterin's face and torso appeared over the vid plate. She was wearing that flattering slate-blue thing again. "Ah," she said happily. "There you are. That's better."

"Well, not quite." He touched his fingers to his lips and transferred the kiss in pantomime to the image of hers. Cool ghost, alas, not warm flesh. Belatedly, he asked, "Where are you?" Alone, he trusted.

"In my cabin on the *Prince Xav*. Admiral Vorpatril gave me a nice one. I think he evicted some poor senior officer. Are you all right? Have you had your dinner?"

"Dinner?"

"Oh, dear, I know that look. Make Lieutenant Smolyani at least open you a meal tray before you go off again."

"Yes, love." He grinned at her. "Practicing that maternal drill?"

"I was thinking of it more as a public service. Have you found something interesting and useful?"

"Interesting is an understatement. Useful—well— I'm not sure." He described his find on the *Idris*, in only slightly more colorful terms than the ones he'd just sent off to Gregor.

Ekaterin's eyes grew wide. "Goodness! And here I was all excited because I thought I'd found a fat clue for you! I'm afraid mine's just gossip, by comparison."

"Gossip away, do."

"Just something I picked up over dinner with Vorpatril's officers. They seemed a pleasant group, I must say."

I'll bet they made themselves pleasant. Their guest was beautiful, cultured, a breath of home, and the first female most of them had spoken to in weeks. And married to the Imperial Auditor, heh. *Eat your hearts out, boys.*

"I tried to get them to talk about Lieutenant Solian, but hardly anyone knew the man. Except that one fellow remembered that Solian had had to step out of a weekly fleet security officers' meeting because he'd sprung a nosebleed. I gather that Solian was more embarrassed and annoyed than alarmed. But it occurred to me that it might be a chronic thing with him. Nikki had them for a while, and I had them occasionally for a couple of years when I was a girl, though mine went away on their own. But if Solian hadn't taken himself to his ship's medtech to get fixed yet, well, it might be another way someone could have obtained a tissue sample from him for that manufactured blood." She paused. "Actually, now I think on it, I'm not so sure that *is* a help to you. Anyone might have grabbed his used nose rag out of the trash, wherever he'd been. Although I supposed that if his nose was bleeding, at least he had to have been alive at the time. It seemed a little hopeful, anyway." Her thoughtful frown deepened. "Or maybe not."

"*Thank* you," said Miles sincerely. "I don't know if it's hopeful or not either, but it gives me another reason to see the medtechs next. Good!" He was rewarded with a smile. He added, "And if you come up with any thoughts on Dubauer's cargo, feel free to share. Although only with me, for the moment."

"I understand." Her brows drew down. "It is stunningly strange. Not strange that the cargo exists—I mean, if all the haut children are conceived and genetically engineered centrally, the way your friend the haut Pel described it to me when she came as an envoy to Gregor's wedding, the haut women geneticists have to be exporting thousands of embryos from the Star Crèche all the time."

"Not all the time," Miles corrected. "Once a year. The annual haut child ships to the outlying satrapies are all dispatched at the same time. It gives all the top haut-lady planetary consorts like Pel, who are charged with conducting them, a chance to meet and consult with each other. Among other things."

She nodded. "But to bring this cargo all the way here—and with only one handler to look after them . . . If your Dubauer, or whoever it is, really does have a thousand babies in tow, I don't care if they're normal human or ghem or haut or what, it had better have several hundred nursemaids waiting for them somewhere."

"Truly." Miles rubbed his forehead, which was aching again, and not just from the exploding possibilities.

Ekaterin was right about that meal tray, as usual. If Solian could have tossed away a blood sample anywhere, any time . . .

"Oh, ha!" He rummaged in his trouser pocket and pulled out his handkerchief, forgotten there since this morning, and opened it on the heavy brown stain. Blood sample, indeed. He didn't have to wait for ImpSec HQ to get back to him on *this* identification. He would have undoubtedly remembered this accidental specimen eventually without the prompting. Whether before or after the efficient Roic had cleaned his clothes and returned them ready to don again, now, that was another question, wasn't it? "Ekaterin, I love you dearly. And I need to talk to the *Prince Xav*'s surgeon *right now*." He made frantic kissing motions at her, which elicited that entrancing enigmatic smile of hers, and cut the com.

CHAPTER TEN

Miles made an urgent heads-up call to the *Prince Xav*; a short delay followed while Bel negotiated clearance for the *Kestrel*'s message drone. Half a dozen armed Union Militia patrol vessels still floated protectively between Graf Station and Vorpatril's fleet lying in frustrated exile several kilometers off. It would not have done for Miles's precious sample to be shot out of space by some quaddie militia guard with a double quota of itchy trigger fingers. Miles didn't relax until the *Prince Xav* reported the capsule safely retrieved and taken inboard.

He finally settled down at the *Kestrel*'s wardroom table with Bel, Roic, and some military-issue ration trays. He ate mechanically, barely tasting the admittedly not-very-tasty hot food, one eye on the vid display still fast forwarding through the *Idris*'s lock records. Dubauer, it appeared, had never once left the vessel to so much as stroll about the station during the whole of the time the ship had been in dock, until forcibly removed with the other passengers to the stationside hostel by the quaddies.

Lieutenant Solian had left five times, four of them duty excursions for routine cargo checks, the fifth, most interestingly, after his work shift on his last day. The vid showed a good view of the back of his head, departing, and a clear shot of his face, returning about forty minutes later. Despite freezing the image, Miles could not certainly identify any of the spots or shadows on Solian's dark-green Barrayaran military tunic as nose-bloodstains, even in close-up. Solian's expression was set and frowning as he glanced up straight at the security vid pickup, part of his charge, after all—perhaps automatically checking its function. The young man didn't look relaxed, or happy, or as though he were looking forward to some interesting station leave, although he had been due some. He looked . . . intent on something.

It was the last documented time Solian had been seen alive. No sign of his body had been found when Brun's men had searched the *Idris* the next day, and they had searched thoroughly, requiring each passenger with cargo, including Dubauer, to unlock their cabins and holds for inspection. Hence Brun's strongly held theory that Solian must have smuggled himself out undetected. "So where did he go out to, during that forty minutes he was off the ship?" Miles asked in aggravation.

"He didn't cross my customs barriers, not unless someone rolled him in a damned carpet and carried him," said Bel positively. "And I don't have a record of anyone lugging in a carpet. We looked. He had pretty free access to the six loading bays in that sector, and any ships then in dock. Which were all your four, at the time."

"Well, Brun swears he doesn't have vids of him

boarding any of the other vessels. I suppose I'd better check everyone else who entered or left any of the ships during that period. Solian could have sat down for a quiet, unobserved chat—or more sinister exchange—with someone in any number of nooks in those loading bays. With or without a nosebleed."

"The bays aren't that closely controlled or patrolled," Bel admitted. "We let crew and passengers use the empty ones for exercise spaces or games, sometimes."

"Hm." Someone had certainly used one to play games with that synthesized blood, later.

After their utilitarian dinner, Miles had Bel conduct him back through the customs checkpoints to the hostel where the impounded ships' crews were housed. These digs were notably less luxurious and more crowded than the ones devoted to the paying galactic passengers, and the edgy crews had been stuck in them for days with nothing but the holovid and each other for entertainment. Miles was instantly pounced upon by assorted senior officers, both from the two Toscane Corporation ships and the two independents caught up in this fracas, demanding to know how soon he was going to obtain their release. He cut through the hubbub to request interviews with the medtechs assigned to the four ships, and a quiet room to conduct them in. Some shuffling produced, at length, a back office and a quartet of nervous Komarrans.

Miles addressed the *Idris*'s medtech first. "How hard would it be for an unauthorized person to gain access to your infirmary?"

The man blinked. "Not hard at all, Lord Auditor. I mean, it's not locked. In case of an emergency, people might need to be able to get in right away, without hunting me up. I might even *be* the emergency." He paused, then added, "A few of my medications and some equipment are kept in code-locked drawers, with tighter inventory controls, of course. But for the rest, there's no need. In dock, who comes on and off the ship is controlled by ship's security, and in space, well, that takes care of itself."

"You haven't had trouble with theft, then? Equipment going for a walk, supplies disappearing?"

"Very little. I mean, the ship is public, but it's not that *kind* of public. If you see what I mean."

The medtechs from the two independent ships reported similar protocols when in space, but when in dock both were required to keep their little departments secured when they were not themselves on duty there. Miles reminded himself that one of these people might have been bribed to cooperate with whoever had undertaken the blood synthesis. Four suspects, eh. His next inquiry ascertained that all four ship's infirmaries did indeed keep portable synthesizers in inventory as standard equipment.

"If someone snuck in to one of your infirmaries to synthesize some blood, would you be able to tell that your equipment had been used?"

"If they cleaned up after themselves . . . maybe not," said the *Idris's* tech. "Or—how much blood?"

"Three to four liters."

The man's anxious face cleared. "Oh, yes. That is, if they used my supplies of phyllopacks and fluids, and didn't bring in their own. I'd have noticed if *that* much were gone."

"How soon would you notice?"

"Next time I looked, I suppose. Or at the monthly inventory, if I didn't have occasion to look before then."

"*Have* you noticed?"

"No, but—that is, I haven't looked."

Except that a suitably bribed medtech ought to be perfectly capable of fudging the inventory of such bulky and noncontrolled items. Miles decided to turn up the heat. He said blandly, "The reason I ask is that the blood that was found on the loading bay floor that kicked off this unfortunate—and expensive—chain of events, while it was indeed initially DNA typed as Lieutenant Solian's, was found to be synthesized. Quaddie customs claim to have no record of Solian ever crossing into Graf Station, which suggests, although it does not alas prove, that the blood might have been synthesized on the outboard side of the customs barrier too. I think we had better check each of your supply inventories, next."

The medtech from the *Idris*'s Toscane-owned sister ship, the *Rudra*, frowned suddenly. "There was—" She broke off.

"Yes?" Miles said encouragingly.

"There was that funny passenger, who came in to ask me about my blood synthesizer. I just figured he was one of the nervous sorts of travelers, although when he explained himself, I also thought he probably had good reason to be."

Miles smiled carefully. "Tell me more about your funny passenger."

"He'd just signed on to the *Rudra* here at Graf Station. He said he was worried, if he had any accidents en route, because he couldn't take standard blood substitutes on account of being so heavily gengineered. Which he was. I mean, I believed him about the blood compatibility problems. That's why we carry the synthesizers, after all. He had the longest fingers—with webs. He told me he was an amphibian, which I didn't *quite* believe, till he showed me his gill slits. His ribs opened out in the most astonishing fashion. He said he has to keep spraying his gills with moisturizer, when he travels, because the air on ships and stations is too dry for him." She stopped, and swallowed.

Definitely not "Dubauer," then. Hm. Another player? But in the same game, or a different one?

She continued in a scared voice, "I ended up showing him my synthesizer, because he seemed so worried and kept asking questions about it. I mainly worried about what sorts of tranquilizers were going to be safe to use on him, if he turned out to be one of those people who gets hysterical eight days out."

Leaping about and whooping, Miles told himself firmly, would likely just frighten the young woman more. He did sit up and favor her with a perky smile, which made her shrink back in her chair only slightly. "When was this? What day?"

"Um . . . two days before the quaddies made us all evacuate the ship and come here."

Three days after Solian's vanishing. *Better and better.* "What was the passenger's name? Could you identify him again?"

"Oh, sure—I mean, webs, after all. He told me his name was Firka."

As if casually, Miles asked, "Would you be willing to repeat this testimony under fast-penta?"

She made a face. "I suppose so. Do I have to?"

Neither panicked nor too eager; good. "We'll see. Physical inventory next, I think. We'll start with the *Rudra's* infirmary." And just in case he was being led up the path by his nose, the others to follow.

More delays ensued, while Bel negotiated over the comconsole with Venn and Watts for the temporary release from house arrest of the medtechs as expert witnesses. Once those arrangements had been approved, the visit to the *Rudra's* infirmary was gratifyingly short, direct, and fruitful.

The medtech's supply of synthetic blood base was down by four liters. A phyllopack, with its hundreds of square meters of primed reaction surface stacked in microscopic layers in a convenient insert, was gone. And the blood synthesizing machine had been improperly cleaned. Miles smiled toothily as he personally scraped a tinge of organic residue from its tubing into a plastic bag for the delectation of the *Prince Xav*'s surgeon.

It all rang sufficiently true that he set Roic to collecting copies of the *Rudra*'s security records, with particular reference to Passenger Firka, and sent Bel off with the techs to cross-check the other three infirmaries without him. Miles returned to the *Kestrel* and handed off his new sample to Lieutenant Smolyani to convey promptly to the *Prince Xav*, then settled down to run a search for Firka's present location. He tracked him to the second of the two hostels taken up with the impounded ships' passengers, but the quaddie on security duty there reported that the man had signed out for the evening before dinner and had not yet returned. Firka's prior venture out that day had been around the time of the passengers' meeting; perhaps he'd been one of the men in the back of the room, although Miles certainly hadn't noticed a webbed hand raised for questions. Miles left orders with quaddie hostel security to call him or Armsman Roic when the passenger returned, regardless of the time.

Frowning, he called the first hostel to check on Dubauer. The Betan/Cetagandan herm/ba/whatever had indeed returned safely from the *Idris*, but had left again after dinner. Not in itself unusual: few of the trapped passengers stayed in their hostel when they could vary their evening boredom by seeking entertainment elsewhere on the station. But hadn't Dubauer just been the person who'd been too frightened to traverse Graf Station alone without an armed escort? Miles's frown deepened, and he left orders to this quaddie duty guard to notify him when Dubauer, too, came back.

He rescanned the *Idris*'s security vids on fast forward while waiting Roic's return. Paused close-up views of the hands of a number of otherwise unexceptionable visitors to the ship revealed no webs. It was nearing station midnight when Roic and Bel checked in.

Bel was yawning. "Nothing exciting," the herm reported. "I think we got it in one. I sent the medtechs back to the hostel with a security escort to tuck 'em into bed. What's next?"

Miles chewed gently on the side of his finger. "Wait for the surgeon to report identifications on the two samples I sent over to the *Prince Xav*. Wait for Firka and Dubauer to return to their hostels, or else go running all over the station looking for them. Or better yet, make Venn's patrollers do it, except that I don't really want to divert them from hunting for my assassin till they nail the fellow."

Roic, who had begun to look alarmed, relaxed again. "Good thinking, m'lord," he murmured gratefully.

"Sounds like a golden opportunity to sleep, to me," opined Bel.

Miles, to his irritation, was finding Bel's yawns contagious. Miles had never quite mastered their old mercenary colleague Commodore Tung's formidable ability to sleep anywhere, any time a break in the action permitted. He was sure he was still too keyed up to doze. "A nap, maybe," he granted grudgingly.

Bel, intelligently, at once seized the chance to go home to Nicol for a time. Overriding the herm's argument that it *was* a bodyguard, Miles made Bel take a quaddie patroller along. Regretfully, Miles decided to wait until he had heard back from the surgeon to call and wake up Chief Venn; he could not afford mistakes in quaddie eyes. He cleaned up and lay down himself in his tiny cabin for whatever sleep he could snatch. If he had a choice between a good night's uninterrupted sleep, and early news, he'd prefer news.

Venn would presumably let him know at once if Security effected an arrest of the quaddie with the rivet gun. Some space transfer stations were deliberately designed to be hard to hide in. Unfortunately, Graf wasn't one of them. Its architecture could only be described as an agglomeration. It had to be full of forgotten crannies. Best chance of catching the fellow would be if he attempted to leave; would he be cool enough to go to some den and lie low, instead? Or, having missed his target the first time—whoever his target had been—hot enough to circle back for another pass? Smolyani had disengaged the *Kestrel* from its lock and taken up position a few meters off the side of the station, just in case, while the Lord Auditor slept.

Replacing the question of who would want to shoot a harmless elderly Betan herm shepherding, well, sheep, with the question of who would want to shoot a Cetagandan ba smuggling a secret human—or superhuman—cargo of inestimable value, at least to the Star Crèche . . . opened up the range of possible complications in an extremely disturbing fashion. Miles had already quietly decided that Passenger Firka was due for an early rendezvous with fast-penta, with quaddie cooperation if Miles could get it, or without. But, upon reflection, it was doubtful that the truth drug would work on a ba. He entertained brief, wistful fantasies of older interrogation methods. Something from the ancestral era of Mad Emperor Yuri, perhaps, or great-great-grandfather Count Pierre "Le Sanguinaire" Vorrutyer.

He rolled over in his narrow bunk, conscious of how lonely the silence of his cabin was without the reassuring rhythmic breath of Ekaterin overhead. He had gradually become used to that nightly presence. This

marriage thing was getting to be a habit, one of his
better ones. He touched the chrono on his wrist, and
sighed. She was probably asleep by now. Too late to
call and wake her just to listen to his blither. He
counted over the days to Aral Alexander and Helen
Natalia's decanting. Their travel margin was narrowing each day he fooled around here. His brain was putting together a twisted jingle to an old nursery tune,
something about fast-penta and puppy dog tails early
in the morning, when he mercifully drifted off.

"M'lord?"

Miles snapped alert at Roic's voice on the cabin
intercom. "Yes?"

"The *Prince Xav*'s surgeon is on the secured comconsole. I told him to hold, you'd wish to be wakened."

"Yes." Miles glanced at the glowing numerals of the
wall chrono; he'd been asleep about four hours. Plenty
enough for now. He reached for his jacket. "On my
way."

Roic, again—no, still—in uniform, waited in the
increasingly familiar little wardroom.

"I thought I told you to get some sleep," Miles said.
"Tomorrow—today, it is now, could be a long one."

"I was checking through the *Rudra*'s security vids,
m'lord. Think I might have something."

"All right. Show me them after this, then." He slid
into the station chair, powered up the security cone,
and activated the com vid image.

The senior fleet surgeon, who by the collar tabs on
his green uniform held a captain's rank, looked to be one
of the young and fit New Men of Emperor Gregor's
progressive reign; by his bright, excited eyes, he wasn't
regretting his lost night's sleep much. "My Lord Auditor.
Captain Chris Clogston here. I have your blood work."

"Excellent. What have you found?"

The surgeon leaned forward. "The most interesting was the stain on that handkerchief of yours. I'd say it was Cetagandan haut blood, without question, except that the sex chromosomes are decidedly odd, and instead of the extra pair of chromosomes where they usually assemble their genetic modifications, there are two extra pairs."

Miles grinned. *Yes!* "Quite. An experimental model. Cetagandan haut indeed, but this one is a ba— genderless—and almost certainly from the Star Crèche itself. Freeze a portion of that sample and mark it top secret, and send it along home to ImpSec's bio-labs by the first available courier, with my compliments. I'm sure they'll want it on file."

"Yes, my lord."

No wonder Dubauer had tried to retrieve that blood-ied handkerchief. Quite aside from blowing its cover, high-level Star Crèche gene work was not the sort of thing the haut ladies cared to have circulating at large, not unless they'd released it themselves, filtered through a few select Cetagandan ghem clans via their haut trophy wives and mothers. Granted, the haut ladies saved their greatest vigilance for the genes they gated *in* to their well-guarded genome, generations-long work of art that it was. Miles wondered how tidy a profit one might make, offering pirate copies of those cells he'd inadvert-ently collected. Or maybe not—this ba wasn't, clearly, their *latest* work. A near-century out of date, in fact.

Their *latest* work lay in the hold of the *Idris*. Urk.

"The other sample," Clogston went on, "was Solian II—that is, Lieutenant Solian's synthesized blood. Identical to the earlier specimen—same batch, I'd say."

"Good! Now we're getting somewhere." *Where, for God's sake?* "Thank you, Captain. This is invaluable. Go get some sleep, you've earned it."

The surgeon, disappointment writ plainly on his face at this dismissal without further explication, signed off.

Miles turned back to Roic in time to catch him stifling a yawn. The armsman looked embarrassed, and sat up straighter.

"So what do we have?" Miles prompted.

Roic cleared his throat. "The passenger Firka actually joined the *Rudra* after it was first due to leave, during that delay for repairs."

"Huh. Suggests it wasn't part of a long-laid itinerary, then . . . maybe. Go on."

"I've filtered out quite a few records of the fellow passing on and off the ship, before it was impounded and the passengers evicted. Using his cabin as his hostel, it seems, which a lot of folks do to save money. Two of his trips bracket times Lieutenant Solian was away from the *Idris*—one overlaps his last routine cargo inspection, and t'other exactly brackets that last forty minutes we can't account for."

"Oh, very nice. So what does this self-declared amphibian look like?"

Roic fiddled a moment with the console and brought up a clear full-length shot from the *Rudra*'s lock vid records.

The man was tall, with pale unhealthy-looking skin and dark hair shaved close to his skull in a patchy, unflattering fuzz, like lichen on a boulder. Big nose, small ears, a lugubrious expression on his rubbery face—he looked strung out, actually, eyes dark and ringed. Long, skinny arms and legs; a loose tunic or poncho concealed the details of his big upper torso. His hands and feet were especially distinctive, and Miles zoomed in for close-ups. One hand was half-concealed in a cloth glove with the fingertips cut out, which hid the webs from a casual glance, but the other was ungloved and half-raised, and the webs showed distinctly, a dark rose color between the over-long fingers. The feet were concealed in soft boots or buskins, tied at the ankles, but they too were about double the length of a normal foot, though no wider. Could the fellow spread his webbed toes, when in the water, as he spread his webbed fingers, to make a broad flipper?

He recalled Ekaterin's description of the passenger who had accosted her and Bel on their outing, that first day—*he had the longest, narrowest hands and feet*. Bel should get a look at this shortly. Miles let the vid run. The fellow had a somewhat shambling gait when he walked, lifting and setting down those almost clownish feet.

"Where did he come from?" Miles asked Roic.

"His documentation *claims* he's an Aslunder." Roic's voice was heavy with disbelief.

Aslund was one of Barrayar's fairly near nexus neighbors, an impoverished agricultural world in a local space cul-de-sac off the Hegen Hub. "Huh. Almost our neck of the woods."

"I dunno, m'lord. His Graf Station customs records show him disembarking from a ship he'd joined at Tau Ceti, which arrived here on the day before our fleet was originally due to leave. Don't know if he originated there or not."

"I'd bet not." Was there a water-world being settled somewhere on the fringes of the nexus, whose colonists had chosen to alter their children instead of their environment? Miles hadn't heard of one, but it had to happen sometime. Or was Firka a one-off project, an experiment or prototype of some sort? He'd certainly run into a few of those, before. Neither exactly squared with an origin on Aslund. Though he might have immigrated there . . . Miles made a note to request an ImpSec background search on the fellow in his next report, even though any results were likely to trickle back too late to be of any immediate use. At least, he certainly hoped he'd have this mess wrapped up and shipped out before then.

"He originally tried to get a berth on the *Idris*, but there wasn't room," Roic added.

"Ah!" Or maybe that ought to be, *Huh?*

Miles sat back in his station chair, eyes narrowing. Reasoning in advance of his beloved and much-longed-for fast-penta—posit that this peculiar individual had had some personal contact with Solian before the lieutenant went missing. Posit that he had acquired, somehow, a sample of Solian's blood, perhaps in much the same accidental way that Miles had acquired Dubauer's. Why, then, in the name of reason, would he have subsequently gone to the trouble of running up a fake sample of Solian's blood and dribbling it all over a loading bay and out the airlock?

To cover up a murder elsewhere? Solian's disappearance had already been put down to desertion, by his own commanders. No cover needed: if a murder, it was already nearly the perfect crime at that point, with the investigation about to be abandoned.

A frame? Meant to pin Solian's murder on another? Attractive, but in that case, shouldn't some innocent have been tracked and accused by now? Unless Firka was the innocent, it was a frame with no portrait in it, at present.

To cover up a desertion? Might Firka and Solian be collaborating on Solian's defection? Or . . . when might a desertion not be a desertion? When it was an ImpSec covert ops scam, that's when. Except that Solian was Service Security, not ImpSec: a guard, not a spy or trained agent. Still . . . a *sufficiently* bright, loyal, highly motivated, and ambitious officer, finding himself in some complex imbroglio, might not wait for orders from on high to pursue a fast-moving long shot. As Miles had reason to know.

Of course, taking risky chances like that could get such an officer killed. As Miles also had reason to know.

Regardless of intent, what had the actual effect of the blood bait been? Or what would it have been if Corbeau and Garnet Five's star-crossed romance hadn't run afoul of Barrayaran prejudices and loutishness? The showy scarlet scenario on the loading bay deck would certainly have reaffixed official attention upon Solian's disappearance; it would almost certainly have delayed the fleet's departure, although not as spectacularly as the real events had. Assuming Garnet Five and Corbeau's problems had been accidental. She was an actress of sorts, after all. They had only Corbeau's word about his wrist com.

He said wistfully, "I don't suppose we have a clear shot of this frog-man lugging out half a dozen liter jugs at any point?"

"Afraid not, m'lord. He went back and forth with lots of packages and boxes at various times, though; they could well have been hid inside something."

Gah. The acquisition of facts was supposed to clarify thought. This was just getting murkier and murkier. He asked Roic, "Has quaddie security from either of the hostels called yet? Are Dubauer or Firka back yet?"

"No, m'lord. No calls, that is."

Miles called both to cross-check; neither of his two passengers of interest had yet returned. It was over four hours after midnight, now, 0420 on the twenty-four-hour, Earth-descended clock that Quaddiespace still kept, generations after their ancestors' unmodified ancestors had departed the home world.

After he'd cut the com, Miles asked querulously, "So where the hell have they gone, all night?"

Roic shrugged. "If it was t' obvious thing, I wouldn't look for them to be back till breakfast."

Miles considerately declined to take notice of Roic's distinct blush. "Our frog-man, maybe, but I guarantee the ba didn't go looking for feminine companionship. There's nothing obvious about any of this." Decisively, Miles reached for the call pad again.

Instead of Chief Venn, the image of a quaddie woman in a Security gray uniform appeared against the dizzying radial background of Venn's office. Miles wasn't sure what her rank markings decoded to, but she looked sensible, middle-aged, and harried enough to be fairly senior.

"Good morning," he began politely. "Where's Chief Venn?"

"Sleeping, I hope." The expression on her face suggested she was going to do her loyal best to keep it that way, too.

"At a time like this?"

"The poor man had a double shift and a half yester . . ." She squinted at him, and seemed to come to some recognition. "Oh. Lord Auditor Vorkosigan. I'm Chief Venn's third-shift supervisor, Teris Three. Is there anything I can do for you?"

"Night duty officer, eh? Very good. Yes, please. I wish to arrange for the detainment and interrogation, possibly with fast-penta, of a passenger from the *Rudra*. His name's Firka."

"Is there some criminal charge you wish to file?"

"Material witness, to start. I have found reason to suspect he may have something to do with the blood on the floor of the docking bay that started this mess. I want very much to find out for sure."

"Sir, we can't just go around arresting and drugging anyone we please, here. We need a formal charge. And if the transient doesn't volunteer to be interrogated, you'll have to get an adjudicator's order for the fast-penta."

That problem, Miles decided, he would bounce to Sealer Greenlaw. It sounded like her department. "All right, I charge him with suspected littering. Incorrect disposal of organics has to be some kind of illegal, here."

Despite herself, the corner of her mouth twitched. "It's a misdemeanor. Yes, that would do," she admitted.

"Any pretext that will fix it for you is all right by me. I *want* him, and I want him as quickly as you can lay hands on him. Unfortunately, he signed out of his hostel at about seventeen-hundred yesterday, and hasn't been seen since."

"Our security work gang is seriously overstretched, here, on account of yesterday's . . . unfortunate incident. Can this wait till morning, Lord Auditor Vorkosigan?"

"No."

For a moment, he thought she was going to go all bureaucratic on him, but after screwing up her lips in a thoughtfully aggravated way for a moment, she relented. "Very well. I'll put out a detention order on him, pending Chief Venn's review. But you'll have to see to the adjudicator as soon as we pick him up."

"Thank you. I promise you won't have any trouble recognizing him. I can download IDs and some vid shots to you from here, if you wish."

She allowed as how that would be useful, and the task was done.

Miles hesitated, mulling over the even more disturbing dilemma of Dubauer. There was not, to be sure, any obvious connection between the two problems. Yet. Perhaps the interrogation of Firka would reveal one?

Leaving Venn's myrmidon to get on with it, Miles cut the com. He leaned back in his station chair for a moment, then brought up the vids of Firka and reran them a couple of times.

"So," he said after a time. "How the devil did he keep those long, floppy feet out of the blood puddles?"

Roic stared over his shoulder. "Floater?" he finally said. "He'd have to be damned near double-jointed to fold those legs up in one, though."

"He *looks* damned near double-jointed." But if Firka's toes were as long and prehensile as his fingers suggested, might he have been able to manipulate the joystick controls, designed for quaddie lower hands, with his feet? In this new scenario, Miles needn't picture the person in the floater horsing a heavy body around, merely emptying his gurgling liter jugs overboard and supplying some artistic smears with a suitable rag.

After a few cross-eyed moments trying to imagine this, Miles dumped Firka's vid shots into an image manipulator and installed the fellow in a floater. The supposed amphibian didn't quite have to be double-jointed or break his legs to fit in. Assuming his lower body was rather more flexible than Miles's or Roic's, it folded pretty neatly. It looked a bit painful, but possible.

Miles stared harder at the image above the vid plate.

The first question one addressed in describing a person on Graf Station wasn't "man or woman"? It was "quaddie or downsider"? The very first cut, by which one discarded half or more of the possibilities from further consideration.

He pictured a blond quaddie in a dark jacket, speeding up a corridor in a floater. He pictured that quaddie's belated pursuers, whizzing past a shaven-headed downsider in light garb, walking the other way. That was all it would take, in a sufficiently harried moment. Step out of the floater, turn one's jacket inside out, stuff the wig in a pocket, leave the machine with a couple of others sitting waiting, stroll away . . . It would be much harder to work it the other way around, of course, for a quaddie to impersonate a downsider.

He stared at Firka's hollow, dark-ringed eyes. He pulled up a suitable mop of blond ringlets from the imager files and applied it to Firka's unhandsome head.

A fair approximation of the dark-eyed barrel-chested quaddie with the rivet gun? Glimpsed for a fraction of a second, at fifteen meters range, and truth to tell most of Miles's attention had been on the spark-spitting, chattering, hot-brass-chucking object in his hands . . . had those hands been webbed?

Fortunately, he could draw upon a second opinion. He called up Bel Thorne's home code from the comconsole.

Unsurprisingly, at this ungodly hour, the visual didn't come on when Nicol's sleepy voice answered. "Hello?"

"Nicol? Miles Vorkosigan here. Sorry to drag you out of your sleep sack. I need to talk to your housemate. Boot it out and make it come to the vid. Bel's had more sleep than I have, by now."

The visual came up. Nicol righted herself and drew a fluffy lace garment closer about her with a lower hand; this section of the apartment she shared with Bel was evidently on the free fall side. It was too dim to make out much beyond her floating form. She rubbed her eyes. "What? Isn't Bel with you?"

Miles's stomach went into free fall, for all that the *Kestrel*'s grav was in good working order. "No . . . Bel left over six hours ago."

Her frown sharpened. The sleep drained from her face, to be replaced by alarm. "But Bel didn't come home last night!"

CHAPTER ELEVEN

Graf Station Security Post One, housing most of the security police administrative offices including Chief Venn's, lay entirely on the free fall side of the station. Miles and Roic, trailed by a flustered quaddie guard from the *Kestrel*'s lock, floated into the post's radially arranged reception space, from which tubular corridors led off at odd angles. The place was still night-quiet, although shift change was surely due soon.

Nicol had beaten Miles and Roic there, but not by much. She was still awaiting the arrival of Chief Venn under the concerned eye of a uniformed quaddie whom Miles took to be the equivalent of a night desk sergeant. The quaddie officer's wariness increased when they entered, and one lower hand moved unobtrusively to touch a pad on his console; as if casually, and very promptly, another armed quaddie officer drifted down from one of the corridors to join his comrade.

Nicol wore a plain blue T-shirt and shorts, hastily donned with no artistic touches. Her face was pale with worry. Her lower hands clenched each other. She returned a short grateful nod to Miles's under-voiced greeting.

Chief Venn arrived at last and gave Miles a look unloving but resigned. He had apparently slept, if not enough, and had pessimistically dressed for the day; no secret hope of getting back into the sleep sack showed in his neat attire. He waved off the armed guard and gruffly invited the Lord Auditor and company to follow him to his office. The third-shift supervisor Miles had spoken with a while ago—might as well start calling it *last night*—brought coffee bulbs along with her end-of-shift report. Meticulously, she handed the bulbs out to the downsiders, instead of launching them through the air and expecting them to be caught the way she served her crew chief and Nicol. Miles turned the bulb's thermal control to the limit of the red zone and sucked the hot bitter brew with gratitude, as did Roic.

"This panic may be premature," Venn began after his own first swallow. "Portmaster Thorne's nonappearance may have some very simple explanation."

And what were the top three complicated explanations in Venn's mind right now? The quaddie wasn't sharing, but then, neither was Miles. Bel had been missing for over six hours. Miles considered the difference between, say, six hours without food, or six hours without oxygen. By now this panic might just as easily be posthumous, but Miles didn't care to say so aloud in front of Nicol. "I am extremely concerned."

"Thorne could be asleep somewhere else." Venn glanced somewhat enigmatically at Nicol. "Have you checked with likely friends?"

"The portmaster stated explicitly that it was heading home to Nicol to rest, when it left the *Kestrel* about midnight," said Miles. "A well-earned rest by that time,

I might add. Your own guards should be able to confirm the exact time of Thorne's departure from my ship."

"We will, of course, provide you with another liaison officer to assist you in your inquiries, Lord Vorkosigan." Venn's voice was a little distant; buying time to think, was how Miles read him. He might be playing deliberately obtuse as well. Miles did not mistake him for actually obtuse, not when he'd cut his sleep shift short and come in for this within little more than minutes.

"I don't want another. I want Thorne. You mislay too damned many downsiders around here. It's beginning to seem bloody careless." Miles took a deep breath. "It has to have crossed your mind by now, as it has mine, that there were three persons in the line of fire in the hostel lobby yesterday afternoon. We all assumed that I was the obvious target. What if it was something less obvious? What if it was Thorne?"

Teris Three made a stemming motion at him with an upper hand, and interjected, "Speaking of that, the trace on that hot riveter came in a few hours ago."

"Oh, good," said Venn, turning to her with relief. "What have we got?"

"It was sold for cash three days back, from an engineering supply store near the free fall docks. Carried out, not delivered. The purchaser didn't fill out the warranty questionnaire. The clerk wasn't sure which customer took it, because it was a busy hour."

"Quaddie or downsider?"

"He couldn't say. Could have been either, it seems."

And if certain webbed hands had been covered with gloves as in the vid shot, they might well have been overlooked. Venn grimaced, his hopes for a break plainly frustrated.

The night supervisor glanced at Miles. "Lord Vorkosigan here also called, to request that we detain one of the passengers from the *Rudra*."

"Find him yet?" asked Miles.

She shook her head.

"Why do you want him?" asked Venn, frowning.

Miles repeated his own night's news about his interrogation of the medtechs and finding traces of Solian's synthesized blood in the *Rudra*'s infirmary.

"Well, that explains why *we* were having no luck at the station hospitals and clinics," grumbled Venn. Miles imagined him totting up his department's wasted quaddie-hours from the fruitless search, and let the grumble pass.

"I also flushed out one suspect, in the course of the conversation with the *Rudra*'s tech. All circumstantial speculation so far, but fast-penta is the drug to cure that." Miles described the unusual Passenger Firka, his own insufficient but nagging sense of recognition, and his suspicions about the creative use of a floater. Venn looked grimmer and grimmer. Just because Venn reflexively resisted being stampeded by a Barrayaran dirtsucker, Miles decided, didn't mean he wasn't listening. What he made of it all, through his provincial Quaddiespace cultural filters, was much harder to guess.

"But what about *Bel*?" Nicol's voice was tight with suppressed anguish.

Venn was obviously less immune to a plea from a beautiful fellow quaddie. He met his night supervisor's inquiring look and nodded agreement.

"Well, what's one more?" Teris Three shrugged. "I'll put out a call to all patrollers to start looking for Portmaster Thorne, too. As well as the fellow with the webs."

Miles nibbled on his lower lip in worry. Sooner or

later, that live cargo secreted aboard the *Idris* must draw the ba back to it. "Bel—Portmaster Thorne *did* get back to you people last night about resealing the *Idris*, did it not?"

"Yes," said Venn and the night supervisor together. Venn gave her a short apologetic nod and continued, "Did that Betan passenger Thorne was trying to help get its animal fetuses taken care of all right?"

"Dubauer. Um, yes. They're fine for now. But, ah . . . I think I'd like to have you pick up Dubauer, as well as Firka."

"Why?"

"It left its hostel and vanished yesterday evening close to the same time that Firka went out, and also hasn't returned. And Dubauer was the third of our little triumvirate of targets yesterday. Let's just call it protective custody, for starters."

Venn screwed up his lips for a moment, considering this, and eyed Miles with shrewd disfavor. He'd have to be less bright than he appeared not to suspect Miles wasn't telling him everything. "Very well," he said at last. He waved a hand at Teris Three. "Let's go ahead and collect the whole set."

"Right." She glanced at the chrono on her left lower wrist. "It's oh-seven-hundred." Shift change, presumably. "Shall I stay?"

"No, no. I'll take over. Get the new missing-person traces started, then go get some rest." Venn sighed. "Tonight may be no better."

The night supervisor gave him an acknowledging thumbs-up with both lower hands and slipped out of the little office chamber.

"Would you prefer to wait at home?" Venn said suggestively to Nicol. "You'd be more comfortable there, I'm sure. We'll undertake to call you as soon as we find your partner."

Nicol took a breath. "I would rather be here," she said sturdily. "Just in case . . . just in case something happens soon."

"I'll keep you company," Miles volunteered. "For a little while, anyway." There, let Venn try to shift *his* diplomatic mass.

Venn at least managed to get them shifted out of his office by conducting them to a private waiting space, advertising it as more undisturbed. More undisturbed for Venn, anyway.

Miles and Nicol were left regarding each other in troubled silence. What Miles most wanted to know was if Bel had any other ImpSec business in train at present that might have impinged unexpectedly last night. But he was almost certain Nicol knew nothing of Bel's second source of income—and risk. Besides, that was wishful thinking. If any business had impinged, it was most probably the current mess. Which was now messy enough to raise every hackle Miles owned to quivering attention.

Bel had escaped its former career very nearly unscathed, despite Admiral Naismith's sometimes-lethal nimbus. For the Betan herm to have come all this way, to have come so close to regaining a private life and future, only to have its past reach out like some blind fate and swat it down *now* . . . Miles swallowed guilt and worry, and refrained from blurting some ill-timed and incoherent apology to Nicol. Something had certainly come upon Bel last night, but Bel was quick and clever and experienced; Bel could cope. Bel had always coped before.

But even the luck you made for yourself ran out sometimes. . . .

Nicol broke the stretched silence by asking some random question of Roic about Barrayar, and the armsman returned clumsy but kind small talk to distract her from her nerves. Miles glanced at his wrist com. Was it too early to call Ekaterin?

What the bloody hell was next on his agenda, anyway? He'd planned to spend this morning conducting fast-penta interrogations. All the threads he'd thought he'd had in hand, winding in nicely, had come to these disturbingly similar cut ends; Firka vanished, Dubauer vanished, and now Bel vanished too. And Solian, don't forget him. Graf Station, for all its maze-like non-design, wasn't that big a place. Were they all sucked into the same oubliette? How many oubliettes could the damned labyrinth have?

To his surprise, his frustrated fretting was interrupted by the night supervisor sticking her head in through one of the round doors. Hadn't she been leaving?

"Lord Auditor Vorkosigan, may we see you for a moment?" she asked in a polite tone.

He excused himself to Nicol and floated after her, Roic trailing dutifully. She led the way back through a corridor to Venn's nearby office. Venn was finishing up a comconsole call, saying, "He's here, he's hot, and he's all over me. It's *your* job to handle him." He glanced over his shoulder and cut the com. Above the vid plate, Miles just glimpsed Sealer Greenlaw's form, wrapped in what might be a bathrobe, vanish with a sparkle.

When the door hissed closed again behind them, the supervisor turned in midair and stated, "The patroller that you detailed to escort Postmaster Thorne last night reports that Thorne dismissed him when they got to the Joint."

"The what?" said Miles. "When? *Why?*"

She glanced at Venn, who opened a hand in a go-ahead gesture. "The Joint is one of our main corridor hubs on the free fall side, with a bubble-car transfer station and a public garden—a lot of people meet there, to eat or whatever after their work shifts. Thorne evidently encountered Garnet Five at about oh-one-hundred, coming the other way, and went off to have some kind of conversation."

"Yes? They're friends, I believe."

Venn shifted in what Miles recognized after a belated moment as embarrassment, and said, "Do you happen to know how good of friends? I didn't wish to discuss this in front of that distressed young lady. But Garnet Five is known to, um, favor exotic downsiders, and the Betan herm is, after all, a Betan herm. Simple explanations, after all."

Half a dozen mildly outraged arguments coursed through Miles's mind, to be promptly rejected. He wasn't supposed to know Bel that well. Not that someone who did know Bel would be in the least shocked by Venn's delicate suggestion . . . no. Bel's sexual tastes might be eclectic, but the herm wasn't the sort to betray the trust of a friend. Had never been. *We all change.* "You might ask Boss Watts," he temporized. He caught Roic's rolling eye and head-jerk in the direction of Venn's comconsole, affixed to the curving office wall. Miles continued smoothly, "Better still, call Garnet Five. If Thorne's there, the mystery is solved. If not, she might at least know where Thorne was headed." He tried to decide which would be the worse cause for dismay. The memory of the hot rivets parting his hair inclined him to hope for the first result, despite Nicol.

Venn opened an upper hand in acknowledgment of the point, and half-turned to tap out a search-code on his comconsole with a lower. Miles's heart jumped as Garnet Five's serene face and crisp voice came on, but it was only an answering program. Venn's brows twitched; he left a brief request that she contact him at her earliest convenience, and cut the com.

"She could just be asleep," said the night-shift woman wistfully.

"Send a patroller to check," said Miles a little tightly. Remembering he was supposed to be a diplomat, he added, "If you please."

Teris Three, looking as though a vision of her sleep sack was receding before her eyes, departed again. Miles and Roic returned to Nicol, who turned anxious eyes upon them as they floated back into the waiting chamber. Miles barely hesitated before reporting the patroller's sighting to her.

"Can you think of any reason for them to have met?" he asked her.

"Lots," she answered without reserve, confirming Miles's secret judgment. "I'm sure she'd want news from Bel about Ensign Corbeau, or anything happening that might affect his chances. If she crossed trajectories with Bel coming home through the Joint, she'd be sure to grab the chance to try to get some news. Or she might have just wanted an ear to vent at. Most of her other friends are not too sympathetic about her romance, after the Barrayaran attack and the fire."

"All right, that might account for the first hour. But no more. Bel was tired. Then what?"

She turned all four hands out in helpless frustration. "I can't imagine."

Miles's own imagination was all too wildly active. *Need data dammit* was becoming his private mantra here. He left Roic to make more distracting small talk with Nicol and, feeling a trifle selfish, took himself to the side of the chamber to call Ekaterin on his wrist com.

Her voice was sleepy but cheerful, and she stoutly maintained that she'd been awake already, and just about to get up. They exchanged a few verbal caresses that were no one's business but their own, and he described what he'd found as a result of the gossip she'd collected about Solian's nosebleeds, which seemed to please her greatly.

"So where are you now, and what have you had for breakfast?" she asked.

"Breakfast is delayed. I'm at the Station Security HQ." He hesitated. "Bel Thorne went missing last night, and they're putting together a search for it."

A little silence greeted this, and her return remark was as carefully neutral in tone as his own. "Oh. That's very worrisome."

"Yes."

"You *are* keeping Roic with you at all times, aren't you?"

"Oh, yes. The quaddies have armed guards trailing me around now, too."

"Good." Her breath drew in. "Good."

"The situation's getting pretty murky over here. I may have to send you home after all. We have four more days to decide, though."

"Well. In four more days we can talk about it, then."

Between his desire not to alarm her further, and hers not to distract him unduly, the conversation grew limping, and he mercifully tore himself from the calming sound of her voice to let her go bathe and dress and obtain her own breakfast.

He wondered if he and Roic ought, after all, to escort Nicol home, and perhaps after that try quartering the station themselves in the hope of some random encounter. Now, there was a tactically bankrupt plan if ever he'd evolved one. Roic would have a fully justifiable, painfully polite fit at the suggestion. It would feel just like old times. But suppose there was some way to make it less random . . .

The night supervisor's voice floated in from the corridor. Dear God, was the poor woman never to get home to sleep? "Yes, they're in here, but don't you think you ought to see the medtech next to—"

"I have to see Lord Vorkosigan!"

Miles jerked to full alertness as he identified the sharp, breathless female voice as Garnet Five's. The blond quaddie practically tumbled through the round door from the corridor. She was trembling and haggard, almost greenish, an unpleasant contrast to her rumpled carmine doublet. Her eyes, huge and dark-ringed, flicked over the waiting trio. "Nicol, oh, Nicol!" She flew to her friend in a fierce three-armed hug, the immobilized fourth wavering slightly.

Nicol, looking bewildered, dutifully hugged her back, but then pushed her away and asked urgently, "Garnet, have you seen Bel?"

"Yes. No. I'm not sure. This is just insane. I thought we were both knocked out together, but when I came to, Bel wasn't there any more. I thought Bel might have waked up first and gone for help, but the security crew"—she nodded to her escort—"says not. Haven't you heard anything?"

"Came to? Wait—who knocked you out? Where? Are you hurt?"

"I have the most horrible headache. It was some sort of drug mist. Icy cold. It didn't smell like anything, but it tasted bitter. He sprayed it in our faces. Bel yelled, 'Don't breathe, Garnet!' but of course had to breathe to yell. I felt Bel go all limp, and then everything sort of drained away. When I woke up, I was so sick I almost threw up, ugh!"

Nicol and Teris Three both grimaced in sympathy. Miles gathered this was the security woman's second time through this recitation, but her focus didn't flag.

"Garnet," Miles interjected, "please, take a deep breath, calm down, and begin at the beginning. A patroller reported he saw you and Bel somewhere in the Joint last night. Is that correct?"

Garnet Five scrubbed her pallid face with her upper hands, inhaled, and blinked; a little returning color relieved her gray-greenness. "Yes. I bumped into Bel coming out of the bubble-car stop. I wanted to know if Bel had asked—if you'd said anything—if anything had been decided about Dmitri."

Nicol nodded in bleak satisfaction.

"I bought us those peppermint teas that Bel likes at the Kabob Kiosk, hoping to get it to talk to me. But we hadn't been there five minutes when Bel went all distracted by this other pair who came in. One was a quaddie Bel knew from the Docks and Locks crew— Bel said he was someone it'd been keeping an eye on, because it suspected him of handling stolen stuff from the ships. The other was this really funny-looking downsider."

"Tall, lanky fellow with webbed hands and long feet, and a big barrel chest? Looks sort of like his mother might have married the Frog Prince, but the kiss didn't quite work out?" Miles asked.

Garnet Five stared. "Why, yes. Well, I'm not sure about the chest—he was wearing this loose, flippy cape-thing. How did you know?"

"This is about the third time he's turned up in this case. You might say he's riveted my attention. But go on, then what?"

"I couldn't get Bel to stay on the subject. Bel made me turn around and sit facing the pair, so Bel could keep its back to them, and made me report what they were doing. I felt silly, like we were play-ing spies."

No, not playing. . . .

"They had some sort of argument, then the quaddie from Dock and Locks spotted Bel and left in a hurry.

The other fellow, the funny downsider, left too, and then Bel insisted on following him."

"And Bel left the bistro?"

"We both left together. I wasn't going to be dumped, and besides, Bel said, *Oh, all right, come along, you may be useful*. I think the downsider must have been some sort of spacer, because he wasn't as awkward as most tourists usually are on the free fall side. I didn't think he saw us, following, but he must have, because he wandered down Cross Corridor, weaving in and out of any shops that were open at that hour but not buying anything. Then he suddenly zigzagged over to the portal to the grav side. There weren't any floaters in the rack, so Bel boosted me onto its back and kept on after the fellow. He ducked into this utility section, where the shops on the next corridor—over on the grav side—move freight and supplies in and out of their back doors. He seemed to vanish around a corner, but then he just popped out in front of us and waved this little tube in our faces, that spit out that nasty spray. I was afraid it was a poison, and we were both dead, but evidently not." She hesitated in stricken doubt. "Anyway, I woke up."

"Where?" asked Miles.

"There. Well, not quite there—I was all in a heap stuck to the floor inside a recycle bin behind one of the shops, on top of a bundle of cartons. It wasn't locked, fortunately. That horrible downsider couldn't have stuffed me into it if it had been, I suppose. I had a bad time trying to climb out. The stupid lid kept pressing down. It almost smashed my fingers. I hate gravity. Bel wasn't anywhere around. I looked, and called. And then I had to walk on three hands back to the main corridor, till I could find help. I grabbed the first patroller I came to, and she brought me right here."

"You must have been out cold for six or seven hours, then," Miles calculated aloud. How different were quaddie metabolisms from those of Betan herms? Not to mention body mass, and the erratic dosage inhaled by two variously dodging persons. "You should be seen by a physician right away, and get a blood sample drawn while there are still traces of the drug in your system. We might be able to identify it, and maybe its place of origin, if it isn't just a local product."

The night supervisor endorsed this idea emphatically, and permitted the downsider visitors, as well as Nicol, to whom Garnet Five still clung, to trail along as she escorted the shaken blond quaddie to the post's infirmary. When Miles had assured himself that Garnet Five had been taken into competent medical hands, and plenty of them, he turned back to Teris Three.

"It isn't just my airy theories any more," he told her. "You have a valid assault charge on this Firka fellow. Can't you step up the search?"

"Oh, yes," she answered grimly. "This one's going out on all the com channels, now. He attacked a *quaddie. And* he released toxic volatiles into the *public air.*"

Miles left the two quaddie women safely ensconced in the security post's infirmary. He then leaned on the night supervisor to supply him with the patroller who'd brought in Garnet Five to take him on an inspection of the scene of the crime, such as it was. The supervisor temporized, more delays ensued, and Miles harassed Crew Chief Venn in a nearly undiplomatic manner. But at length, he was issued a different quaddie patroller who did indeed escort him and Roic to the spot where Garnet Five had been so uncomfortably cached.

The dimly lit utility corridor had a flat floor and squared-off walls, and while not exactly cramped, shared its cross section with a great deal of duct work, which Roic had to bend to avoid. Around an obliquely angled turn, they found three quaddies, one in a Security uniform and two in shorts and shirts, working behind a stretched-out plastic ribbon printed with the Graf Station Security logo. Forensics techs at last, and about time. The young male rode in a floater broadly stenciled with a Graf Station technical school identification number. An intent-looking middle-aged female piloted a floater that bore the mark of one of the station clinics.

The shorts-and-shirt man in the tech school floater, hovering carefully, finished a laser scan for fingerprints along the edge and top of a large square bin sticking out into the corridor at a convenient height to bang the shins of the unwary passerby. He moved aside, and his colleague moved into place and began to run over the surfaces with what looked to be a standard sort of skin cell- and fiber-collecting hand-vac.

"Was that the bin where Garnet Five was hidden?" Miles asked the quaddie officer who was supervising.

"Yes."

Miles leaned forward, only to be waved back by the intently vacuuming tech. After extracting promises to be informed of any interesting cross-matches in the evidence, he strolled up and down the corridor instead, hands scrupulously tucked in his pockets, looking for . . . what? Cryptic messages written in blood on the walls? Or in ink, or spit, or snot, or *something*. He checked the floor, ceiling, and ducts, too, at Bel-height and lower, angling his head to catch odd reflections. Nothing.

"Were all these doors locked?" he asked the patroller who shadowed them. "Have they been checked yet? Could someone have bunged Bel—dragged Portmaster Thorne inside one?"

"You'll have to ask the officer in charge, sir," the quaddie guard replied, exasperation leaking into his service-issue neutral tone. "I only just got here with you."

Miles stared at the doors and their key pads in frustration. He couldn't very well go down the row trying them all, not unless the scanner man was finished. He returned to the bin.

"Finding anything?" he inquired.

"Not—" The medical quaddie glanced aside at the officer in charge. "Was this area swept before I got here?"

"Not as far as I know, ma'am," said the officer.

"Why do you ask?" Miles inquired instantly.

"Well, there isn't very much. I would have expected more."

"Try further away," suggested the scanner tech.

She cast him a somewhat bemused look. "That's not quite the point. In any case, after you." She gestured down the corridor, and Miles hurriedly confided his worries about the doors to the officer in charge.

The crew dutifully scanned everything, including, at Miles's insistence, the ductwork above, where the assailant might have braced himself in near-concealment to drop upon his victims. They tried each door. Fingers tapping impatiently on his trouser seam, Miles followed them up and down the corridor as they completed their survey. All doors proved locked . . . at least, they were now. One hissed open as they passed, and a blinking shopkeeper with legs poked his head through; the quaddie officer interrogated him briefly, and he in turn helped rouse his neighbors to cooperate in the search. The quaddie woman collected lots of little plastic bags of nothing much. No unconscious hermaphrodite was discovered in any bin, hallway, utility closet, or shop adjoining the passageway.

The utility corridor ran for about another ten meters before opening discreetly into a broader cross-corridor lined with shops, offices, and a small restaurant. The scene would have been quieter partway into third shift last night, but by no means reliably deserted, and just as well lit. Miles pictured the lanky Firka lugging or dragging Bel's compact but substantial form down the public way . . . wrapped in something for concealment? It would almost have to be. It would take a strong man to lug Bel far. Or . . . someone in a floater. Not necessarily a quaddie.

Roic, looming at his shoulder, sniffed. The spicy smells wafting into the corridor, into which the eatery cannily vented its bakery ovens, reminded Miles of his duty to feed his troops. Troop. The disgruntled quaddie guard could fend for himself, Miles decided.

The place was small, clean, and cozy, the sort of cheap café where the local working people ate. It was evidently past the breakfast rush and not yet time for lunch, because it was occupied only by a couple of legged young men who might be shop assistants, and a quaddie in a floater who, judging by her crowded tool belt, was an electrician on break. They stared covertly at the Barrayarans—more at tall Roic in his not-from-around-here brown-and-silver uniform than at short Miles in his unobtrusive gray civvies. Their quaddie security guard distanced himself slightly—with their party but not of it—and ordered coffee in a bulb.

A legged woman doubled as server and cook, assembling food on the plates with practiced speed. The spicy breads, apparently a specialty of the place, appeared handmade, the slices of vat protein unexceptionable, and the fresh fruit startlingly exquisite. Miles selected a large golden pear, its skin touched with a rose blush, unblemished; its flesh, when he cut into it, proved pale, perfect, and dripping with perfumed juice. If only they had more time, he'd love to sic Ekaterin onto the local agriculture—whatever plant-like matrix this had grown from had to have been genetically engineered to thrive in free fall. The Empire's space stations could use such stocks—if the Komarran traders hadn't snagged them already. Miles's plan to slip seeds into his pocket to smuggle home was thwarted by the fruit being seedless.

A holovid in the corner with the sound turned low had been mumbling to itself, ignored by everyone, but a sudden rainbow of blinking lights advertised an official safety bulletin. Heads turned briefly, and Miles followed the stares to find being displayed the shots of Passenger Firka from the *Rudra*'s locks that he had downloaded earlier to Station Security. He didn't need the sound to guess the content of the serious-looking quaddie woman's speech that followed: suspect wanted for questioning, may be armed and dangerous, if you see this dubious downsider call this code at once. A couple of shots of Bel followed, as the putative kidnapping victim, presumably; they were taken from yesterday's interviews after the assassination attempt in the hostel, which a newscaster came on to re-cap.

"Can you turn it up?" Miles asked belatedly.

The newscaster was just winding down; even as the café server aimed her remote, her image was replaced with an advertisement for an impressive selection of work gloves.

"Oh, sorry," said the server. "It was a repeat anyway. They've been showing it every fifteen minutes for the past hour." She provided Miles with a verbal summary of the alarm, which matched Miles's guess in most particulars.

So, on just how many holovids all over the station was this now appearing? It would be an order of magnitude harder for a wanted man to hide, with an order of magnitude more pairs of eyes looking for him . . . but was Firka himself seeing this? If so, would he panic, becoming more hazardous to anyone who crossed him? Or perhaps turn himself in, claiming it was all some sort of misunderstanding? Roic, studying the vid, frowned and drank more coffee. The sleep-deprived armsman was holding up all right for the moment, but Miles figured he would be dragging dangerously by mid-afternoon.

Miles had an unpleasant sensation of sinking in a quicksand of diversions and losing his grip on his initial mission. Which had been what? Oh, yes, free the fleet. He suppressed an internal snarl of *Screw the fleet, where the hell's Bel?* But if there was any way to use this disturbing development to pry his ships from quaddie hands, it was not apparent to him right now.

They returned to Security Post One to find Nicol waiting for them in the front reception space with the air of a hungry predator at a water hole. She pounced on Miles the moment he appeared.

"Did you find Bel? Did you see any sign?"

Miles shook his head in regret. "Neither hide nor hair. Well, there might be hairs—we'll know when the forensics tech gets her analysis done—but that won't tell us anything we don't already know from Garnet Five's testimony." The truth of which Miles didn't doubt. "I do have a better mental picture of the possible course of events, now." He wished it made more sense. The first part—Firka wishing to delay or shake his pursuers—was sensible enough. It was the blank afterward that puzzled.

"Do you think," Nicol's voice grew smaller, "he carried Bel away to murder someplace else?"

"In that case, why leave a witness alive?" He tossed this off instantly for her reassurance; upon reflection, he found it reassuring too. Maybe. But if not murder,

what? What did Bel have or know that someone else
might want? Unless, like Garnet Five, Bel had come
to consciousness on its own, and gone off. But . . . if
Bel had wandered away in some state of dazed or sick
confusion, it should have been picked up by the
patrollers or some solicitous fellow stationers by now.
And if it had gone in hot pursuit of something, it
should have reported in. *To me, at least, dammit . . .*

"If Bel was," Nicol began, and stopped. A startling
crowd heaved through the main entry port, and paused
for orientation.

A pair of husky male quaddies in the orange work
shirts and shorts of Docks and Locks managed the two
ends of a three-meter length of pipe. Firka occupied
the middle.

The unhappy downsider's wrists and ankles were
lashed to the pipe with swathes of electrical tape,
bending him in a U, with another rectangle of tape
plastered across his mouth, muffling his moans. His
eyes were wide, and rolled in panic. Three more
quaddies in orange, panting and rumpled, one with
a red bruise starting around his eye, bobbed along
beside as outriders.

The work crew took aim and floated with their
squirming burden through free fall to fetch up with
a thump at the reception desk. A quartet of uniformed
security quaddies appeared from another portal to
gather and stare at this unwilling prize; the desk
sergeant hit his intercom, and lowered his voice to
speak into it in a rapid undertone.

The spokes-quaddie for the posse bustled forward,
a smile of grim satisfaction on his bruised face. "We
caught him for you."

CHAPTER TWELVE

"Where?" Miles asked.

"Number Two Freight Bay," the spokes-quaddie answered. "He was trying to get Pramod Sixteen, here"—his nod indicated one of the husky quaddies holding an end of the pipe, who nodded back in confirmation—"to take him out in a pod around the security zone to the galactic jumpship docks. So you can add attempted bribery of an airseal tech to violate regs to his list of charges, I'd say."

Ah, ha. Another way to get around Bel's customs barriers . . . Miles's mind jumped back to the missing Solian.

"Pramod told him he was making arrangements, and slipped out and called me. I rounded up the boys, and we made sure he'd come along and explain himself to you." The spokes-quaddie gestured to Chief Venn, who'd floated in hastily from the office corridor and was taking in the scene with unsurprised satisfaction.

The web-fingered downsider made a plaintive noise,

beneath his electrical tape, but Miles took it more for protest than explanation.

Nicol put in urgently, "Did you see any sign of Bel?"

"Oh, hi, Nicol." The spokes-quaddie shook his head in regret. "We asked the fellow, but we didn't get an answer. If you all don't have better luck with him, we have a few more ideas we can try." His scowl suggested that these might run to the illicit utilization of airlocks, or perhaps innovative applications of freight-handling equipment definitely not covered in the manufacturer's warranties. "I bet we could make him stop screaming and start talking before his air ran out."

"I think we can take it from here, thanks," Chief Venn assured him. He glanced without favor at Firka, wriggling on his pole. "Although I'll keep your offer in mind."

"Do you know Portmaster Thorne?" Miles asked the Docks and Locks quaddie. "Do you work together?"

"Bel's one of our best supervisors," the quaddie replied. "About the most sensible downsider we've ever gotten. We don't care to lose it, eh?" He gave Nicol a nod.

She ducked her head in mute gratitude.

The citizens' arrest was duly recorded. The quaddie patrollers who'd assembled looked cautiously over the long, squirming captive, and elected to take him pole and all, for the moment. The Docks and Locks crew, with justifiable self-satisfaction, also presented the duffel bag Firka had been carrying.

So here was Miles's most wanted suspect, if not presented on a platter, at least *en brochette*. Miles itched to tear that tape off his rubbery face and start squeezing.

Sealer Greenlaw arrived while this was going forth, accompanied by a new quaddie man, dark-haired and fit-looking though not especially young. He wore neat, subdued garb much like that of Boss Watts and Bel, but black instead of slate blue. She introduced him as Adjudicator Leutwyn.

"So," said Leutwyn, staring curiously at the tape-secured suspect. "This is our one-man crime wave. Do I understand he, too, came in with the Barrayaran fleet?"

"No, Adjudicator," said Miles. "He joined the *Rudra* here on Graf Station, at the last minute. Actually, he didn't sign aboard until after the ship had originally been due to leave. I'd very much like to know why. I strongly suspect him of synthesizing and planting the blood in the loading bay, of attempting to assassinate . . . someone, in the hostel lobby yesterday, and of attacking Garnet Five and Bel Thorne last night. Garnet Five, at least, had a fairly close look at him, and should be able to confirm that identification shortly. But by far the most urgent question is, what has happened to Portmaster Thorne? Hot pursuit of a kidnap victim in danger is sufficient pretext for nonvoluntary penta interrogations in most jurisdictions, surely."

"Here as well," the adjudicator admitted. "But a fast-penta examination is a delicate undertaking. I've found, in the half dozen I've monitored, that it's not nearly the magic wand most people think it is."

Miles cleared his throat in fake diffidence. "I am tolerably familiar with the techniques, Adjudicator. I've conducted or sat in on over a hundred penta-assisted interrogations. And I've had it given to me twice." No need to go into his idiosyncratic drug reaction that had made those two events such dizzyingly surreal and notably uninformative occasions.

"Oh," said the quaddie adjudicator, sounding impressed despite himself, possibly especially with that last detail.

"I'm keenly aware of the need to keep the examination from being a mob scene, but you also need the right leading questions. I believe I have several."

Venn put in, "We haven't even processed the suspect yet. Me, I want to see what he's got in that bag."

The adjudicator nodded. "Yes, carry on, Chief Venn. I'd like further clarification, if I can get it."

Mob scene or no, they all followed the quaddie patrollers who maneuvered the unfortunate Firka, pole and all, into a back chamber. A pair of the patrollers, after first clapping proper restraints around the bony wrists and ankles, recorded retinal patterns and took laser scans of the fingers and palms. Miles had one curiosity satisfied when they also pulled off the prisoner's soft boots; the finger-length toes, prehensile or nearly so, flexed and stretched, revealing wide rose-colored webs between. The quaddies scanned them, too—of *course* the quaddies would routinely scan all four extremities—then cut through the bulky lashings of tape.

Meanwhile another patroller, assisted by Venn, emptied and inventoried the duffel. They removed an assortment of clothes, mostly in dirty wads, to find a large new chef's knife, a stunner with a dubiously corroded discharged power pack but no stunner permit, a long crowbar, and a leather folder full of small tools. The folder also contained a receipt for an automated hot riveter from a Graf Station engineering supply store, complete with incriminating serial numbers. It was at this point that the adjudicator stopped looking so carefully reserved and started to look grim instead. When the patroller held up something that looked at first glance to be a scalp, but when shaken out proved a brassy short blond wig of no particular quality, the evidence seemed almost redundant.

Of more interest to Miles was not one, but a dozen sets of identifying documentation. Half of them proclaimed their bearers to be natives of Jackson's Whole; the others were from local space systems all adjoining the Hegen Hub, a wormhole-rich, planet-poor system that was one of the Barrayaran Empire's nearest and most strategically important nexus neighbors. Jump routes from Barrayar to both Jackson's Whole and the Cetagandan Empire passed, via Komarr and the independent buffer polity of Pol, through the Hub.

Venn ran the handful of IDs through a holovid station affixed to the chamber's curving wall, his frown deepening. Miles and Roic both maneuvered to watch over his shoulder.

"So," Venn growled after a bit, "which one really *is* the fellow?"

Two sets of documentation for "Firka" included physical vid shots of a man very different in appearance from their moaning captive: a big, bulky, but perfectly normal human male from either Jackson's Whole, no House affiliation, or Aslund, another Hegen Hub neighbor, depending on which—if either—ID was to be believed. Yet a third Firka ID, the one the present Firka seemed to have used to travel from Tau Ceti to Graf Station, portrayed the prisoner himself. Finally, his vid shots also matched up with the IDs of a person named Russo Gupta, also hailing from Jackson's Whole and lacking a proper House affiliation. That name, face, and associated retina scans came up again on a jumpship engineer's license that Miles recognized as originating from a certain Jacksonian organization of the sub-economy he had dealt with in his covert ops days. Judging from the long file of dates and customs stamps appended, it had passed as genuine elsewhere. And recently. *A record of his travels, good!*

Miles pointed. "That is almost certainly a forgery."

The clustering quaddies looked genuinely shocked. Greenlaw said, "A false engineer's license? That would be *unsafe*."

"If it's from the place I think, you could get a false neurosurgeon's license to go with it. Or any other job you cared to pretend to have, without going through all that tedious training and testing and certification." Or, in this case, really have—now, there was a disturbing thought. Although on-the-job apprenticeship and self-teaching might cover some of the gaps over time . . . *someone* had been clever enough to modify that hot riveter, after all.

Under no circumstances could this pale, lanky mutie pass for a stout, pleasantly ugly, red-haired woman named either Grace Nevatta of Jackson's Whole—no House affiliation—or Louise Latour of Pol, depending on which set of IDs she favored. Nor for a short, head-wired, mahogany-skinned jumpship pilot named Hewlet.

"Who *are* all these people?" Venn muttered in aggravation.

"Why don't we just ask?" suggested Miles.

Firka—or Gupta—had finally stopped struggling and just lay in midair, nostrils flexing with his panting above the blue rectangle of tape over his mouth. The quaddie patroller finished recording his last scans and reached for a corner of the tape, then paused uncertainly. "I'm afraid this is going to hurt a bit."

"He's probably sweated enough underneath the tape to loosen it," Miles offered. "Take it in one quick jerk. It'll hurt less in the long run. That's what I'd want, if I were him."

A muffled mew of disagreement from the prisoner turned into a shrill scream as the quaddie followed this plan. All right, so, the frog prince hadn't sweated as much around the mouth as Miles had guessed. It was still better to have the damned tape off than on.

But despite the noises he'd been making the prisoner did not follow up this liberation of his lips with outraged protests, swearing, complaints, or raving threats. He just kept panting. His eyes were peculiarly glassy—a look Miles recognized, of a man who'd been wound up far too tight for far too long. Bel's loyal stevedores might have roughed him up a bit, but he hadn't acquired *that* look in the brief time he'd been in quaddie hands.

Chief Venn held up a double handful, left and left, of IDs before the prisoner's eyes. "All right. Which one are you really? You may as well tell us the truth. We'll be cross-checking it all anyway."

With surly reluctance, the prisoner muttered, "I'm Guppy."

"Guppy? Russo Gupta?"

"Yeah."

"Who are these others?"

"Absent friends."

Miles wasn't quite sure if Venn had caught the intonation. He put in, "Dead friends?"

"Yeah, that too." Guppy/Gupta stared away into a distance Miles calculated as light-years.

Venn looked alarmed. Miles was torn between anxiety to proceed and an intense desire to sit down and study the place and date stamps on all those IDs, real and fake, before decanting Gupta. A world of revelation lay therein, he was fairly sure. But greater urgencies drove the sequencing now.

"Where is Portmaster Thorne?" Miles asked.

"I told those thugs before. I never heard of him."

"Thorne is the Betan herm you sprayed with knockout mist last night in a utility passage off Cross Corridor. Along with a blond quaddie woman named Garnet Five."

The surly look deepened. "Never seen either of 'em."

Venn turned his head and nodded to a patroller, who flitted off. A few moments later she returned through one of the chamber's other portals, ushering Garnet Five. Garnet's color looked vastly better now, Miles was relieved to note, and she had obviously managed to obtain whatever female grooming equipment she used to touch herself back up to her high-visibility norm.

"Ah!" she said cheerfully. "You caught him! Where's Bel?"

Venn inquired formally, "Is this the downsider who committed chemical assault on you and the portmaster, and released illicit volatiles into the public atmosphere last night?"

"Oh, yes," said Garnet Five. "I couldn't possibly mistake him. I mean, look at the webs."

Gupta clenched his lips, his fists, and his feet, but further pretense was clearly futile.

Venn lowered his voice to a quite nicely menacing official growl. "Gupta, where is Portmaster Thorne?"

"I don't know where the blighted nosy herm is! I left it in the bin right next to hers. It was all right then. I mean, it was breathing and all. They both were. I made sure. The herm's probably still sleeping it off in there."

"No," said Miles. "We checked all the bins in the passage. The portmaster was gone."

"Well, *I* don't know where it went after that."

"Would you be willing to repeat that assertion under fast-penta, and clear yourself of a kidnapping charge?" Venn inquired cannily, angling for a voluntary interrogation.

Gupta's rubbery face set, and his eyes shifted away. "Can't. I'm allergic to the stuff."

"Is that so?" said Miles. "Let's just check, shall we?" He dug in his trouser pocket and drew out the strip of test patches he'd borrowed earlier from the *Kestrel*'s ImpSec supplies, in anticipation of just such an opportunity. Granted, he hadn't anticipated the added urgency of Bel's alarming vanishing act. He held up the strip and explained to Venn and the adjudicator, who was monitoring all this with a judicial frown, "Security-grade penta allergy skin test. If the subject has any of the six kinds of artificially induced anaphylaxes or even a mild natural allergy, the welt pops right up." By way of reassurance to the quaddie officials, he peeled off one of the burr-like patches and slapped it on the back of his own wrist, displaying it with a heartening wriggle of his fingers. The sleight of hand was sufficient that no one except the prisoner protested when he leaned over and pressed another to Gupta's arm. Gupta let out a yowl of horror that won him only stares; he reduced it to a pitiable whimper under the bemused eyes of the onlookers.

Miles peeled off his own patch to reveal a distinct reddish prickle. "As you see, I do have a slight endogenous sensitivity." He waited a few moments longer, to drive home the point, then reached over and peeled the patch off Gupta. The rather sickly natural—mushrooms were natural, right?—skin tone was unaffected.

Venn, getting into the rhythm of the thing like an old ImpSec hand, leaned toward Gupta and said, "That's two lies, so far, then. You can stop lying now. Or you can stop lying shortly. Either way will do." He raised narrowed eyes to his fellow quaddie official. "Adjudicator Leutwyn, do you rule that we have sufficient cause for an involuntary chemically assisted interrogation of this transient?"

The adjudicator looked less than wholly enthusiastic, but he replied, "In light of his admitted connection to the worrisome disappearance of a valued Station employee, yes, there can be no question. I do remind you that subjecting detainees in your charge to unnecessary physical discomfort is against regs."

Venn glanced at Gupta, hanging miserably in air. "How can he be uncomfortable? He's in free fall."

The adjudicator pursed his lips. "Transient Gupta, aside from your restraints, are you in any special discomfort at this time? Do you require food, drink, or downsider sanitary facilities?"

Gupta jerked his wrists against their soft bonds, and shrugged. "Naw. Well, yes. My gills are getting dry. If you're not gonna let me loose, I need somebody to spray them. The stuff's in my bag."

"This?" The female quaddie patroller held out what appeared to be a perfectly ordinary plastic sprayer, of the sort that Miles had seen Ekaterin use to mist some of her plants. She wriggled it, and it gurgled.

"What's in it?" asked Venn suspiciously.

"Water, mostly. And a bit of glycerin," said Gupta.

"Go ahead and check it," said Venn aside to his patroller. She nodded and floated out; Gupta watched her depart with some mistrust, but no particular alarm.

"Transient Gupta, it appears you're going to be our guest for a while," said Venn. "If we remove your restraints, are you going to give us any trouble, or are you going to behave yourself?"

Gupta was silent a moment, then vented an exhausted sigh. "I'll behave. Much good it'll do me either way."

A patroller floated forward and unshackled the prisoner's wrists and ankles. Only Roic seemed less than pleased with this unnecessary courtesy, tensing with a hand on a wall grip and one foot planted to a bit of bulkhead not occupied by equipment, ready to launch himself forward. But Gupta only chafed his wrists and bent to rub his ankles, and looked grudgingly grateful.

The patroller returned with the bottle, handing it to her chief. "The lab's chemical sniffer says it's inert. Should be safe," she reported.

"Very well." Venn pitched the bottle to Gupta, who despite his odd long hands caught it readily, with little downsider clumsiness, a fact Miles was sure the quaddie noted.

"Um." Gupta gave the crowd of onlookers a slightly embarrassed glance, and hitched up his loose poncho. He stretched and inhaled, and the ribs on his big barrel chest drew apart; flaps of skin parted to reveal red slashes. The substance beneath seemed spongy, rippling in the misting like densely laid feathers.

God almighty. He really does have gills under there. Presumably, the bellows-like movement of the chest helped pump water through, when the amphibian was immersed. Dual systems. So did he hold his breath, or did his lungs shut down involuntarily? By what mechanism was his blood circulation switched from one oxygenating interface to the other? Gupta pumped the bottle and sprayed mist into the red slits, handing it back and forth from right side to left, and seemed to draw some comfort thereby. He sighed, and the slits closed back down, his chest appearing merely ridged and scarred. He smoothed the drifting poncho back into place.

"Where *are* you from?" Miles couldn't help asking.

Gupta grew surly again. "Guess."

"Well, Jackson's Whole, by the weight of the evidence, but which House made you? Ryoval, Bharaputra, another? And were you a one-off, or part of a set? First-generation gengineered, or from a self-reproducing line of, of water people?"

Gupta's eyes widened in surprise. "You know Jackson's Whole?"

"Let's say, I've had several painfully educational visits there."

The surprise became edged with faint respect, and a certain lonely eagerness. "House Dyan made me. I *was* part of a set, once—we were an underwater ballet troupe."

Garnet Five blurted in unflattering astonishment, "*You* were a dancer?"

The prisoner hunched his shoulders. "No. They made me to be submersible stage crew. But House Dyan suffered a hostile takeover by House Ryoval— just a few years before Baron Ryoval was assassinated, pity *that* didn't happen sooner. Ryoval broke up the troupe for other, um, tasks, and decided he had no alternate use for me, so I was out of a job and out of protection. Could have been worse. He mighta kept me. I drifted around and took what tech jobs I could get. One thing led to another."

In other words, Gupta had been born into Jacksonian techno-serfdom, and dumped out on the street when his original owner-creators had been engulfed by their vicious commercial rival. Given what Miles knew of the late, unsavory Baron Ryoval, Gupta's fate was perhaps happier than that of his mer-cohort. By the known date of Ryoval's death, that last vague remark about things leading to things covered at least five years, maybe as many as ten.

Miles said thoughtfully, "You weren't shooting at *me* at all yesterday, then, were you. Nor at Portmaster Thorne." Which left . . .

Gupta blinked at him. "Oh! *That's* where I saw you before. Sorry, no." His brow corrugated. "So what were you doing there, then? You're not one of the passengers. Are you another Stationer squatter like that officious bloody Betan?"

"No. My name is"—he made an instant, almost subliminal decision to drop all the honorifics— "Miles. I was sent out to look after Barrayaran concerns when the quaddies impounded the Komarran fleet."

"Oh." Gupta grew uninterested.

What the devil was keeping that fast-penta? Miles softened his voice. "So what happened to your friends, Guppy?"

That fetched the amphibian's attention again. "Double-crossed. Subjected, injected, infected . . . rejected. We were all taken in. Damned Cetagandan bastard. That wasn't the Deal."

Something inside Miles went on overdrive. *Here's the connection, finally.* His smile grew charming, sympathetic, and his voice softened further. "Tell me about the Cetagandan bastard, Guppy."

The hovering mob of quaddie listeners had stopped rustling, even breathing more quietly. Roic had drawn back to a shadowed spot opposite Miles. Gupta glanced around at the Graf Stationers, and at Miles and himself, the only legged persons now in view in the center of the circle. "What's the use?" The tone was not a wail of despair, but a bitter query.

"I *am* Barrayaran. I have a special stake in Cetagandan bastards. The Cetagandan ghem-lords left five million of my grandfather's generation dead behind them, when they finally gave up and pulled out of Barrayar. I still have his bag of ghem-scalps. For certain kinds of Cetagandans, I might know a use or two you'd find interesting."

The prisoner's wandering gaze snapped to his face and locked there. For the first time, he'd won Gupta's total attention. For the first time, he'd hinted he might have something that Guppy really wanted. Wanted? Burned for, lusted for, desired with mad obsessive hunger. His glassy eyes were ravenous for . . . maybe revenge, maybe justice—in any case, blood. But the frog prince clearly lacked personal expertise in retribution. The quaddies didn't deal in blood. Barrayarans . . . had a more sanguinary reputation. Which, for the first time this mission, might actually prove some *use*.

Gupta took a long breath. "I don't know *what* kind this one was. Is. He was like nothing I'd ever met before. Cetagandan bastard. He *melted* us."

"Tell me," Miles breathed, "everything. Why you?"

"He came to us . . . through our usual cargo agents. We thought it would be all right. We had a ship. Gras-Grace and Firka and Hewlet and me had this ship. Hewlet was our pilot, but Gras-Grace was the brains. Me, I had a knack for fixing things. Firka kept the books, and fixed regs, and passports, and nosy officials. Gras-Grace and her three husbands, we called us. We were a collection of rejects, but maybe we added up to one real spouse for her, I don't know. One for all and all for one, because it was damn sure that a crew of refugee Jacksonians, without a House or a Baron, wasn't going to get a break from anyone *else* in the nexus."

Gupta was getting wound up in his story. Miles, listening with utmost care, prayed Venn would have the sense not to interrupt. Ten people hovered around them in this chamber, yet he and Gupta, mutually hypnotized by the increasing intensity of his confession, might almost be floating in a bubble of time and space altogether removed from this universe. "So where did you pick up this Cetagandan and his cargo, anyway?"

Gupta glanced up, startled. "You know about the cargo?"

"If it's the same one now aboard the *Idris*, yes, I've had a look. I found it rather disturbing."

"What's he got in there, really? I only saw the outsides."

"I'd rather not say, at this time. What did he," Miles elected not to go into the confusions of ba gender just now, "tell you it was?"

"Gengineered mammals. Not that we asked questions. We got paid extra for not asking questions. That was the Deal, we thought."

And if there was anything that the ethically elastic inhabitants of Jackson's Whole held nearly sacred, it was the Deal. "A good bargain, was it?"

"Looked like. Two or three more runs like that, we could have paid off the ship and owned it free and clear."

Miles took leave to doubt that, if the crew was in debt for their jumpship to a typical Jacksonian financial House. But perhaps Guppy and his friends had been terminal optimists. *Or terminally desperate.*

"The gig looked easy enough. Just take a little mixed-freight run through the fringes of the Cetagandan Empire. We jumped in through the Hegen Hub, via Vervain, and skirted round to Rho Ceta. All those arrogant, suspicious bastard inspectors who boarded us at the jump points turned up nothing to hold against us, though they'd have liked to, because there wasn't anything aboard but what our filed manifest said. Gave old Firka a good chuckle. Till we were heading out for the last jumps, for Rho Ceta through those empty buffer systems just before the route splits to Komarr. We made one little mid-space rendezvous there that didn't appear on our flight plan."

"What kind of ship did you rendezvous with? Jumpship, or just a local space crawler? Could you tell for sure, or was it disguised or camouflaged?"

"Jumpship. I don't know what else it might have really been. It looked like a Cetagandan government ship. It had lots of fancy markings, anyway. Not big, but fast—fresh and classy. The Cetagandan bastard moved his cargo all by himself, with float pallets and hand tractors, but he sure didn't waste any time. The moment the locks were closed, they went off."

"Where? Could you tell?"

"Well, Hewlet said they had an odd trajectory. It was that uninhabited binary system a few jumps out from Rho Ceta, I don't know if you know it—"

Miles nodded in encouragement.

"They went inbound, deeper into the grav well. Maybe they were planning to swing around the suns and approach one of the jump points from a disguised trajectory, I don't know. That would make sense, given all the rest of it."

"Just the one passenger?"

"Yeah."

"Tell me more about him."

"Not much to tell—then. He kept to himself, ate his own rations in his own cabin. He didn't talk to me at all. He had to talk to Firka, on account of Firka was fixing his manifest. By the time we reached the first Barrayaran jump point inspection, it had a whole new provenance. He was somebody else by then, too."

"Ker Dubauer?"

Venn twitched at this first mention of the familiar name in his hearing, and opened his mouth and inhaled, but closed it again without diverting Guppy's flow. The unhappy amphibian was in full spate now, pouring out his troubles.

"Not yet, he wasn't. He musta become Dubauer during his layover on the Komarran transfer station, I figure. I didn't track him by his identity, anyway. He was too good for that. Fooled you Barrayarans, didn't he?"

Indeed. An apparent Cetagandan agent of the highest caliber had passed through Barrayar's key nexus trade crossroad like so much smoke. *ImpSec* would have a seizure when *this* report arrived. "How did you follow him here, then?"

The first smile-like expression Miles had seen on the rubbery face ghosted across Gupta's lips. "I was ship's engineer. I tracked him by his cargo's mass. It was kind of distinctive, when I went to look, later."

The ghastly smile faded into a black frown. "When we dumped him and his pallets off on the Komarran transfer station's loading bay, he seemed happy. Downright cordial. He went around to each of us for the first time, and gave us our no-problems bonuses personally. He shook Hewlet's and Firka's hands. He asked to see my webbing, so I spread my fingers for him, and he leaned over and gripped my arm and seemed real interested, and thanked me. He gave Gras-Grace a pat on her cheek, and smiled at her in this sappy way. He *smirked* as he touched her. *Knowing*. Since she was holding the bonus chit in her hand, she sort of smiled back and didn't deck him, though I could see it was a near thing. And then we bailed out. Hewlet and I wanted to take station leave and spend some of our bonus, but Gras-Grace said we could party later. And Firka said the Barrayaran Empire wasn't a healthy place for the likes of us to linger in." A distracted laugh that had nothing to do with humor puffed from his lips. So. That startling scream when Miles had touched the test patch to Guppy's skin hadn't been overreaction, exactly. It had been a flashback. Miles suppressed a shudder. *Sorry, sorry.*

"It was six days out from Komarr, past the jump to Pol, before the fevers began. Gras-Grace guessed it first, from the way it started. She always was the quickest of us. Four little pink wheals, like some kind of bug bites, on the backs of Hewlet and Firka's hands, on her cheek, on my arm where the Cetagandan bastard had touched me. They swelled up to the size of eggs, and throbbed, though not as much as our heads. It only took an hour. My head hurt so bad I could hardly see, and Gras-Grace, who wasn't doing any better, helped me to my cabin so's I could get into my tank."

"Tank?"

"I'd rigged up a big tank in my cabin, with a lid I could lock down from the inside, because the gravity on that old ship wasn't any too reliable. It was really comfortable to rest in, my own kind of water bed. I could stretch all the way out, and turn around. Good filtration system on the water, nice and clean, and extra oxygen sparkling up through it from a bubbler I'd rigged, all pretty with colored lights. And music. I miss my tank." He heaved a sigh.

"You . . . appear to have lungs, as well. Do you hold your breath underwater, or what?"

Gupta shrugged. "I have these extra sphincter muscles in my nose and ears and throat that shut down automatically, when my breathing switches over. That's always kind of an awkward moment, the switch; my lungs don't always seem to want to stop. Or start again, sometimes. But I can't stay in my tank forever, or I'd end up pissing in the water I breathe. That's what happened then. I floated in my tank for . . . hours, I'm not sure how many. I don't think I was quite in my right mind, I hurt so bad. But then I had to piss. Really bad. So I had to get out.

"I damn near passed out when I stood. I threw up on the floor. But I could walk. I made it to my cabin's head, finally. The ship was still running, I could feel the right vibrations through my feet, but it had gone all quiet. Nobody talking or arguing or snoring, no music. No laughing. I was cold and wet. I put on a robe—it was one of hers that Gras-Grace had given me, because she claimed being fat made her hot, and

I was always too cold. She said it was because my designers gave me frog genes. For all I know, that might be true.

"I found her body . . ." He stopped. The light-years-gone look in his eyes intensified. "About five steps down the corridor. At least, I thought it was her. It was her braid, floating on the . . . At least, I thought it was a body. The size of the puddle seemed about right. It stank like . . . What kind of hell-disease liquefies *bones*?"

He inhaled, and continued unsteadily, "Firka had made it to the infirmary, for all the good it had done him. He was all flaccid, like he was deflating. And dripping. Over the side of the bunk. He stank worse than Gras-Grace. And he was *steaming*.

"Hewlet—what was left of him—was in his pilot's chair in Nav and Com. I don't know why he crawled up there, maybe it was a comfort to him. Pilots are strange that way. His pilot's headset kind of held his skull braced, but his face . . . his features . . . they were just sliding off. I thought he might have been trying to send an emergency message, maybe. *Help us. Biocontamination aboard*. But maybe not, because nobody ever came. Later I thought maybe he'd sent too much, and the rescuers stayed away on purpose. Why should the good citizens risk anything for *us*? Just Jacksonian smuggler scum. Better off dead. Saves the trouble and expense of prosecution, eh?" He looked at no one, now.

Miles feared he was falling silent, spent. But there was so much more, desperately important, to know . . . He dared to play out a lead—"So. No shit, there you were, trapped on a drifting ship with three dissolving corpses including a dead jump pilot. How did you get away?"

"The ship . . . the ship was no good to me now, not

without Hewlet. And the others. Let the bastard financiers have it, biocontamination and all. Murdered dreams. But I figured I was everybody's heir, by that time. Nobody had anybody else, not to speak to. I would've wanted them to have my stuff, if it had been the other way around. I went round and collected everybody's movables, spare cash, credit chits—Firka had a huge cache. He would. And he had all our doctored IDs. Gras-Grace, well, she probably gave hers away, or lost it gambling, or spent it on toys, or let it slip through her fingers somehow. Which made her smarter than Firka, in the long run. Hewlet, I guess he'd drunk most of his. But there was enough. Enough to travel to the ends of the nexus, if I was clever about it. Enough to catch up with that Cetagandan bastard, stern chase or no. With that heavy cargo, I didn't figure he'd be traveling all that fast.

"I took it all and loaded it in an escape capsule. Decontaminated it all, and me, a dozen times first, trying to get that horrible death smell off. I wasn't . . . I wasn't at my best and brightest, I don't think, but I wasn't *that* far gone. Once I was in the capsule, it wasn't so hard. They're designed to get injured idiots to safety, automatically following the local space beacons . . . I got picked up three days later by a passing ship, and told a bullshit story about our ship coming apart—they believed *that* when they looked up the Jacksonian registry. I'd stopped crying by then." Tears were glistening at the corners of his eyes now. "Didn't mention the bio-shit, or they'd have jugged me good. They dropped me at the nearest Polian jump point station. From there I slipped away from the safety investigators and got me on the first ship I could bound for Komarr. I tracked the Cetagandan bastard's cargo by its mass to the Komarran trade fleet that had just pulled out. Ran a search to find a route that would catch me up to it at the first possible place. Which was here." He stared around, blinking at his quaddie audience as if surprised to find them all still in the room.

"How did Lieutenant Solian get sucked into it?" Miles had been waiting with nerves stretched to twanging to ask that one.

"I thought I could just lie in wait and ambush the Cetagandan bastard as soon as he came off the *Idris*. But he never came off. Stayed holed up in his cabin, I guess. Smart scum. I couldn't get through customs or the ship's security—I wasn't a registered passenger or a guest of one, though I tried to butter up a few. Scared the shit out of me when the fellow I tried to bribe to get me on board threatened to turn me in. Then I got smart and got me a berth on the *Rudra*, to at least get me legal entry past customs into those loading bays. And to be sure I'd be able to follow along if the fleet pulled out suddenly, which it was overdue to do by then. I wanted to kill him myself, for Gras-Grace and Firka and Hewlet, but if he was going to get away, I thought, if I turned him in to the Barrayarans as a Cetagandan spy, maybe . . . something interesting might happen, anyway. Something he wouldn't like. I didn't want to leave my trace on the vid call record, so I caught the *Idris*'s security officer in person when he was out in the loading bay. Tipped him off. I wasn't sure if he believed me or not, but I guess he went to check." Gupta hesitated. "He musta run into the Cetagandan bastard. I'm sorry. I'm afraid I got him melted. Like Gras-Grace and . . ." His litany ended in a shaken gulp.

"Is that when Solian had the nose bleed? When you were tipping him off?" Miles asked.

Gupta stared. "What are you, some kind of psychic?"

Check. "Why the faked blood on the docking bay floor?"

"Well . . . I'd heard the fleet was pulling out. They were saying that the poor bugger I'd got melted was supposed to have deserted, and they were writing him off, just like . . . like he didn't have a House or a Baron to put up any stake for him, and nobody cared. But I was afraid the Cetagandan bastard would pull another mid-space transfer, and I'd be stuck on the *Rudra*, and he'd get away . . . I thought it would focus attention back on the *Idris*, and what might be on it. I didn't dream those military morons would attack the quaddie station!"

"There were concatenating circumstances," Miles said primly, made conscious, for the first time in what seemed a small eternity of evoked horrors, of the hovering quaddie officialdom. "You certainly triggered events, but you could not possibly have anticipated them." He, too, blinked and looked around. "Er . . . did you have any questions, Chief Venn?"

Venn was giving him a most peculiar stare. He shook his head, slowly, from side to side.

"Uh . . ." A young quaddie patroller Miles had barely noticed enter during Guppy's urgent soliloquy held out a small, glittering object to his chief. "I have the fast-penta dose you ordered, sir . . . ?"

Venn took it and gazed over at Adjudicator Leutwyn.

Leutwyn cleared his throat. "Remarkable. I do believe, Lord Auditor Vorkosigan, that is the first time I've ever seen a fast-penta interrogation conducted without the fast-penta."

Miles glanced at Guppy, curled around himself in air, shivering a little. Smears of water still glistened at the corners of his eyes. "He . . . really wanted to tell somebody his story. He's been dying to for weeks. There was just no one in the entire nexus he could trust."

"Still isn't," gulped the prisoner. "Don't get a swelled

head, Barrayaran. I know nobody's on *my* side. But I missed my one shot, and he saw me. I was safe when he thought I was melted like the others. I'm a dead frog now, one way or another. But if I can't take him with me, maybe somebody else can."

CHAPTER THIRTEEN

Chief Venn said, "So . . . this Cetagandan bastard Gupta here is raving about, that he says killed three of his friends and maybe your Lieutenant Solian—you really think this is the same as the Betan transient, Dubauer, that you wanted us to pick up last night? So is he a herm, or a man, or what?"

"Or what," answered Miles. "My medical people established from a blood sample I accidentally collected yesterday that Dubauer is a Cetagandan ba. The ba are neither male, female, nor hermaphrodite, but a gender-less servant . . . caste, I guess is the best word, of the Cetagandan haut lords. More specifically, of the haut ladies who run the Star Crèche, at the core of the Celestial Garden, the Imperial residence on Eta Ceta." Who almost never left the Celestial Garden, with or without their ba servitors. *So what's this ba doing way out here, eh?* Miles hesitated, then went on, "This ba appears to be conducting a cargo of a thousand of what I suspect are the latest genetically modified haut fetuses in uterine replicators. I don't know where, I don't know why, and I don't know who for, but if Guppy's telling us the straight story, the ba has killed four people, including our missing security officer, and tried to kill Guppy, to keep its secret and cover its tracks." *At least four people.*

Greenlaw's expression had grown stiff with dismay. Venn regarded Gupta, frowning. "I guess we'd better put out a public arrest call on Dubauer, then, too."

"No!" Miles cried in alarm.

Venn raised his brows at him.

Miles explained hastily, "We're talking about a possible trained Cetagandan agent who may be carrying sophisticated bioweapons. It's already extremely stressed by the delays into which this dispute with the trade fleet has plunged it. It's just discovered it's made one bad mistake at least, because Guppy here is still alive. I don't care how superhuman it is, it has to be rattled by now. The last thing you want to do is send a bunch of feckless civilians up against it. Nobody should even approach the ba who doesn't know exactly what they're doing and what they're facing."

"And *your* people brought this creature here, onto *my* station?"

"Believe me, if any of my people had known what the ba was before this, it would never have made it past Komarr. The trade fleet are dupes, innocent carriers, I'm sure." Well, he wasn't *that* sure—checking that airy assertion was going to be a high-priority problem for counterintelligence, back home.

"Carriers . . ." Greenlaw echoed, looking hard at Guppy. All the quaddies in the room followed her stare. "Could this transient still be carrying that . . . whatever it was, infection?"

Miles took a breath. "Possibly. But if he is, it's too damned late already. Guppy has been running all over

Graf Station for days, now. Hell, if he's infectious, he's just spread a plague along a route through the nexus touching half a dozen planets." *And me. And my fleet. And maybe Ekaterin too.* "I see two points of hope. One, by Guppy's testimony, the ba had to administer the thing by actual touch."

The patrollers who'd handled the prisoner looked apprehensively at each other.

"And secondly," Miles went on, "if the disease or poison is something bioengineered by the Star Crèche, it's likely to be highly controlled, possibly deliberately self-limiting and self-destructing. The haut ladies don't like to leave their trash lying around for anyone to pick up."

"But I got better!" cried the amphibian.

"Yes," said Miles. "Why? Obviously, something in your unique genetics or situation either defeated the thing, or held it at bay long enough to keep you alive past its period of activity. Putting you in quarantine is about useless by now, but the next highest priority after nailing the ba has got to be running you through the medical wringer, to see if what you have or did can save anyone else." Miles drew breath. "May I offer the facilities of the *Prince Xav*? Our medical people do have some specific training in Cetagandan bio-threats."

Guppy blurted to Venn in panic, "Don't give me to them! They'll dissect me!"

Venn, who had brightened at this offer, shot the prisoner an exasperated look, but Greenlaw said slowly, "I know something of the ghem and the haut, but I've never heard of these ba, or the Star Crèche."

Adjudicator Leutwyn added warily, "Cetagandans of any stripe haven't much come in my way."

Greenlaw continued, "What makes you think their work is so safe, so restricted?"

"Safe, no. Controlled, maybe." How far did he need

to back up his explanation to make the dangers clear to them? It was vital that the quaddies be made to understand, and believe. "The Cetagandans . . . have this two-tiered aristocracy that is the bafflement of non-Cetagandan military observers. At the core are the haut lords, who are, in effect, one giant genetics experiment in producing the post-human race. This work is conducted and controlled by the haut women geneticists of the Star Crèche, the center where all haut embryos are created and modified before being sent back to their haut constellations—clans, parents—on the outlying planets of the empire. Unlike most prior historical versions of this sort of thing, the haut ladies didn't start by assuming they'd reached the perfected end already. They do not, at present, believe themselves to be done tinkering. When they are—well, who knows what will happen? What are the goals and desires going to be of the true post-human? Even the haut ladies don't try to second-guess their great-great-great-whatever grandchildren. I will say, it makes it uncomfortable to have them as neighbors."

"Didn't the haut try to conquer you Barrayarans, once?" asked Leutwyn.

"Not the haut. The ghem-lords. The buffer race, if you will, between the haut and the rest of humanity. I suppose you could think of the ghem as the haut's bastard children, except that they aren't bastards. In that sense, anyway. The haut leak selected genetic lines into the ghem via trophy haut wives—it's a complicated system. But the ghem-lords are the military arm of the empire, always anxious to prove their worth to their haut masters."

"The ghem, I've seen," said Venn. "We get them through here now and then. I thought the haut were, well, sort of degenerate. Aristocratic parasites. Afraid to get their hands dirty. They don't *work*." He gave a very quaddie sniff of disdain. "Or fight. You have to wonder how long the ghem-soldiers will put up with them."

"On the surface, the haut appear to dominate the ghem through pure moral suasion. Overawe by their beauty and intelligence and refinement, and by making themselves the source of all kinds of status rewards, culminating in the haut wives. All this is true. But beneath that . . . it is strongly suspected that the haut hold a biological and biochemical arsenal that even the ghem find terrifying."

"I haven't heard of anything like that being *used*," said Venn in a tone of skepticism.

"Oh, you bet you haven't."

"Why didn't they use it on you Barrayarans, back then, if they had it?" said Greenlaw slowly.

"That is a problem much studied, at certain levels of my government. First, it would have alarmed the neighborhood. Bioweapons aren't the only kind. The Cetagandan Empire apparently wasn't ready to face a posse of people scared enough to combine to burn off their planets and sterilize every living microbe. More importantly, we think it was a question of goals. The ghem-lords wanted the territory and the wealth, the personal aggrandizement that would have followed successful conquest. The haut ladies just weren't that interested. Not enough to waste their resources—not resources of weapons per se, but of reputation, secrecy, of a silent threat of unknown potency. Our intelligence services have amassed maybe half a dozen cases in the past thirty years of suspected use of haut-style bioweapons, and in every instance, it was a Cetagandan internal matter." He glanced at Greenlaw's intensely disturbed face and added in what he hoped didn't sound like hollow reassurance, "There was no spread or bio-backsplash from those incidents that we know of."

Venn looked at Greenlaw. "So do we take this prisoner to a clinic, or to a cell?"

Greenlaw was silent for a few moments, then said, "Graf Station University clinic. Straight to the infectious isolation unit. I think we want our best experts in on this, and as quickly as possible."

Gupta objected, "But I'll be an open target! I was hunting the Cetagandan bastard—now he—it, whatever—will be hunting me!"

"I agree with this evaluation," Miles said quickly. "Wherever you take Gupta, the location should be kept absolutely secret. The fact that he's even been taken into custody should be suppressed—dear God, this arrest hasn't gone out on your news services already, has it?" Piping the word of Gupta's location to every nook of the station . . .

"Not formally," said Venn uneasily.

It scarcely mattered, Miles supposed. Dozens of quaddies had seen the web-fingered man brought in, including everybody that Bel's crew of roustabouts had passed on the way. The Docks and Locks quaddies would certainly brag of their catch to everyone they knew. The gossip would be all over.

"I strongly urge—beg!—you to put out word of his daring escape, then. Complete with follow-up bulletins asking all the citizens to keep an eye out for him again." The ba had killed four to keep its secret—would it be willing to kill fifty thousand?

"A disinformation campaign?" Greenlaw's lips pursed in repugnance.

"The lives of everyone on the station might well depend on it. Secrecy is your best hope of safety. And Gupta's. After that, guards—"

"My people are already spread to their limit," Venn protested. He gave Greenlaw a beseeching look.

Miles opened a hand in acknowledgment. "Not

patrollers. Guards who know what they're doing, trained in bio-defense procedures."

"We'll have to draw on Union Militia specialists," said Greenlaw in a decisive tone. "I'll put in the request. But it will take them . . . some time, to get here."

"In the meanwhile," said Miles, "I can loan you some trained personnel."

Venn grimaced. "I have a detention block full of your personnel. I'm not much impressed with their training."

Miles suppressed a wince. "Not *them*. Military medical corps."

"I will consider your offer," said Greenlaw neutrally.

"Some of Vorpatril's senior medical men must have some expertise in this area. If you won't let us take Gupta out to the safety of one of our vessels, please, let them come aboard the station to help you."

Greenlaw's eyes narrowed. "All right. We will accept up to four such volunteers. Unarmed. *Under* the direct supervision and command of our own medical experts."

"Agreed," said Miles instantly.

It was the best compromise he was likely to get, for the moment. The medical end of this problem, terrifying as it was, would have to be left to the specialists; it was out of Miles's range of expertise. Catching the ba before it could do any more damage, now . . .

"The haut are not immune to stunner fire. I . . . recommend"—he could not order, he could not demand, most of all, he could not scream—"you *quietly* inform all of your patrollers that the ba—Dubauer—be stunned on sight. Once it's down, we can sort things out at our leisure."

Venn and Greenlaw exchanged looks with the

adjudicator. Leutwyn said in a constricted voice, "It would be against regs to so ambush the suspect if it is not in process of a crime, resisting arrest, or fleeing."

"Bioweapons?" muttered Venn.

The adjudicator swallowed. "Make damned sure your patrollers don't miss their first shot."

"Your ruling is noted, sir."

And if the ba stayed out of sight? Which it had certainly managed to do for most of the past twenty-four hours. . . .

What did the ba want? Its cargo freed, and Guppy dead before he could talk, presumably. What did the ba know, at this point? Or not know? It didn't know that Miles had identified its cargo . . . did it? *Where the hell is Bel?*

"Ambush," Miles echoed. "There are two places where you could set up an ambush for the ba. Wherever you take Guppy—or better still, wherever the ba *believes* you've taken Guppy. If you don't want to put it about that he's escaped, then take him to a concealed location, with a second, less secret one set up for bait. Then, another trap at the *Idris*. If Dubauer calls in requesting permission to go aboard again, which the last time we met, it fully intended to do, you should grant the petition. Then nail it as it enters the loading bay."

"That's what *I* was going to do," put in Gupta in a resentful voice. "If you people had just let well enough alone, this could have been all over by now."

Miles privately agreed, but it would hardly do to say so out loud; someone might point out just who had put on the pressure for Gupta's arrest.

Greenlaw was looking grimly thoughtful. "I wish to inspect this alleged cargo. It is possible that it violates enough regs to merit impoundment quite separately from the issue of its carrier ship."

The adjudicator cleared his throat. "That could grow legally complex, Sealer. More complex. Cargoes not off-loaded for transfer, even if questionable, are normally allowed to pass through without legal comment. They're considered to be the territorial responsibility of the polity of registration of the carrier, unless they are an imminent public danger. A thousand fetuses, if that's what they are, constitute . . . what menace?"

Impounding them could prove a horrific danger, Miles thought. It would certainly lock Cetagandan attention upon Quaddiespace. Speaking from both historical and personal experience, this was not necessarily a good thing.

"I want to confirm this for myself, too," said Venn. "And give my guards their orders in person, and figure out where to place my sharpshooters."

"And you need me along, to get into the cargo hold," Miles pointed out.

Greenlaw said, "No, just your security codes."

Miles smiled blandly at her.

Her jaw tightened. After a moment, she growled, "Very well. Let's go, Venn. You too, Adjudicator. And," she sighed briefly, "you, Lord Auditor Vorkosigan."

Gupta was wrapped in bio-barriers by the two quaddies who had handled him before—a logical choice, if not much to their liking. They donned wraps and gloves themselves and towed him out without allowing him to touch anything else. The amphibian suffered this without protest. He looked utterly exhausted.

Garnet Five left with Nicol for Nicol's apartment, where the two quaddie women planned to support each other while awaiting word of Bel. *"Call me,"* Nicol pleaded in an under-voice to Miles as they floated out. Miles nodded his promise, and prayed silently that it would not prove to be one of those hard calls.

His brief vid call out to the *Prince Xav* and Admiral Vorpatril was hard enough. Vorpatril was almost as white as his hair by the time Miles had finished bringing him up to date. He promised to expedite a selection of medical volunteers at emergency speed.

The procession to the *Idris* finally included Venn, Greenlaw, the adjudicator, two quaddie patrollers, Miles, and Roic. The loading bay was as dim and quiet as—had it only been yesterday? One of the two quaddie guards, watched bemusedly by the other, was out of his floater and crouched on the floor. He was evidently playing a game with gravity involving a scattering of tiny bright metal caltrops and a small rubber ball, which seemed to consist of bouncing the ball off the floor, catching it again, and snatching up the little caltrops between bounces. To make it more interesting for himself, he was switching hands with each iteration. At the sight of the visitors, the guard hastily pocketed the game and scrambled back into his floater.

Venn pretended not to see this, simply inquiring after any events of note during their shift. Not only had no unauthorized persons attempted to get past them, the investigation committee was the first live persons the bored men had seen since relieving the prior shift. Venn lingered with his patrollers to make his arrangements for the stunner ambush of the ba, should it appear, and Miles led Roic, Greenlaw, and the adjudicator aboard the ship.

The gleaming rows of replicator racks in Dubauer's leased cargo hold appeared unchanged from yesterday. Greenlaw grew tense about the lips, guiding her floater around the hold on an initial overview, then pausing to stare down the aisles. Miles thought he could almost see her doing the multiplication in her head. She and Leutwyn then hovered by Miles's side as he activated a few control panels to demonstrate the replicators' contents.

It was almost a repeat of yesterday, except . . . a number of the readout indicators showed amber instead of green. Closer examination revealed them as measures of an array of stressor-signals, including adrenaline levels. Was the ba right about the fetuses reaching some sort of biological limit in their containers? Was this the first sign of dangerous overgrowth? As Miles watched, a couple of the light bars dropped back on their own from amber to a more encouraging green. He went on to call up the vid monitor images of the individual fetuses for Greenlaw's and the adjudicator's views. The fourth one he activated showed amniotic fluid cloudy with scarlet blood when the lights came on. Miles caught his breath. *How . . . ?*

That surely wasn't normal. The only possible source of blood was the fetus itself. He rechecked the stressor levels—this one showed a lot of amber—then stood on tiptoe and peered more closely at the image. The blood appeared to be leaking from a small, jagged gash on the twitching haut infant's back. The low red lighting, Miles reassured himself uneasily, made it look worse than it was.

Greenlaw's voice by his ear made him jump. "Is there something wrong with that one?"

"He appears to have suffered some sort of mechanical injury. That . . . shouldn't be possible, in a sealed replicator." He thought of Aral Alexander, and Helen Natalia, and his stomach knotted. "If you have any quaddie experts in replicator reproduction, it might not be a bad idea to get them in here to look at these." He doubted this was a specialty where the military medicos from the *Prince Xav* were likely to be much help.

Venn appeared at the door of the hold, and

Greenlaw repeated most of Miles's orienting patter for his benefit. Venn's expression was most disturbed as he regarded the replicators. "That frog fellow wasn't lying. This is *very* strange."

Venn's wrist com buzzed, and he excused himself to float to the side of the room and engage in some low-voiced conversation with whatever subordinate was reporting in. At least, it began as low-voiced, until Venn bellowed, "*What? When?*"

Miles abandoned his worried study of the injured haut infant and edged over to Venn.

"About 0200, sir," a distressed voice responded from the wrist com.

"This wasn't authorized!"

"Yes, it was, Crew Chief, duly. Portmaster Thorne authorized it. Since it was the same passenger it had brought on board yesterday, the one who had that live cargo to tend, we didn't think anything was odd."

"What time did they *leave?*" Venn asked. His face was a mask of dismay.

"Not on our shift, sir. I don't know what happened after that. I went straight home and went to bed. I didn't see the search bulletin for Portmaster Thorne on the news stream till I got up for breakfast just a few minutes ago."

"Why didn't you pass this on in your end-of-shift report?"

"Portmaster Thorne *said* not to." The voice hesitated. "At least . . . the passenger suggested we might want to leave this off the record, so that we wouldn't have to deal with all the other passengers demanding access too if they heard about it, and Portmaster Thorne nodded and said *Yes.*"

Venn winced, and took a deep breath. "It can't be helped, Patroller. You reported as soon as you knew. I'm glad you at least picked up the news right away.

We'll take it from here. Thank you." Venn cut the channel.

"What was that all about?" asked Miles. Roic had strolled up to loom over his shoulder.

Venn clutched his head with his upper hands, and groaned, "My night-shift guard on the *Idris* just woke up and saw the news bulletin about Thorne being missing. *He* says Thorne came here last night about oh-two-hundred and passed Dubauer through the guards."

"Where did Thorne go after that?"

"Escorted Dubauer aboard, apparently. Neither of them came off while my night-shift crew was watching. Excuse me. I need to go talk to my people." Venn grabbed his floater control and swung hastily out of the cargo hold.

Miles stood stunned. How could Bel have gone from an uncomfortable, but relatively safe, nap in a recycling bin to *this* action in little more than an hour? Garnet Five had taken six or seven hours to wake up. His high confidence in his judgment of Gupta's account was suddenly shaken.

Roic, eyes narrowing, asked, "Could your herm friend have gone renegade, m'lord? Or been bribed?"

Adjudicator Leutwyn looked to Greenlaw, who looked sick with uncertainty.

"I would sooner doubt . . . myself," said Miles. And that was slandering Bel. "Although the portmaster might have been bribed with a nerve disruptor muzzle pressed to its spine, or something equivalent." He wasn't sure he wanted to even try to imagine the ba's bioweapon equivalent. "Bel *would* play for time."

"How could this ba find the portmaster when we couldn't?" asked Leutwyn.

Miles hesitated. "The ba wasn't hunting Bel. The ba was hunting Guppy. If the ba had been closing

in last night when Guppy counterattacked his shad-
owers . . . the ba might have come along immediately
after, or even been a witness. And allowed itself to
be diverted, or swapped its priorities, in the face of
the unexpected opportunity to gain access to its cargo
through Bel."

What priorities? What did the ba want? Well,
Gupta dead, certainly, doubly so now that the amphibian was witness to both its initial clandestine
operation, and to the murders by which the ba had
attempted to completely erase its trail. But for the
ba to have been so close to its target, and yet veer
off, suggested that the other priority was overwhelm-
ingly more important to it.

The ba had spoken of utterly destroying its purport-
edly animal cargo; the ba had also spoken of taking
tissue samples for freezing. The ba had spoken lie upon
lie, but suppose this was the truth? Miles wheeled to
stare down the aisle of racks. The image formed
itself in his mind: of the ba working all day, with
relentless speed and concentration. Loosening the lid
of each replicator, stabbing through membrane, fluid,
and soft skin with a sampling needle, lining the needles
up, row on row, in a freezer unit the size of a small
valise. Miniaturizing the essence of its genetic payload
to something it could carry away in one hand. At the
cost of abandoning their originals? *Destroying the
evidence?*

Maybe it has, and we just can't see the effects yet.
If the ba could make adult-sized bodies steam away
their own liquids within hours and turn to viscous
puddles, what could it do with such tiny ones?

The Cetagandan wasn't stupid. Its smuggling scheme
might have gone according to plan, but for the slipup
with Gupta. Who had followed the ba here, and drawn
in Solian—whose disappearance had led to the muddle

with Corbeau and Garnet Five, which had led to the
bungled raid on the quaddie security post, which had
resulted in the impoundment of the fleet, including the
ba's precious cargo. Miles knew exactly how it felt to
watch a carefully planned mission slide down the toilet in a flush of random mischance. How would the
ba respond to that sick, heart-pounding desperation?
Miles had almost no sense of the person, despite
meeting it twice. The ba was smooth and slick and self-
controlled. It could kill with a touch, smiling.

But if the ba was paring down its payload to a
minimum mass, it certainly wouldn't saddle its escape
with a prisoner.

"I think," said Miles, and had to stop and clear a
throat gone dry. Bel would play for time. But suppose time and ingenuity ran out, and no one came,
and no one came, and no one came . . . "I think Bel
might still be aboard the *Idris*. We must search the
ship. At once."

Roic stared around, looking daunted. "All of it,
m'lord?"

He started to cry *Yes!* but his laggard brain converted it to, "No. Bel had no access codes beyond
quaddie control of the airlock. The ba had codes only
for this hold and its own cabin. Anything that was
locked before, should still be. For the first pass, check
unsecured spaces only."

"Shouldn't we wait for Chief Venn's patrollers?"
asked Leutwyn uneasily.

"If anyone even tries to come aboard who hasn't
been exposed already, I swear I'll stun them myself
before they can get through the airlock. I'm not fool-
ing." Miles's voice was husky with conviction.

Leutwyn looked taken aback, but Greenlaw, after a
frozen moment, nodded. "I quite see your point, Lord
Auditor Vorkosigan. I must agree."

They spread out in pairs, the intent-looking Green-law followed by the somewhat bewildered adjudicator, Roic determinedly keeping to Miles's shoulder. Miles tried the ba's cabin first, to find it as empty as before. Four other cabins had been left unlocked, three presumably because they had been cleared of possessions, the last apparently through sheer carelessness. The infirmary was sealed, as it had been left after Bel's inspection with the medtechs last evening. Nav and Com was fully secured. On the deck above, the kitchen was open, as were some of the recreation areas, but no cheeky Betan herm or unnaturally decomposed remains were to be found. Greenlaw and Leutwyn passed through, to report that all of the other holds in the huge long cylinder shared by the ba's cargo were still properly sealed. Venn, they discovered, had taken over a comconsole in the passenger lounge; upon being apprised of Miles's new theory, he paled and attached himself to Greenlaw. Five more nacelles to check.

On the deck below the passengers' zone, most of the utility and engineering areas remained locked. But the door to the department of Small Repairs opened at Miles's touch on its control pad.

Three adjoining chambers were full of benches, tools, and diagnostic equipment. In the second chamber, Miles came upon a bench holding three deflated bod pods marked with the *Idris*'s logo and serial numbers. These tough-skinned human-sized balloons were furnished with enough air recycling equipment and power to keep a passenger alive in a pressurization emergency until rescue arrived. One had only to step inside, zip it up, and hit the power-on button. Bod pods required a minimum of instruction, mostly because there wasn't bloody much you could do once you were trapped inside one. Every cabin, hold, and corridor on the ship had them, stored in emergency lockers on the walls.

On the floor beside the bench, one bod pod stood fully inflated, as if it had been left there in the middle of testing by some tech when the ship had been evacuated by the quaddies.

Miles stepped up to one of the pod's round plastic ports and peered through.

Bel sat inside, cross-legged, stark naked. The herm's lips were parted, and its eyes glazed and distant. So still was that form, Miles feared he was looking at death already, but then Bel's chest rose and fell, breasts trembling with the shivers racking its body. On the blank face a fevered flush bloomed and faded.

No, God, no! Miles lunged for the pod's seal, but his hand stopped and fell back, clenching so hard his nails bit into his palm like knives. *No . . .*

CHAPTER FOURTEEN

Step One. Seal the biocontaminated area.

Had the entry lock been closed behind them when their party entered the *Idris*? Yes. Had anyone opened it since?

Miles raised his wrist com to his lips and spoke Venn's contact code. Roic stepped closer to the bod pod, but stopped at Miles's upflung hand; he ducked his head and peered past Miles's shoulder, and his eyes widened.

The few seconds of delay while the wrist com's search program located Venn seemed to flow by like cold oil. Finally, the crew chief's edgy voice: "Venn here. What now, Lord Vorkosigan?"

"We've found Portmaster Thorne. Trapped in a bod pod in the engineering section. The herm appears dazed and very ill. I believe we have an urgent bio-contamination emergency here, at least Class Three and possibly as bad as Class Five." The most extreme level, biowarfare plague. "Where are you all now?"

"In the Number Two freight nacelle. The sealer and the adjudicator are with me."

"No one has attempted to leave or enter the ship since we boarded? You didn't go out for any reason?"

"No."

"You understand the necessity for keeping it that way till we know what the devil we're dealing with?"

"What, do you think I'd be insane enough to carry some hell-plague back onto *my own station?*"

Check. "Very good, Crew Chief. I see we are of one mind in this." *Step Two. Alert the medical authority in your district.* To each their own. "I'm going to report this to Admiral Vorpatril and request medical assistance. I presume Graf Station has its own emergency protocols."

"Just as soon as you get off my com link."

"Right. At the earliest feasible moment, I also intend to break the tube seals and move the ship a little way out of its docking cradle, just to be sure. If you or the Sealer would warn station traffic control, plus clear whatever shuttle Vorpatril sends, that would be most helpful. Meanwhile—I strongly urge you to seal the locks between your nacelle and this central section until . . . until we know more. Find the nacelle's atmosphere controls and put yourselves on internal circulation, if you can. I haven't . . . quite figured out what to do about this damned bod pod yet. Nai—Vorkosigan out."

He cut the com and stared in anguish at the thin wall between him and Bel. How good a biocontamination barrier was a sealed bod pod's skin? Probably quite good, for something not purpose-built for the task. A new and horrible idea of just where to look for Solian, or rather, whatever organic smear of the lieutenant might now remain, presented itself inescapably to Miles's imagination.

With that jump of deduction came new hope and new terror. Solian had been disposed of weeks ago, probably aboard this very vessel, at a time when passengers and crew had been moving freely between the station and the ship. No plague had broken out yet. If Solian had been dissolved by the same nightmare method Gupta testified had claimed his shipmates, inside a bod pod, which was then folded and set out of the way ... leaving Bel in the pod with the seals unbroken might make everyone perfectly safe.

Everyone, of course, except Bel. ...

It was unclear if the incubation or latency period of the infection was adjustable, although what Miles was seeing now suggested it was. Six days for Gupta and his friends. Six hours for Bel? But the disease or poison or bio-molecular device, whatever it was, had killed the Jacksonians quickly once it became active, in just a few hours. How long did Bel have until intervention became futile? Before the herm's brains began turning to some bubbling gray slime along with its body ... ? Hours, minutes, too late already? And what intervention could help?

Gupta survived this. Therefore, survival is possible. His mind dug into that historical fact like pitons into a rock face. *Hang on and climb, boy.*

He held his wrist com to his lips and called up the emergency channel to Admiral Vorpatril.

Vorpatril responded almost immediately. "Lord Vorkosigan? The medical squad you requested reached the quaddie station a few minutes ago. They should be reporting in to you there momentarily to assist with the examination of your prisoner. Haven't they presented themselves yet?"

"They may have, but I'm now aboard the *Idris*, along with Armsman Roic. And, unfortunately, Sealer Greenlaw, Adjudicator Leutwyn, and Chief Venn. We've ordered the ship sealed. We appear to have a biocontamination incident aboard." He repeated the description of Bel he'd given Venn, with a few more details.

Vorpatril swore. "Shall I send a personnel pod to take you off, my lord?"

"Absolutely not. If there's anything contagious loose in here—which, while not certain, is not yet ruled out—it's um . . . already too late."

"I'll divert my medical squad to you at once."

"Not all of them, dammit. I want some of our people in with the quaddies, working on Gupta. It is of the highest urgency to find out why he survived. Since we may be stuck in here for a while, don't tie up more men than required. But do send me bright ones. In Level Five biotainer suits. You can send any equipment they want aboard with them, but nothing and no one goes back off this ship till this thing is locked down." Or until the plague took them all . . . Miles had a vision of the *Idris* towed away from the station and abandoned, the untouchable final tomb of all aboard. A damned *expensive* sepulchre, there was that consolation. He had faced death before and, once at least, lost, but the lonely ugliness of this one shook him badly. There would be no cheating with cryochambers this time, he suspected. Not for the last victims to go, certainly. "Volunteers only, you understand me, Admiral?"

"That I do," said Vorpatril grimly. "I'm on it, my Lord Auditor."

"Good. Vorkosigan out."

How much time did Bel have? Half an hour? Two hours? How much time would it take Vorpatril to muster his new set of medical volunteers and all their complex cargo? More than half an hour, Miles was fairly certain. And what could they do when they got here?

Besides his genetic engineering, what had been different from the others about Gupta?

His tank? Breathing through his gills . . . Bel didn't have gills, no help there. Cooling water, flowing over the froggish body, his fan-like webs, through the blood-filled, feathery gills, chilling his blood . . . could some of this bio-dissolvent's hellish development be heat-sensitive or temperature-triggered?

An ice-water bath? The vision sprang to his mind's eye, and his lips drew back on a fierce grin. A low-tech, but provably fast, way to lower body temperature, no question about it. He could personally guarantee the effects. *Thank you, Ivan.*

"My lord?" said Roic uncertainly to his apparent transfixed paralysis.

"We run like hell now. You go to the galley and check for ice. If there isn't any, start whatever machine they have full blast. Then meet me in the infirmary." He had to move fast; he didn't have to be stupid about it. "They may have biotainer gear there."

By the expression on Roic's face, he was notably not following any of this, but at least he followed Miles, who boiled out and down the corridor. They rose up the lift tube the two flights to the level that housed galley, infirmary, and recreation areas. More out of breath than he cared to reveal, Miles waved Roic on his way and galloped to the infirmary at the far end of the central nacelle. A frustrating pause while he tapped out the locking code, and he was through into the little sickbay.

The facilities were scant: two small wards, although both with at least Level Three bio-containment capabilities, plus an examining room equipped for minor surgery and also harboring the pharmacy. Major surgeries and severe injuries were expected to be transported to one of the military escort ship's more seriously equipped sickbays. Yes, one of the ward's bathrooms included a sterilizable treatment tub; Miles pictured unhappy passengers with skin infestations soaking therein. Lockers full of emergency equipment. He jerked them all open. There was the blood synthesizer, there a drawer of mysterious and unnerving objects perhaps designed for female patients, there was a narrow float pallet for patient transport, standing on end in a tall locker with two biotainer suits, yes! One too large for Miles, the other too small for Roic.

He could wear the too-large suit; it wouldn't be the first time. The other would be impossible. He couldn't justify endangering Roic so . . .

Roic jogged in. "Found the ice maker, m'lord. Nobody seems to have turned it off when the ship was evacuated. It's packed full."

Miles pulled out his stunner and dropped it on the examining table, then began to skin into the smaller biotainer suit.

"What t'hell do you think you're doing, m'lord?" asked Roic warily.

"We're going to bring Bel up here. Or at least, I am. It's where the medics will want to do treatments anyway." If there were any treatments. "I have an idea for some quick-and-dirty first aid. I think Guppy might have survived by the water in his tank keeping his body temperature down. Head for engineering. Try to find a pressure suit that will fit you. If—*when* you find the suit, let me know, and put it on at once. Then meet me back where Bel is. Move!"

Roic, face set, moved. Miles used the precious seconds to run to the galley and scoop a plastic waste bin full of ice, and drag it back to the infirmary on the float pallet to dump in the tub. Then a second bin full. Then his wrist com buzzed.

"Found a suit, m'lord. It'll just fit, I think." Roic's

voice wavered as, presumably, his arm moved about. Some rustling and faint grunting indicated a successful test. "Once I'm in, I won't be able to use my secured wrist com. I'll have to access you over some public channel."

"We'll have to live with that. Make contact with Vorpatril on your suit com as soon as you're sealed in; be sure his medics can communicate when they bring their pod to one of the outboard locks. Make sure they don't try to come through the same freight nacelle where the quaddies have taken refuge!"

"Right, m'lord."

"Meet you in Small Repairs."

"Right, m'lord. Suiting up now." The channel went muffled.

Regretfully, Miles covered his own wrist com with the biotainer suit's left glove. He tucked his stunner into one of the sealable outer pockets on the thigh, then adjusted his oxygen flow with a few taps on the suit's control vambrace on his left arm. The lights in the helmet faceplate display promised him he was now sealed from his environment. The slight positive pressure within the overlarge suit puffed it out plumply. He slopped toward the lift tube in the loose boots, towing the float pallet.

Roic was just clumping down the corridor as Miles maneuvered the pallet through the door of Small Repairs. The armsman's pressure suit, marked with the *Idris*'s engineering department's serial numbers, was certainly as much protection as Miles's gear, although its gloves were thicker and more clumsy. Miles motioned Roic to bend toward him, touching his faceplate to Roic's helmet.

"We're going to reduce the pressure in the bod pod to partially deflate it, roll Bel onto the float pallet, and run it upstairs. I'm not going to unseal the pod till we're in the ward with the molecular barriers activated."

"Shouldn't we wait for the *Prince Xav*'s medics for that, m'lord?" asked Roic nervously. "They'll be here soon enough."

"No. Because I don't know how soon too late is. I don't dare vent Bel's pod into the ship's atmosphere, so I'm going to try to rig a line to another pod as a catchment. Help me look for sealing tape, and something to use for an air pipe."

Roic gave him a rather frustrated gesture of acknowledgment, and began a survey of benches and drawers.

Miles peered in the port again. "Bel? Bel!" he shouted through faceplate and bod skin. Muffled, yes, but he should be audible, dammit. "We're going to move you. Hang on in there."

Bel sat unchanged, apparently, from a few minutes ago, still glazed and unresponsive. It might not be the infection, Miles tried to encourage himself. How many drugs had the herm been hit with last night, to assure its cooperation? Knocked out by Gupta, stimulated to consciousness by the ba, tanked with hypnotics, presumably, for the walk to the *Idris* and the scam of the quaddie guards. Maybe fast-penta after that, and some sedatives to keep Bel quiescent while the poison took hold, who knew?

Miles shook out one of the other pods onto the floor nearby. If the residue of Solian lay therein, well, this wasn't going to make it any *more* contaminated, now was it? And would Bel's remains have escaped notice for as long as Solian's, if Miles hadn't come along so soon—was that the ba's plan? Murder and dispose of the body in one move. . . .

He knelt to the side of Bel's bod pod and opened the access panel to the pressurization control unit. Roic handed down a length of plastic tubing and strips of tape. Miles wrapped, prayed, and turned assorted valve controls. The air pump vibrated gently. The pod's round outline softened and slumped. The second pod expanded, after a flaccid, wrinkled fashion. He closed valves, cut lines, sealed, wished for a few liters of disinfectant to splash around. He held the fabric up away from the lump that was Bel's head as Roic lifted the herm onto the pallet.

The pallet moved at a brisk walking pace; Miles longed to run. They maneuvered the load into the infirmary, into the small ward. As close as possible to the rather cramped bathroom.

Miles motioned Roic to bend close again.

"All right. This is as far as you go. We don't both need to be in here for this. I want you to exit the room and turn on the molecular barriers. Then stand ready to assist the medics from the *Prince Xav* as needed."

"M'lord, are you sure you wouldn't rather we do it t'other way around?"

"I'm sure. Go!"

Roic exited reluctantly. Miles waited till the lines of blue light indicating that the barriers had been activated sprang into being across the doorway, then bent to unzip the pod and fold it back from Bel's tensed, trembling body. Even through his gloves, Bel's bare skin felt scorching hot.

Edging both the pallet and himself into the bathroom involved some awkward clambering, but at last he had Bel positioned to shift into the waiting vat of ice and water. Heave, slide, splash. He cursed the pallet and lunged over it to hold Bel's head up. Bel's body jerked in shock; Miles wondered if his shakily theorized palliative would instead give the victim heart failure. He shoved the pallet back out the door, and out of the way, with one foot. Bel was now trying to curl into a fetal position, a more heartening response than the open-eyed coma Miles had observed so far. Miles pulled the bent limbs down one by one and held them under the ice water.

Miles fingers grew numb with the cold, except where they touched Bel. The herm's body temperature seemed scarcely affected by this brutal treatment. Unnatural indeed. But at least Bel stopped growing hotter. The ice was melting noticeably.

It had been some years since Miles had last glimpsed Bel nude, in a field shower or donning or divesting space armor in a mercenary warship locker room. Fifty-something wasn't old, for a Betan, but still, gravity was clearly gaining on Bel. *On all of us.* In their Dendarii days Bel had taken out its unrequited lust for Miles in a series of half-joking passes, half-regretfully declined. Miles repented his younger sexual reticence altogether, now. Profoundly. *We should have taken our chances back then, when we were young and beautiful and didn't even know it.* And Bel had been beautiful, in its own ironic way, living and moving at ease in a body athletic, healthy, and trim.

Bel's skin was blotched, mottled red and pale; the herm's flesh, sliding and turning in the ice bath under Miles's anxious hands, had an odd texture, by turns swollen tight or bruised like crushed fruit. Miles called Bel's name, tried his best old *Admiral Naismith Commands You* voice, told a bad joke, all without penetrating the herm's glazed stupor. It was a bad idea to cry in a biotainer suit, almost as bad as throwing up in a pressure suit. You couldn't blot your eyes, or wipe your snot.

And when someone touched you unexpectedly on the shoulder, you jumped as though shot, and they looked at you funny, through their faceplate and yours.

"Lord Auditor Vorkosigan, are you all right?" said the *Prince Xav's* biotainer-swaddled surgeon, as he knelt beside him at the vat's edge.

Miles swallowed for self-control. "I'm fine, so far. This herm's in a very bad way. I don't know what they've told you about all this."

"I was told that I might be dealing with a possible Cetagandan-designed bioweapon in hot mode, that had killed three so far with one survivor. The part about there being a survivor made me really wonder about the first assertion."

"Ah, you didn't get a chance to see Guppy yet, then." Miles took a breath and ran through a brief recap of Gupta's tale, or at least the pertinent biological aspects of it. As he spoke, his hands never stopped shoving Bel's arms and legs back down, or ladling watery ice cubes over the herm's burning head and neck. He finished, "I don't know if it was Gupta's amphibian genetics, or something he did, that allowed him to survive this hell-shit when his friends didn't. Guppy said their dead flesh *steamed*. I don't know what all this heat's coming from, but it can't be just fever. I couldn't duplicate the Jacksonian's bioengineering, but I thought I could at least duplicate the water tank trick. Wild-assed empiricism, but I didn't think there was much time."

A gloved hand reached past him to raise Bel's eyelids, touch the herm here and there, press and probe. "I see that."

"It's *really important*"—Miles took another gulp of air to stabilize his voice—"it's really important that this patient survive. Thorne's not just any stationer. Bel was . . ." He realized he didn't know the surgeon's security clearance. "Having the portmaster die on our watch would be a diplomatic disaster. Another one, that is. And . . . and the herm saved my life yesterday. I owe—Barrayar owes—"

"My lord, we'll do our best. I have my top squad here; we'll take over now. Please, my Lord Auditor, if you could please step out and let your man decontaminate you?"

Another suited figure, doctor or medtech, appeared through the bathroom door and held out a tray of instruments to the surgeon. Perforce Miles moved aside, as the first sampling needle plunged past him into Bel's unresponsive flesh. No room left in here even for his shortness, he had to admit. He withdrew.

The spare ward bunk had been turned into a lab bench. A third biotainer-clad figure was rapidly shifting what looked a promising array of equipment from boxes and bins piled high on a float pallet onto this makeshift surface. The second tech returned from the bathroom and started feeding bits of Bel into the various chemical and molecular analyzers on one end of the bunk even as the third man arranged more devices on the other.

Roic's tall, pressure-suited figure stood waiting just past the molecular barriers across the ward door. He was holding a high-powered laser-sonic decontaminator, familiar Barrayaran military issue. He raised an inviting hand; Miles returned the acknowledgment.

Nothing further was to be gained in here by dithering more at the medical squad. He'd just distract them and get in their way. He suppressed his unstrung urge to explain to them Bel's superior right, by old valor and love, to survive. Futile. He might as well rail at the microbes themselves. Even the Cetagandans had not yet devised a weapon that triaged for virtue before slaughtering its victims.

I promised to call Nicol. God, why did I promise that? Learning Bel's present status would surely be more terrifying for her than knowing nothing. He would wait a little longer, at least till he received the first report from the surgeon. If there was hope by then, he could impart it. If there was none . . .

He stepped slowly through the buzzing molecular barrier, raising his arms to turn about beneath the even stronger sonic-scrubber/laser-dryer beam from Roic's decontaminator. He had Roic treat every part of him, including palms, fingers, the soles of his feet, and, nervously, the insides of his thighs. The suit protected him from what would otherwise be a nasty scorching, leaving skin pink and hair exploded off. He didn't motion Roic to desist till they'd gone over each square centimeter. Twice.

Roic pointed to Miles's control vambrace and bellowed through his faceplate, "I have the ship's com link relay up and running now, m'lord. You should be able to hear me through Channel Twelve, if you'll switch over. T'medics are all on Thirteen."

Hastily, Miles switched on the suit com. "Can you hear me?"

Roic's voice sounded now beside his ear. "Yes, m'lord. Much better."

"Have we blown the tube seals and pulled away from the docking clamps yet?"

Roic looked faintly chagrined. "No, m'lord." At Miles's chin raised in inquiry, he added, "Um . . . you see, there's only me. I've never piloted a jumpship."

"Unless you're actually jumping, it's just like a shuttle," Miles assured him. "Only bigger."

"I've never piloted a shuttle, either."

"Ah. Well, come on, then. I'll show you how."

They threaded their way to Nav and Com; Roic tapped their passage through the code locks. All right, Miles admitted, looking around at the various station chairs and their control banks, so it *was* a big ship. It was only going to be a ten-meter flight. He was a bit out of practice even on pods and shuttles, but really, given some of the pilots he'd known, how hard could it be?

Roic watched in earnest admiration while he concealed his hunt for the tube seal controls—ah, there. It took three tries to get in touch with station traffic control, and then with Docks and Locks—if only Bel had been here, he would have instantly delegated this task to . . . He bit his lip, rechecking the all-clear from the loading bay—it would be the cap on this mission's multitude of embarrassments to pull away from the station yanking out the docking clamps, decompressing the loading bay, and killing some unknown number of quaddie patrollers on guard therein. He scooted from the communications station to the pilot's chair, shoving the jump helmet up out of the way and clenching his gloved hands briefly before activating the manual controls. A little gentle pressure from the side verniers, a little patience, and a countering thrust from the opposite side left the vast bulk of the *Idris* floating in space a neat stone's throw from the side of Graf Station. Not that a stone thrown out there would do anything but keep on going forever . . .

No bio-plague can cross that gap, he thought with satisfaction, then instantly thought of what the Cetagandans might do with spores. *I hope.*

It occurred to him belatedly that if the *Prince Xav*'s surgeon sounded an all-clear from the biocontamination alert, docking once again was going to be a critically more delicate task. *Well, if he clears the ship, we can import a pilot then.* He glanced at the time on a wall digital. Barely an hour had passed since they'd found Bel. It seemed a century.

"You're a pilot, as well?" a surprised, muffled female voice sounded.

Miles swung around in the pilot's chair to find the three quaddies in their floaters hovering in the control room's doorway. All now wore quaddie-shaped bio-tainer suits in pale medical green. His eye rapidly sorted them out. Venn was bulkier, Sealer Greenlaw a little shorter. Adjudicator Leutwyn brought up the rear.

"Only in an emergency," he admitted. "Where did you get the suits?"

"My people sent them across from the station in a drone pod," said Venn. He, too, wore his stunner holstered on the outside of his suit.

Miles would have preferred to keep the civilians safely locked down in the freight nacelle, but there was clearly no help for that now.

"*Which* is still attached to the lock, yes," Venn overrode Miles's opening mouth.

"Thank you," said Miles meekly.

He wanted desperately to rub his face and scrub his itching eyes, but couldn't. What was next? Had he done all he could to contain this thing? His eye fell on the decontaminator, slung over Roic's shoulder. It would probably be a good idea to take that back down to Engineering and sterilize their tracks.

"M'lord?" said Roic diffidently.

"Yes, Armsman?"

"I been thinking. The night guard saw the port-master and the ba enter the ship, but nobody reported anybody leaving. We found Thorne. I was wondering how the ba got off the ship."

"*Thank* you, Roic, yes. And how long ago. Good question to pursue next."

"Whenever one of the *Idris*'s hatches opens, its lock vid recorders start up automatically. We should ought to be able to access t'lock records from here, I'd think, same as from Solian's security office." Roic cast a somewhat desperate eye around the intimidating array of stations. "Somewhere."

"We should indeed." Miles abandoned the pilot's chair for the flight engineer's station. A little poking among the controls, and a short delay while one of Roic's library of override codes pacified the lockdowns, and Miles was able to bring up a duplicate file of the sort of airlock security records they'd found in Solian's office and spent so many bleary-eyed hours studying. He set the search to present the data in reverse order of time.

The most recent usage was first up on the vid plate, a nice shot of the automated drone pod docking at the outboard personnel lock serving the number two freight nacelle. An anxious-looking Venn scooted into the lock in his floater. He shuttled in and out handing back green suits folded in plastic bags to waiting hands, plus an assortment of other objects: a big box of first aid supplies, a tool kit, a decontaminator somewhat resembling Roic's, and what might be some weapons with rather more authority than stunners. Miles cut the scene short and sent the search back in time.

Mere minutes before that was the Barrayaran military medical patrol arriving in a small shuttle from the *Prince Xav*, entering via one of the number four nacelle personnel locks. The three medical officers and Roic were all clearly identifiable, hastily unloading equipment.

A freight lock in one of the Necklin drive nacelles popped up next, and Miles caught his breath. A figure in a bulky extravehicular-repairs suit marked with serial numbers from the *Idris*'s engineering section lumbered heavily past the vid pickup, and departed into the vacuum with a brief puff of suit jets. The quaddies bobbing at Miles's shoulder murmured and pointed; Greenlaw muffled an exclamation, and Venn choked on a curse.

The next record back in time was of themselves—

the three quaddies, Miles, and Roic—entering the ship from the loading bay for their inspection, however many hours ago it had been. Miles tapped instantly back to the mystery figure in the engineering suit. What time . . . ?

Roic exclaimed, "Look, m'lord! He—it—was getting away not twenty minutes before we found t'portmaster! The ba must've still been aboard when we came on!" Even through his faceplate, his face took on a greenish tinge.

Had Bel's conundrum in the bod pod been a fiendishly engineered delaying tactic? Miles wondered if the knotted feeling in his stomach and tightness in his throat could be the first sign of a bioengineered plague. . . .

"Is that our suspect?" asked Leutwyn anxiously. "Where did he go?"

"What is the range on those heavy suits of yours, do you know, Lord Auditor?" asked Venn urgently.

"Those? Not sure. They're meant to allow men to work outside the ship for hours at a time, so I'd guess, if they were fully topped up with oxygen, propellant, and power . . . damned near the range of a small personnel pod." The engineering repair suits resembled military space armor, except with an array of built-in tools instead of built-in weapons. Too heavy for even a strong man to walk in, they were fully powered. The ba might have ridden in one around to any point on Graf Station. Worse, the ba might have ridden out to a mid-space pickup by some Cetagandan co-agent, or perhaps by some bribed or simply bamboozled local helper. The ba might be thousands of kilometers away by now, with the gap widening every second. Heading for entry to another quaddie habitat under yet another faked identity, or even for rendezvous with a passing jumpship and escape from Quaddiespace altogether.

"Station Security is on full emergency alert," said

Venn. "I have all my patrollers and all of the Sealer's militia on duty out looking for the fellow—the person. Dubauer *can't* have gotten back aboard the station unobserved." A tremor of doubt in Venn's voice undercut the certainty of this statement.

"I've ordered the station onto a full biocontamination quarantine," said Greenlaw. "All incoming ships and vehicles have been waved off or diverted to Union, and none now in dock are cleared to leave. If the fugitive did get back aboard already—it isn't leaving." Judging by the sealer's congealed expression, she was by no means sure if this was a good thing. Miles sympathized. Fifty thousand potential hostages . . . "If it's fled somewhere else . . . if our people can't locate this fugitive promptly, I'm going to have to extend the quarantine throughout Quaddiespace."

What would be the most important task for the ba, now that the flag had been dropped? It had to realize that the tight secrecy it had relied on for protection thus far was irremediably ruptured. Did it realize how close on its heels its pursuers had come? Would it still wish to murder Gupta to assure the Jacksonian smuggler's silence? Or would it abandon that hunt, cut losses, and run if it could? Which direction was it trying to move, back in, or out?

Miles's eye fell on the vid image of the work suit, frozen above the plate. Did that suit have the kind of telemetry space armor did? More to the point—did it have the kind of remote control overrides some space armor did?

"Roic! When you were down in the engineering suit lockers hunting for that pressure suit, did you see an automated command-and-control station for these powered repair units?"

"I . . . there's a control room down there, yes, m'lord. I passed it. I don't know what all might be in it."

"I have an idea. Follow me."

He levered himself from the station chair and left
Nav and Com at a sloppy jog, his biotainer suit
sliding aggravatingly around him. Roic strode after; the
curious quaddies followed in their floaters.

The control room was scarcely more than a booth,
but it featured a telemetry station for exterior maintenance and repairs. Miles slid into its station chair,
and cursed the tall person who'd fixed it at a height
that left his boots dangling in air. On permanent
display were several real-time vid shots of critical
portions of the ship's outlying anatomy, including
directional antenna arrays, the mass shield generator,
and the main normal-space thrusters. Miles sorted
through a bewildering mess of data from structural
safety sensors scattered throughout the ship. Finally,
the work suit control program came up.

Six suits in the array. Miles called up visual telemetry from their helmet vids. Five returned views of
blank walls, the insides of their respective storage
lockers. The sixth returned a lighter image, but more
puzzling, of a curving wall. It remained as static as the
vistas from the suits in storage.

Miles pinged the suit for full telemetry download.
The suit was powered up but quiescent. The medical
sensors were basic, just heart rate and respiration—
and turned off. The life-support readouts claimed the
rebreather was fully functional, the interior humidity
and temperature were exactly on-spec, but the system
appeared to be supporting no load.

"It can't be very far away," Miles said over his
shoulder to his hovering audience. "There's zero time
lag in my com linkup."

"*That's* a relief," sighed Greenlaw.

"Is it?" muttered Leutwyn. "Who for?"

Miles stretched shoulders aching with tension, and

bent again to the displays. The powered suit had to have an exterior control override somewhere; it was a common safety feature on these civilian models, in case its occupant should suddenly become injured, ill, or incapacitated . . . ah. There.

"What are you doing, m'lord?" asked Roic uneasily.

"I believe I can take control of the suit via the emergency overrides, and bring it back aboard."

"Wit' t' ba inside? Is that a *good* idea?"

"We'll know in a moment."

He gripped the joysticks, slippery under his gloves, gained control of the suit's jets, and tried a gentle puff. The suit slowly began to move, scraping along the wall and then turning away. The puzzling view resolved itself—he was looking at the outside of the *Idris* itself. The suit had been hidden, tucked in the angle between two nacelles. No one inside the suit fought back at this hijacking. A new and extremely disturbing thought crept up on Miles.

Carefully, Miles brought the suit back around the outside of the ship to the nearest lock to Engineering, on the outboard side of one of the Necklin rod nacelles, the same lock from which it had exited. Opened the lock, brought the suit inside. Its servos kept it upright. The light reflected from its faceplate, concealing whatever was within. Miles did not open the interior lock door.

"Now what?" he said to the room at large.

Venn glanced at Roic. "Your armsman and I have stunners, I believe. If you control the suit, you control the prisoner's movements. Bring it in, and we'll arrest the bastard."

"The suit has manual capacities, too. Anyone in it who was . . . alive and conscious should have been able to fight me." Miles cleared a throat thick with worry. "I was just wondering if Brun's searchers checked inside these suits when they were looking for Solian, that first day he went missing. And, um . . . what he's like—what condition his body might be in by now."

Roic made a small noise, and emitted an under-voiced, plaintive protest of *M'lord!* Miles wasn't sure of the exact interpretation, but he thought it might have something to do with Roic wanting to keep his last meal in his stomach, and not all over the inside of his helmet.

After a brief, fraught pause, Venn said, "Then we'd better go have a look. Sealer, Adjudicator—wait here."

The two senior officials didn't argue.

"Would you like to stay with 'em, m'lord?" Roic suggested tentatively.

"We've all been looking for that poor bastard for weeks," Miles replied firmly. "If this is him, I want to be the first to know." He did allow Roic and Venn to precede him from engineering through the locks into the Necklin field generator nacelle, though.

At the lock, Venn drew his stunner and took position. Roic peered through the port on the airlock's inner door. Then his hand swept down to the lock control, the door slid open, and he strode in. He reappeared a moment later, half-dragging the heavy toppling work suit. He laid it faceup on the corridor floor.

Miles ventured closer and stared down at the faceplate.

The suit was empty.

CHAPTER FIFTEEN

"Don't open it!" cried Venn in alarm.

"Wasn't planning to," Miles replied mildly. *Not for any money*.

Venn floated closer, stared down over Miles's shoulder, and swore. "The bastard's got away already! But to the station, or to a ship?" He edged back, tucked his stunner away in a pocket of his green suit, and began to gabble into his helmet com, alerting both Station Security and the quaddie militia to pursue, seize, and search anything—ship, pod, or shuttle—that had so much as shifted its parking zone off the side of the station in the past three hours.

Miles envisioned the escape. Might the ba have ridden the repairs suit back aboard the station before Greenlaw had called down the quarantine? Yes, maybe. The time window was narrow, but possible. But in that case, how had it returned the suit to the hiding place outside the *Idris*? It would make more sense for the ba to have been picked up by a personnel pod—plenty

enough of them zipping around out there at all hours—
and have prodded the suit back to its concealment with
a tractor beam, or had it towed there by someone in
another powered suit and tucked out of sight.

But the *Idris*, like all the other Barrayaran and
Komarran ships, was under surveillance by the
quaddie militia. How cursory was that outside guard?
Surely not that inattentive. Yet a person, a tall person,
sitting in that engineering control booth manipulat-
ing the joysticks, might well have walked the suit out
this airlock and quickly around the nacelle, popping
it away out of sight deftly enough to evade notice by
the militia guardians. Then risen from the station
chair, and . . . ?

Miles's palms itched, maddeningly, inside his gloves,
and he rubbed them together in a futile attempt to gain
relief. He'd have traded blood for the chance to rub his
nose. "Roic," he said slowly. "Do you remember what
this," he prodded the repair suit with his toe, "had in
its hand when it went out the airlock?"

"Um . . . nothing, m'lord." Roic twisted slightly and
shot Miles a puzzled look, through his faceplate.

"That's what I thought." *Right.*

If Miles was guessing correctly, the ba had turned
aside from the imminent murder of Gupta to seize the
chance of using Bel to get back aboard the *Idris* and
do—what?—with its cargo. Destroy it? It would surely
not have taken the ba this long to inoculate the
replicators with some suitable poison. It might even
have been able to do them twenty at a time, introduc-
ing the contaminant into the support system of each
rack. Or—even more simply, if all it had wanted was
to kill its charges—it might have just turned off all the
support systems, a work of mere minutes. But taking
and marking individual cell samples for freezing, yes,
that could well have taken all night, and all day too.

If the ba had risked everything to do that, would it then leave the ship *without* its freezer case firmly in hand?

"The ba's had over two hours to effect an escape. Surely it wouldn't *linger* . . ." muttered Miles. But his voice lacked conviction. Roic, at least, caught the quaver at once; his helmet turned toward Miles, and he frowned.

They needed to count pressure suits, and check every lock to see if any of the vid monitors had been manually disabled. No, too slow—that would be a fine evidence-collecting task to delegate if one had the manpower, but Miles felt painfully bereft of minions just now. And in any case, so what if another suit was found to be gone? Pursuing loose suits was a job that the quaddies around the station were already turning to, by Venn's order. But if no other suit *was* gone . . .

And Miles himself had just turned the *Idris* into a trap.

He gulped. "I was about to say, we need to count suits, but I've a better idea. I believe we should return to Nav and Com, and shut the ship down in sections from there. Collect all the weapons at our disposal, and do a systematic search."

Venn jerked around in his float chair. "What, do you think this Cetagandan agent could still be aboard?"

"M'lord," said Roic in an uncharacteristically sharp voice, "what t'matter with your *gloves*?"

Miles stared down, turning up his hands. His breath congealed in his chest. The thin, tough fabric of his biotainer gloves was shredding away, hanging loose in strings; beneath the lattice, his palms showed red. Their itching seemed to redouble. His breath let loose again in a snarl of "*Shit!*"

Venn bobbed closer, took in the damage with widening eyes, and recoiled.

Miles held his hands up, and apart. "Venn. Go collect Greenlaw and Leutwyn and take over Nav and Com. Secure yourselves and the infirmary, in that order. Roic. Go ahead of me to the infirmary. Open the doors for me." He choked back an unnecessary scream of *Run!*; Roic, with an indrawn breath audible over the suit com, was already moving.

He dodged through the half-dark ship in Roic's long-legged wake, touching nothing, expecting every lumping heartbeat to rupture inside him. Where had he collected this hellish contamination? Was anyone else affected? Everyone else?

No. It had to have been the power-suit control joysticks. They'd slid greasily under his gloved hands. He had gripped them tighter, intent upon the task of bringing the suit back inboard. He'd taken the bait . . . Now, more than ever, he was certain the ba had walked an empty suit out the airlock. And then set a snare for any smartass who figured it out too soon.

He plunged through the door to the infirmary, past Roic, who stood aside, and straight on through the blue-lit inner door to the bio-sealed ward. A medtech's suited form jumped in surprise. Miles called up Channel 13 and rapped out, "Someone please . . ." then stopped. He'd meant to cry, *Turn on the water for me!* and hold his hands under the sluice of a sink, but where did the water then *go*? "Help," he finished in a smaller voice.

"What is it, my Lord Audi—" the chief surgeon began, stepping from the bathroom; then his glance took in Miles's upraised hands. *"What happened?"*

"I think I hit a booby trap. As soon as you have a free tech, have Armsman Roic take him down to Engineering and collect a sample from the repair suit remote controller there. It appears to have been painted with some powerful corrosive or enzyme and . . . and I don't know what else."

"Sonic scrubber," Captain Clogston snapped over his shoulder to the tech monitoring the makeshift lab bench. The man hastened to rummage among the stacks of supplies. He turned back, powering on the device; Miles held out both his burning hands. The machine roared as the tech ran the directed beam of vibration over the afflicted areas, its powerful vacuum sucking the loosened detritus both macroscopic and microscopic into the sealed collection bag. The surgeon leaned in with a scalpel and tongs, slicing and tearing away the remaining shreds of gloves, which were also sucked into the receptacle.

The scrubber seemed effective; Miles's hands stopped feeling worse, though they continued to throb. Was his skin breached? He brought his now-bare palms closer to his faceplate, impeding the surgeon, who hissed under his breath. Yes. Red flecks of blood welled in the creases of the swollen tissue. *Shit. Shit. Shit. . . .*

Clogston straightened and glanced around, lips drawn back in a grimace. "Your biotainer suit's compromised all to hell, my lord."

"There's another pair of gloves on the other suit," Miles pointed out. "I could cannibalize them."

"Not yet." Clogston hurried to slather Miles's hands with some mystery goo and wrap them in biotainer barriers, sealed to his wrists. It was like wearing mittens over handfuls of snot, but the burning pain eased. Across the room, the tech was scraping fragments of contaminated glove into an analyzer. Was the third man in with Bel? Was Bel still in the ice bath? Still alive?

Miles took a deep, steadying breath. "Do you have any kind of a diagnosis on Portmaster Thorne yet?"

"Oh, yes, it came up right away," said Clogston in a

somewhat absent tone, still sealing the second wrist wrap. "The instant we ran the first blood sample through. What the hell we can *do* about it is not yet obvious, but I have some ideas." He straightened again, frowning deeply at Miles's hands. "The herm's blood and tissues are crawling with artificial—that is, bioengineered—parasites." He glanced up. "They appear to have an initial, latent, asymptomatic phase, where they multiply rapidly throughout the body. Then, at some point—possibly triggered by their own concentration— they switch over to producing two chemicals in different vesicles within their own cellular membrane. The vesicles engorge. A rise in the victim's body temperature triggers the bursting of the sacs, and the chemicals in turn undergo a violently exothermic reaction with each other—killing the parasite, damaging the host's surrounding tissues, and stimulating more nearby parasites to go off. Tiny, pin-point bombs all through the body. It's"—his tone went reluctantly admiring—"extremely elegant. In a hideous sort of way."

"Did—did my ice-water bath treatment help Thorne, then?"

"Yes, absolutely. The drop in core temperature stopped the cascade in its tracks, temporarily. The parasites had almost reached critical concentration."

Miles's eyes squeezed shut in brief gratitude. And opened again. "Temporarily?"

"I still haven't figured out how to get rid of the damned things. We're trying to modify a surgical shunt into a blood filter to both mechanically remove the parasites from the patient's bloodstream, and chill the blood to a controlled degree before returning it to the body. I think I can make the parasites respond selectively to an applied electrophoresis gradient across the shunt tube, and pull them right on out of the bloodstream."

"Won't that do it, then?"

Clogston shook his head. "It doesn't get the parasites lodged in other tissues, reservoirs of reinfection. It's not a cure, but it might buy time. I think. The cure must somehow kill every last one of the parasites in the body, or the process will just start up again." His lips twisted. "Internal vermicides could be tricky. Injecting something to kill already-engorged parasites within the tissues will just release their chemical loads. A very little of that micro-insult will play hell with circulation, overload repair processes, cause intense pain—it's . . . it's tricky."

"Destroy brain tissue?" Miles asked, feeling sick.

"Eventually. They don't seem to cross the blood-brain barrier very readily. I believe the victim would be conscious to a, um, very late phase of the dissolution."

"Oh." Miles tried to decide whether that would be good, or bad.

"On the bright side," offered the surgeon, "I may be able to downgrade the biocontamination alarm from Level Five to Level Three. The parasites appear to need direct blood-to-blood contact to effect transference. They don't seem to survive long outside a host."

"They can't travel through the air?"

Clogston hesitated. "Well, maybe not until the host starts coughing blood."

Until, not *unless*. Miles noted the word choice. "I'm afraid talk of a downgrade is premature anyway. A Cetagandan agent armed with unknown bioweapons—well, unknown except for this one, which is getting too damned familiar—is still on the loose out there." He inhaled, carefully, and forced his voice to calm. "We've found some evidence suggesting that the agent still may be hiding aboard this ship. You need to secure your work zone from a possible intruder."

Captain Clogston cursed. "Hear that, boys?" he called to his techs over his suit com.

"Oh, great," came a disgusted reply. "Just what we need right now."

"Hey, at least it's something we can *shoot*," another voice remarked wistfully.

Ah, Barrayarans. Miles's heart warmed. "On sight," he confirmed. These were *military* medicos; they all bore sidearms, bless them.

His eye flicked over the ward and the infirmary chamber beyond, summing weak points. Only one entry, but was that weakness or strength? The outer door was definitely the vantage to hold, protecting the ward beyond; Roic had taken up station there quite automatically. Yet traditional attack by stunner, plasma arc, or explosive grenade seemed . . . insufficiently imaginative. The place was still on ship's air circulation and ship's power, but this of all sections had to have its own emergency reservoirs of both.

The military-grade Level Five biotainer suits the medicos wore also doubled as pressure suits, their air circulation entirely internal. The same was not true of Miles's cheaper suit, even before he'd lost his gloves; his atmosphere pack drew air from the environs, through filters and cookers. In the event of a pressurization loss, his suit would turn into a stiff, unwieldy balloon, perhaps even rupture at a weak point. There were bod pod lockers on the walls, of course. Miles pictured being trapped in a bod pod while the action went on without him.

Given that he was already exposed to . . . whatever, peeling out of his biotainer suit long enough to get into something tighter couldn't make things any worse, could it? He stared at his hands and wondered why he wasn't dead yet. Could the glop he'd touched have been only a simple corrosive?

Miles clawed his stunner out of his thigh pocket, awkwardly with his mittened hand, and walked back through the blue bars of light marking the bio-barrier. "Roic. I want you to dash back down to Engineering and grab me the smallest pressure suit you can find. I'll guard this point till you get back."

"M'lord," Roic began in a tone of doubt.

"Keep your stunner out; watch your back. We're all here, so if you see anything move that isn't quaddie green, shoot first."

Roic swallowed manfully. "Yes, well, see that you *stay* here, m'lord. Don't go haring off on your own without me!"

"I wouldn't dream of it," Miles promised.

Roic departed at the gallop. Miles readjusted his awkward grip on the stunner, made sure it was set to maximum power, and took a stance partly sheltered by the door, staring up the central corridor at his body-guard's retreating form. Scowling.

I don't understand this.

Something didn't add up, and if he could just get ten consecutive minutes not filled with lethal new tactical crises, maybe it would come to him. . . . He tried not to think about his stinging palms, and what ingenious microbial sneak assault might even now be stealing through his body, maybe even making its way into his brain.

An ordinary imperial servitor ba ought to have died before abandoning a charge like those haut-filled replicators. And even if this one had been trained as some sort of special agent, why spend all that critical time taking samples from the fetuses that it was about to desert or maybe even destroy? Every haut infant ever made had its DNA kept on file back in the central gene banks of the Star Crèche. They could make more, surely. What made *this* batch so irreplaceable?

His train of thought derailed itself as he imagined little gengineered parasites multiplying frenetically through his bloodstream, *blip-blip-blip-blip. Calm down, dammit.* He didn't actually know if he'd even been inoculated with the same evil disease as Bel. *Yeah, it might be something even worse.* Yet surely some Cetagandan designer neurotoxin—or even some quite ordinary off-the-shelf poison—ought to cut in much faster than this. *Although if it's a drug to drive the victim mad with paranoia, it's working really well.* Was the ba's repertoire of hell-potions limited? If it had any, why not many? Whatever stimulants or hypnotics it had used on Bel need not have been anything out of the ordinary, by the norms of covert ops. How many other fancy bio-tricks did it have up its sleeve? Was Miles about to personally demonstrate the next one?

Am I going to live long enough to say good-bye to Ekaterin? A good-bye kiss was right out, unless they pressed their lips to opposite sides of some really thick window of glass. He had so much to say to her; it seemed impossible to find where to start. Even more impossible by voice alone, over an open, unsecured public com link. *Take care of the kids. Kiss them for me every night at bedtime, and tell them I loved them even if I never saw them. You won't be alone—my parents will help you. Tell my parents . . . tell them . . .*

Was this damned thing starting up already, or were the hot panic and choking tears in his throat entirely self-induced? An enemy that attacked you from the inside out—you could try to turn yourself inside out to fight it, but you wouldn't succeed—filthy weapon! *Open channel or not, I'm calling her now. . . .*

Instead, Venn's voice sounded in his ear. "Lord Vorkosigan, pick up Channel Twelve. Your Admiral Vorpatril wants you. Badly."

Miles hissed through his teeth and keyed his helmet com over. "Vorkosigan here."

"Vorkosigan, you idiot—!" The admiral's syntax had shed a few honorifics sometime in the past hour. "What the hell is going on over there? Why don't you answer your wrist com?"

"It's inside my biotainer suit and inaccessible right now. I'm afraid I had to don the suit in a hurry. Be aware, this helmet link is an open access channel and unsecured, sir." Dammit, where did that *sir* drop in from? Habit, sheer old bad habit. "You can ask for a brief report from Captain Clogston over his military suit's tight-beam link, but keep it *short*. He's a very busy man right now, and I don't want him distracted."

Vorpatril swore—whether generally or at the Imperial Auditor was left nicely ambiguous—and clicked off.

Faintly echoing through the ship came the sound Miles had been waiting for—the distant clanks and hisses of airseal doors shutting down, sealing the ship into airtight sections. The quaddies had made it to Nav and Com, good! Except that Roic wasn't back yet. The armsman would have to get in touch with Venn and Greenlaw and get them to unseal and reseal his passage back up to—

"Vorkosigan." Venn's voice sounded again in his ear, strained. "Is that you?"

"Is what me?"

"Shutting off the compartments."

"Isn't it," Miles tried, and failed, to swallow his voice back down to a more reasonable pitch. "*Aren't you in Nav and Com yet*?"

"No, we circled back to the Number Two nacelle to pick up our equipment. We were just about to leave it."

Hope flared in Miles's hammering heart. "Roic," he called urgently. "Where are you?"

"Not in Nav and Com, m'lord," Roic's grim voice returned.

"But if we're here and he's there, who's doing *this*?" came Leutwyn's unhappy voice.

"Who do you *think*?" Greenlaw ripped back. Her breath huffed out in anguish. "Five people, and not one of us thought to see the door locked behind us when we left—dammit!"

A small, bleak grunt, like a man being hit with an arrow, or a realization, sounded in Miles's ear: Roic.

Miles said urgently, "Anyone who holds Nav and Com has access to all these ship-linked com channels, or will, shortly. We're going to have to switch off."

The quaddies had independent links to the station and Vorpatril through their suits; so did the medicos. Miles and Roic would be the ones plunged into communications limbo.

Then, abruptly, the sound in his helmet went dead. *Ah. Looks like the ba has found the com controls. . . .*

Miles leapt to the environmental control panel for the infirmary to the left of the door, opened it, and hit every manual override in it. With this outer door shut, they could retain air pressure, although circulation would be blocked. The medicos in their suits would be unaffected; Miles and Bel would be at risk. He eyed the bod pod locker on the wall without favor. The bio-sealed ward was already functioning on internal circulation, thank God, and could remain so— as long as the power stayed on. But how could they keep Bel cold if the herm had to retreat to a pod?

Miles hurried back into the ward. He approached Clogston, and yelled through his faceplate, "We just lost our ship-linked suit coms. Keep to your tight-beam military channels only."

"I heard," Clogston yelled back.

"How are you coming on that filter-cooler?"

"Cooler part's done. Still working on the filter. I wish I'd brought more hands, although there's scarcely room in here for more butts."

"I've almost got it, I think," called the tech, crouched over the bench. "Check that, will you, sir?" He waved in the direction of one of the analyzers, a collection of lights on its readout now blinking for attention.

Clogston dodged around him and bent to the machine in question. After a moment he murmured, "Oh, *that's* clever."

Miles, crowding his shoulder close enough to hear this, did not find it reassuring. "What's clever?"

Clogston pointed at his analyzer readout, which now displayed incomprehensible strings of letters and numbers in cheery colors. "I didn't see how the parasites could possibly survive in a matrix of that enzyme that ate your biotainer gloves. But they were microencapsulated."

"What?"

"Standard trick for delivering drugs through a hostile environment—like your stomach, or maybe your bloodstream—to the target zone. Only this time, used to deliver a disease. When the microencapsulation passes out of the unfriendly environment into the—chemically speaking—friendly zone, it pops open, releasing its load. No loss, no waste."

"Oh. Wonderful. *Are* you saying I now have the same shit Bel has?"

"Um." Clogston glanced up at a chrono on the wall. "How long since you were first exposed, my lord?"

Miles followed his glance. "Half an hour, maybe?"

"They *might* be detectable in your bloodstream by now."

"Check it."

"We'll have to open your suit to access a vein."

"Check it now. *Fast*."

Clogston grabbed a sampler needle; Miles peeled back the biotainer wrap from his left wrist, and gritted his teeth as a biocide swab stung and the needle poked. Clogston was pretty deft for a man wearing biotainer gloves, Miles had to concede. He watched anxiously as the surgeon delicately slipped the needle into the analyzer.

"How long will this take?"

"Now that we have the template of the thing, no time at all. If it's positive, that is. If this first sample shows negative, I'd want a recheck every thirty minutes or so to be sure." Clogston's voice slowed, as he studied his readout. "Well. Um. A recheck won't be necessary."

"Right," Miles snarled. He yanked open his helmet and pushed back his suit sleeve. He bent to his secured wrist com and snapped, "Vorpatril!"

"Yes!" Vorpatril's voice came back instantly. Riding his com channels—he must be on duty in either the *Prince Xav*'s own Nav and Com, or maybe, by now, its tactics room. "Wait, what are you doing on this channel? I thought you had no access."

"The situation has changed. Never mind that now. What's happening out there?"

"What's happening in *there*?"

"The medical team, Portmaster Thorne, and I are holed up in the infirmary. For the moment, we're still in control of our environment. I believe Venn, Greenlaw, and Leutwyn are trapped in the Number Two freight nacelle. Roic may be somewhere in Engineering. And the ba, I believe, has seized Nav and Com. Can you confirm that last?"

"Oh, yes," groaned Vorpatril. "It's talking to the quaddies on Graf Station right now. Making threats and demands. Boss Watts seems to have inherited their hot seat. I have a strike team scrambling."

"Patch it in here. I have to hear this."

A few seconds delay, then the ba's voice sounded. The Betan accent was gone; the academic coolness was fraying. "—name does not matter. If you wish to get the Sealer, the Imperial Auditor, and the others back alive, these are my requirements. A jump pilot for this ship, delivered immediately. Free and unimpeded passage from your system. If either you or the Barrayarans attempt to launch a military assault against the *Idris*, I will either blow up the ship with all aboard, or ram the station."

Boss Watts's voice returned, thick with tension, "If you attempt to ram Graf Station, we'll blow you up *ourselves*."

"Either way will do," the ba's voice returned dryly.

Did the ba know *how* to blow up a jumpship? It wasn't exactly easy. Hell, if the Cetagandan was a hundred years old, who knew what all it knew how to do? Ramming, now—with a target that big and close, any layman could manage it.

Greenlaw's stiff voice cut in; her com link presumably was patched through to Watts in the same way that Miles's was to Vorpatril. "Don't do it, Watts. Quaddiespace *cannot* let a plague-carrier like this pass through to our neighbors. A handful of lives can't justify the risk to thousands."

"Indeed," the ba continued after a slight hesitation, still in that same cool tone. "If you do succeed in killing me, I'm afraid you will win yourselves another dilemma. I have left a small gift aboard the station. The experiences of Gupta and Portmaster Thorne should give you an idea of what sort of package it is. You *might* find it before it ruptures, although I'd say your odds are poor. Where are your thousands now? Much closer to home."

True threat or bluff? Miles wondered frantically. It

certainly fit the ba's style as demonstrated so far—Bel in the bod pod, the booby trap with the suit-control joysticks—hideous, lethal puzzles tossed out in the ba's wake to disrupt and distract its pursuers. *It sure worked on me, anyway.*

Vorpatril cut in privately on the wrist com, in an unnecessarily lowered, tense tone, overriding the exchange between the ba and Watts. "Do you think the bastard's bluffing, m'lord?"

"Doesn't matter if it's bluffing or not. I want it *alive.* Oh, God do I ever want it alive. Take that as a top priority and an order in the Emperor's Voice, Admiral."

After a small and, Miles hoped, thoughtful pause, Vorpatril returned, "Understood, my Lord Auditor."

"Ready your strike team, yes . . ." Vorpatril's best strike force was locked in quaddie detention. What was the *second* best one like? Miles's heart quailed. "But *hold* it. This situation is extremely unstable. I don't have any clear sense yet how it will play out. Put the ba's channel back on." Miles returned his attention to the negotiation in progress—no—winding up?

"A jump pilot." The ba seemed to be reiterating. "Alone, in a personnel pod, to the Number Five B lock. And, ah—naked." Horribly, there seemed to be a smile in that last word. "For obvious reasons."

The ba cut the com.

CHAPTER SIXTEEN

Now what?

Delays, Miles guessed, while the quaddies on Graf Station either readied a pilot or ran the risks of stalling about delivering one into such a hazard, and suppose none volunteered? While Vorpatril marshaled his strike team, while the three quaddie officials trapped in the freight nacelle—well, didn't sit on their hands, Miles bet—*while this infection gains on me*, while the ba did—what?

Delay is not my friend.

But it was his gift. What time was it, anyway? Late evening—still the same day that had started so early with the news of Bel's disappearance? Yes, though it hardly felt possible. Surely he had entered some time warp. Miles stared at his wrist com, took a deep, terrified breath, and called up Ekaterin's code. Had Vorpatril told her anything of what was happening yet, or had he kept her comfortably ignorant?

"Miles!" she answered at once.

"Ekaterin, love. Where, um . . . are you?"

"The tactics room, with Admiral Vorpatril."

Ah. That answered that question. In a way, he was relieved that he didn't have to deliver the whole litany of bad news himself, cold. "You've been following this, then."

"More or less. It's been very confusing."

"I'll bet. I . . ." He couldn't say it, not so baldly. He dodged, while he mustered courage. "I promised to call Nicol when I had news of Bel, and I haven't had a chance. The news, as you may know, is not good; we found Bel, but the herm has been deliberately infected with a bioengineered Cetagandan parasite that may . . . may prove lethal."

"Yes, I understand. I've been hearing it all, here in the tactics room."

"Good. The medics are doing their best, but it's a race against time and now there are these other complications. Will you call Nicol and redeem my word for me? There's not *no* hope, but . . . she needs to know it doesn't look so good right now. Use your judgment how much to soften it."

"My judgment is that she should be told plain truth. The whole of Graf Station is in an uproar now, what with the quarantine and biocontamination alert. She needs to know exactly what's going on, and she has a right to know. I'll call her at once."

"Oh. Good. Thank you. I, um . . . you know I love you."

"Yes. Tell me something I don't know."

Miles blinked. This wasn't getting easier; he rushed it in a breath. "Well. There's a chance I may have screwed up pretty badly, here. Like, I may not get out of this one. The situation here is pretty unsettled, and, um . . . I'm afraid my biotainer suit gloves were sabotaged by a nasty little Cetagandan booby trap I triggered. I seem to have got myself infected with the same biohazard that's taken Bel down. The stuff doesn't appear to act very quickly, though."

In the background, he could just hear Admiral Vorpatril's voice, cursing in choice barracks language not at all consonant with the respect due to one of His Majesty Gregor Vorbarra's Imperial Auditors. From Ekaterin, silence; he strained to hear her breathing. The sound reproduction on these high-grade com links was so excellent, he could hear when she let her breath out again, through those pursed, exquisite warm lips he could not see or touch.

He began again. "I'm . . . I'm sorry that . . . I wanted to give you—this wasn't what I—I never wanted to bring you grief—"

"Miles. Stop that babbling at once."

"Oh . . . uh, yes?"

Her voice sharpened. "If you die on me out here, I will not be grieved, I will be *pissed*. This is all very fine, love, but may I point out that you don't have *time* to indulge in angst right now. You're the man who used to rescue hostages for a living. You are *not allowed* to not get out of this one. So stop worrying about me and start paying attention to what you are doing. Are you listening to me, Miles Vorkosigan? Don't you dare die! I won't have it!"

That seemed definitive. Despite everything, he grinned. "Yes, dear," he sang back meekly, heartened. This woman's Vor ancestresses had defended bastions in war, oh, yes.

"So stop talking to me and get back to work. Right?"

She almost kept the shaken sob out of that last word.

"Hold the fort, love," he breathed, with all the tenderness he knew.

"Always." He could hear her swallow. "Always."

She cut her link. He took it as a hint.

Hostage rescue, eh? *If you want something done right, do it yourself.* Come to think of it, did this ba have any idea of what Miles's former line of work had been? Or did it assume Miles was just a diplomat, a bureaucrat, another frightened civilian? The ba could not know which of the party had triggered its booby trap on the repair suit remote controls, either. Not that this biotainer suit hadn't been useless for space assault purposes even before it had been buggered all to hell. But what tools were available here in this infirmary that might be put to uses their manufacturers had never envisioned? And what personnel?

The medical crew had military training, right enough, and discipline. They also were up to their collective elbows in other tasks of the highest priority. Miles's very last desire was to pull them away from their cramped, busy lab bench and critical patient care to go play commando with him. *Although it may come to that.* Thoughtfully, he began walking about the infirmary's outer chamber, opening drawers and cupboards and staring at their contents. A muddy fatigue was beginning to drag at his edgy, adrenaline-pumped high, and a headache was starting behind his eyes. He studiously ignored the terror of it.

He glanced through the blue light bars into the ward. The tech hurried from the bench, heading toward the bathroom with something in his hands that trailed looping tubes.

"Captain Clogston!" Miles called.

The second suited figure turned. "Yes, my lord?"

"I'm shutting your inner door. It's supposed to close on its own in the event of a pressure change, but I'm not sure I trust any remote-controlled equipment on this ship at the moment. Are you prepared to move your patient into a bod pod, if necessary?"

Clogston gave him a sketchy salute of acknowledgment with a gloved hand. "Almost, my lord. We're starting construction on the second blood filter. If the first one works as well as I hope, we should be ready to rig you up very soon, too."

Which would tie him down to a bunk in the ward. He wasn't ready to lose mobility yet. Not while he could still move and think on his own. *You don't have much time then. Regardless of what the ba does.* "Thank you, Captain," Miles called. "Let me know." He slid the door shut with the manual override.

What could the ba know, from Nav and Com? More importantly, what were its blind spots? Miles paced, considering the layout of this central nacelle: a long cylinder divided into three decks. This infirmary lay at the stern on the uppermost deck. Nav and Com was far forward, at the other end of the middle deck. The internal airseal doors of all levels lay at the three evenly spaced intersections to the freight and drive nacelles, dividing each deck longitudinally into quarters.

Nav and Com had security vid monitors in all the outer airlocks, of course, and safety monitors on all the inner section doors that closed to seal the ship into airtight compartments. Blowing out a monitor would blind the ba, but also give warning that the supposed prisoners were on the move. Blowing out *all* of them, or all that could be reached, would be more confusing . . . but still left the problem of giving warning. How likely was the ba to carry out its harried, or perhaps insane, threat of ramming the station?

Dammit, this was so *unprofessional* . . . Miles halted, arrested by his own thought.

What were the standard operating procedures for a Cetagandan agent—anyone's agent, really—whose covert mission was going down the toilet? Destroy all the evidence: try to make it to a safe zone, embassy, or neutral territory. If that wasn't possible, destroy the evidence and then sit tight and endure arrest by the locals, whoever the locals might be, and wait for one's own side to either bail or bust one out, depending. For the really, really critical missions, destroy the evidence and commit suicide. This last was seldom ordered, because it was even more seldom carried out. But the Cetagandan ba were so conditioned to loyalty to their haut masters—and mistresses—Miles was forced to consider it a more realistic possibility in the present case.

But splashy hostage-taking among neutrals or neighbors, blaring the mission all over the news, most of all—*most* of all, the public use of the Star Crèche's most private arsenal . . . This wasn't the modus operandi of a trained agent. This was goddamned *amateur* work. And Miles's superiors used to accuse *him* of being a loose cannon—hah! Not any of his most direly inspired messes had ever been as forlorn as this one was shaping up to be—for both sides, alas. This gratifying deduction did not, unfortunately, make the ba's next action more predictable. Quite the reverse.

"M'lord?" Roic's voice rose unexpectedly from Miles's wrist com.

"Roic!" cried Miles joyfully. "Wait. What the hell are you doing on this link? You shouldn't be out of your suit."

"I might ask you the same question, m'lord," Roic returned rather tartly. "If I had time. But I had to get out of t' pressure suit anyway to get into this work suit. I think . . . yes. I can hang the com link in my helmet. There." A slight chink, as of a faceplate closing. "Can you still hear me?"

"Oh, yes. I take it you're still in Engineering?"

"For now. I found you a real nice little pressure suit, m'lord. And a lot of other tools. Question is how to get it to you."

"Stay away from all the airseal doors—they're monitored. Have you found any cutting tools, by chance?"

"I'm, uh . . . pretty sure that's what these are, yes."

"Then move as far to the stern as you can get, and cut straight up through the ceiling to the middle deck. Try to avoid damaging the air ducts and grav grid and control and fluid conduits, for now. Or anything else that would make the boards light up in Nav and Com. Then we can place you for the next cut."

"Right, m'lord. I was thinking something like that might do."

A few minutes ran by, with nothing but the sound of Roic's breathing, broken with a few under-voiced obscenities as, by trial and error, he discovered how to handle the unfamiliar equipment. A grunt, a hiss, a clank abruptly cut off.

The rough-and-ready procedure was going to play hell with the atmospheric integrity of the sections, but did that necessarily make things any worse, from the hostages' point of view? And a pressure suit, oh bliss! Miles wondered if any of the powered work suits had been sized extra-small. Almost as good as space armor, indeed.

"All right, m'lord," came the welcome voice from his wrist com. "I've made it to the middle deck. I'm moving back now . . . I'm not exactly sure how close I am under you."

"Can you reach up to tap on the ceiling? Gently. We don't want it to reverberate through the bulkheads all the way to Nav and Com." Miles threw himself prone, opened his faceplate, tilted his head, and listened. A faint banging, apparently from out in the corridor. "Can you move farther toward the stern?"

"I'll try, m'lord. It's a question of getting these ceiling panels apart . . ." More heavy breathing. "There. Try now."

This time, the rapping seemed to come from nearly under Miles's outstretched hand. "I think that's got it, Roic."

"Right, m'lord. Be sure you're not standing where I'm cutting. I think Lady Vorkosigan would be right peeved with me if I accidentally lopped off any of your body parts."

"I think so too." Miles rose, ripped up a section of friction matting, skittered to the side of the infirmary's outer chamber, and held his breath.

A red glow in the bare deck plate beneath turned yellow, then white. The dot became a line, which grew, wavering in an irregular circle back to its beginning. A thump, as Roic's gloved paw, powered by his suit, punched up through the floor, tearing the weakened circle from its matrix.

Miles nipped over and stared down, and grinned at Roic's face staring up in worry through the faceplate of another repair suit. The hole was too small for that hulking figure to squeeze through, but not too small for the pressure suit he handed up through it.

"Good job," Miles called down. "Hang on. I'll be right with you."

"M'lord?"

Miles tore off the useless biotainer suit and crammed himself into the pressure suit in record time. Inevitably, the plumbing was female, and he left it unattached. One way or another, he didn't think he would be suited up for very long. He was flushed and sweating, one moment too hot, the next too cold, though whether from incipient infection or just plain overdriven nerves he scarcely knew.

The helmet supplied no place to hang his wrist com, but a bit of medical tape solved that problem in a moment. He lowered the helmet over his head and locked it into place, breathing deeply of air that no one controlled but him. Reluctantly, he set the suit's temperature to chilly.

Then he slid to the hole and dangled his legs through. "Catch me. Don't squeeze too hard—remember, you're powered."

"Right, m'lord."

"Lord Auditor Vorkosigan," came Vorpatril's uneasy voice. "What are you doing?"

"Reconnoitering."

Roic caught his hips, lowering him with exaggerated gentleness to the middle deck. Miles glanced up the corridor, past the larger hole in its floor, to the airseal doors at the far end of this sector. "Solian's security office is in this section. If there's any control board on this bloody ship that can monitor without being monitored in turn, it'll be in there."

He tiptoed down the corridor, Roic lumbering in his wake. The deck creaked beneath the armsman's booted feet. Miles tapped out the now-familiar code to the office door; Roic barely squeezed through behind him. Miles slid into the late Lieutenant Solian's station chair and flexed his fingers, contemplating the console. He drew a breath and bent forward.

Yes, he could siphon off views from the vid monitors of every airlock on the ship—simultaneously, if desired. Yes, he could tap into the safety sensors on the airseal doors. They were designed to take in a good view of anyone near—as in, frantically pounding on— the doors. Nervously, he checked the one for this middle rear section. The vista, if the ba was even looking at it with so much else going on, did not extend as far as Solian's office door. Whew. Could he bring up a view of Nav and Com, perhaps, and spy secretly upon its current occupant?

Roic said apprehensively, "What are you thinking of doing, m'lord?"

"I'm thinking that a surprise attack that has to stop to bore through six or seven bulkheads to get to the target isn't going to be surprising enough. Though we may come to that. I'm running out of time." He blinked, hard, then thought *to hell with it* and opened his faceplate to rub his eyes. The vid image unblurred in his vision, but still seemed to waver around the edges. Miles didn't think the problem was in the vid plate. His headache, which had started as a stabbing pain between his eyes, seemed to be spreading to his temples, which throbbed. He was shivering. He sighed and closed the faceplate again.

"That bio-shit—the admiral said you got t' same bio-shit the herm has. The crap that melted Gupta's friends."

"When did you talk to Vorpatril?"

"Just before I talked to you."

"Ah."

Roic said lowly, "I should've been t' one to run those remote controls. Not you."

"It had to be me. I was more familiar with the equipment."

"Yes." Roic's voice went lower. "You should've brought Jankowski, m'lord."

"Just a guess—based on long experience, mind you . . ." Miles paused, frowning at the security display. All right, so Solian didn't have a monitor in every cabin, but he had to have private access to Nav and Com if he had anything . . . "But I suspect there will be enough heroism before this day is done to go around. I don't think we're going to have to ration it, Roic."

"'S not what I meant," said Roic, in a dignified tone.

Miles grinned blackly. "I know. But think of how hard it would have been on Ma Jankowski. And all the not-so-little Jankowskis."

A soft snort from the com link taped inside Miles's

helmet apprised him that Ekaterin was back, listening in. She would not interrupt, he suspected.

Vorpatril's voice sounded suddenly, breaking his concentration. The admiral was sputtering. "The spineless scoundrels! The four-armed bastards! My Lord Auditor!" Ah, Miles was promoted again. "The goddamn little mutants are giving this sexless Cetagandan plague-vector a jump pilot!"

"What?" Miles's stomach knotted. Tighter. "They found a volunteer? Quaddie, or downsider?" There couldn't be that large a pool of possibilities to choose from. The pilots' surgically installed neuro-controllers had to fit the ships they guided through the wormhole jumps. However many jump pilots were currently quartered—or trapped—on Graf Station, chances were that most would be incompatible with the Barrayaran systems. So was it the *Idris*'s own pilot or relief pilot, or a pilot from one of the Komarran sister ships . . . ?

"What makes you think he's a volunteer?" snarled Vorpatril. "I can't bloody *believe* they're just handing . . ."

"Maybe the quaddies are up to something. What do they say?"

Vorpatril hesitated, then spat, "Watts cut me out of the loop a few minutes ago. We were having an argument over whose strike team should go in, ours or the quaddie militia's, and when. And under whose orders. Both at once with no coordination struck me as a supremely bad idea."

"Indeed. One perceives the potential hazards." The ba was beginning to seem a trifle outnumbered. But then there were its bio-threats . . . Miles's nascent sympathy died as his vision blurred again. "We *are* guests in their polity . . . hang on. Something seems to be happening at one of the outer airlocks."

Miles enlarged the security vid image from the lock that had suddenly come alive. Docking lights framing the outer door ran through a series of checks and go-aheads. The ba, he reminded himself, was probably looking at this same view. He held his breath. Were the quaddies, under the mask of delivering the demanded jump pilot, about to attempt to insert their own strike force?

The airlock door slid open, giving a brief glimpse of the inside of a tiny, one-person personnel pod. A naked man, the little silver contact circles of a jump pilot's neural implant gleaming at mid-forehead and temples, stepped through into the lock. The door slid shut again. Tall, dark-haired, handsome but for the thin pink scars running, Miles could now see, all over his body in a winding swathe. Dmitri Corbeau. His face was pale and set.

"The jump pilot has just arrived," Miles told Vorpatril.

"*Dammit*. Human or quaddie?"

Vorpatril was really going to have to work on his diplomatic vocabulary. . . . "Downsider," Miles answered, in lieu of any more pointed remark. He hesitated, then added, "It's Ensign Corbeau."

A stunned silence: then Vorpatril hissed, "Son-of-a-bitch . . . !"

"H'sh. The ba is finally coming on." Miles adjusted the volume, and opened his faceplate again so that Vorpatril could overhear too. As long as Roic kept his suit sealed, it was . . . no worse than ever. *Yeah, and how bad is that, again?*

"Turn toward the security module and open your mouth," the ba's voice instructed coolly and without preamble over the lock vid monitor. "Closer. Wider." Miles was treated to a fair view of Corbeau's tonsils. Unless Corbeau harbored a poison-filled tooth, no weapons were concealed therein.

"Very well . . ." The ba continued with a chill

series of directions for Corbeau to go through a humiliating sequence of gyrations which, while not as thorough as a body cavity search, gave at least some assurance that the jump pilot carried nothing *there*, either. Corbeau obeyed precisely, without hesitation or argument, his expression rigid and blank.

"Now release the pod from the docking clamps."

Corbeau rose from his last squat and stepped through the lock to the personnel hatch entry area. A chink and a clank—the pod, released but unpowered, drifted away from the side of the *Idris*.

"Now listen to these instructions. You will walk twenty meters toward the bow, turn left, and wait for the next door to open for you."

Corbeau obeyed, still almost expressionless, except for his eyes. His gaze darted about, as if he searched for something, or was trying to memorize his route. He passed out of sight of the lock vids.

Miles considered the peculiar pattern of old worm scars across Corbeau's body. He must have rolled, or been rolled, across a bad nest. A story seemed written in those fading hieroglyphs. A young colonial boy, perhaps the new boy in camp or town—tricked or dared or maybe just stripped and pushed? To rise again from the ground, crying and frightened, to the jangle of some cruel mockery . . .

Vorpatril swore, repetitively, under his breath. "Why Corbeau? Why *Corbeau*?"

Miles, who was frantically wondering the same thing, hazarded, "Perhaps he volunteered."

"Unless the bloody quaddies bloody sacrificed him. Instead of risking one of their own. Or . . . maybe he's figured out another way to desert."

"I . . ." Miles held his words for a long moment of thought, then let them out on a breath, "think that would be doing it the hard way." It was a sticky suspicion, though. Just *whose* ally might Corbeau prove?

Miles caught Corbeau's image again as the ba walked him through the ship toward Nav and Com, briefly opening and closing airseal doors. He passed through the last barrier and out of vid range, straight-backed, silent, bare feet padding quietly on the deck. He looked . . . cold.

Miles's attention was jerked aside by the flicker of another airlock sensor alarm. Hastily, he called up the image of another lock—just in time to see a quaddie in a green biotainer suit whap the vid monitor mightily with a spanner while beyond, two more green figures sped past. The image shattered and went dark. He could still hear, though—the beep of the lock alarm, the hiss of a lock door opening—but no hiss when it closed. Because it did not close, or because it closed on vacuum? Air, and sound, returned as the lock cycled. The lock, therefore, had opened on vacuum; the quaddies had made their getaway into space around the station.

That answered his question about their biotainer suits—unlike the *Idris*'s cheaper issue, they were vacuum-rated. In Quaddiespace, that made all kinds of sense. Half a dozen station locks offered refuge within little more than a few hundred meters; the fleeing quaddies would have their pick, in addition to whatever pods or shuttles hovered nearby able to swoop down on them and take them inboard.

"Venn and Greenlaw and Leutwyn just escaped out an airlock," he reported to Vorpatril. "*Good* timing." Shrewd timing, to go just when the ba was both distracted by the arrival of its pilot and, with the real possibility of a getaway now in hand, less inclined to carry out the station-ramming threat. It was exactly the right move, to leak hostages from the enemy's grip at every opportunity. Granted, this use of Corbeau's arrival was ruthlessly calculated in the extreme. Miles could not be sorry. "Good. Excellent! Now this ship is entirely cleared of civilians."

"Except for you, m'lord," Roic pointed out, started to say something else, intercepted the dark look Miles cast over his shoulder, and ran down in a mumble.

"Ha," muttered Vorpatril. "Maybe *this* will change Watts's mind." His voice lowered, as if directed away from his audio pickup, or behind his hand. "What, Lieutenant?" Then murmured, "Excuse me," Miles was not certain to whom.

So, only Barrayarans left aboard now. Plus Bel—on the ImpSec payroll, therefore an honorary Barrayaran for all mortal accounting purposes. Miles smiled briefly despite it all as he considered Bel's probable outraged response to such a suggestion. The best time to insert a strike force would be before the ship started to move, rather than to attempt to play catch-up in mid-space. At some point, Vorpatril was probably going to stop waiting for quaddie permission to launch his men. At some point, Miles would agree.

Miles returned his attention to the problem of spying on Nav and Com. If the ba had knocked out the monitor the way the passing quaddies just had, or even merely thrown a jacket over the vid pickup, Miles would be out of luck . . . ah. Finally. An image of Nav and Com formed over his vid plate. But *now* he had no sound. Miles gritted his teeth and bent forward.

The vid pickup was apparently centered over the door, giving a good view over the half dozen empty station chairs and their dark consoles. The ba was there, still dressed in the Betan garb of its discarded alias, jacket and sarong and sandals. Although a pressure suit—one—abstracted from the *Idris*'s supplies lay nearby, flung over the back of a station chair. Corbeau, still vulnerably naked, was seated in the pilot's chair, but had not yet lowered his headset. The ba held up a hand, said something; Corbeau frowned fiercely, and flinched, as the ba pressed a hypospray briefly against the pilot's upper arm and stepped back with a flash of satisfaction on its strained face.

Drugs? Surely even the ba was not mad enough to drug a jump pilot upon whose neural function it would shortly be betting its life. Some disease inoculation? The same problem applied, although something latent might do—*Cooperate, and later I will let you have the antidote.* Or pure bluff, a shot of water, perhaps. The hypospray seemed altogether too crude and obvious as a Cetagandan drug administration method; it hinted at bluff to Miles's mind, though perhaps not to Corbeau's. One had no choice but to turn control over to the pilot when he lowered his headset and plugged the ship into his mind. It made pilots hard to effectively threaten.

It did rather put paid to Vorpatril's paranoid fear that Corbeau had turned traitor, volunteering for this as a way to get a free ride out of his quaddie detention cell and his dilemmas. Or did it? Regardless of prior or secret agreements, the ba would not simply trust when it could, it would think, guarantee.

Over his wrist com, muffled as from a distance, Miles heard a sudden, startling bellow from Admiral Vorpatril: "*What?* That's impossible. Have they gone mad? Not *now* . . ."

After a few more moments passed without further enlightenment, he murmured, "Um, Ekaterin? Are you still there?"

Her breath drew in. "Yes."

"What's going on?"

"Admiral Vorpatril was called away by his communications officer. Some sort of priority message from

Sector Five headquarters just arrived. It seems to be something very urgent."

On the vid image in front of him, Miles watched as Corbeau began to run through preflight checks, moving from station to station under the hard, watchful eyes of the ba. Corbeau made sure to move with disproportionate care; apparently, from the movement of his rather stiff lips, explaining each move before he touched a console. And slowly, Miles noted. Rather more slowly than necessary, if not quite slowly enough to be obvious about it.

Vorpatril's voice, or rather, Vorpatril's heavy breathing, returned at last. The admiral appeared to have run out of invective. Miles found that considerably more disturbing than his previous naval bellowing.

"My lord." Vorpatril hesitated. His voice dropped to a sort of stunned growl. "I have just received Priority One orders from Sector Five HQ to marshal my escort ships, abandon the Komarran fleet, and head for fleet rendezvous off Marilac at maximum possible speed."

Not with my wife, you don't, was Miles's first gyrating thought.

Then he blinked, freezing in his seat.

The *other* function of the military escorts Barrayar donated to the Komarran trade fleets was to quietly and unobtrusively maintain an armed force dispersed through the nexus. A force that could, in the event of a truly dire emergency, be collected rapidly so as to present a convincing military threat at key strategic points. In a crunch it might otherwise be too slow, or even diplomatically or militarily impossible, to get any force from the homeworlds through the wormhole jumps of intervening local space polities to the mustering places where it could do Barrayar some good. But the trade fleets were out there already.

The planet of Marilac was a Barrayaran ally at the back door of the Cetagandan Empire, from Barrayar's point of view, in the complex web of wormhole jump routes that strung the nexus together. A second front, as Rho Ceta's immediate neighborly threat to Komarr was considered the first front. Granted, the Cetagandans had the shorter lines of communication and logistics between the two points of contact. But the strategic pincer still beat hell out of the sound of one hand clapping, particularly with the potential addition of Marilacan forces. The Barrayarans would only be marshaling at Marilac in order to offer a threat to Cetaganda.

Except that, when Miles and Ekaterin had left Barrayar on this belated honeymoon trip, relations between the two empires had been about as—well, cordial was perhaps not quite the right term—about as unstrained as they had been in years. What the *hell* could have changed that, so profoundly, and so quickly?

Something has stirred up the Cetagandans around Rho Ceta, Gregor had said.

A few jumps out from Rho Ceta, Guppy and his smuggler friends had off-loaded a strange live cargo from a Cetagandan government ship, one with lots of fancy markings. A screaming-bird pattern, perhaps? Along with one, and only one person—one survivor? After which the ship had tilted away, on a dangerous in-bound course for the system's suns. What if that trajectory hadn't been a swing around? What if it had been a straight dive, with no return?

"Sonuvabitch," breathed Miles.

"My lord?" said Vorpatril. "If—"

"*Quiet*," snapped Miles.

The admiral's silence was shocked, but it held.

Once a year, the most precious cargoes of the haut race left the Star Crèche on the capital world of Eta

Ceta. Eight ships, bound each for one of the planets of the Empire so curiously ruled by the haut. Each carrying that year's cohort of haut embryos, genetically modified and certified results of all the contracts of conception so carefully negotiated, the prior year, between the members of the great constellations, the clans, the carefully cultivated gene-lines of the haut race. Each load of a thousand or so nascent lives conducted by one of the eight most important haut ladies of the Empire, the planetary consorts who were the steering committee of the Star Crèche. All most private, most secret, most never-to-be-discussed with outsiders.

How was it that a ba agent could not go back for more copies, if it lost such a cargo of future haut lives in transit?

When it wasn't an agent at all. When it was a *renegade*.

"The crime isn't murder," Miles whispered, his eyes widening. "The crime is *kidnapping*."

The murders had come subsequently, in an increasingly panicked cascade, as the ba, with good reason, attempted to bury its trail. Well, Guppy and his friends had surely been planned to die, as eyewitnesses to the fact that one person had not gone down with the rest on the doomed ship. A ship hijacked, if briefly, before its destruction—all the best hijackings were inside jobs, oh, yes. The Cetagandan government must be going *insane* over this.

"My lord, are you all right—?"

Ekaterin's voice, in a fierce whisper: "No, don't interrupt him. He's thinking. He just makes those funny leaking noises when he's thinking."

From the Celestial Garden's point of view, a Star Crèche child-ship had disappeared on what should have been a safe route to Rho Ceta. Every rescue force and intelligence agent the Cetagandan empire *owned* would have been flung into the case. If it were not for Guppy, the tragedy might have passed as some mysterious malfunction that had sent the ship tumbling, out of control and unable to signal, to its fiery doom. No survivors, no wreckage, no loose ends. But there *was* Guppy. Leaving a messy trail of wildly suggestive evidence behind him with every flopping footfall.

How far behind could the Cetagandans be, by now? Too close for the ba's comfort, obviously; it was a wonder, when Guppy had popped up on the hostel railing, that the ba hadn't just died of heart failure without any need for the rivet gun. But the ba's trail, marked by Guppy with blazing flares, led straight through from the scene of the crime to the heart of a sometimes-enemy empire—Barrayar. What were the Cetagandans making of it all?

Well, we have a clue now, don't we?

"Right," breathed Miles, then, more crisply, "Right. You're recording all this, I trust. So my first order in the Emperor's Voice, Admiral, is to countermand your rendezvous orders from Sector Five. That was what you were about to ask for, yes?"

"Thank you, my Lord Auditor, yes," said Vorpatril gratefully. "Normally, that would be a call I would rather die than disregard, but . . . given our present situation, they are going to have to wait a little." Vorpatril wasn't self-dramatizing; this was delivered as a plain statement of fact. "Not too long, I hope."

"They are going to have to wait a lot. This is my next order in the Emperor's Voice. Clear copy everything—*everything*—you have on record here from the past twenty-four hours and squirt it back on an open channel, at the highest priority, to the Imperial Residence, to the Barrayaran high command on Barrayar, to ImpSec HQ, and to ImpSec Galactic Affairs on

Komarr. And," he took a breath, and raised his voice to override Vorpatril's outraged cry of *Clear copy! At a time like this?* "marked from Lord Auditor Miles Vorkosigan of Barrayar to the most urgent, personal attention of ghem-General Dag Benin, Chief of Imperial Security, the Celestial Garden, Eta Ceta, personal, urgent, most urgent, by Rian's hair this one's real, Dag. Exactly those words."

"*What?*" screamed Vorpatril, then hastily lowered his tone to an anguished repeat, "What? A rendezvous at Marilac can only mean imminent war with the Cetagandans! We can't hand them that kind of intelligence on our position and movements—gift-wrapped!"

"Obtain the complete, unedited Graf Station Security recording of the interrogation of Russo Gupta and send it along too, as soon as you possibly can. Sooner."

New terror shook Miles, a vision like a fever dream: the grand façade of Vorkosigan House, in the Barrayaran capital of Vorbarr Sultana, with plasma fire raining down upon it, its ancient stone melting like butter; two fluid-filled canisters exploding in steam. Or a fog of plague, leaving all the House's protectors dead in heaps in the halls, or fled to die in the streets; two almost ripe replicators running down unattended, stopping, slowly chilling, their tiny occupants dying for lack of oxygen, drowning in their own amniotic fluid. His past and his future, all destroyed together . . . Nikki, too—would he be swept up with the other children in some frantic rescue, or left uncounted, unmissed, fatally alone? Miles had fancied himself growing into a good stepfather to Nikki—that was called into deep question now, eh? *Ekaterin, I'm sorry . . .*

It would be hours—days—before the new tight-beam could get back to Barrayar and Cetaganda. Insanely upset people could make fatal mistakes in mere minutes. Seconds . . . "And if you are a praying man, Vorpatril, pray that no one will do anything stupid before it gets there. And that we will be believed."

"Lady Vorkosigan," Vorpatril whispered urgently. "Could he be hallucinating from the disease?"

"No, no," she soothed. "He's just thinking too fast, and leaving out all the intervening steps. He does that. It can be very frustrating. Miles, love, um . . . for the *rest* of us, would you mind unpacking that a little more?"

He took a breath—and two or three more—to stop his trembling. "The ba. It's not an agent on a mission. It's a criminal. A renegade. Perhaps insane. I believe it hijacked the annual haut child-ship to Rho Ceta, sent the vessel into the nearest sun with all aboard— probably murdered already—and made off with its cargo. Which trans-shipped through Komarr, and which left the Barrayaran Empire on a trade ship belonging to Empress Laisa *personally*—and just how incriminating *that* particular detail is going to look to certain minds inside the Star Crèche, I shrink to imagine. The Cetagandans think *we* stole their babies, or colluded in the theft, and, dear God, murdered a *planetary consort*, and so they are about to make war on us by *mistake*!"

"Oh," said Vorpatril blankly.

"The ba's whole safety lay in perfect secrecy, because once the Cetagandans got on the right trail they would never rest till they tracked this crime down. But the perfect plan cracked when Gupta didn't die on schedule. Gupta's frantic antics drew Solian in, drew you in, drew me in . . ." His voice slowed. "Except, what in the world does the ba want those haut infants *for*?"

Ekaterin offered hesitantly, "Could it be stealing them for someone else?"

"Yes, but the ba aren't *supposed* to be subornable."

"Well, if not for pay or some bribe, maybe black-mail or threat? Maybe threat to some haut to whom the ba *is* loyal?"

"Or maybe some faction in the Star Crèche," Miles supplied. "Except . . . the ghem-lords do factions. The haut lords do factions. The Star Crèche has always moved as one—even when it was committing arguable treason, a decade ago, the haut ladies took no separate decisions."

"The *Star Crèche* committed treason?" echoed Vorpatril in astonishment. "This certainly didn't get out! Are you sure? I never heard of any mass executions that high in the Empire back then, and I should have." He paused, and added in a baffled tone, "How could a bunch of haut-lady baby-makers commit treason, anyway?"

"It didn't quite come off. For various reasons." Miles cleared his throat.

"Lord Auditor Vorkosigan. This is your com link, yes? Are you there?" a new voice, and a very welcome one, broke in.

"Sealer Greenlaw!" Miles cried happily. "Have you made it to safety? All of you?"

"We are back aboard Graf Station," replied the Sealer. "It seems premature to call it safety. And you?"

"Still trapped aboard the *Idris*. Although not totally without resources. Or ideas."

"I urgently need to speak to you. You can override that hothead Vorpatril."

"Ah, my com link is sustaining an open audio link with Admiral Vorpatril now, ma'am. You can speak to both of us at once, if you like," Miles put in hastily, before she could express herself even more freely.

She hesitated only fractionally. "Good. We absolutely need Vorpatril to hold, repeat, *hold* any strike force of his. Corbeau confirms the ba *does* have some sort of a remote control or deadman switch on his person, apparently linked back to the biohazard it has hidden aboard Graf Station. The ba is not bluffing."

Miles glanced up in surprise at his silent vid of Nav and Com. Corbeau was seated now in the pilot's station chair, the control headset lowered over his skull, his expressionless face even more absent. "*Corbeau* confirms! How? He was stark naked—the ba is watching him every second! Subcutaneous com link?"

"There was no time to find and insert one. He undertook to blink the ship's running lights in a pre-arranged code."

"Whose idea was that?"

"His."

Quick colonial boy. The pilot was on their side. Oh, but that was good to know. . . . Miles's shivering was turning to shudders.

"Every adult quaddie on Graf Station not on emergency duty is out looking for the bio-bomb now," Greenlaw continued, "but we have no idea what it looks like, or how big it is, or if it is disguised as something else. Or if there is more than one. We are trying to evacuate as many children as possible into what ships and shuttles we have on hand, and seal them off, but we can't even be sure of *them*, really. If you people do anything to set this mad creature off—if you launch an unauthorized strike force before this vicious threat is found and safely neutralized—I swear I will give our militia the order to shoot them out of space myself. Do you copy, Admiral? Confirm."

"I hear you," said Vorpatril reluctantly. "But ma'am—the Imperial Auditor himself has been infected with one of the ba's lethal bio-agents. I cannot—I will not—if I have to sit here and do nothing while listening to him die—"

"There are fifty *thousand* innocent lives on Graf Station, Admiral—Lord Auditor!" Her voice failed for a second; returned stiffly. "I am sorry, Lord Vorkosigan."

"I'm not dead yet," Miles replied rather primly. A new and most unwelcome sensation struggled with the tight fear grinding in his belly. He added, "I'm going to switch off my com link for just a moment. I'll be right back."

Motioning Roic to keep still, Miles opened the door to the security office, stepped into the corridor, opened his faceplate, leaned over, and vomited onto the floor. *No help for it.* With an angry swipe, he turned his suit temperature back up. He blinked back the green dizziness, wiped his mouth, went back inside, seated himself again, and called his link back on. "Continue."

He let Vorpatril's and Greenlaw's arguing voices fade from his attention, and studied his view of Nav and Com more closely. One object had to be there, somewhere . . . ah. There it was, a small, valise-sized cryo-freezer case, set carefully down next to one of the empty station chairs near the door. A standard commercial model, no doubt bought off the shelf from some medical supplier here on Graf Station sometime in the past few days. All of *this*, this entire diplomatic mess, this extravagant trail of deaths winding across half the nexus, two empires teetering on the verge of war, came down to *that*. Miles was reminded of the old Barrayaran folktale, about the evil mutant magician who kept his heart in a box to hide it from his enemies.

Yes . . .

"Greenlaw," Miles broke in. "Do you have any way to signal *back* to Corbeau?"

"We designated one of the navigation buoys that broadcasts to the channels of the pilots on cyber-neuro

control. We can't get voice communication through it—
Corbeau wasn't sure how it would emerge, in his
perceptions. We are certain we can get some kind of
simple code blink or beep through it."

"I have a simple message for him. Urgent. Get it
through if you possibly can, however you can. Tell him
to open all the inner airseal doors in the middle deck
of the central nacelle. Kill the security vids there, too,
if he can."

"Why?" she asked suspiciously.

"We have personnel trapped there who are going to
die shortly if he doesn't," Miles replied glibly. Well, it
was true.

"Right," she rapped back. "I'll see what we can do."

He cut his outgoing voice link, turned in his station chair, and made a throat-cutting motion for Roic
to do the same. He leaned forward. "Can you hear
me?"

"Yes, m'lord." Roic's voice was muffled, through the
work suit's thicker faceplate, but sufficiently audible;
they neither of them had to shout, in this quiet, little
space.

"Greenlaw will never order or permit a strike force
to be launched to try to capture the ba. Not hers, not
ours. She can't. There are too many quaddie lives up
for grabs. Trouble is, I don't think this placating
approach will make her station any safer. If this ba
really murdered a planetary consort, it'll not even blink
at a few thousand quaddies. It'll promise cooperation
right up to the last, then hit the release switch on its
bio-bomb and jump, just for the off chance that the
chaos in its wake will delay or disrupt pursuit an extra
day or three. Are you with me so far?"

"Yes, m'lord." Roic's eyes were wide.

"If we can get as close as the door to Nav and Com
unseen, I think we have a chance of jumping the ba

ourselves. Specifically, *you* will jump the ba; I will supply a distraction. You'll be all right. Stunner and nerve disruptor fire will pretty much bounce off that work suit. Needler spines wouldn't penetrate immediately either, if it comes to that. And it would take longer than the seconds you'll need to cross that little room for plasma arc fire to burn through it."

Roic's lips twisted. "What if he just fires at you? That pressure suit's not *that* good."

"The ba won't fire at me. That, I promise you. The Cetagandan haut, and their siblings the ba, are physically stronger than anyone but the dedicated heavy-worlders, but they're not stronger than a power suit. Go for his hands. Hold them. If we get that far, well, the rest will follow."

"And Corbeau? The poor bastard's starkers. Nothing's gonna stop anything fired at him."

"Corbeau," said Miles, "will be the ba's last choice of targets. Ah!" His eyes widened, and he whirled about in his station chair. At the edge of the vid image, half a dozen tiny images in the array were quietly going dark. "Get to the corridor. Get ready to run. As silently as you can."

From his com link, Vorpatril's volume-reduced voice pleaded heartrendingly for the Imperial Auditor to please reopen his outgoing voice contact. He urged Lady Vorkosigan to request the same.

"Leave him alone," Ekaterin said firmly. "He knows what he's doing."

"What *is* he doing?" Vorpatril wailed.

"Something." Her voice fell to a whisper. Or perhaps it was a prayer. "Good luck, love."

Another voice, somewhat offsides, broke in: Captain Clogston. "Admiral? Can you reach Lord Auditor Vorkosigan? We've finished preparing his blood filter and are ready to try it, but he's disappeared out of the infirmary. He was right here a few minutes ago . . ."

"Do you hear that, Lord Vorkosigan?" Vorpatril tried somewhat desperately. "You are to report to the infirmary. Now."

In ten minutes—five—the medics could have their way with him. Miles pushed up from his station chair— he had to use both hands—and followed Roic into the corridor outside Solian's office.

Up ahead in the dimness, the first airseal door across the corridor hissed quietly aside, revealing the cross-corridor to the other nacelles beyond. On the far side, the next door began to slide.

Roic started trotting. His steps were unavoidably heavy. Miles half-jogged behind. He tried to think how recently he had used his seizure-stimulator, how much at risk he was right now for falling down in a fit from a combination of bad brain chemistry and terror. Middling risky, he decided. No automatic weapons for him this trip anyway. No weapons at all, but for his wits. They seemed a meager arsenal, just at the moment.

The second pair of doors opened for them. Then the third. Miles prayed they were not walking into another clever trap. But he didn't think the ba would have any way of tapping, or even guessing, this oblique line of communication. Roic paused briefly, stepping behind the last door edge, and peered ahead. The door to Nav and Com was shut. He gave a short nod and continued forward, Miles in his shadow. As they drew closer, Miles could see that the control panel to the left of the door had been burned out by some cutting tool, cousin, no doubt, to the one Roic had used. The ba had gone shopping in Engineering, too. Miles pointed at it; Roic's face lightened, and a corner of his mouth turned up. *Someone* hadn't forgotten to lock the door behind them when they'd last left after all, it appeared.

Roic pointed to himself, to the door; Miles shook his head and motioned him to bend closer. They touched helmets.

"Me first. Gotta grab that case before the ba can react. 'Sides, I need *you* to pull back the door."

Roic looked around, inhaled, and nodded.

Miles motioned him back down to touch helmets one more time. "And, Roic? I'm glad I didn't bring Jankowski."

Roic smiled. Miles stepped aside.

Now. Delay was no one's friend.

Roic bent, splayed his gloved hands across the door, pressed, and pulled. The servos in his suit whined at the load. The door creaked unwillingly aside.

Miles slipped through. He didn't look back, or up. His world had narrowed to one goal, one object. The freezer case—there, still on the floor beside the absent communication officer's station chair. He pounced, grabbed, lifted it up, clutched it to his chest like a shield, like the hope of his heart.

The ba was turning, yelling, lips drawn back, eyes wide, its hand snaking for a pocket. Miles's gloved fingers felt for the catches. If locked, toss the case toward the ba. If unlocked . . .

The case snapped open. Miles yanked it wide, shook it hard, swung it.

A silver cascade, the better part of a thousand tiny tissue-sampling cryo-storage needles, arced out of the case and bounced randomly across the deck. Some shattered as they struck, making tiny crystalline singing noises like dying insects. Some spun. Some skittered, disappearing behind station chairs and into crevices. Miles grinned fiercely.

The yell became a scream; the ba's hands shot out

toward Miles as if in supplication, in denial, in despair. The Cetagandan began to stumble toward him, gray face working in shock and disbelief.

Roic's power-suited hands locked down over the ba's wrists and hoisted. Wrist bones crackled and popped; blood spurted between the tightening gloved fingers. The ba's body convulsed as it was lifted up. Wild eyes rolled back. The scream transmuted into a weird wail, trailing away. Sandal-clad feet kicked and drummed uselessly at the heavy shin plating of Roic's work suit; toenails split and bled, without effect. Roic stood stolidly, hands up and apart, racking the ba helplessly in the air.

Miles let the freezer case fall from his fingers. It hit the deck with a thump. With a whispered word, he called back the outgoing audio in his com link. "We've taken the ba prisoner. Send relief troops. In biotainer suits. They won't need their guns now. I'm afraid the ship's an unholy mess."

His knees were buckling. He sank to the deck himself, giggling uncontrollably. Corbeau was rising from his pilot's chair; Miles motioned him away with an urgent gesture. "Stay back, Dmitri! I'm about to . . ."

He wrenched his faceplate open in time. Barely. The vomiting and spasms that wrung his stomach this time were much worse. *It's over. Can I please die now?*

Except that it wasn't over, not nearly. Greenlaw had played for fifty thousand lives. Now it was Miles's turn to play for fifty million.

CHAPTER SEVENTEEN

Miles arrived back in the *Idris's* infirmary feet first. He was carried by two of the men from Vorpatril's strike force, which had been hastily converted to, mostly, a medical relief team, and as such cleared by the quaddies. His porters almost fell down the unsightly hole Roic had left in the floor. Miles seized back personal control of his locomotion long enough to stand up, under his own power, and lean rather unsteadily against the wall by the door to the bio-isolation ward. Roic followed, carefully holding the ba's remote trigger in a biotainer bag. Corbeau, stiff-faced and pale, brought up the rear dressed in a loose medical tunic and drawstring pants, and shepherded by a medtech with the ba's hypospray in another biotainer sack.

Captain Clogston came out through the buzzing blue barriers and looked over his new influx of patients and assistants. "Right," he announced, glowering at the gap in the deck. "This ship is so damned befouled, I'm declaring the whole thing a Level Three

Biocontamination Zone. So we may as well spread out and get comfortable, boys."

The techs made a human chain to pass the analyzing equipment quickly to the outer chamber. Miles snared the chance for a few brief, urgent words with the two men with medical markings on their suits who stood apart from the rest—the *Prince Xav's* military interrogation officers. Not really in disguise, merely discreet—and, Miles had to allow, they *were* medically trained.

The second ward was declared a temporary holding cell for their prisoner, the ba, who followed in the procession, bound to a float pallet. Miles scowled as the pallet drifted past, towed on its control lead by a watchful, muscular sergeant. The ba was strapped down tightly, but its head and eyes rolled oddly, and its saliva-flecked lips writhed.

Above almost anything else, it was essential to keep the ba in Barrayaran hands. Finding where the ba had hidden its filthy bio-bomb on Graf Station was the first priority. The haut race had some genetically engineered immunity to the most common interrogation drugs and their derivatives; if fast-penta didn't work on this one, it would give the quaddies very little in the way of interrogation procedures to fall back upon that would pass Adjudicator Leutwyn's approval. In this emergency, military rules seemed more appropriate than civilian ones. *In other words, if they'll just leave us alone we'll pull out the ba's fingernails* for *them.*

Miles caught Clogston by the elbow. "How is Bel Thorne doing?" he demanded.

The fleet surgeon shook his head. "Not well, my Lord Auditor. We thought at first the herm was improving, as the filters cut in—it seemed to return to consciousness. But then it became restless.

Moaning and trying to talk. Out of its head, I think.
It keeps crying for Admiral Vorpatril."

Vorpatril? Why? Wait— "Did Bel say Vorpatril?"
Miles asked sharply. "Or just, *the Admiral*?"

Clogston shrugged. "Vorpatril's the only admiral
around right now, although I suppose the portmaster
could be hallucinating altogether. I hate to sedate
anyone so physiologically distressed, especially when
they've just fought their way *out* of a drug fog. But
if that herm doesn't calm down, we'll have to."

Miles frowned and hurried into the isolation ward.
Clogston followed. Miles pulled off his helmet, fished
his wrist com back out of it, and clutched the vital
link safely in his hand. A tech was making up the
hastily cleared second bunk, readying it for the
infected Lord Auditor, presumably.

Bel now lay on the first bunk, dried off and
dressed in a pale green Barrayaran military-issue
patient tunic, which seemed at first heartening
progress. But the herm was gray-faced, lips purple-
blue, eyelids fluttering. An IV pump, not dependent
upon potentially erratic ship's gravity, infused yellow
fluid rapidly into Bel's right arm. The left arm was
strapped to a board; plastic tubing filled with blood
ran from under a bandage and into a hybrid appli-
ance bound around with quantities of plastic tape. A
second tube ran back again, its dark surface moist
with condensation.

" 'S balla," Bel moaned. " 'S balla."

The fleet surgeon's lips pursed in medical displeasure
behind his faceplate. He edged forward to glance at
a monitor. "Blood pressure's way up, too. I think it's
time to knock the poor bugger back out."

"Wait." Miles elbowed to the edge of Bel's bunk to
put himself in Bel's line of sight, staring down at the
herm in wild hope. Bel's head jerked. The eyelids

flickered up; the eyes widened. The blue lips tried to move again. Bel licked them, took a long inhalation, and tried once more. "Adm'ral! Portent. 'S basti'd hid it in the balla. Tol' me. Sadist'c basti'd."

"Still going on about Admiral Vorpatril," Clogston muttered in dismay.

"Not Admiral Vorpatril. Me," breathed Miles. Did that witty mind still exist, in the bunker of its brain? Bel's eyes were open, shifting to try to focus on him, as if Miles's image wavered and blurred in the herm's sight.

Bel knew a portent. No. Bel was trying to say something important. Bel wrestled death for the possession of its own mouth to try to get the message out. Balla? Ballistic? Balalaika? No—ballet!

Miles said urgently, "The ba hid its bio-bomb at the ballet—in the Minchenko Auditorium? Is that what you're trying to say, Bel?"

The straining body sagged in relief. "Yeh. Yeh. Get 's word out. In the lights, I thin'."

"Was there only one bomb? Or were there more? Did the ba say, could you tell?"

"Don' know. 'S homemade, I thin'. Check. Purch'ses . . ."

"Right, got it! Good work, Captain Thorne." *You always were the best, Bel.* Miles turned half away and spoke forcefully into his wrist com, demanding to be patched through to Greenlaw, or Venn, or Watts, or *somebody* in authority on Graf Station.

A ragged female voice finally replied, "Yes?"

"Sealer Greenlaw? Are you there?"

Her voice steadied. "Yes, Lord Vorkosigan? Do you have something?"

"Maybe. Bel Thorne reports the ba said that it hid the bio-bomb somewhere in the Minchenko Auditorium. Possibly behind some lights."

Her breath drew in. "Good. We'll concentrate our trained searchers in there."

"Bel also thinks the bomb was something the ba rigged itself, recently. It may have made purchases on Graf Station in the persona of Ker Dubauer that could give you a clue as to how many it could have devised."

"Ah! Right! I'll get Venn's people on it."

"Note, Bel's in pretty bad shape. Also, the ba could have been lying. Get back to me when you know something."

"Yes. Yes. Thank you." Hastily, she cut her com. It occurred to Miles to wonder if she was locked down in protective bio-isolation right now too, as he was about to be, trying to shape the critical moment at a similar frustrating remove.

"Basti'd," Bel muttered. "Paralyzed me. Put me in s' damn bod pod. Tol' me. *Then* zipped it up. Left me to die, 'magining . . . Knew . . . it knew about Nicol 'n me. Saw my vid cube. Where's m' vid cube?"

"Nicol is safe," Miles assured Bel. Well, as much as any quaddie on Graf Station at the moment—if not safe, at least *warned*. Vid cube? Oh, the little imager full of Bel's hypothetical children. "Your vid cube is put away safely." Miles had no idea if this last was true or not—the cube might be still in Bel's pocket, destroyed with the herm's contaminated clothes, or stolen by the ba. But the assertion gave Bel ease. The exhausted herm's eyes closed again, and its breathing steadied.

In a few hours, I'm going to look like that.

Then you'd better not waste any time now, eh?

With a vast distaste, Miles suffered a hovering tech to help him off with his pressure suit and underwear— to be taken away and incinerated, Miles supposed. "If you're tying me down here, I want a comconsole set up by my bunk immediately. No, you can't have that." Miles fended off the tech, who was now trying to pry loose his com link, then paused to swallow. "And something for nausea. All right, put it around my *right* arm, then."

Horizontal was scarcely better than vertical. Miles smoothed down his own pale green tunic and gave up his left arm to the surgeon, who personally attended to piercing his vein with some medical awl that felt the size of a drinking straw. On the other side a tech pressed a hypospray against his right shoulder—a potion that would kill the dizziness and the cramping in his stomach, he hoped. But he didn't yelp until the first spurt of filtered blood returned to his body. "*Crap*, that's cold. I *hate* cold."

"Can't be helped, my Lord Auditor," Clogston murmured soothingly. "We have to lower your body temperature at least three degrees. It will buy time."

Miles hunched, uncomfortably reminded that they didn't have a fix for this yet. He stifled a gush of terror, escaping under pressure from the place he'd kept it locked for the past hours. Not for one second would he allow himself to believe that there was no cure to be had, that this bio-shit would drag him under and this time he wouldn't come back up . . . "Where's Roic?" He raised his right wrist to his lips. "Roic?"

"I'm in the outer chamber, m'lord. I'm afraid to carry this triggering device through the bio-barrier till we're sure it's disarmed."

"Right, good thinking. One of those fellows out there should be the bomb disposal tech I requested. Find him and give it to him. Then ride herd on the interrogation for me, will you?"

"Yes, m'lord."

"Captain Clogston."

The doctor glanced down from where he fiddled with the jury-rigged blood filter. "My lord?"

"The moment you have a medtech—no, a doctor.

The moment you have some qualified men free, send them to the cargo hold where the ba has the replicators. I want them to run samples, try to see if the ba has contaminated or poisoned them in any way. Then make sure the equipment's all running all right. It's *very important* that the haut infants all be kept alive and well."

"Yes, Lord Vorkosigan."

If the haut babies were inoculated with the same vile parasites presently rioting through his own body, might the replicators' temperature be turned down to chill them all, and slow the disease process? Or would such cold stress the infants, damage them . . . he was borrowing trouble, reasoning in advance of his data. A trained agent, conditioned to the correct disconnect between action and imagination, might have performed such an inoculation, cleaning up every bit of incriminating high-haut DNA before abandoning the scene. But this ba was an amateur. This ba had another sort of conditioning altogether. *Yes, but that conditioning must have gone very wrong somehow, or this ba wouldn't have got this far . . .*

Miles added as Clogston turned away, "And give me word on the condition of the pilot, Corbeau, as soon as you have it." The retreating suited figure raised a hand in acknowledgment.

In a few minutes, Roic entered the ward; he had doffed the bulky powered work suit, and now wore more comfortable military-issue Level Three biotainer garb.

"How's it going over there?"

Roic ducked his head. "Not well, m'lord. T' ba has gone into some sort of strange mental state. Raving, but nothing to the point, and the intelligence fellows say its physiological state is all out of kilter as well. They're trying to stabilize it."

"The ba *must* be kept alive!" Miles struggled half-up, a vision of having himself carried into the next chamber to take charge running through his head. "We have to get it back to Cetaganda. To prove Barrayar is innocent."

He sank back and eyed the humming device filtering his blood hung by his left side. Pulling out parasites, yes, but also draining the energy the parasites had stolen from him to create themselves. Siphoning off the mental edge he desperately needed right now.

He remarshaled his scattering thoughts, and explained to Roic the news Bel had imparted. "Return to the interrogation room and give them the word on this development. See if they can get any cross-confirmation on the hiding place in the Minchenko Auditorium, and especially see if they can get anything that would suggest if there is more than one device. Or not."

"Right." Roic nodded. He glanced over Miles's growing array of medical attachments. "By the way, m'lord. Had you happened to mention your seizure disorder to the surgeon yet?"

"Not yet. There hasn't been time."

"Right." Roic's lips screwed up thoughtfully, in an editorial fashion that Miles chose to ignore. "I'll see to it then, shall I, m'lord?"

Miles hunched. "Yeah, yeah."

Roic trod out of the ward on both his errands.

The remote comconsole arrived; a tech swung a tray across Miles's lap, laid the vid plate frame upon it, and helped him sit mostly up, with extra pillows at his back. He was starting to shiver again. All right, good, the device was Barrayaran military issue, not just scavenged from the *Idris*. He had a securable visual link again now. He entered codes.

Vorpatril's face was a moment or two coming up;

riding herd on all this from the *Prince Xav*'s tactics room, the admiral no doubt had a few other demands on his attention at the moment. He appeared at last with a, "*Yes*, my lord!" His eyes searched the image of Miles on his vid display. He apparently was not reassured by the view. His jaw tightened in dismay. "Are you all—" he began, but edited this fatuity on the fly to, "How bad is it?"

"I can still talk. And while I can still talk, I need to record some orders. While we're waiting on the quaddies' search for the bio-bomb—are you following the latest on that?" Miles brought the admiral up to the moment on Bel's intelligence about the Minchenko Auditorium, and went on. "Meanwhile, I want you to select and prepare the fastest ship in your escort that has a sufficient capacity for the load it's going to be carrying. Which will be me, Portmaster Thorne, a medical team, our prisoner the ba and guards, Guppy the Jacksonian smuggler if I can pry him out of quaddie hands, and a thousand working uterine replicators. With qualified medical attendants."

"And me," put in Ekaterin's voice firmly from offsides. Her face leaned briefly into range of Vorpatril's vid pickup, and she frowned at him. She'd seen her husband looking like death on a plate more than once before, though; perhaps she wouldn't be as disturbed as the admiral clearly was. Having an Imperial Auditor get melted to steaming slime on his watch would be a notable black mark, not that Vorpatril's career wasn't in a shambles over this episode already.

"My courier ship will travel in convoy, carrying Lady Vorkosigan." He cut across Ekaterin's beginning objection: "I may well need *one* spokesperson along who isn't in medical quarantine."

She settled back with a dubious "Hm."

"But I want to make damned sure we're not impeded

by any hassles along the way, Admiral, so have your fleet department start working immediately on our passage clearances in all the local space polities we're going to have to cross. Speed. Speed is of the essence. I want to get away the moment we're sure the ba's devil-device has been cleared from Graf Station. At least with us carrying all these biohazards, no one is going to want to stop and board us for inspections."

"To Komarr, my lord? Or Sergyar?"

"No. Calculate the shortest possible jump route directly to Rho Ceta."

Vorpatril's head jerked back in startlement. "If the orders I received from Sector Five HQ mean what we think, you'll hardly get passage *there*. Reception by plasma fire and fusion shells the moment you pop out of the wormhole, would be what I'd expect."

"*Unpack*, Miles," Ekaterin's voice drifted in.

He grinned briefly at the familiar exasperation in her voice. "By the time we arrive there, I will have arranged our clearances with the Cetagandan Empire." *I hope.* Or else they were all going to be in more trouble than Miles ever wanted to imagine. "Barrayar is bringing their kidnapped haut babies back to them. On the end of a long stick. I get to be the stick."

"Ah," said Vorpatril, his gray brows rising in speculation.

"Give a head's-up to my ImpSec courier pilot. I plan to start the moment we have everyone and everything transferred aboard. You can start on the everything part now."

"Understood, my lord." Vorpatril rose and vanished out of vid range. Ekaterin moved back in, and smiled at him.

"Well, we're making some progress at last," Miles said to her, with what he hoped seemed good cheer, and not suppressed hysteria.

Her smile twisted up on one side. Her eyes were warm, though. "Some progress? What do you call an avalanche, I wonder?"

"No arctic metaphors, please. I'm cold enough. If the medicos get this . . . infestation under control en route, perhaps they'll clear me for visitors. We'll want the courier ship later, anyway."

A medtech appeared, drew a blood sample from the outbound tube, added an IV pump to the array, raised the bed rails, then bent and began tying down the left arm board.

"Hey," objected Miles. "How am I supposed to unravel all this mess with one hand tied behind my back?"

"Captain Clogston's orders, m'lord Auditor." Firmly, the tech finished securing his arm. "Standard procedure for seizure risk."

Miles gritted his teeth.

"Your seizure-stimulator is with the rest of your things aboard the *Kestrel*," Ekaterin observed dispassionately. "I'll find it and send it across as soon as I transfer back aboard."

Prudently, Miles limited his response to, "Thank you. Check back with me before you dispatch it—there may be a few other things I'll need. Let me know when you're safely aboard."

"Yes, love." She touched her fingers to her lips and held them up, passing them through his image before her. He returned the gesture. His heart chilled a little as her image winked out. How long before they dared touch flesh to warm flesh again? *What if it's never . . . ? Damn, but I'm cold.*

The tech departed. Miles hunched down in his bed. He supposed it would be futile to ask for blankets. He imagined little tiny bio-bombs set to go off all through his body, sparking like a Midsummer fireworks display seen at a distance out over the river in Vorbarr Sultana, cascading to a grand, lethal finale. He imagined his flesh decomposing into corrosive ooze while he yet lived in it. He needed to think about something else.

Two empires, both alike in indignation, maneuvering for position, massing deadly force behind a dozen wormhole jumps, each jump a point of contact, conflict, catastrophe . . . that was no better.

A thousand almost-ripe haut fetuses, turning in their little chambers, unaware of the distance and dangers they had passed through, and the hazards still to come—*how* soon would they have to be decanted? The picture of a thousand squalling infants dropped upon a few harried Barrayaran military medicos was almost enough to make him smile, if only he wasn't so primed to start screaming.

Bel's breath, in the next bunk, was thick and labored. Speed. For every reason, speed. Had he set in motion everyone and everything that he could? He ran down checklists in his aching head, lost his place, tried again. How long had it been since he'd slept? The minutes crawled by with tortuous slowness. He imagined them as snails, hundreds of little snails with Cetagandan clan markings coloring their shells, going past in procession, leaving slime-trails of lethal biocontamination . . . a crawling infant, little Helen Natalia, cooing and reaching for one of the pretty, poisonous creatures, and he was all tied up and pierced with tubes and couldn't get across the room fast enough to stop her . . .

A bleep from his lap link, thank God, snapped him awake before he could find out where *that* nightmare was going. He was still pierced with tubes, though. What time was it? He was losing track altogether. His usual mantra—*I can sleep when I'm dead*—seemed a little too apropos.

An image formed over the vid plate. "Sealer Green-law!" Good news, bad news? *Good*. Her lined face was radiant with relief.

"We found it," she said. "It's been contained."

Miles blew out his breath in a long exhalation. "Yes. Excellent. Where?"

"In Minchenko Auditorium, just as the portmaster said. Attached to the wall in a stage light cell. It did seem to have been put together hastily, but it was deadly clever for all of that. Simple and clever. It was scarcely more than a little sealed plastic balloon, filled with some sort of nutrient solution, my people tell me. And a tiny charge, and the electronic trigger for it. The ba had stuck it to the wall with ordinary packing tape, and sprayed it with a little flat black paint. No one would notice it in the ordinary course of events, not even if they had been working on the lights, unless they put a hand right on it."

"Homemade, then. On the spot?"

"It would seem so. The electronics, which were off-the-shelf items—and the tape, for that matter—are all quaddie-make. They match with the purchases recorded to Dubauer's credit chit the evening after the attack in the hostel lobby. All the parts are accounted for. There seems to have been only the one device." She ran her upper hands through her silver hair, massaging her scalp wearily, and squeezed shut eyes bounded beneath by little dark half-moons of shadow.

"That . . . fits with the timetable as I see it," said Miles. "Right up until Guppy popped up with his rivet gun, the ba evidently thought it had gotten away clean with its stolen cargo. And with Solian's death. Everything calm and perfect. Its plan was to pass through Quaddiespace quietly, without leaving a trace. It would not have had any reason before then to rig such a device. But from that botched murder attempt on, it was running scared, having to improvise rapidly. Curious bit of foresight, though. It can't have *planned* to be trapped on the *Idris* the way it was, surely."

She shook her head. "It planned something. The explosive charge had two leads to its trigger. One was a receiver for the signal device the ba had in its pocket. The other was a simple sound sensor. Set to a fairly high decibel level. That of an auditorium full of applause, for example."

Miles's teeth snapped shut. *Oh, yes.* "Thus masking the pop of the charge, and blowing out contaminant to the maximum number of people at once." The vision was instant, and horrifying.

"So we think. People come in from other stations all over Quaddiespace to see performances of the Minchenko Ballet. The contagion could have spread back out with them through half the system before it became apparent."

"Is it the same—no, it can't be what the ba gave to me and Bel. Can it? Was it lethal, or merely something debilitating, or what?"

"The sample is in the hands of our medical people now. We should know soon."

"So the ba set up its bio-bomb . . . after it knew real Cetagandan agents would be following, after it knew it would be compelled to abandon the utterly incriminating replicators and their contents . . . I'll *bet* it put the bomb together and slapped it out there in a hurry." Maybe it was revenge. Revenge upon the quaddies for all the forced delays that had so wrecked the ba's perfect plan . . . ? By Bel's report, the ba was not above such motivations; the Cetagandan had displayed a cruel humor, and a taste for bifurcating strategies. If the ba hadn't run into the troubles on the *Idris*, would it have retrieved the device, or would it simply have quietly left the bomb behind to go off on its own? Well, if Miles's own men couldn't get the whole story out of their prisoner, he damned well knew some people who could.

"Good," he breathed. "We can go now."

Greenlaw's weary eyes opened. "What?"

"I mean—with your permission, Madame Sealer." He adjusted his vid pickup to a wider angle, to take in his sinister medical setting. Too late to adjust the color balance toward a more sickly green. Also, possibly, redundant. Greenlaw's mouth turned down in dismay, looking at him.

"Admiral Vorpatril has received an extremely alarming military communiqué from home . . ." Swiftly, Miles explained his deduction about the connection of suddenly increased tensions between Barrayar and its dangerous Cetagandan neighbor to the recent events on Graf Station. He talked carefully around the tactical use of trade fleet escorts as rapid-deployment forces, although he doubted the sealer missed the implications.

"My plan is to get myself, the ba, the replicators, and as much evidence as I can amass of the ba's crimes back to Rho Ceta, to present to the Cetagandan government, to clear Barrayar of whatever accusation of collusion is driving this crisis. As fast as possible. Before some hothead—on either side—does something that, to put it bluntly, makes Admiral Vorpatril's late actions on Graf Station look like a model of restraint and wisdom."

That won a snort from her; he forged on. "While the ba and Russo Gupta both committed crimes on Graf, they committed crimes in the Cetagandan and Barrayaran empires first. I submit we have clear prior claim. And worse—their mere continued presence on Graf Station is dangerous, because, I promise you, sooner or later their furious Cetagandan victims will be following them up. I think you've had enough of a taste of their medicine to make the prospect of a swarm of *real* Cetagandan agents descending upon you unwelcome indeed. Cede us both criminals, and any retribution will chase after us instead."

"Hm," she said. "And your impounded trade fleet? Your fines?"

"Let . . . on my authority, I am willing to transfer ownership of the *Idris* to Graf Station, in lieu of all fines and expenses." He added prudently, "As is."

Her eyes sprang wide. She said indignantly, "The ship's *contaminated*."

"Yes. So we can't take it anywhere anyway. Cleaning it up could be a nice little training exercise for your biocontrol people." He decided not to mention the holes. "Even with that expense, you'll come out ahead. I'm afraid the passengers' insurance will have to eat the value of any of their cargo that can't be cleared. But I'm really hopeful that most of it will not need to be quarantined. And you can let the rest of the fleet go."

"And your men in our detention cells?"

"You let one of them out. Are you sorry? Can you not allow Ensign Corbeau's courage to redeem his comrades? That has to be one of the bravest acts I've ever witnessed, him walking naked and knowing into horror to save Graf Station."

"That . . . yes. That was remarkable," she conceded. "By any people's standards." She regarded him thoughtfully. "You went in after the ba too."

"Mine doesn't count," Miles said automatically. "I was already . . ." he cut the word, *dead*. He was not, dammit, dead yet. "I was already infected."

Her brows rose in bemused curiosity. "And if you hadn't been, what would you have done?"

"Well . . . it *was* the tactical moment. I have a kind of gift for timing, you see."

"And for doubletalk."

"That, too. But the ba was just my job."

"Has anyone ever told you that you are quite mad?"

"Now and then," he admitted. Despite everything, a slow smile turned his lips. "Not so much since I was appointed an Imperial Auditor, though. Useful, that."

She snorted, very softly. Softening? Miles trotted out the next barrage. "My plea is humanitarian, too. It is my belief—my hope—that the Cetagandan haut ladies will have some treatment up their capacious sleeves for their own product. I propose to take Portmaster Thorne with us—at our expense—to share the cure that I now so desperately seek for myself. It's only justice. The herm was, in a sense, in my service when it took this harm. In my work gang, if you like."

"Huh. You Barrayarans do look after your own, at least. One of your few saving graces."

Miles opened his hands in an equally ambiguous acknowledgment of this mixed compliment. "Thorne and I both now labor under a deadline that waits on no committee debate, I'm afraid, and no one's permission. The present palliative," he gestured awkwardly at the blood filter, "buys a little time. As of this moment, no one knows if it will buy enough."

She rubbed her brow, as if it ached. "Yes, certainly . . . certainly you must . . . oh, hell." She took a breath. "All right. Take your prisoners and your evidence and the whole damned lot—and Thorne— and go."

"And Vorpatril's men in detention?"

"Them, too. Take them *all* away. Your ships can all go, bar the *Idris*." Her nose wrinkled in distaste. "But we will discuss the residue of your fines and expenses further, after the ship is evaluated by our inspectors.

Later. Your government can send someone for the task. Not you, by preference."

"*Thank* you, Madame Sealer," Miles sang in relief. He cut the com, and collapsed back on his pillows. The ward seemed to be spinning around his head, very slowly, in short jerks. It wasn't, he decided after a moment, a problem with the room.

Captain Clogston, who had been waiting by the door for the Auditor to complete this high-level negotiation, advanced to glower at his cobbled-together blood filter some more. He then transferred his glower to Miles. "Seizure disorder, eh? I'm glad *someone* told me."

"Yes, well, we wouldn't want you to mistake it for an exotic new Cetagandan symptom. It's pretty routine. If it happens, don't panic. I come up on my own in about five minutes. Usually gives me a sort of hangover, afterwards, not that I'd be able to tell the difference at the moment. Never mind. What can you tell me about Ensign Corbeau?"

"We checked the ba's hypospray. It was filled with water."

"Ah! Good! I thought so." Miles smiled in wolfish satisfaction. "Can you pronounce him clear of bio-horrors, then?"

"Given that he's been running around this plague-ship bare-ass naked, not until we're sure we have identified all possible hazards that the ba might have released. But nothing came up on the first blood and tissue samples we took."

A hopeful—Miles tried not to think, *overly optimistic*—sign. "Can you send the ensign in to me? Is it safe? I want to talk to him."

"We now believe that what you and the herm has isn't virulently contagious through ordinary contact.

Once we're sure the ship's clear of anything else, we'll all be able to get out of these suits, which will be a relief. Although the parasites might transfer sexually— we'll have to study that."

"I don't like Corbeau *that* much. Send him in, then."

Clogston gave Miles an odd look, and moved off. Miles wasn't sure if the captain had missed the feeble joke, or merely considered it too feeble to merit a response. But that *transfer sexually* theory kicked off a whole new cascade of unpleasant, unwelcome speculation in Miles's mind. What if the medicos found they could keep him alive indefinitely, but not get rid of the damned things? Would he never be able to touch any more of Ekaterin than her holovid image for the rest of his life . . . ? It also suggested a new set of questions to put to Guppy about his recent travels—well, the quaddie doctors were competent, and receiving copies of the Barrayarans' medical downloads; their epidemiologists were doubtless already on it.

Corbeau pushed through the bio-barriers. He was now somewhat desultorily arrayed in a disposable mask and gloves, in addition to the medical tunic and some patient slippers. Miles sat up, pushed away his tray, and unobtrusively twitched open his own tunic, letting the paling spiderweb of old needle-grenade scars silently suggest whatever they might to Corbeau.

"You asked for me, my Lord Auditor?" Corbeau ducked his head in a nervous jerk.

"Yes." Miles scratched his nose thoughtfully with his one free hand. "Well, hero. That was a very good career move you just made."

Corbeau hunched a little, mulishly. "I didn't do it for my career. Or for Barrayar. I did it for Graf Station, and the quaddies, and Garnet Five."

"And glad I am of it. Nevertheless, people will doubtless be wanting to pin gold stars on you.

Cooperate with me, and I won't make you receive them in the costume you were wearing when you earned them."

Corbeau gave him a baffled, wary look.

What was the matter with all his jokes today, anyway? Flat, flatter, flattest. Maybe he was violating some sort of unwritten Auditor protocol, and messing up everyone else's lines.

The ensign said, in a notably uninviting voice, "What do you want me to do? My lord."

"More urgent concerns—to put it mildly—are going to compel me to leave Quaddiespace before my assigned diplomatic mission is quite complete. Nevertheless, with the true cause and course of our recent disasters here finally dragged out into the light, what follows should be easier." *Besides, there's nothing like the threat of imminent death to force one to delegate.* "It is very plain that Barrayar is overdue to have a full-time diplomatic consulate officer assigned to the Union of Free Habitats. A bright young man who . . ." *is shacked up with a quaddie girl*, no, *married to*, wait, that wasn't what they called it here, *is partners with*, yes, very likely, but it hadn't happened yet. Although Corbeau was thrice a fool if he didn't grab this opportunity to fix things with Garnet Five for good and all. "Likes quaddies," Miles continued smoothly, "and has earned both their respect and gratitude by his personal valor, and has no objection to a long assignment away from home—two years, was it? Yes, two years. Such a young man might be particularly well placed to argue effectively for Barrayar's interests in Quaddiespace. In my personal opinion."

Miles couldn't tell if Corbeau's mouth was open, behind his medical mask. His eyes had grown rather wide.

"I can't imagine," said Miles, "that Admiral Vorpatril

would have any objection to releasing you to this detached duty. Or at any rate, to not having to deal with you in his command structure after all these . . . complex events. Not that I'd planned to give him a Betan vote in my Auditorial decrees, mind you."

"I . . . I don't know anything about diplomacy. I was trained as a pilot."

"If you went through military jump pilot training, you have already shown that you can study hard, learn fast, and make confident, rapid decisions affecting other people's lives. Objection overruled. You will, of course, have a consulate budget to hire expert staff to assist you in specialized problems, in law, in the economics of port fees, in trade matters, whatever. But you'll be expected to learn enough as you go to judge whether their advice is good for the Imperium. And if, at the end of two years, you do decide to muster out and stay here, the experience would give you a major boost into Quaddiespace private-sector employment. If there's any problem with all this from your point of view—or from Garnet Five's, very level-headed woman, by the way, don't let her get away—it's not apparent to me."

"I'll"—Corbeau swallowed—"think about it. My lord."

"Excellent." And not readily stampeded, either, good. "Do so." Miles smiled and waved dismissal; warily, Corbeau withdrew. As soon as he was out of earshot, Miles murmured a code into his wrist com.

"Ekaterin, love? Where are you?"

"In my cabin on the *Prince Xav*. The nice young yeoman is getting ready to help carry my things to the shuttle. Yes, thank you, that too . . ."

"Right. I've just about cracked us loose from Quaddiespace. Greenlaw was reasonable, or at least, too exhausted to argue any more."

"She has all my sympathy. I don't think I have a functional nerve left, right now."

"Don't need your nerves, just your usual grace. The moment you can get to a comconsole, call up Garnet Five. I want to appoint that heroic young idiot Corbeau to be Barrayaran consul here, and make him clean up all this mess I have to leave in my wake. It's only fair; he certainly helped create it. Gregor *did* specifically ask that I assure that Barrayaran ships could dock here again someday. The boy is wobbling, however. So pitch it to Garnet Five, and make sure that *she* makes sure Corbeau says yes."

"Oh! What a splendid idea, love. They would make a good team, I think."

"Yep. Her for beauty, and um . . . her for brains."

"And him for courage, surely. I think it might work out. I must think what to send them for a wedding present, to convey my personal thanks."

"Partnering present? I don't know, ask Nicol. Oh. Speaking of Nicol." Miles glanced aside at the sheeted figure in the next bunk. Crucial message delivered, Thorne had fallen back into what Miles hoped was sleep and not incipient coma. "I'm thinking that Bel really ought to have someone to ride along and take care of it. Or of things for it. Some kind of support trooper, anyway. I expect the Star Crèche will have a fix for their own weapon—they'd have to, lab accidents, after all." *If we get there in time.* "But this looks like something that's going to involve a certain amount of really unpleasant convalescence. I'm not exactly looking forward to it myself." *But consider the alternative . . .* "Ask her if she's willing. She could ride in the *Kestrel* with you, be some company, anyway." And if neither he nor Bel got out of this alive, mutual support.

"Certainly. I'll call her from here."

"Call me again when you're safe aboard the *Kestrel*, love." *Often and often.*

"Of course." Her voice hesitated. "Love you. Get some rest. You sound like you need it. Your voice has that down-in-a-well sound it gets when . . . There *will* be time." Determination flashed through her own audible fatigue.

"I wouldn't dare die. There's this fierce Vor lady who threatened she'd kill me if I did." He grinned weakly and cut the com.

He drowsed for a time in dizzy exhaustion, fighting the sleep that tried to overtake him, because he couldn't be sure it wasn't the ba's hell-disease gaining on him, and he might not wake up. He marked a subtle change in the sounds and voices that penetrated from the outer chamber, as the medical team switched over to evacuation-mode. In time, a tech came and took Bel away on a float pallet. In a little more time, the pallet was returned, and Clogston himself and another medtech shifted the Imperial Auditor and all his growing array of life-support trappings aboard.

One of the intelligence officers reported to Miles, during a brief delay in the outer chamber.

"We finally found the remains of Lieutenant Solian, my Lord Auditor. What there was of them. A few kilograms of . . . well. Inside a bod pod, folded up and put back in its wall locker in the corridor just outside the cargo hold where the replicators were."

"Right. Thank you. Bring it along. As is. For evidence, and for . . . the man died doing his job. Barrayar owes him . . . debt of honor. Military burial. Pension, family . . . figure it all out later . . ."

His pallet rose again, and the corridor ceilings of the *Idris* flowed past his blurred gaze for the last time.

CHAPTER EIGHTEEN

"Are we there yet?" Miles mumbled muzzily.

He blinked open eyes that were not, oddly enough, gluey and sore. The ceiling above him didn't waver and bend in his vision as though seen mirage-like through rising desert heat. Breath drawn through his flaring nostrils flowed in coolly and without clogging impediment. No phlegm. No tubes. No tubes?

The ceiling was unfamiliar. He groped for memory. Fog. Biotainered angels and devils, tormenting him; someone demanding he piss. Medical indignities, mercifully vague now. Trying to talk, to give orders, till some hypospray of darkness had shut him down.

And before that: near desperation. Sending frantic messages racing ahead of his little convoy. The return stream of days-old accounts of wormholes blockaded, outlanders interned by both sides, assets seized, ships massing, telling its own tale to Miles's mind, worse for the details. He knew too damned much about the details. *We can't have a war now, you fools! Don't you know there are children almost present?* His left arm jerked, encountering no resistance except for a smooth coverlet beneath his clutching fingers. " . . . there yet?"

Ekaterin's lovely face bent over him from the side. Not half-hidden behind biotainer gear. He feared for a moment that this was only a holovid projection, or some hallucination, but the real warm kiss of breath from her mouth, carried on a puff of laughter, reassured him of her present solidity even before his hesitant hand touched her cheek.

"Where's your mask?" he asked thickly. He heaved up on one elbow, fighting off a wave of dizziness.

He certainly wasn't in the Barrayaran military ship's crowded, utilitarian sickbay to which he'd been transferred from the *Idris*. His bed was in a small but elegantly appointed chamber that screamed of Cetagandan aesthetics, from the arrays of live plants through the serene lighting to the view out the window of a soothing seashore. Waves creamed gently up a pale sandy beach seen through strange trees casting delicate fingers of shade. Almost certainly a vid projection, since the subliminals of the atmosphere and sounds of the room also murmured *spaceship cabin* to him. He wore a loose, silky garment in subdued gray hues, only its odd accessibilities betraying it as a patient gown. Above the head of his bed, a discreet panel displayed medical readouts.

"Where *are* we? What's happening? Did we stop the war? Those replicators they found on their end—it's a trick, I know it—"

The final disaster—his speeding ships intercepting tight-beamed news from Barrayar of diplomatic talks broken off upon the discovery, in a warehouse outside Vorbarr Sultana, of a thousand empty replicators apparently stolen from the Star Crèche, their occupants gone. Supposed occupants? Even Miles hadn't been sure. A baffling nightmare of implications. The Barrayaran government had of course hotly denied any knowledge of how they came to be there, or where their contents were now. And was not believed . . .

"The ba—Guppy, I promised—all those haut babies—I've got to—"

"*You* have got to lie still." A firm hand to his chest pushed him back down. "All the most urgent matters have been taken care of."

"Who by?"

She colored faintly. "Well . . . me, mostly. Vorpatril's ship captain probably shouldn't have let me override him, technically, but I decided not to point that out to him. You're a bad influence on me, love."

What? What? "How?"

"I just kept repeating your messages, and demanding they be put through to the haut Pel and ghem-General Benin. Benin was brilliant. Once he had your first dispatches, he figured out that the replicators found in Vorbarr Sultana were decoys, smuggled out of the Star Crèche by the ba a few at a time over a year ago in preparation for this." She frowned. "It was apparently a deliberate sleight of hand by the ba, meant to cause just this sort of trouble. A backup plan, in case anyone figured out that not everyone had died on the child-ship, and traced the trail as far as Komarr. It almost worked. Might have worked, if Benin hadn't been so painstaking and levelheaded. I gather that the internal political circumstances of his investigation were extremely difficult by then. He really put his reputation on the line."

Possibly even his life, if Miles read between these simple lines. "All honor unto him, then."

"The military forces—theirs and ours—have all gone off alert and are standing down, now. The Cetagandans have declared it an internal, civil matter."

He eased back, vastly relieved. "Ah."

"I don't think I could have gotten through to them without the haut Pel's name." She hesitated. "And yours."

"Ours."

Her lips curved up at that. "*Lady Vorkosigan* did seem a title to conjure with. It gave both sides pause. That, and yelling the truth over and over. But I couldn't have held it together without the name."

"May I suggest that the name couldn't have held it together without you?" His free hand tightened around hers, on the coverlet. Hers tightened back.

He started up again. "Wait—shouldn't you be in biotainer gear?"

"Not any more. Lie *down*, drat it. What's the last thing you remember?"

"My last *clear* memory is of being on the Barrayaran ship about four days out from Quaddiespace. Cold."

Her smile didn't change, but her eyes grew dark with memory. "Cold is right. The blood filters fell behind, even with four of them running at once. We could see the life just *draining* out of you; your metabolism couldn't keep up, couldn't replace the resources being siphoned off even with the IVs and nutrient tubes running flat out, and multiple blood transfusions. Captain Clogston couldn't think of any other way to suppress the parasites but to put you, Bel, *and* them into stasis. A cold hibernation. The next step would have been cryofreeze."

"Oh, no. Not again . . . !"

"It was the ultimate fallback, but it wasn't needed, thank heavens. Once you and Bel were sedated and chilled enough, the parasites stopped multiplying. The captains and crews of our little convoy were very good about rushing us along as fast as was safe, or a little faster. Oh—yes, we're here; we arrived in orbit around Rho Ceta . . . yesterday, I guess it was."

Had she slept since then? Not much, Miles suspected. Her face, though cheerful now, was drawn with fatigue. He reached for it again, to lightly touch her lips with two fingers as he habitually did her holovid image.

"I remember that you wouldn't let me say good-bye to you properly," he complained.

"I figured it would give you more motivation to fight your way back to me. If only for the last word."

He snorted a laugh, and let his hand fall back to the coverlet. The artificial gravity probably wasn't turned up to two gees in this chamber, despite his arm feeling as though it were hung with lead weights. He had to admit, he didn't feel exactly . . . chipper. "What, then, am I all clear of those hell-parasites?"

Her smile returned. "All better. Well, that is, that frightening Cetagandan lady doctor the haut Pel brought with her has pronounced you cured. But you're still very debilitated. You're supposed to rest."

"Rest, I can't rest! What else is happening? Where's Bel?"

"Sh, sh. Bel's alive too. You can see Bel soon, and Nicol too. They're in a cabin just down the corridor. Bel took . . ." She frowned hesitantly. "Took more damage from this than you did, but is expected to recover, mostly. In time."

Miles didn't quite like the sound of that.

Ekaterin followed his glance around. "Right now we're aboard the haut Pel's own ship—that is, her Star Crèche ship, that she brought from Eta Ceta. The women from the Star Crèche had you and Bel carried across to treat you here. The haut ladies wouldn't let any of our men aboard to guard you, not even Armsman Roic at first, which caused the most stupid argument; I was ready to slap everybody concerned, till they finally decided that Nicol and I could come with you.

Captain Clogston was very upset that he wouldn't be allowed to attend. He wanted to hold back giving them the replicators till they cooperated, but you can bet I put my foot down on *that* idea."

"Good!" And not just because Miles had wanted those little time bombs off Barrayaran hands at the earliest possible instant. He could not imagine a more psychologically repugnant or diplomatically disastrous ploy, at this late hour. "I remember trying to calm down that idiot Guppy, who was hysterical about being carried back to the Cetagandans. Making promises . . . I hope I wasn't lying through my chattering teeth. Was it true he was still harboring a reservoir of parasites? Did they fix him, too? Or . . . not? I swore on my name that if he'd cooperate in testifying, Barrayar would protect him, but I expected to be conscious when we arrived. . . ."

"Yes, the Cetagandan doctor treated him, too. She claims the latent residue of parasites wouldn't have fired up again, but really, I don't think she was sure. Apparently, no one has ever survived this bioweapon before. I gathered the impression that the Star Crèche wants Guppy for research purposes even more than Cetagandan Imperial Security does for criminal charges, and if they have to arm wrestle for him, the Star Crèche will win. Our men did carry out your order; he's still being held on the Barrayaran ship. Some of the Cetagandans aren't too pleased about that, but I told them they'd have to deal with you on the subject."

He hesitated, and cleared his throat. "Um . . . I also seem to remember recording some messages. To my parents. And Mark and Ivan. And to little Aral and Helen. I hope you didn't . . . you didn't send them off already, did you?"

"I set them aside."

"Oh, good. I'm afraid I wasn't very coherent by then."

"Perhaps not," she admitted. "But they were very moving, I thought."

"I put it off too long, I guess. You can erase them now."

"Never," she said, quite firmly.

"But I was babbling."

"Nevertheless, I'm going to save them." She stroked his hair, and her smile twisted. "Perhaps they can be recycled someday. After all . . . next time, you might not have time."

The door to the chamber slid aside, and two tall, willowy women entered. Miles recognized the senior of them at once.

The haut Pel Navarr, Consort of Eta Ceta, was perhaps the number-two woman in the strange secret hierarchy of the Star Crèche, after the Empress, haut Rian Degtiar herself. In appearance, she was unchanged from when Miles had first met her a decade ago, except perhaps for her hairstyle. Her immensely long, honey-blond hair was gathered today into a dozen braids, hanging from a level running around the back of her head from one ear to the other, their decorated ends swinging around her ankles along with her skirt hem and draperies. Miles wondered if the unsettling, faintly Medusa-like effect was intended. Her skin was still pale and perfect, but she could not, even for an instant, be mistaken for young. Too much calm, too much control, too much cool irony . . .

Outside the innermost sanctuaries of the Celestial Garden, the high haut women normally moved in the privacy and protection of personal force bubbles, screened from unworthy eyes. The fact that she strode here unveiled was alone enough to tell Miles that he now lay in a Star Crèche reserve. The dark-haired woman beside her was old enough to have streaks of silver in the hair looping down her back among her long robes, and skin that, while unblemished, was distinctly softened with age. Chill, deferential, unknown to Miles.

"Lord Vorkosigan." The haut Pel gave him a relatively cordial nod. "I am pleased to find you awake. Are you quite yourself again?"

Why, who was I before? He was afraid he could guess. "I think so."

"It was quite a surprise to me that we should meet again this way, although not, under the circumstances, an unwelcome one."

Miles cleared his throat. "It was all a surprise to me, too. Your babies in their replicators—you have them back? Are they all right?"

"My people completed their examinations last night. All seems to be well with them, despite their horrific adventures. I'm sorry that the same was not so for you."

She gave a nod to her companion; the woman proved to be a physician, who, with a few brusque murmurs, completed a brief medical examination of their Barrayaran guest. Signing off her work, Miles guessed. His leading questions about the bioengineered parasites met polite evasion, and then Miles wondered if she were physician—or ordnance designer. Or veterinarian, except that most veterinarians he'd met showed signs of actually liking their patients.

Ekaterin was more determined. "Can you give me any idea of what long-term side-effects we should watch for from this unfortunate exposure, for the Lord Auditor and Portmaster Thorne?"

The woman motioned for Miles to refasten his garment, and turned to speak over his head. "Your *husband*," she made the term sound utterly alien, in her mouth, "does suffer some muscular and circulatory micro-scarring. Muscle tone should recover gradually over time to near his prior levels. However, added to his earlier cryo-trauma, I would expect greater chance of circulatory mishaps later in his life. Although as short-lived as you people are, perhaps the few decades difference in life expectancy will not seem significant."

Quite the reverse, madam. Strokes, thromboses, blood clots, aneurysms, Miles supposed was what this translated to. Oh, joy. Just add them to the list, along with needler guns, sonic grenades, plasma fire, and nerve disruptor beams. And hot rivets and hard vacuum.

And seizures. So, what interesting synergies might be expected when this circulatory micro-scarring crossed paths with his seizure disorder? Miles decided to save that question for his own physicians, later. They could use a challenge. He was going to be a damned research project, again. Military as well as medical, he realized with a chill.

The haut woman continued to Ekaterin, "The Betan suffered notably more internal damage. Full recovery of muscle tone may never occur, and the herm will need to be on guard against circulatory stress of all kinds. A low- or zero-gravity environment might be the safest for it during its convalescence. I gathered from its partner, the quaddie female, that this may actually be easy to provide."

"Whatever Bel needs will be arranged," Miles vowed. For such a debilitating injury in the Emperor's service, it shouldn't even take an Imperial Auditor to get ImpSec off Bel's neck, and maybe rustle up a little medical pension in the bargain.

The haut Pel gave a tiny jerk of her chin. The physician favored the planetary consort with an obeisant bow, and excused herself.

Pel turned back to Miles. "As soon as you feel sufficiently recovered, Lord Auditor Vorkosigan, ghem-General Benin begs the opportunity to speak with you."

"Ah! Dag Benin's here? Good! I want to talk to him, too. Does he have the ba in his custody yet? Has it been made crystal clear that Barrayar was an innocent dupe in your ba's illicit travels?"

Pel replied, "The ba was of the Star Crèche; the ba has been returned to the Star Crèche. It is an internal matter, although we are, of course, grateful to ghem-General Benin for his assistance dealing with any persons outside our purview who may have aided the ba in its . . . mad flight."

So, the haut ladies had their stray back. Miles suppressed a slight twinge of pity for the ba. Pel's quelling tone of voice did not invite further questions from outlander barbarians. Tough. Pel was the most venturesome of the planetary consorts, but his likelihood of ever getting her alone, face-to-face, after this moment was slight, and her likelihood of discussing the matter frankly in front of anyone else even slighter.

He forged on. "I finally deduced the ba must be a renegade, and not, as I'd first thought, an agent of the Star Crèche. I'm most curious about the mechanics of this bizarre kidnapping. Guppy—the Jacksonian smuggler, Russo Gupta—could only give me an exterior view of events, and that only from his first point of contact, when the ba off-loaded the replicators from what I assume was the annual child-ship to Rho Ceta, yes?"

Pel inhaled, but conceded stiffly, "Yes. The crime was long planned and prepared, it now appears. The ba slew the Consort of Rho Ceta, her handmaidens, and the crew of the ship by poison just after their last jump. They were all dead by the time of the rendezvous. It set the ship's auto-navigation to take the vessel into the sun of the system thereafter. To the ba's credit, this was intended as a befitting pyre, of sorts," she conceded grudgingly.

Given his prior exposure to the arcana of haut funeral practices, Miles could almost follow this evident point in the prisoner's favor without his brain cramping. Almost. But Pel spoke of the ba's intention as fact, not conjecture; therefore, the haut ladies had already had more luck in their interrogation of the deranged ba in one night than Miles's security people had gained on their whole voyage here. *Luck, I suspect, has nothing to do with it.* "I thought the ba should have been carrying a greater variety of bioweapons, if it had any time to loot the child-ship before the vessel was abandoned and destroyed."

Pel was normally rather sunny, as haut planetary consorts went, but this elicited a freezing frown. "*These* matters are *altogether* not for discussion outside the Star Crèche."

"Ideally, no. But unfortunately, your . . . private items managed to travel quite a way outside the Star Crèche indeed. As I can personally testify. They became a source of very public concern for us, when apprehending the ba on Graf Station. At the time I left there, no one was certain if we'd identified and neutralized every contagion, or not. "

Reluctantly, Pel admitted, "The ba had planned to steal the complete array. But the haut lady in charge of the consort's . . . supplies, although dying, managed to destroy them before her death. As was her duty." Pel's eyes narrowed. "*She* will be remembered among us."

The dark-haired woman's opposite number, perhaps? Did the chilly physician guard a similar arsenal on Pel's behalf, perhaps aboard this very ship? *Complete array*, eh. Miles filed that tacit admission silently away, for later sharing with ImpSec's highest echelons, and swiftly redirected the conversation.

"But what was the ba actually trying to do? Was it acting alone? If it was, how did it defeat its loyalty programming?"

"That is an internal matter, too," she repeated darkly.

"Well, I'll tell you *my* guesses," Miles burbled on, before she could turn away and end the exchange. "I believe this ba to be very closely related to Emperor Fletchir Giaja, and therefore, to his late mother. I'm guessing this ba was one of the old Dowager Empress Lisbet's close confidants during her reign. Her bio-treason, her plan to split the haut into competing subgroups, was defeated after her death—"

"Not *treason*," haut Pel objected faintly. "As such."

"Unsanctioned unilateral redesign, then. For some reason, this ba was not purged with the others of her inner cadre after her death—or maybe it was, I don't know. Demoted, perhaps? But anyway, I'm guessing this whole escapade was some sort of misguided effort to complete its dead mistress's—or mother's—vision. Am I close?"

The haut Pel eyed him with extreme distaste. "Close enough. It is truly done now, in any case. The emperor will be pleased with you—again. Some token of his gratitude may well be forthcoming at the child-ship landing ceremonies tomorrow, to which you and your lady-wife are invited. The first outlanders—ever—to be so honored."

Miles waved aside this little distraction. "I'd trade all the honors for some scrap of understanding."

Pel snorted. "You *haven't* changed, have you? Still insatiably curious. To a fault," she added pointedly.

Ekaterin smiled dryly.

Miles ignored Pel's hint. "Bear with me. I don't think I've quite got it, yet. I suspect the haut—and the ba—are not so post-human yet as to be beyond self-deception, all the more subtle for their subtlety.

I saw the ba's face, when I destroyed that freezer case of genetic samples in front of it. Something shattered. Some last, desperate . . . something." He had slain men's bodies, and bore the mark, and knew it. He did not think he'd ever before slain a soul, yet left the body breathing, bereft and accusing. *I have to understand this.*

Pel was clearly not pleased to go on, but she understood the depth of a debt that could not be paid off with such trivialities as medals and ceremonies. "The ba, it seems," she said slowly, "desired more than Lisbet's vision. It planned a new empire—with itself as both emperor *and* empress. It stole the haut children of Rho Ceta not just as a core population for its planned new society, but as . . . mates. Consorts. Aspiring to even more than Fletchir Giaja's genetic place, which, while part of the goal of haut, does not imagine itself the whole. Hubris," she sighed. "Madness."

"In other words," breathed Miles, "the ba wanted children. In the only way it could . . . conceive."

Ekaterin's hand, which had drifted to his shoulder, tightened.

"Lisbet . . . should not have told it so much," said Pel. "She made a pet of this ba. Treated it almost as a *child*, instead of a servitor. Hers was a powerful personality, but not always . . . wise. Perhaps . . . self-indulgent in her old age, as well."

Yes—the ba was Fletchir Giaja's sibling, perhaps the Cetagandan emperor's near-clone. Elder sibling. Test run, and the test judged successful—and decades of observant service in the Celestial Garden thereafter, with the question always hovering—so why was not the ba, instead of its brother, given all that honor, power, wealth, fertility?

"One last question. If you will. What was the ba's name?"

Pel's lips tightened. "It shall be nameless now. And forevermore."

Erased. *Let the punishment fit the crime.*

Miles shivered.

The luxurious lift van banked over the palace of the Imperial Governor of Rho Ceta, the sprawling complex shimmering in the night. The vehicle began to drop into the vast dark garden, laced with veins of lights along its roads and paths, which lay to the east of the buildings. Miles stared in fascination out his window as they swooped down, then up over a small range of hills, trying to guess if the landscape was natural, or artificially carved out of Rho Ceta's surface. Partly carved, at any rate, for on the opposite side of the rise a grassy bowl of an amphitheater sheltered in the slope, overlooking a silky black lake a kilometer across. Beyond the hills on the lake's other side, Rho Ceta's capital city made the night sky glow amber.

The amphitheater was lit only by dim, glowing globes lavishly spread across its width: a thousand haut lady force bubbles, set to mourning white, damped to the barest visible luminosity. Among them, other pale figures moved softly as ghosts. The view turned from his sight as the driver of the van swung it about and brought it down to a gentle landing a few meters inward from the lake shore at one edge of the amphitheater.

The van's internal lighting brightened just a little, in red wavelengths designed to help maintain the passengers' dark adaptation. In the aisle across from Miles and Ekaterin, ghem-General Benin turned from his window. It was hard to read his expression beneath the formalized swirls of black-and-white face paint that marked him as an Imperial ghem-officer, but Miles took it for pensive. In the red light, his uniform glowed like fresh blood.

All in all, and even taking into account his sudden close personal introduction to Star Crèche bioweapons, Miles wasn't sure if he'd have cared to trade recent nightmares with Benin. The past weeks had been exhausting for the senior officer of the Celestial Garden's internal security. The child-ship, carrying Star Crèche personnel who were his special charge, vanishing en route without a trace; garbled reports leaking back from Guppy's scrambled trail hinting not only at breathtaking theft, but possible biocontamination from the Crèche's most secret stores; the disappearance of that trail into the heart of an enemy empire.

No wonder that by the time he had arrived in Rho Cetan orbit last night to interrogate Miles in person—with exquisite courtesy, to be sure—he'd looked as tired, even under the face paint, as Miles felt. Their contest for the possession of Russo Gupta had been brief. Miles certainly sympathized with Benin's strong desire, with the ba plucked from his hands by the Star Crèche, for *someone* to take his frustrations out on—but, first, Miles had given his Vor word, and secondly, he discovered, he could apparently do no wrong on Rho Ceta this week.

Nevertheless, Miles wondered where to drop Guppy when this was all over. Housing him in a Barrayaran jail was a useless expense to the Imperium. Turning him loose back on Jackson's Whole was an invitation for him to return to his old haunts, and employment—no benefit to the neighbors, and a temptation to Cetagandan vengeance. He could think of one other nicely distant place to deposit a person of such speckled background and erratic talents, but was it fair to do that to Admiral Quinn . . . ? Bel had laughed, evilly, at the suggestion, till it had to stop to breathe.

Despite Rho Ceta's key place in Barrayaran strategic and tactical considerations, Miles had never set foot on the world before. He didn't now, either, at least not right away. Grimacing, he allowed Ekaterin and ghem-General Benin to help him from the van into a floater. In the ceremony to come, he planned to stand on his feet, but a very little experimentation had taught him that he had better conserve his endurance. At least he wasn't alone in his need for mechanical aid. Nicol hovered, shepherding Bel Thorne. The herm sat up and managed its own floater controls, only the oxygen tube to its nose betraying its extreme debilitation.

Armsman Roic, his Vorkosigan House uniform pressed and polished, took up station behind Miles and Ekaterin, at his very stiffest and most silent. Spooked half to death, Miles gauged. Miles couldn't blame him.

Deciding he represented the whole of the Barrayaran Empire tonight, and not just his own House, Miles had elected to wear his plain civilian gray. Ekaterin seemed tall and graceful as a haut in some flowing thing of gray and black; Miles suspected under-the-table female sartorial help from Pel, or one of Pel's many minions. As ghem-General Benin led the party forward, Ekaterin paced beside Miles's floater, her hand resting lightly upon his arm. Her faint, mysterious smile was as reserved as ever, but it seemed to Miles as though she walked with a new and firm confidence, unafraid in the shadowed dark.

Benin stopped at a small group of men, glimmering up out of the murk like specters, who were gathered a few meters from the lift van. Complex perfumes drifted from their clothing through the damp air, distinct, yet somehow not clashing. The ghem-general meticulously introduced each member of the party to the current haut governor of Rho Ceta, who was of the Degtiar constellation, cousin in some kind to the present Empress. The governor, too, was dressed, as were all the haut men present, in the loose white tunic and trousers of full mourning, with a multilayered white over-robe that swept to his ankles.

The former occupant of this post, whom Miles had once met, had made it plain that outlander barbarians were barely to be tolerated, but this man swept a low and apparently sincere bow, his hands pressed formally together in front of his chest. Miles blinked, startled, for the gesture more resembled the bow of a ba to a haut than the nod of a haut to an outlander.

"Lord Vorkosigan. Lady Vorkosigan. Portmaster Thorne. Nicol of the Quaddies. Armsman Roic of Barrayar. Welcome to Rho Ceta. My household is at your service."

They all returned suitably civil murmurs of thanks. Miles considered the wording—*my household*, not *my government*, and was reminded that what he was seeing tonight was a *private* ceremony. The haut governor was momentarily distracted by the lights on the horizon of a shuttle dropping from orbit, his lips parting as he peered up into the glowing night sky, but the craft banked disappointingly away toward the opposite side of the city. The governor turned back, frowning.

A few minutes of polite small talk between the haut governor and Benin—formal wishes for the continued health of the Cetagandan emperor and his empresses, and somewhat more spontaneous-sounding inquiries after mutual acquaintances—was broken off again as another shuttle's lights appeared in the wide predawn dark. The governor swung around to stare again. Miles glanced back over the silent crowd of haut men and haut lady bubbles scattered like white flower petals across the bowl of the hillside. They emitted no cries, they scarcely seemed to move, but Miles felt rather than heard a sigh ripple across their ranks, and the tension of their anticipation tighten.

This time, the shuttle grew larger, its lights

brightening as it boomed down across the lake, which foamed in its path. Roic stepped back nervously, then forward again nearer to Miles and Ekaterin, watching the bulk of it loom almost above them. Lights on its sides picked out upon the fuselage a screaming-bird pattern, enameled red, that glowed like flame. The craft landed on its extended feet as softly as a cat, and settled, the chinks and clinks of its heated sides contracting sounding loud in the breathless, waiting stillness.

"Time to stand up," Miles whispered to Ekaterin, and grounded his floater. She and Roic helped hoist him out of it to his feet, and step forward to stand at attention. The close-cut grass, beneath his booted soles, felt like thick fine carpeting; its scent was damp and mossy.

A wide cargo hatch opened, and a ramp extended itself, illuminated from beneath in a pale, diffuse glow. First down it drifted a haut lady bubble—its force field not opaque, as the others, but transparent as gauze. Within, its float chair could be seen to be empty.

Miles murmured to Ekaterin, "Where's Pel? Thought this was all her . . . baby."

"It's for the Consort of Rho Ceta who was lost with the hijacked ship," she whispered back. "The haut Pel will be next, as she conducts the children in the dead consort's place."

Miles had met the murdered woman, briefly, a decade ago. To his regret, he could remember little more of her now than a cloud of chocolate-brown hair that had tumbled down about her, stunning beauty camouflaged in an array of other haut women of equal splendor, and a ferocious commitment to her duties. But the float chair seemed suddenly even emptier.

Another bubble followed, and yet more, and ghem-women and ba servitors. The second bubble drew up beside the haut governor's group, grew transparent, and then winked out. Pel in her white robes sat regally in her float chair.

"Ghem-General Benin, as you are charged, please convey now the thanks of Emperor the haut Fletchir Giaja to these outlanders who have brought our Constellations' hopes home to us."

She spoke in a normal tone, and Miles didn't see the voice pickups, but a faint echo back from the grassy bowl told him their words were being conveyed to all assembled here.

Benin called Bel forward; with formal words of ceremony, he presented a high Cetagandan honor to the Betan, a paper bound in ribbon, written in the Emperor's Own Hand, with the odd name of the Warrant of the Celestial House. Miles knew Cetagandan ghem-lords who would have traded their own mothers to be enrolled on the year's Warrant List, except that it wasn't nearly that easy to qualify. Bel dipped its floater for Benin to press the beribboned roll into its hands, and though its eyes were bright with irony, murmured thanks to the distant Fletchir Giaja in return, and kept its sense of humor, for once, under full control. It probably helped that the herm was still so exhausted it could barely hold its head upright, a circumstance for which Miles had not expected to be grateful.

Miles blinked, and suppressed a huge grin, when Ekaterin was next called forward by ghem-General Benin and bestowed with a like beribboned honor. Her obvious pleasure was not without its edge of irony either, but she returned an elegantly worded thank you.

"My Lord Vorkosigan," Benin spoke.

Miles stepped forward a trifle apprehensively.

"My Imperial Master, the Emperor the haut Fletchir Giaja, reminds me that true delicacy in the giving of gifts considers the tastes of the recipient. He therefore charges me only to convey to you his personal thanks, in his own Breath and Voice."

First prize, the Cetagandan Order of Merit, and what an embarrassment *that* medal had been, a decade ago. Second prize, *two* Cetagandan Orders of Merit? Evidently not. Miles breathed a sigh of relief, only slightly tinged with regret. "Tell your Imperial Master from me that he is entirely welcome."

"My Imperial Mistress, the Empress the haut Rian Degtiar, Handmaiden of the Star Crèche, also charged me to convey to you her own thanks, in her own Breath and Voice."

Miles bowed perceptibly lower. "I am at *her* service in this."

Benin stepped back; the haut Pel moved forward. "Indeed. Lord Miles Naismith Vorkosigan of Barrayar, the Star Crèche calls you up."

He'd been warned about this, and talked it over with Ekaterin. As a practical matter, there was no point in refusing the honor; the Star Crèche had to have about a kilo of his flesh on private file already, collected not only during his treatment here, but from his memorable visit to Eta Ceta all those years back. So with only a slight tightening of his stomach, he stepped forward, and permitted a ba servitor to roll back his sleeve and present the tray with the gleaming sampling needle to the haut Pel.

Pel's own white, long-fingered hand drove the sampling needle into the fleshy part of his forearm. It was so fine, its bite scarcely pained him; when she withdrew it, barely a drop of blood formed on his skin, to be wiped away by the servitor. She laid the needle into its own freezer case, held it high for a moment of public display and declaration, closed it, and set it away in a compartment in the arm of her float chair. The faint murmur from the throng in the amphitheater did not seem to be outrage, though there was, perhaps, a tinge of amazement. The highest honor any Cetagandan could achieve, higher even than the bestowal of a haut bride, was to have his or her genome formally taken up into the Star Crèche's banks—for disassembly, close examination, and possible selective insertion of the approved bits into the haut race's next generation.

Miles, rolling his sleeve back down, muttered to Pel, "It's prob'ly nurture, not nature, y'know."

Her exquisite lips resisted an upward crook to form the silent syllable, *Sh*.

The spark of dark humor in her eye was veiled again as if seen through the morning mist as she reactivated her force shield. The sky to the east, across the lake and beyond the next range of hills, was turning pale. Coils of fog curled across the waters of the lake, its smooth surface growing steel gray in reflection of the predawn luminescence.

A deeper hush fell across the gathering of haut as through the shuttle's door and down its ramp floated array after array of replicator racks, guided by the ghem-women and ba servitors. Constellation by constellation, the haut were called forth by the acting consort, Pel, to receive their replicators. The Governor of Rho Ceta left the little group of visiting dignitaries/heroes to join with his clan, as well, and Miles realized that his humble bow, earlier, had not been any kind of irony after all. The white-clad crowd assembled were not the whole of the haut race residing on Rho Ceta, just the fraction whose genetic crosses, arranged by their clan heads, bore fruit this day, this year.

The men and women whose children were here delivered might never have touched or even seen each other till this dawn, but each group of men accepted from the Star Crèche's hands the children of their getting. They floated the racks in turn to the waiting array of white bubbles carrying their genetic partners. As each constellation rearranged itself around its replicator racks, the force screens turned from dull mourning white to brilliant colors, a riotous rainbow. The rainbow bubbles streamed away out of the amphitheater, escorted by their male companions, as the hilly horizon across the lake silhouetted itself against the dawn fire, and above, the stars faded in the blue.

When the haut reached their home enclaves, scattered around the planet, the infants would be given up again into the hands of their ghem nurses and attendants for release from their replicators. Into the nurturing crèches of their various constellations. Parent and child might or might not ever meet again. Yet there seemed more to this ceremony than just haut protocol. *Are we not all called on to yield our children back to the world, in the end?* The Vor did, in their ideals at least. *Barrayar eats its children*, his mother had once said, according to his father. Looking at Miles.

So, Miles thought wearily. *Are we heroes here today, or the greatest traitors unhung?* What would these tiny, high haut hopefuls grow into, in time? Great men and women? Terrible foes? Had he, all unknowing, saved here some future nemesis of Barrayar—enemy and destroyer of his own children still unborn?

And if such a dire precognition or prophecy had been granted to him by some cruel god, could he have acted any differently?

He sought Ekaterin's hand with his own cold one; her fingers wrapped his with warmth. There was enough light for her to see his face, now. "Are you all right, love?" she murmured in concern.

"I don't know. Let's go home."

EPILOGUE

They said good-bye to Bel and Nicol at Komarr orbit.

Miles had ridden along to the ImpSec Galactic Affairs transfer station offices here for Bel's final debriefing, partly to add his own observations, partly to see that the ImpSec boys did not fatigue the herm unduly. Ekaterin attended too, both to testify and to make sure Miles didn't fatigue himself. Miles was hauled away before Bel was.

"Are you sure you two don't want to come along to Vorkosigan House?" Miles asked anxiously, for the fourth or fifth time, as they gathered for a final farewell on an upper concourse. "You missed the wedding, after all. We could show you a very good time. My cook alone is worth the trip, I promise you." Miles, Bel, and of course Nicol hovered in floaters. Ekaterin stood with her arms crossed, smiling slightly. Roic wandered an invisible perimeter as if loath to give over his duties to the unobtrusive ImpSec guards. The armsman had been on continuous alert for so long, Miles thought, he'd forgotten how to take a shift off. Miles understood the feeling. Roic was due at least two weeks of uninterrupted home leave when they returned to Barrayar, Miles decided.

Nicol's brows twitched up. "I'm afraid we might disturb your neighbors."

"Stampede the horses, yeah," said Bel.

Miles bowed, sitting; his floater bobbed slightly. "My horse would like you fine. He's extremely amiable, not to mention much too old and lazy to stampede anywhere. And I personally guarantee that with a Vorkosigan liveried armsman at your back, not the most benighted backcountry hick would offer you insult."

Roic, passing nearby in his orbit, added a confirming nod.

Nicol smiled. "Thanks all the same, but I think I'd rather go someplace where I don't *need* a bodyguard."

Miles drummed his fingers on the edge of his floater. "We're working on it. But look, really, if you—"

"Nicol is tired," said Ekaterin, "probably homesick, and she has a convalescing herm to look after. I expect she'll be glad to get back to her own sleepsack and her own routine. Not to mention her own music."

The two exchanged one of those League of Women looks, and Nicol nodded gratefully.

"Well," said Miles, yielding with reluctance. "Take care of each other, then."

"You, too," said Bel gruffly. "I think it's time you gave up those hands-on ops games, hey? Now that you're going to be a daddy and all. Between this time and the last time, Fate has got to have your range bracketed. Bad idea to give it a third shot, I think."

Miles glanced involuntarily at his palms, fully healed by now. "Maybe so. God knows Gregor probably has a list of domestic chores waiting for me as long as a quaddie's arms all added together. The last one was wall-to-wall committees, coming up with, if you can believe it, new Barrayaran bio-law for the Council of Counts to approve. It took a year. If he starts another one with, 'You're half Betan, Miles, you'd be just the man'— I think I'll turn and run."

Bel laughed; Miles added, "Keep an eye on young Corbeau for me, eh? When I toss a protégé in to sink or swim like that, I usually prefer to be closer to hand with a life preserver."

"Garnet Five messaged me, after I sent to tell her Bel was going to live," said Nicol. "She says they're doing all right so far. At any rate, Quaddiespace hasn't declared all Barrayaran ships *non grata* forever or anything yet."

"That means there's no reason you two couldn't come back someday," Bel pointed out. "Or at any rate, stay in touch. We are both free to communicate openly now, I might observe."

Miles brightened. "If discreetly. Yes. That's true."

They exchanged some un-Barrayaran hugs all around; Miles didn't care what his ImpSec lookouts thought. He floated, holding Ekaterin's hand, to watch the pair progress out of sight toward the commercial ship docks. But even before they'd rounded the corner he felt his face pulled around, as if by a magnetic force, in the opposite direction—toward the military arm of the station, where the *Kestrel* awaited their pleasure.

Time ticked in his head. "Let's go."

"Oh, yes," said Ekaterin.

He had to speed his floater to keep up with her lengthening stride up the concourse.

Gregor waited to greet Lord Auditor and Lady Vorkosigan upon their return, at a special reception at the Imperial Residence. Miles trusted whatever reward the Emperor had in mind would be less disturbingly arcane than that of the haut ladies. But Gregor's party was going to have to be put off a day or two. The word from their obstetrician back at Vorkosigan House was that the children's sojourn in their replicators was stretched to nearly its maximum safe extension. There had been enough oblique medical disapproval in the tone of the message, it didn't even need Ekaterin's nervous jokes about ten-month twins and how glad she was now for replicators to get him aimed in the right direction, and no more damned interruptions.

He'd undergone these homecomings what seemed a thousand times, yet this one felt different than any before. The groundcar from the military shuttleport, Armsman Pym driving, pulled up under the porte-cochère of Vorkosigan House, looming stone pile that it ever was. Ekaterin bustled out first and gazed longingly toward the door, but paused to wait for Miles.

When they'd left Komarr orbit five days ago he'd traded in the despised floater for a slightly less despised cane, and spent the journey hobbling incessantly up and down what limited corridors the *Kestrel* provided. His strength was returning, he fancied, if more slowly than he'd hoped. Maybe he would look into getting a swordstick like Commodore Koudelka's for the interim. He pulled himself to his feet, swung the cane in briefly jaunty defiance, and offered Ekaterin his arm. She rested her hand lightly upon it, covertly ready to grab if needed. The double doors swung open on the grand old black-and-white paved entry hall.

The mob was waiting, headed by a tall woman with roan-red hair and a delighted smile. Countess Cordelia Vorkosigan actually hugged her daughter-in-law first. A white-haired, stocky man advanced from

the antechamber to the left, face luminous with pleasure, and stood in line for his chance with Ekaterin
before turning to his son. Nikki clattered down the
sweeping stairway and into his mother's arms, and
returned her tight hug with only a tinge of embarrassment. The boy had grown at least three centime-
ters in the past two months. When he turned to
Miles, and copied the Count's handshake with dauntingly grown-up resolve, Miles found himself looking
up into his stepson's face.

A dozen armsmen and servants stood around grinning; Ma Kosti, the peerless cook, pressed a splendid
bunch of flowers on Ekaterin. The Countess handed
off an awkwardly worded but sincere message of felici-
tation for their impending parenthood from Miles's
brother Mark, at graduate school on Beta Colony, and
a rather more fluent one from his Grandmother
Naismith there. Ekaterin's older brother, Will Vorvayne,
unexpectedly present, took vids of it all.

"Congratulations," Viceroy Count Aral Vorkosigan
was saying to Ekaterin, "on a job well done. Would you
like another? I'm sure Gregor can find you a place in
the diplomatic corps after this, if you want it."

She laughed. "I think I have at least three or four
jobs already. Ask me again in, oh, say about twenty
years." Her glance went to the staircase leading to the
upper floors, and the nursery.

Countess Vorkosigan, who caught the look, said,
"Everything is waiting and ready as soon as you are."

After the briefest of washups in their second-floor
suite, Miles and Ekaterin made their way down a
servitor-crowded hallway to rendezvous with the core
family again in the nursery. With the addition of the
birth team—an obstetrician, two medtechs, and a
bio-mechanic—the small chamber overlooking the
back garden was as full as it could hold. It seemed

as public a birth as those poor monarchs' wives in the old histories had ever endured, except that Ekaterin had the advantage of being upright, dressed, and dignified. All of the cheerful excitement, none of the blood or pain or fear. Miles decided that he approved.

The two replicators, released from their racks, stood side by side on a table, full of promise. A medtech was just finishing fiddling with a cannula on one. "Shall we proceed?" inquired the obstetrician.

Miles glanced at his parents. "How did *you* all do this, back then?"

"Aral lifted one latch," said his mother, "and I lifted the other. Your grandfather, General Piotr, lurked menacingly, but he came around to a wider way of thinking later." His mother and his father exchanged a private smile, and Aral Vorkosigan shook his head wryly.

Miles looked to Ekaterin.

"It sounds good to me," she said. Her eyes were brilliant with joy. It lifted Miles's heart to think that *he* had given her that happiness.

They advanced to the table. Ekaterin went around, and the techs scrambled out of her way; Miles hooked his cane over the edge, supported himself with one hand, and raised the other to match Ekaterin's. A double snap sounded from the latches. They moved down and repeated the gesture with the second replicator.

"Good," Ekaterin whispered.

Then they had to stand out of the way, watching with irrational anxiety as the obstetrician popped the first lid, swept the exchange tube matting aside, slit the caul, and lifted the pink squirming infant out into the light. A few heart-stopping moments clearing air passages, draining and cutting the cord; Miles breathed again when little Aral Alexander did, and blinked his blurring lashes. He felt less self-conscious when he noticed his father wipe his eyes. Countess Vorkosigan gripped her skirts at her sides, forcibly making hungry grandmotherly hands wait their turn. The Count's hand on Nikki's shoulder tightened, and Nikki in his front-and-center viewpoint lifted his chin and grinned. Will Vorvayne bobbed around trying to get better vid angles, until his little sister put on her firmest Lady Ekaterin Vorkosigan voice and quashed his attempts at stage directing. He looked startled, but backed off.

By some tacit assumption, Ekaterin got first dibs. She held her new son and watched as the second replicator yielded up her very first daughter. Miles leaned on his cane at her elbow, his eyes devouring the astonishing sight. A baby. A *real* baby. *His*. He'd thought his children had seemed real enough, when he'd touched the replicators in which they grew. That was nothing like this. Little Aral Alexander was so small. He blinked and stretched. He breathed, actually breathed, and placidly smacked his tiny lips. He had a notable amount of black hair. It was wonderful. It was . . . terrifying.

"Your turn," said Ekaterin, smiling at Miles.

"I . . . I think I'd better sit down, first." He half-fell into an armchair brought hastily forward for him. Ekaterin tucked the blanket-wrapped bundle into his panicked arms. The Countess hovered over the back of the chair like some maternal vulture.

"He seems so small."

"What, four point one kilos!" chortled Miles's mother. "He's a little bruiser, he is. You were half that size when you were taken out of the replicator." She continued with an unflattering description of Miles at that moment that Ekaterin not only ate up, but *encouraged*.

A lusty yowl from the replicator table made Miles

start; he looked up eagerly. Helen Natalia announced her arrival in no uncertain terms, waving freed fists and howling. The obstetrician completed his examination and pressed her rather hastily into her mother's reaching arms. Miles stretched his neck. Helen Natalia's dark, wet wisps of hair were going to be as auburn as promised, he fancied, when they dried.

With two babies to go around, all the people lined up to hold them would have their chances soon enough, Miles decided, accepting Helen Natalia, still making noise, from her grinning mother. They could wait a few more moments. He stared at the two bundles more than filling his lap in a kind of cosmic amazement.

"We *did* it," he muttered to Ekaterin, now perching on the chair arm. "Why didn't anybody stop us? Why aren't there more regulations about this sort of thing? What fool in their right mind would put *me* in charge of a baby? Two babies?"

Her brows drew together in quizzical sympathy. "Don't feel bad. I'm sitting here thinking that eleven years suddenly seems longer than I realized. I don't remember *anything* about babies."

"I'm sure it'll all come back to you. Like, um, like flying a lightflyer."

He had been the end point of human evolution. At this moment he abruptly felt more like a missing link. *I thought I knew everything. Surely I knew nothing.* How had his own life become such a surprise to him, so utterly rearranged? His brain had whirled with a thousand plans for these tiny lives, visions of the future both hopeful and dire, funny and fearful. For a moment, it seemed to come to a full stop. *I have no idea who these two people are going to be.*

Then it was everyone else's turn, Nikki, the Countess, the Count. Miles watched enviously his father's sure grip of the infant on his shoulder. Helen Natalia actually stopped screaming there, reducing the noise level to one of more generalized, desultory complaint.

Ekaterin slipped her hand into his and gripped tightly. It felt like free falling into the future. He squeezed back, and soared.

MILES VORKOSIGAN/NAISMITH:
HIS UNIVERSE AND TIMES

Chronology	Events	Chronicle
Approx. 200 years before Miles's birth	Quaddies are created by genetic engineering.	*Falling Free*
During Beta-Barrayaran War	Cordelia Naismith meets Lord Aral Vorkosigan while on opposite sides of a war. Despite difficulties, they fall in love and are married.	*Shards of Honor*
The Vordarian Pretendership	While Cordelia is pregnant, an attempt to assassinate Aral by poison gas fails, but Cordelia is affected; Miles Vorkosigan is born with bones that will always be brittle and other medical problems. His growth will be stunted.	*Barrayar*
Miles is 17	Miles fails to pass physical test to get into the Service Academy. On a trip, necessities force him to improvise the Free Dendarii Mercenaries into existence; he has unintended but unavoidable adventures for four months. Leaves the Dendarii in Ky Tung's competent hands and takes Elli Quinn to Beta for rebuilding of her damaged face; returns	*The Warrior's Apprentice*

Chronology	Events	Chronicle
	to Barrayar to thwart plot against his father. Emperor pulls strings to get Miles into the Academy.	
Miles is 20	Ensign Miles graduates and immediately has to take on one of the duties of the Barrayaran nobility and act as a detective and judge in a murder case. Shortly afterwards, his first military assignment ends with his arrest. Miles has to rejoin the Dendarii to rescue the young Barrayaran emperor. Emperor accepts Dendarii as his personal secret service force.	"The Mountains of Mourning" in *Borders of Infinity* *The Vor Game*
Miles is 22	Miles and his cousin Ivan attend a Cetagandan state funeral and are caught up in Cetagandan internal politics.	*Cetaganda*
	Miles sends Commander Elli Quinn, who's been given a new face on Beta, on a solo mission to Kline Station.	*Ethan of Athos*
Miles is 23	Now a Barrayaran Lieutenant, Miles goes with the Dendarii to smuggle a scientist out of Jackson's	"Labyrinth" in *Borders of Infinity*

Chronology	Events	Chronicle
	Whole. Miles's fragile leg bones have been replaced by synthetics.	
Miles is 24	Miles plots from within a Cetagandan prison camp on Dagoola IV to free the prisoners. The Dendarii fleet is pursued by the Cetagandans and finally reaches Earth for repairs. Miles has to juggle both his identities at once, raise money for repairs, and defeat a plot to replace him with a double. Ky Tung stays on Earth. Commander Elli Quinn is now Miles's right-hand officer. Miles and the Dendarii depart for Sector IV on a rescue mission.	"The Borders of Infinity" in *Borders of Infinity* *Brothers in Arms*
Miles is 25	Hospitalized after previous mission, Miles's broken arms are replaced by synthetic bones. With Simon Illyan, Miles undoes yet another plot against his father while flat on his back.	*Borders of Infinity*
Miles is 28	Miles meets his clone brother Mark again, this time on Jackson's Whole.	*Mirror Dance*

Chronology	Events	Chronicle
Miles is 29	Miles hits thirty; thirty hits back.	*Memory*
Miles is 30	Emperor Gregor dispatches Miles to Komarr to investigate a space accident, where he finds old politics and new technology make a deadly mix.	*Komarr*
	The Emperor's wedding sparks romance and intrigue on Barrayar, and Miles plunges up to his neck in both.	*A Civil Campaign*
Miles is 32	Miles and Ekaterin's honeymoon journey is interrupted by an Auditorial mission to Quaddiespace, where they encounter old friends, new enemies, and a double handful of intrigue.	*Diplomatic Immunity*
Miles is 39	Miles and Roic go to Kibou-daini.	*Cryoburn*

PRAISE FOR
LOIS McMASTER BUJOLD

What the critics say:

The Warrior's Apprentice: "Now here's a fun romp through the spaceways—not so much a space opera as space ballet... It has all the 'right stuff.' A lot of thought and thoughtfulness stand behind the all-too-human characters. Enjoy this one, and look forward to the next."   —Dean Lambe, *SF Reviews*

"The pace is breathless, the characterization thoughtful and emotionally powerful, and the author's narrative technique and command of language compelling. Highly recommended."   —*Booklist*

Brothers in Arms: "...she gives it a genuine depth of character, while reveling in the wild turnings of her tale... Bujold is as audacious as her favorite hero, and as brilliantly (if sneakily) successful."   —*Locus*

"Miles Vorkosigan is such a great character that I'll read anything Lois wants to write about him... a book to re-read on cold rainy days."   —Robert Coulson, *Comics Buyers Guide*

Borders of Infinity: "Bujold's series hero Miles Vokosigan may be a lord by birth and an admiral by rank, but a bone disease that has left him hobbled and in frequent pain has sensitized him to the suffering of outcasts in her very hierarchical era.... Playing off of Miles's reserve and cleverness, Bujold draws outrageous and outlandish foils to color her high-minded adventures."   —*Publishers Weekly*

Falling Free: "In *Falling Free* Lois McMaster Bujold has written her fourth straight superb novel.... How to break down a talent like Bujold's into analyzable components? Best not to try. Best to say: 'Read, or you will be missing something extraordinary.'"
—Roland Green, *Chicago Sun-Times*

The Vor Game: "The chronicles of Miles Vokosigan are far too witty to be literary junk food, but they rouse the kind of craving that makes popcorn magically vanish during a double feature."   —Faren Miller, *Locus*

MORE PRAISE FOR
LOIS McMASTER BUJOLD

What the readers say:

"My copy of *Shards of Honor* is falling apart I've reread it so often…. I'll read whatever you write. You've certainly proved yourself a grand storyteller.

—Lisa Kolbe, Colorado Springs, CO

"I experience the stories of Miles Vorkosigan as almost viscerally uplifting… But certainly, even the weightiest theme would have less impact than a cinder on snow were it not for a rousing good story, and good story-telling with it. This is the second thing I want to thank you for… I suppose if you boiled down all I've said to its simplest expression, it would be that I immensely enjoy and admire your work. I submit that, as literature, your work raises the overall level of the science fiction genre, and spiritually, you work cannot avoid positively influencing all who read it."

—Glen Stonebreaker, Gaithersburg, MD

"'The Mountains of Mourning' [in *Borders of Infinity*] was one of the best-crafted, and simply best, works I'd ever read. When I finished it, I immediately turned back to the beginning and read it again, and I can't remember the last time I did that."

—Betsy Bizot, Lisle, IL

"I can only hope that you will continue to write, so that I can continue to read (and of course buy) your books, for they make me laugh and cry and think … rare indeed."

—Steven Knott, Major, USAF

What do you say?

Cordelia's Honor
pb • 0-671-57828-6 • $7.99
Contains *Shards of Honor* and Hugo-award winner *Barrayar* in one volume.

Young Miles
trade pb • 0-671-87782-8 • $17.00
pb • 0-7434-3616-4 • $7.99
Contains *The Warrior's Apprentice*, Hugo-award winner *The Vor Game*, and Hugo-award winner "The Mountains of Mourning" in one volume.

Cetaganda
0-671-87744-5 • $7.99

Miles, Mystery and Mayhem
pb • 0-7434-3618-0 • $7.99
Contains *Cetaganda*, *Ethan of Athos* and "Labyrinth" in one volume.

Brothers in Arms
pb • 1-4165-5544-7 • $7.99

Miles Errant
trade pb • 0-7434-3558-3 • $15.00
Contains "The Borders of Infinity," *Brothers in Arms* and *Mirror Dance* in one volume.

Mirror Dance
pb • 0-671-87646-5 • $7.99

Memory
hc • 0-671-87743-7 • $22.00
pb • 0-671-87845-X • $7.99